I0671606

INSTITUTIONALISED:

Beyond the Stanford Experiment

Being a Tale of Debility, Dependency, Dread, Debauchery and Exploitation

Garth. P. ToynTanen

Institutionalised: Beyond the Stanford Experiment
By Garth. P. ToynTanen

First Published 2008

Copyright © 2008 Garth. P. ToynTanen

The moral rights of the author have been asserted.

All rights reserved. No part of this publication may be reproduced, stored in a retrieval system or transmitted in any form or by any means, electronic, mechanical or otherwise without the written permission of the Publisher.

ISBN 978-0-9558501-0-3

CONTENTS

FOREWORD

Way back in the sunny August of 1971 an experiment was begun at the prestigious Stanford University in California; it was an experiment that was destined to become a classic in the field of psychology and to inspire several fictional works in a variety of genres and guises, of which this is one.

The Stanford Experiment, as it became known, had been conceived to investigate to what extent the brutality and oppressive conditions so often associated with the prison system were a manifestation of the interaction of two groups of people of differing innate natures, i.e. the prison guards and the prisoners, rather than due to the prison environment *per se*. So, to put it simply, the question was: do prisoners and guards behave the way they do because they are somehow 'guard-like' or 'prisoner-like' people to begin with or do their respective group behaviours merely reflect the situation within which they find themselves?

To further investigate the latter hypothesis a study was set up wherein student volunteers were randomly assigned to one of two groups, either prison guards or inmates, and as such left to their own devices, although under the observation of the researchers, living together in a mocked-up prison in the university basement.

The original experiment had to be called to a halt after only six days had elapsed, despite the original concept having called for it to run for two weeks. Even over this short period the two groups had been observed to have become increasingly polarised; the guard's behaviour towards their charges was becoming dominant to the verge of sadism and that of the prisoners increasingly apathetic, depressed and submissive to the point whereupon it was feared that to have continued would have been to have risked inflicting permanent psychological damage.

The above study was ostensibly that of the behavioural responses to captivity and its effects on both the inmates and those given authority over them. It may be hypothesised that, in part, the compliant behaviour of the prisoner group is explainable in terms of an extreme manifestation of social compliance. The latter being the tendency for individuals to obey those that they have been primed by society to see as trustworthy and/or in authority even if their received instructions might run counter to their common-sense, ethics, moral sense or innate nature.

Such an affect was classically examined in the so-called 'Milgram experiment', a psychology experiment conducted in the 1960s whereby subjects were instructed to press a button that they understood would inflict a painful electric shock on another research subject in a separate room. Despite hearing what appeared to be the screams of agony emitted by the 'victim' and despite their unease and growing reluctance to inflict further punishment on a fellow human being, such sadistic behaviour being diametrically opposed to their innate nature, the test subjects nevertheless continued to press the button when instructed to do so by an authoritative-looking, white-coated, medical researcher.

1

Foreword

In the context of the aforementioned Stanford experiment, it should be noted that even those that objected most vehemently to their treatment would quite docilely return to their cells when instructed to do so by their 'guards'.

But what if...? What if the Stanford experiment had *not* been truncated? What if the guards had *not* been composed of randomly assigned test subjects themselves, what if those guards had in fact been hand-picked, especially selected for certain behavioural and personality traits, psychometrically tested to eliminate any that might find ethical, moral, or emotional conflict in fulfilling such a role? What if none were eliminated based on the grounds of the likelihood of their gaining sexual satisfaction from such a role and the dangers inherent therein, perhaps such even being encouraged and exploited so as to ensure the maintenance of the required research conditions; few motivations being greater than that of sexual gratification.

What if a woman of considerable affluence, influence and resources, a woman of misplaced philanthropic intent, being concerned of the number of homeless young women she sees drifting aimlessly through the city, should have made the acquaintance of a brilliant young female psychologist, her career frustrated by what she perceives as a blinkered lack of academic freedom? And then again, what if our aforementioned philanthropist should be of equally frustrated aspiration?

Consider: Everywhere around her she sees young women seeking independence and finding only the freedom for corruption. Runaways, dreamers, girls of otherwise good character, striving to distance themselves from some domestic upheaval, perhaps, yet finding at the end of the rainbow anything *but* a pot of gold.

Every night she tours the city offering help, every night she sees young women drifting hopelessly, drawn with tragic inevitability towards what she quaintly perceives as 'moral peril', the temptations of the street both sexual and pharmacological. She offers a warm and secure home, a renewed education, some hope for the future and, in return, she asks only that they might adhere to certain standards, learn basic etiquette and manners and obey simple rules; in short, take on board a modicum of *discipline*.

A few have taken up her offer, fewer have remained long; in their misguided way preferring to cling to their freedom and independence. To our philanthropist, though, it is her *duty* to remove from them what she sees as 'that modern and excessive freedom of choice that has allowed for their temptation, allowed them the *flexibility* to be moulded by sin in its own image'.

What if our philanthropist was to fund her new acquaintance's work, what if, in collaboration, the 'Stanford Experiment' was to live again but this time as an end in itself?

To the psychologist is provided the scaffold within which to structure further layers of research, and a secure cache of compliant young subjects.

To the philanthropist, at long last, is gifted the ability to save these young women from their 'freedom'. She would rescue them from the twin dangers of their own vanity and the sinful temptations of the modern world. She can at last provide them with the security that they undoubtedly crave and yet consciously deny. She can provide them with the discipline and the education they so blatantly need.

2

Ah! Yes! The discipline; they might not appreciate the wisdom or advantage of her intervention but nevertheless, in her view, they must be helped and, in her view, the first step, logically, has to be the curtailment of that sin-nourishing freedom, to be quickly followed by the curbing of those lesser, but related, nourishments of vanity and over-inflated self-belief.

And the girls will stay, this time they shall stay; the depersonalising institutional environment, the staff uniforms and the power of social compliance will see to it that they do. To our philanthropist, then, incarceration is the only option if she is to truly help these girls, it's all for their own good after all.

This, then, is our scenario: a psychology experiment in private hands and out-of-control. Attractive, feminine, inmates whose only sin, in truth, has been to strive for independence; and to have been attractive to certain eyes. A staff of amoral, dominant, women, skilled in psychiatric nursing and have a strong predilection towards young girls. A world of strict discipline and punishment, both physical and psychological.

Into this maelstrom let's now toss two or three young women, thought by those around them to be better incarcerated than interfering in business and financial affairs beyond their ken, pass over their strings to a corrupt solicitor, and be assured that they are now free of interference through any ethical constraint or mediation and most certainly will *not* be returning home after a mere six days. This, then, is our premise, our story. *This*, then, is *beyond* the Stanford experiment.

It should be pointed out that this is a work finding inspiration through a multiplicity of paths, some far beyond the aforementioned. Among these stands, notably, the work carried out in the 1950s by Dr. D. Ewen Cameron of the Allan Memorial Institute, Montreal, Quebec, Canada. His work, backed by the CIA it might be added, towards the depatterning of subjects, the latter meaning to break up existing patterns of behaviour so as to leave the subject more amenable to attitudinal change, was likened at the time to 'the creation of a vegetable' (The reader is directed to the book: *A Father, a Son and the CIA* by Harvey Weinstein. (James Lorimer & Company, Publishers. Toronto, 1988)).

It should be obvious to all, but it must be stated nevertheless, that the following is a work of fiction. The characters that inhabit these pages are themselves fictional, i.e. they do not exist and any resemblance to *any* person living or dead, whether by name or by description, is purely coincidental and unintentional.

It should go without saying that the author does not condone behaviour such as exhibited within these pages and believes that corporal and psychological punishment, such as depicted herein, should neither be applied nor suffered at any time, by anybody under any circumstances, other than in a world of pure fantasy.

The author believes that paedophilic behaviour is deplorable, it is neither depicted nor implied in any way within these pages; nothing here pertains to anything that should in any way be construed as childhood. Where the term 'girl' is used it is as a denigrating label applied to an adult woman not in control of her own affairs i.e. that is under the authority of those around her; throughout, the terms 'girl' and 'young woman' are used quite interchangeably therefore.

3

Foreword

A few other terms have been used herein that may be unfamiliar or of ambiguous meaning to some and for this reason there has been provided a short glossary, positioned towards the back of this book.

Now, notwithstanding the above disclaimer, to those of you who would question the plausibility of such a scenario, who might deny that such corrupting perversion of power could ever twist its way through professional echelons, who might baulk at the suggestion that such misguided philanthropy could exist or have existed I leave you with this: In the 19th-century the Rescue Movement came into being. Its founding aim being to tackle the problem of the number of women forced to fall back on prostitution, enabling their rehabilitation by way of the provision of a number of sheltered refuges.

These homes or asylums came to be administered by various orders of the Catholic Church, to be called after St. Mary Magdalene and subsequently, much funding being raised by way of their taking in of laundry work, to become known as Magdalene Laundries.

Originally conceptualised as short-term shelters, these asylums, over time, metamorphosed into long-term institutions taking on an increasingly prison-like character as they did so. At the same time their intake demographic broadened considerably to provide for any woman deemed likely to be in moral danger, a subjective judgement made easily by anyone in their sphere and based on anything from having become pregnant out of wedlock to merely being judged too flirtatious or wayward. They might be sent to such an asylum, often against their will, by their own families, on the word of a guardian or carer or perhaps through the concerned diligence of the local squire, some slighted suitor or -who knows- a catty young stepmother perhaps?

There can be little doubt that discipline was strict; there have been allegations that inmates were abused sexually, psychologically and physically. Isolated behind high walls for an indefinite period the inmates suffered social isolation *within* those walls also, talking was not allowed during work time and was severely limited the rest of the time; the nuns believed silence to be an important part of penance. Corporal punishment was commonplace and by all accounts was often applied with no little hypocrisy; that corruption was rife sexually is anecdotal, that it was financially may be judged by the suggestion, once made, that "the advent of the washing machine has been as instrumental in closing these laundries as have changing attitudes".

Therein lies the shock, with the modernity inherent in the latter quote: It is sobering to reflect that, despite there being reported historically little more extreme in terms of misguided philanthropy than that outlined above, the last Magdalene Asylum was only finally closed down in 1996.

4

PROLOGUE

Leaning forward, the woman smiled; it was a cold smile, a disconcertingly, disturbingly, confidently, cold smile. It spoke of control and the expectancy of control as much as the subsequent silence whispered of calculated manipulation.

"I carry out research into phobias", she said at last. "I have worked for some years at various universities, but the scope of my research has always been limited by the consideration of ethics. I firmly believe that in order to understand how phobias arise in the first place the best approach is to attempt to induce phobias, artificially. Believe me, I understand how that would be considered unethical in today's prevailing 'enlightened' climate but it is frustrating nevertheless, in bygone days researchers suffered far less interference and many great breakthroughs were made as a result."

Mary Stringer could not quite see where this was leading, how it would help with Susan's behavioural problems. "Go on" she said slightly irritated.

Dr Ecclestone was being careful not to appear irritated herself. It was obvious that Mrs Stringer did not really appreciate the scope of her work. Perhaps if she filled in a little background, little of her history? "It is known that some phobic people display a tendency to, over time, develop a nested series of phobias, each seemingly giving birth to the next, you can probably appreciate how debilitating this can become for them. In addition it seems that phobias can be learned while observing the behaviour of others around them, they can arise as the outcome of negative conditioning, where an action, idea, or situation becomes linked with an unpleasant consequence. I believe that, in this way, multiple phobias may sometimes arise, one from another, by way of an existing phobia becoming linked to a novel experience or situation. In a nutshell, then, this is the area of my research."

The woman was still struggling to understand the relevance of all this to her own situation, her incomprehension adding an impatient edge to her already clipped tones. "I must apologise if I'm being obtuse here but I'm not at all sure that I understand in what way I can be of assistance to you or, indeed, how your work could have any possible bearing on my situation. I'm sorry if I've been wasting your time in seeing me today, it's just that I fail to see quite why Lady Marchment recommended I speak to you."

"Please bear with me a while longer, Mrs Stringer." Anne Ecclestone, uncharacteristically for her, betraying her irritation in turn. "I'm sure, from what Lady Marchment has told me that we can be of mutual service to each other. To reiterate, and I'm sure you understand this, the idea of deliberately inducing phobias in otherwise normal subjects is considered unethical, although I think we are missing out on much that could be learnt. The best way for you to appreciate the relevance of my work to your situation is for me to place it in a historic perspective within the framework of my relationship with Lady Marchment."

She went on: "I first made the acquaintance of Lady Marchment at a psychology seminar in California. I had had several setbacks to my research, all of them involving clashes with various ethics committees, and I'd pretty much given up on that particular approach by that time.

Prologue

It was obvious, given that we had met at a rather prestigious scientific gathering, that she had some substantial scientific background and we soon discovered our mutual interest in psychology was along similar lines. Moreover, it later turned out that we shared a similar passion for certain philanthropic work. Naturally at first I was somewhat reticent about discussing my research in much detail with her. However, the more I revealed about my ideas the more her fascination became apparent. She was hugely enthusiastic, expressing an interest in becoming involved in some way, even to the point of suggesting that she might find herself able to fund my work should the right circumstance arise.

She had, and has, a razor intellect, and, although I, myself, did not recognise the implications at the time, she started asking questions specifically about agoraphobia, this seemed to be an area of particular interest to her. Of course I explained about the ethical constraints inherent in my research, but she did not seem put off one iota. Indeed she was most insistent that I should call her as a matter of urgency upon the conclusion of the seminar; it emerged that she had only registered for the second and third days of what was a scheduled five day meeting."

The doctor was in full flow now: "It was around one month later, that I received the 'phone call from Lady Marchment that was to change my life. She had seemed highly excited, saying that she had had some ideas regarding my research, and could I meet her the next day, at what turned out to be a rather nice restaurant I seem to recall. "

Mrs Stringer was not sure she was really following the point, but nevertheless she was loath to interrupt Dr Ecclestone's narration.

The doctor continued; "Lady Marchment told me that she understood that much of medical and drug-related research involved paid volunteers, often students, and that sometimes accommodation was offered for short periods of time. She said that there were many people on the streets that she knew of that were desperate for support, that would be willing to undergo medical research as experimental subjects merely in return for accommodation, especially through the winter months, and she felt sure that the added inducement of ready cash, would ensure a steady supply of such volunteers.

Basically she was offering to supply both the funding and the accommodation required to support my future research work. She explained that her philanthropic work involved running a shelter for teenage girls who had, for one reason or another, run away from home, become homeless or perhaps had been victims of abuse. She said her work helped ensure that these girls remained safe from pharmaceutical and moral harm.

To cut a long story short, as they say, even as she described her proposals I could see that, although the fruits of my research would have to be written up in such a way so as to avoid any moral and ethical implications and repercussions, the opportunity was just too good to pass up."

"I'm still not sure I understand how I can be of assistance to you." It was not that Mary Stringer was particularly slow on the uptake, far from it; she was a highly successful businesswoman in her own right, known for her mental agility in sharp negotiation. This, though, the field of psychology and particularly in this manipulative form, was an entirely alien world to her.

Doctor Ecclestone was only too happy to clarify: "It's not so much how you can help me as how I can assist you and the difficulties you are having with your stepdaughter. Lady Marchment told me that she had suggested that you might consider getting a governess for Susan, she said that you were eager for her to go off to university, once she has completed her A-level study and that really you just wanted her out of the way so as to get on with your life. She has told me the two of you, your stepdaughter and you, don't get on, and that, since her father's illness began, things have been coming to a head between you. As I understand it part of the problem is that the girl begrudges the fact that you have the purse strings and will control her trust fund and her allowance after her father's death"

"Well, yes, true, but only until she reaches the age of majority."

"I know how difficult this must be for you at this time but if you don't mind me asking, how long have the doctors given your husband?" Not that Mrs Stringer appeared to be particularly upset but the doctor thought it prudent to tread delicately nonetheless.

"No, no, not at all; they estimate six to nine months but no more than that." There was little discernible change in the woman's demeanour; the smile still flickered around her lips with little to hint of any upset. Nor was there evidence that might denote denial, the doctor noted with interest.

"I'm sorry to have had to arrange our meeting at this difficult time but there is a window that we really should be taking advantage of, if I've read your situation correctly of course. For what I have in mind, the next few months, up to your husbands demise and immediately thereafter, are absolutely key. The girl is very close to her father I gather?"

"Yes, very, and she has always been pampered beyond belief by her father; he has created a right little Madame."

"So much the better. And she is very independent I think you said?"

"Well, yes, independent, yet quiet and bookish with it. I know that probably doesn't sound so bad to you, a least from how it appears on paper, but she can be arrogant, obstinate. She thinks she is so damn clever, that girl, above everyone else, and above me in particular. And, yes, there is that independent streak, too damn independent if you ask me a bit of discipline would do her good."

"Then get a governess for her, Mary."

"Do governesses still exist? It sounds like something from the nineteenth-century. A Victorian governess? Somehow I just can't imagine *any* modern seventeen-year-old putting up with that, let alone *that* little minx."

"Not at the moment, no. What I mean to say is; not a modern day young woman, no. Not a woman fully flowered, brimming with self-confidence and independence. But, after all, what is the difference between a young woman in her late teens today and a child of exactly the same age living under a governess's guidance in the 19th-century? And believe-you-me it was a common and accepted custom for girls older than Susan to have a governess in that period of history, sometimes up to and, as incredible as it may seem, beyond the age of twenty one. The clue, in actuality, resides within the term I used, and did so quite deliberately; *child*.

Prologue

The only real difference between a girl, such as Susan, today and her counterpart of the 19th-century is one of *perceived* status. These terms, 'young woman', child', these are just psychological states, conditioned by society. What if I was to tell you that I could change all of that?"

Mary Stringer sat silently, content just to listen for now. She no longer felt lost in the subject but, rather, had now begun to develop a very clear picture of the potential inherent in her situation, at least with this woman on her side. The doctor had her full attention.

Dr Ecclestone went on: "Allow me to introduce the right woman to her, give her some time with the girl, then, when the time is right, allow *me* some time with her. I'm convinced that, given time, she will come to accept the guidance of a governess, even if she might not recognise her companion as such initially. In time, though, with the right guidance she will come to not only accept strict discipline but to find herself lost in its absence."

"And how would you accomplish this transformation? Believe me, it would have to be little short of miraculous"

"I'm a psychologist as is the woman I am going to recommend. It's just a matter of psychology, get to know her, befriend the girl, gradually undermine her self-confidence. Given time and the right circumstances, placed in expert hands any woman's independent spirit can be crumbled to dust. Her father's sad condition provides the perfect circumstance and I have at my disposal a pair of hands, endowed of the utmost perfection in their finesse and expertise, in which to place her. You remember what I said earlier about the window of opportunity?"

"Well, yes. You mean my husband's, her father's, illness?"

"Yes, exactly that. I know it seems callous but it really is the perfect opportunity, she is going to be at her lowest ebb, particularly directly after her father's passing on, she is going to need support, possibly counselling, the hand of a friend. I will ensure that it will be there for her when she most needs it.

The woman I have in mind can fulfil all of these functions and more. She will become Susan's friend, her councillor, her support. There is a fine line between guidance and control and it's a fine line across which the girl will eventually drift once placed her hands."

"But how does this fit in with your research exactly?"

"Well, I think in time we could convince Susan to become one of our volunteers. Okay, perhaps initially just for a few months, perhaps just over the winter, before she takes her final exams"

"I can't imagine her agreeing to that, really I can't"

"Oh, I think we could soon convince her to accept some help with her work, perhaps convince her that she is not doing as well as she thinks she is, maybe suggest that we can help her revise for her exams while she is a research subject".

Mary Stringer was al last beginning to warm to this woman. "But what about when she returns home? Would you have the time to continue as her governess?"

"Well, for one thing, it will not be I, personally, that would be acting as her governess of course.

I can be introduced to her later, as a councillor and therapist. As for her returning home at the end of her little winter sojourn, if you would prefer I feel sure that we could convince her to stay on here longer, at the clinic. Of course she would have to postpone her exams and any idea of going on to university but, you know, I think that if we can help her to recognise her limitations she may well come to accept that perhaps university is not really suitable for her after all."

"Well, perhaps, but at least she would be out of my way at university."

"Yes, I'm sure, but out of sight is out of control. And when she has access to her inheritance? I imagine you would want to continue to hold onto those purse strings a little longer, am I right?"

Mary Stringer said nothing, she didn't have to. Her reply was merely a slow knowing nod of affirmation, that and a smile. It was enough.

CHAPTER 1

NEITHER PAST, PRESENT NOR FUTURE

Lady Madison Daisy Bartlett

Erstwhile media mogul and ex fashion bunny she flowed across the floor with a dancer's lithe grace and a businesswoman's smart confidence, her floor length satin-draped gown a wind-swept late summer wheat field shimmer of golden waves echoed by her old-gold streaked brown shoulder length bob that glowed with random highlights and reflected in her honeyed solar-speckled hazel eyes. There was a golden-ish something around everything to do with Daisy Bartlett, or rather Lady Madison Daisy Bartlett as she was now entitled. From the golden glow of her bare shoulders and slender arms, a nod towards some long lost strand of antique exotic ancestry, to her carefully gold lacquered finger and toe nails embellished with the very latest holographic sparkle effects. Beneath the clinging folds of fabric a swelling fluid oscillation of heavy-bedded shadowing spoke of many hours of dedicated gym work as much as of the expense entailed by the finest breast and buttock enhancement that surgery had to offer.

The accessories and trappings were all there, the epitome of the wealthy, if somewhat ostentatious, businesswoman dressed for a fashionista Paris soirée - only the dark brown riding crop occupying her right hand, the latter white leather gloved lest she should suffer discomfort, spoke of different plans for her evening. Now with the full scene unfolding, her swaying walk took on a more threatening aspect, with each step a deliberate flexion of her right wrist brought the switch's leather tongued tip to tap rhythmically against the ludicrously high heel of her hand-tooled golden strap-work open toe shoe.

Before her the blue-uniformed teenager knelt with haunches squatted back on her heels and head bowed, all the time following that swinging tip with a mesmeric fatalistic fascination through saucer eyes as blue as her uniform dress. Small shell pink manicured fingers fidgeted awkwardly between hands rested on an aproned lap of satin-sheened powder-blue and pastel-pink stripes. The long-sleeved frock had long since began to display the irregular darkenings, indicative of nervous tension, spreading along and through the fabric at the sides of the breasts, expansions of sweat following the lines and folds of the soft powder-blue fabric as juxtaposing wetted navy-blue contours around both armpits.

That there should have been such a corruption of her carefully contrived colour scheme had Lady Madison bristling with indignation.

Notwithstanding that the girl's sweat was a perfectly natural response under the circumstances, a physical representation of terror and dread, a terror and dread that Lady Madison herself had carefully and lovingly crafted and instilled in her, nevertheless the slowly spreading staining was earning Lady Madison's ire, it was ruining the entire aesthetic.

Quite with what strange perversity of aesthetic led her to lay such import upon the colour of what, after all, was merely a servant's working dress exactly reflecting the girl's eyes we will never know, suffice it to say that much time and effort had gone into sourcing a fabric that was suitable, practical and that exactly matched those huge, pretty, powder-blue eyes. She had eschewed the traditional black-and-white look and definitely ruled out any influence in the direction of the ' French maid' as being " most unsuitable", feeling compelled to comment in her most haughty of tones: " ... that the little strumpet should ever appear so overtly attractive is quite, quite unthinkable".

No commercially available design could be found quite meeting her criteria and quite able to provide that critical balance between functionality, pleasing aesthetic and, importantly, humility. In the fullness of time Lady Madison herself had been forced to put pen to paper, a task for which she had had no little enthusiasm; indeed a fever set in that had her working practically day and night with an inspired fervour that she had never before achieved, nor since, if she be honest.

Drawing after drawing, each feverishly more outlandish than the previous, poured out of her imagination; through cycle after cycle of evolution, excitement nourished imagination and imagination in its turn stimulated imagination. The result was a froth of domestic femininity, a confection more likely the province of the more fetishistically-extreme transvestite than a real live teenage girl such as was presently facing her ire. That particular blue more than just reiterated those eyes but juxtaposed with the pastel-pink trimmings, details and accessories, emphasised prettily her girlish blonde looks; endowing her with an innocence beyond which she had long ago travelled, totally robbing her eighteen years of any pretence of adulthood while implying total servitude.

A soft and elaborate lacework trimmed the cuffs and collar, both of which were of blue and pink stripe so as to match the apron. The collar was an oversized circular affair lying flat across the shoulders and reaching down at the front to halfway between the dress' second and third buttons and to a similar extent at the rear with its laced edging almost brushing the small neat puffballs of the shoulders at the sides.

The girl's breasts rose and fell with an ever-increasing tempo, emphasised in their shadowy bedded curvature by the close tailoring of the bodice, its glassy-looking plastic buttons nestling neatly in the distinct cleavage thereby formed. Her mistress loomed ever closer, taking her time, always taking her time, letting the humiliation of the situation soak in; punishment was an opportunity. Chastisement was an opportunity to bring the girl deeper under her control, bind her; the mind was to be punished as much as the body, only then could the girl's training be deepened, become truly irrevocable, a permanent and inescapable aspect of her psyche. The cane cracked down on the brown leather stool…

Chapter 1 | Neither Past, Present nor Future

Momentarily the girl started before her response spelt out her resignation in her contrite bending at the waist - the French-plaited golden-tressed head dressed in frilled blue and pink striped cap springing down almost upon the floor, then lifting, so that her lips might meet the proffered riding switch to yield the required gentle kiss, the twin tails of her cap's long striped ribbons lying heaped beneath on the immaculate polished parquet flooring.

From the very first stroke the tears came. She had no resolve, such had left her long ago hand-in-hand with her self-confidence, her pride, her vanity and the majority of her self-respect - the latter she now cursed for it had been through some residual remnant that her present situation had arisen; it was a malady that she knew her mistress had well in hand and would very soon have cured in its entirety.

What possible point was there in resolve, in strength and determination? The six strokes she was to receive were always the minimum tariff, always had been, there was no maximum only the advent of tears, and even then only fully heart-broken weeping, would satisfy her mistress. And she *had* been fully broken or very nearly so; there wasn't much left now - her mistress was an expert who had brought her to heel long before her introduction to corporal punishment and humiliating uniforms, before she had herself realised what was happening to her. It had been a gradual eroding and overpowering of her will. And then there had been that institution, that hospital...

Her knickers had stayed up but merely to aid in the aesthetic, the red swellings enhanced and endowed with a novel beauty beneath the skin tight white satin, any protection was negligible and in any case was offset by a rule that left no freedom to failure: the end came when the tears came, always the tears, always at least six strokes.

The bloomers were the only part of her uniform that was not either pink, blue or both and even these were fastened at the waist and just above each of her knees by blue ribbons threaded through the fabric, those at the knees having to be tied with a neat but obvious bow on the outside of each knee, the ribbon tales dangling to below each knee and well displayed by virtue of her skirt's three-quarter thigh length.

She particularly hated the bloomers; the legs were very full and loose and rustled together noisily as she walked drawing attention to that which she would much rather her skirt kept hidden. Around and between her buttocks, on the other hand, they fitted so as to sheave them as if a second skin, as if sprayed on, every nook, cranny and dimple displayed and she was obliged to ensure that they were kept pulled up tight enough to do so. Lady Madison thought nothing about flipping up her skirt to check and following up with a long hard caning if necessary, as had happened a more than one occasion; now she always not only tied them tightly pulled up as hard as possible but in addition took the precaution of running her index finger along between her buttocks and between her lips at the front, taking care not to linger lest she be punished for self abuse. The fabric was of the thinnest and finest satin she had ever seen or felt, the snow-white colouring displayed the slightest of staining, both inside and out, and her pubic hair could quite clearly be discerned. The latter manifested as a thick bulging triangle now that she was no longer allowed to cut nor trim it.

This was in complete contrast to how they had kept her in hospital; there she had been kept shaved of course but, in its own way, this was every bit as humiliating if not more so.

Lady Madison or, even more humiliatingly, sometimes her housekeeper, would on occasion have her drop her knickers to around her knees, at which point she would be obliged to stand with her legs parted wide enough so as to keep the knickers stretched in position for inspection. Always the gusset would be scrutinised with utmost care; she could, and would, be caned for any staining, the slightest discolouration, they might perceive. And there was always something, she could be sure of that. This, she had long ago realised, was the raison d'etre for the choice of fabric, the colour, the cut, everything; those knickers were specifically designed to humiliate a woman by confronting her with her own femininity.

This was a concept that she had become only all too familiar with during her time in the hospital; an experience from which she had emerged totally ashamed of her own body, of even being a woman. Such checks and inspections were common to all aspects of her uniform, the seams of her pink stockings had to be dead straight, her blue satin pumps had to be kept pristine, the pink ribbon bow that fastened each tied just so.

Yes she had been proud once, this girl, once blessed with a model's figure, potential and, even, ambition. A single word summed her up now, it was embroidered in navy blue thread across the front of her cap and the breast pocket of her dress: MAID. Whatever she had been, whatever she could have been, it had been superseded, wiped out by that most fantastically unnecessary act of embroidery, that one defining word: MAID.

The second stroke slashed in; a redoubling both of effort and of recipient's tears - the woman's anger was obvious now, had the girl the fortitude to face the ornate floor-to-ceiling mirror before her she could barely have failed to recognise the smile of satisfaction curling across her tormentor's lips. First those unsightly darkened swathes of sweat and now the tear stains disfiguring her collar and cuffs - it was unforgivable! Was it not bad enough that the girl had had the temerity to have disobeyed her, or a least to have hesitated long enough as to have qualified as disobedience. True she had dropped to her knees eventually, visibly steeling herself for the ordeal to come, her face a contorted portrait of consternation and of unendurable distaste.

That in itself, that distorted countenance, would have been bad enough. That she should have faced her mistress possessed of an aspect of anything other than that of utmost pleasure, that she should have presented an attitude anything other than that of one to whom servitude gave the utmost pleasure and to whom the intimate pleasure of her mistress represented the very pinnacle of that service, was unforgivable. After all it was not as if she had demanded of the girl some sudden stepwise transition in situation and status, she had put the girl through a carefully orchestrated graduation spread over several months.

Ritual was all important; in gently graduated stages the girl had learnt to kneel and bring her lips to her mistress' feet and then the hem of her skirt in greeting. Later she had she been required to kiss the gusset of her mistresses knickers, taken straight from the draw, before holding them out for her mistress to step into, doing so from bended knees.

Chapter 1 | Neither Past, Present nor Future

Still later the ritual had been expanded to form part of her laundry duties; each and every piece of her mistress's underwear, whether knickers, thong or panty girdle, required the gentlest of kisses placed upon the gusset before progressing to the bowl for washing.

At first it had been sufficient to place her lips to each garments exterior but once judged that she be sufficiently familiar with the flavours and odours she had been progressed to having to kiss the more intimate soiling within.

Throughout these duties she had been placed under the supervision of Lady Madison's housekeeper with whom Lady Madison had been delighted, both with the latter's informed reference to the ritual as the ' pre-wash' and her subsequent functional expansion of it beyond the boundary of mere terminology. There had been some required intervention from Lady Madison's riding crop but as her housekeeper had pointed out: a good minute or two of mouth soaking, pre-wash, did wonders for the more stubborn stains. More recently the girl had progressed to the point of regularly kissing her mistresses knickered crotch. The girl was well used to the sights, tastes and scents, should such a finely-diaphanous barrier of fabric have made such a difference by its removal?

She had begged in the end, the girl, *begged* to be *allowed* to do as had been required of her, pleaded that she might worship her mistress's body. All too late of course, all to no avail - the punishment was to be as much for her display of distaste and reluctance as it was for hesitation and refusal; it was all equally indicative of an attitude requiring of adjustment, an adjustment she was presently undergoing.

Swish-Crrrack! Ssswish-Crrack! The third and fourth strokes slashed in, the riding switch practically bending double as it cut through the air, its flexibility equalled only by its expense. This was very much a whipping, the girl' s screams were evidence enough, dammed-wails that would not have sounded out of place in some mediaeval dungeon rather than echoing from the oak panelled walls of an English country house in the late 20th century. Lady Madison, the title purchased along with the estate, riding switch in leather gloved hand, stood in an ecstasy of appreciative irony surveying the weeping supplicant before her, savouring the scene whilst aiming her next stroke, anticipating the result.

How ironic that the humbling title of maid should be surmounted by the heraldic device of the girl's own family wherever it appeared on her uniform. That her family's crest, for centuries a badge of control, title and possession, should have been turned about so, should have come to represent the control wielded over her, her possession, nay, ownership, *by* the estate rather than *of* the estate, was a humbling crushing irony. How humbling it must have been to have had to embroider it with the skills of her own hands and fingers, fingers only moments removed from setting signature, for what it was worth, to the final papers. Not that such a signature was required or even valid; her sectioning under the mental health act had achieved all that the documentation purported to set out to.

There was the power of attorney to be transferred, the sale of her property to be authorised, the sale of her family's title, her title. That the proceeds, indirectly through the power of attorney, were to come under the control of the purchaser was a most fragrant twist.

14

Then there was the documentation in which the now effectively disinherited and penniless wretch had had to admit to her incapacity, her mental illness and her inability to govern a her own affairs. There was the letter from her psychiatrist releasing her from the hospital with the proviso that she remain under Lady Madison's care and that she could be returned to the clinic at any time should her condition deteriorate. This latter was a most transparent threat, a 'deteriorating condition' could clearly encompass *any* form of disobedience. Anything other than the most docile acceptance of her servile position was to result in her re-incarceration in that place with its unrelenting white walls, therapy sessions and, most of all, the discipline and isolation.

And so, with the grace of Lady Madison's intervention, she lived still within her ancestral pile yet owned nothing, not even the uniform that Lady Madison insisted on. Yet, ironically, in a manner of speaking she herself was now owned, possessed. She was *part* of the estate now, a fact of which she was eternally reminded at each awakening, her first sight ever being that of the hideous uniform patiently awaiting her, hung upon the wall opposite the foot of her bed. The very act of enrobing was now in itself an act of surrender, to be reconfirmed at each break of day.

Ssswish-Crrack! Swisssh-Crrack!: Strokes five and six, the cries were hoarse in her throat now, even her tears were relaxing their flow; she was all cried out, finished. How many? How many more strokes?...

The woman's arm was draped comfortingly around the sobbing girl's shoulders, encouraging and insisting that she rest her head against the amply soft pillowing of her golden satin-sheaved breasts. "There, there, honey" she soothed. "It's not that I don't love you, I love you very much indeed, it is just that you insist on being *so* wilful. Its as if you feel you have to be disobedient from time to time, just on occasion, its as if there is some part of you that just won't give in. It's not as if you have anything to hold out for; you have nothing, you have no future outside of my home or some institution somewhere. The truth is; you just aren't capable of functioning independently, you'd be lost if you were ever returned to society, you silly, silly, girl. Surely they taught you that at the hospital. Sometimes it's just little things, certainly, but it's always there, there's always this little bit of stubbornness in you. Perhaps its pride, I don't know, but we are going to have to work on it together, see if we can't lose those last few vestiges."

She was shepherding the girl slowly across the silk Persian rug that longitudinally dominated the centre of the room, the two women moving together as one towards the thick red velvet drapes that hung down over the French-doors that in turn led out onto the formally arranged garden beyond. Lady Madison kicked aside the puddle of velvet from the foot of the doors, first one side and then the other, simultaneously drawing open the drapes. The afternoon sun poured in, flooding the room with light, forming blinding dusty shafts of almost religious illumination wherever it cut into the more darkened recesses.

"It's not as if you are a prisoner here, I've said that before, many times, there are no locked doors here, see?"

The doors were flung back with a deft movement, the still gently sobbing girl urged towards the green and flowered patchwork opening up before her.

Chapter 1 | Neither Past, Present nor Future

Spread out there lay freedom, potentially at least, albeit notwithstanding the humiliation entailed; the spectacle that a public airing of her uniform would likely provide was not exactly an appealing notion. The garden opened out before her and beyond it, beyond the safe reassuring symmetry of its network of gravel paths and formal flower beds, lay the main road, just half a mile hence. The girl recoiled with such dread-inspired haste as to almost send her mistress sprawling across the room. Her eyes wide with terror she turned away from her agoraphobic torment to run, to hide. She collapsed in the darkest corner she could find, shivering and cringing in a sobbing thumb-sucking foetal heap behind a huge potted palm.

The smile on Lady Madison's lips spoke now of some pity, some compassion, and yet, at the same time, this was a very knowing smile, there was, perhaps, just the vaguest hint of satisfaction to be discerned there.

What with the tour coming up, the meetings and then the cruise, *some* relaxation at last, she was going to be out of the country for pretty much the next six months or so. The girl was coming along fabulously but perhaps some more time spent back in that clinic would still be of benefit, besides who else could provide the special care that the girl now required. After all, she could hardly be expected to take an extreme agoraphobic half way around the globe with her.

Lady Madison Daisy Bartlett sighed; there was always *some* complication to be negotiated, such was the burden that came with success, such was her world.

Annie's World, Matron's World

For others the world is a *very* different place, there are a very different set of trials and tribulations to be faced this day.

Take Annie for example, a runaway once lost amongst the city's sprawl; what if we were to be offered a glimpse into *her* life this particular day, a snapshot as it were? The same day, a far, far different location, environment and routine...

Annie is 21 today. No 'happy birthday, birthday girl' here. For Annie, today shall start like any other and as any other day, Annie is awoken by the harsh shrill ringing of the morning bell. Opening her eyes, the view that greets her she knows only too well. The clinical whiteness of the dormitory walls, the twin rows of hospital style beds. She has spent the last five years of her life waking to this scene.

She climbs quickly from her bed, as do the five other girls. All around is silence save for the soft rustling of latex bed covers and the crinkling of plastic knickers; talking could never be allowable in the dormitory. As do the other girls, Annie meekly kneels on the snow white carpeted floor alongside her bed , hands crossed in front of her, palms facing outwards, head bowed. As are the others, she is waiting for Matron to bring her bed pan. Above her, hanging from a hook on the wall beside her bed, awaits, patiently, her gymslip with its short, knife pleated skirt.

Matron will appear in due course. Her approach heralded in this surreal suffocating silence by the soft rhythmic sighing of her uniform dress against the nylon of her stockings and the occasional softly-cushioned footfall of high healed shoes on carpet. Her dress and demeanour are a study in the art, development and presentation of authority; she is the absolute image of control and domination.

Matron wears her full - skirted blue uniform dress at calf length. From her elasticated nurse's belt with its ornate silver butterfly-wing clasp she hangs her keys to the left and her tawse to the right, the symbols of her rank and authority. She by far prefers to use a tawse to discipline girls - so much more personal than the cane somehow – but a cane hangs above the nurse's station nonetheless.

This, then, is her world. She is queen here, empress, absolute ruler and dictator. The dormitory is her dominion, the girls, 'her girls', subservient serfs and the subjects of her realm. Her rules, her regulations, her stipulations, no matter how petty, are the unquestionable, unassailable law of this land. Unyielding, unbreakable. Unlike her charges, they who, in their turn, kneel, as is only fitting in such a majestic presence, in abject supplication; they are here to be moulded, one and all, broken to her will. The morning ritual is just beginning and ritual is all important here, in *her* world.

Not that there does not exist a higher authority, albeit outside of the immediate environs. Ultimately there is her employer of course but there are other determining forces; she never goes long without reflecting on her good fortune and her gratitude to their mutual benefactor.

From its inception the unit has been gifted with facilities and funding beyond their wildest dreams and set within premises of insurmountable and incomparable perfection of function. Presently the financial aspect still depended on that source; to date the provision of the new workhouse facilities only went so far towards their first stage goal of making the unit self funding, profitability lying some way off in the future.

Many might label as insane the substantial sums that have been poured into the unit, the old fashioned moirés upon which it is structured, the concept of 'protection from moral danger'. However, few are privy and those that *are* support whole heartedly the goals.

Their benefactor is a woman of not insubstantial means, influence and philanthropic drive who, having stepped back from the reins of her businesses, has seized the opportunity to indulge further her unusually active interest in aiding 'runaways' and the homeless. If some might be cynical enough to point the finger at her intention of profitability, labelling it as exploitation, so be it; as she sees it there are many other aspects and benefits to her work. These were young impressionable girls plucked from the jaws of the greatest moral and physical dangers the city had to offer. Some of these girls were barely out of school and generally were lacking even the most basic of qualifications let alone employment prospects; what chance of an education did they have, what chance now? "What these girls need most is a good, stable, secure home, a good education, caring but firm guidance". She is simply a successful business woman in a position to offer exactly that, albeit so far to just a handful of young women but, with the completion of the new wing, she will soon be extending her hand to others. Soon a few more lucky young women will be coming under Lady Marchment's caring regime, to restart their lives in a 'fine, stable and secure home'. A secure home indeed. Lady Marchment sets great store by security, 'protection' as she sees it; few prisons could be more secure. Once a girl has entered Lady Marchment's program she finds that changing her mind is not an option; she has entered a private little world. A world of uniforms, bedpans, petty rules, strict routines and bells. Bells, bells, bells, always bells!…

This, then, is Matron's world; a world within a world, ritualised and controlled. Today though there is disruption; there are girls here other than 'birthday girl' Annie and one of them is having difficulties adjusting.

Humiliation, shame, embarrassment, mortification. These terms and more could easily be applied to Jane's reaction to the situation in which she has found herself this morning, yet no mere words could truly do justice to describe the depths of her despair. She can feel the soggy wetness of the thick knicker-liner, is only too aware of that other soft squigyness confined within her plastic bloomers. She has caught sight of herself in the mirror, kneeling there, and her horror is written across her pretty face. She can see the areas of yellowing and those of the more shaming blackness within the semi -transparent garment. She is acutely aware of the smell and, what is more, she can hear Matron approaching. She can feel tears falling on her upturned palms.

If we could listen in we would hear words of comfort and kindness from Matron, her voice would be soft, no hint of anger nor irritation. We would hear her curt instruction to the nurse to 'clean the girl up' and the nurse's prompt response; "yes, Matron". We might, just might if we were to listen closely enough, make out the occasional soft grunt from girls desperate for control, forced now to wait for their bed pans while the girl is dealt with. There then comes a sequence of events, inevitable under these circumstances.

First there comes the voice of the nurse; "she is ready, Matron."

Then Matron; "thank you, nurse". Then Matron again "bend over, girl".

There is a pause, perhaps a sob, before: CRRACK! "One, t,thank you Matron"; CRRACCK! "T,tt two, tthank yyyou, mmmMatron"; CRRRAACK!! "Th, th, thr, three, th,th,tt thank yy,y you,,'sob', mmmMatron".

A bell rings; six girls take their places squatting over bed pans barely adequate at best. There comes the gasp of the freshly punished girl. She has been lucky, had she failed to count, failed to recite her formula of gratitude there could have been many more than three strokes of Matron's tawse; Matron is apt to re-start her punishments. There are other sounds filling the air now of which the more sensitive might rather not be privy and which the girls, without exception, would rather not anyone hear. Suffice it to say that the bell, although continuing its tintinnabulation throughout is never quite loud enough, particularly under the never distant supervision of Matron and her nurse, strolling up and down between the twin lines of squatting girls as if invigilators in some twisted exam.

Well, what of the rest of the day in Matron's world? For most they will have slipped outside Matron's immediate sphere; there are lessons to be attended. The next two hours Matron spends at her desk; there are reports to be filled in. There are also plans to be drawn up; there are soon to be many changes made, particularly within the framework of the research activities, a bold extension of scope, in fact groundbreaking.

Post lunch and Jane, the girl for whom the morning has proved so vexatious, is scheduled to attend her therapy session with Ms Soames. She has thus been returned to Matron's jurisdiction with the reminder of the latter's authority still throbbing across her rather full buttocks.

She has been left to stand at the foot of her bed to wait for Matron, her compatriots having returned to the class room. She stands with hands on head facing the mirrored wall at the room's far end. There is little scope for anything else.

There are three doors, the two set in to the side walls, one on either side at the room's end toward which she is presently facing, she knows lead to the class room and the examination room, the latter being kept locked. The third door, the one set into the centre of the end wall behind her, the only door in or out of the suite in fact, lies safely beyond the floor to ceiling iron security grille that bisects the entire room at that point and that sets the limit of their living space. The symmetry of its thick bars is disturbed only by its inset gate with its bulky lock beyond which the door itself would, of course, be locked. She knows that through that door and only a short distance along the passageway beyond is to be encountered an identical, if somewhat narrower, grille of equally imposing bars and equipped with an equally robust lock. Besides, in front of her, no more than two bed-widths distant, the nurses station is occupied, as it always is, the woman, a red head, her colouration set off prettily by her light blue uniform, sits with her back to the mirror working on her reports but occasionally glancing up. There is always supervision here in Matron's world.

In due course Matron arrives and takes Jane by the hand. This is one of Matron's little rules; she always insists that a girl holds her hand if moving about the building outside of the 'schooling wing' as the suite is described.

In Ms Soames's office she is told to sit in the deep soft leather armchair in the corner. She knows why she is here and what this is all about. She is reluctant but Matron softly whispers "hush child, be a good girl". Jane feels compelled to sit, suddenly weak and tired. Tired to the bone, she just *has* to sit down for fear she might otherwise collapse, such is the extent of her fatigue.

And so she sits, sinking into the soft leather, her arms resting on the arm rests. Attached to one side of the chair is a table top that can be swung round over the lap of the occupant. On this there sits the television, an innocuous enough device. Matron swings the table top into position; the television screen now occupies practically the whole of the girl's field of vision, the screen only a foot or so from her eyes. It flickers on, a vivid, constantly shifting, coloured, 'herring - bone' pattern appears. Jane looks away, Matron again whispers "hush child, be a good girl" and gently positions the girls head to again face the screen. Try as she might Jane cannot look away; soon she finds she does not even want to. She just wants to relax.

Only the pattern now, the room has receded. For five or six minutes the girl sits gazing at the mesmerising pattern before Ms Soames arrives. Matron smiles in greeting "I think she is ready."

"Good, I take it there is no resistance now?"

"A little, still, I'm afraid." Matron's confident smile is never in danger of fading "…but the trigger phrase seems to quell her quite easily".

Ms Soames approaches the girl from behind and gently begins to soothingly massage her temples with her soft long fingers. Softly, as we listen, we can her voice, but only just.

Chapter 1 | Neither Past, Present nor Future

She is whispering now, whispering deep into the now - so receptive - girl's ear. "Hush child, be a good girl, that's it. Deeply, deeply, deeeeply, that's a good girl, *such* a good girl. There are only us two, just little Jane with her best friend Ms Soames. You must trust and believe, you can trust and believe me can't you, sweatheart?"

"Yes Ms Soames."

"Well child today we are going to learn just how much we should trust, love and obey our betters. You remember how little, how so, *so* small you are, how defenceless, how weak and tired you feel, how difficult decisions are to make, how much better and safer you feel when others can make those decisions for you."

"Yes Ms Soames."

"We are in charge of you for your own good, you understand that now don't you?"

"yes Ms Soames" the girl softly whispers.

"Good girl, you are *such* a good girl"

There is much, much more of course, whispered so sweetly, so maternally, *so* softly that we just can't quite catch it; we have missed much. Perhaps another day, if we listen even more intently. But then again, perhaps it has been for the best; after all, Ms Soames can be *very* persuasive.

Matron leads Jane away from the office. The girl still feels drowsy, she is listless and confused. She is undoubtedly finding Ms Soames's words seemingly completely occupying her mind; it will be quite some time before she will be able to fully concentrate on anything. Clearly, there is little point in returning her to the classroom in this state, accordingly she is led back to the dormitory ward and helped to get ready for bed; an hours afternoon nap will leave her feeling better. Matron leaves the sleeping girl with a recording playing through her bed's headboard speakers. If we listen we may *just* be able to discern Ms Soames's sweet tones, a reiteration of the main points of today's and previous sessions

Ms Soames has prescribed three such therapy sessions per week for the next few weeks. She has been considering, recently, experimenting with techniques she has been thinking of with which to introduce some degree of sexual reorientation and she considers Jane ideal for these trials. She is pleased; under her guidance the girl is developing into a really good 'easy' subject. One or two of the other girls, the more institutionalised ones, are coming along nicely too, notably Annie, with whom we have met earlier, but this girl, Jane, is fast becoming the most responsive.

This then is Matron's world, her immediately influential sphere. We have glimpsed something too, albeit indirectly, of her outer sphere wherein she is undoubtedly influential yet is herself influenced by the ideas and actions of others.

Do we not all inhabit our own little worlds in this way; each life a continuum of influence reaching out in all directions and through time, growing ever more diffuse yet significant nonetheless. Within this we are influenced and, in our turn, are influential. The actions we take, the decisions we make, all have been influenced by events elsewhere and ultimately feed through, influencing future events elsewhere in some way no matter how minor or subtle. A new circumstance is the outcome of the overlap of untold numbers of such influences; spheres overlapping spheres if you will, perhaps infinitely.

Chapter 1 | Neither Past, Present nor Future

It may be argued that no situation or event exists in isolation but is rather like the skin of an onion; a concentric series of causes and effects each orbiting the next.

What then of Matron's world? What of those more distant orbits; the lives she has touched or is destined to touch, the legacies of the past and the developments to come? Time passes, scenes change...

CHAPTER 2

AN INTERTWINING OF FATES

Befriending Her

"… Of course befriending her is only the first stage, but easily the most important; gaining her trust is absolutely key." The doctor was leaning forward across the tooled- leather bounded blotter that dominated the desktop, hands clasped and fingers interlinked, her thumbs tapping together with an excited rapidity that only transiently paused and even then only to be replaced by a circular rubbing of their pads; the latter signalling a pause for thought, the selection of some particularly carefully considered phrasing or, perhaps, an attempt to stall her enthusiasm. If the latter then failure was destined; the mask of professionalism had long since cracked, excitement secretly glinted through fissures and chinks, digits of guilt tentatively probing for a kindred soul.

In Mary Stringer welled up evidence that her enthusiasm had not been misdirected; the woman was clearly intrigued. "And then?" It was not the words, sparse and concise as they were, but rather the delivery that evinced the woman's concordance.

The doctor continued, her intensely blue eyes glittering from behind severe horn-rimmed glasses to betray her further. "Well, if skilfully embedded in everyday conversation, the use of suggestion runs beneath notice, at least at the conscious level, yet through the use of suggestion one can wield great influence. It is insidious and subtle. I can slip seemingly innocuous phrases into casual conversation; you're looking tired, the crowd can be worrying, I can't help but notice that you have a problem with being outdoors don't you? I really think you rather lack in confidence you know."

Mary was trying hard not to seem out of her depth; if her meetings with Marion Marchment and Dr Ecclestone had been a revelation then her introduction to *this* woman had almost been a religious experience, although in truth she could not but entertain a certain scepticism. "And that is enough, simply words and phrases?"

"Yes indeed, that sort of thing, but over time, as I build on the relationship, as her confidence and trust are gained, repeated again and again and developed upon"

"And then what". There was a certain note of incredulity, a cynicism betrayed in her voice, perhaps even impatience, that she hoped wasn't too obvious while knowing the futility of disguise before a psychiatrist of such undoubted talent and experience.

"Well, later one can feign concern, worried that her agoraphobia is developing, worsening."

"Are you really saying that you could convince someone that they suffer some illness, some condition, where none exists?"

"Yes of course, but not to just *think* they have a problem. Given time and patience the condition can actually be made manifest in the subject, as real and as debilitating as in any sufferer. Believe me, I can integrate phrases into everyday conversations designed to nourish those seeds of doubt once sown. I use phrases such as: 'I really can see that you're having problems sweetheart', 'is it that feeling of panic again?' 'I'm really quite worried that if this continues you will become housebound sweetheart,' "I can only help you if you help your self and the first stage in any programme of help is to acknowledge your own problems your limitations'.

In these conversations with the subject my intention is always the same; to gently induce self-doubt, plant little seedlings to grow larger and take root in the subconscious to be gradually accepted as fact.

In a similar way a friendly request may be worded in such a way so as to mask what in actuality is an order: 'I'm not at all sure that jeans really do your figure justice' or 'I think a skirt would be more appropriate don't you, sweetheart?'.

An introduction to Dr Anne Ecclestone would be the next logical step. She is a great friend of mine as well as a respected colleague and one that shares our common interest as it were. She would be an obvious introduction to professional help. Anne has developed a technique, based on the combined use of hypnosis, relaxation techniques and manipulated film images, that she has used to great effect to treat the most deep seated, intractable and debilitating of phobias. She has become a world renown expert, but without a rather, shall we say, cavalier, attitude to certain ethical considerations, and the provision of private financial support, her research would have long ago stagnated."

Mary Stringer was puzzled; clearly this woman had not been told of her previous making of Dr Ecclestone's acquaintance and yet the good doctor herself had arranged this meeting. From her appraisal of the doctor's character at the time she would have said that such an oversight was unlikely in the extreme; a more professional personage she could not imagine. Mary was intrigued; the doctor must have had good reason for not having previously briefed the woman, that much was obvious, but as to her intentions, therein lay the puzzle. She would not interrupt, she might well learn more through a different perspective of the doctor's work. Quite what went on in that clinic of hers? She would learn more: "How so?"

"Well it is well known that multiple phobias can arise in certain individuals, sometimes seeming to extend from some originating seed phobia. In the absence of ethical considerations the best way to investigate the aetiology of such a condition, as I see it, is probably to attempt to induce it artificially. This has been pretty much Anne's approach, for example by exposing her subjects to images calculated to trigger a pre-existing phobia, spiders for example, arachnophobia, cut together and associated with flashes of an otherwise neutral situation, for example an open corn field, a market or perhaps, say, a crowded shopping mall. This, she has shown, can propagate the original concern into the new situation."

"But what possible relevance has this to my stepdaughter?" True, she could guess, she could certainly see the potential, or so she thought, but she wanted it from the doctor's mouth, she wanted it laid out explicitly before her.

Chapter 2 | An Intertwining of Fates

"Imagine, if you will, such an approach applied so as to reinforce the spoken suggestions she would be exposed to in her everyday experience. Agoraphobia taken to the extreme, encouraged, reinforced, well this is tantamount to bondage for the mind if you will. I know for a fact that Anne would like to investigate other ideas.

For example, once convinced of the reality of her panic attacks, the girl could be reminded of times, perhaps, when deciding what to wear has seemed quite impossible, when her inability to make a decision has brought about the build up of that awful panic. Anne is quite interested in the way that some people naturally seem to develop such false memories. I know it is something she would love to investigate by the approach of actually implanting such memories. It has only been ethical considerations that have held back that part of her research but now, thanks to Lady Marchment's support, such limitations are in the past.

But research aside I am sure you can imagine how powerful a technique this could be in developing the sort of mind-set that I am sure you would like to see the young lady adopting. Recognizing and accepting the problems that she would be increasingly encountering with her panic attacks she would gradually become desperate to avoid such attacks at all costs. She would begin to seek to avoid situations which she has learnt are likely to bring about such an attack."

"What sort of situations, what is the point?"

"Well, I would like to start with a programme of suggestions aimed at developing some sort of agoraphobic leanings, I am sure you can imagine the scope for control under such circumstances. Similarly in connection with such common situations as having to decide what to wear. And, of course, each bad experience she suffers consistently reinforces the ideas forming within her mind; Ideas that I will have seeded.

One can imagine her standing before her wardrobe, heart pounding, head spinning, the awful flood of panic filling her every fibre; would this not be something to be avoided at all costs. Likewise the crowded streets, the open fields. Her room, of course, feels safe, perhaps even the corridor beyond, if holding the hand of her nurse or guardian. But walking outside, alone? This has become unthinkable, something filled with dread. In this you can understand my eventual aim; to see the young lady reduced to a childlike dependence, eventually unable to make even the slightest decision for herself."

Mary shuddered; there was something terrible, almost insane here. Fantasy had been one thing, and that was how all this had started out in truth, but this woman was serious, Marion Marchment had been serious when she had recommended her. What she was suggesting was horrific, but what if... The woman was still talking, Mary had to force herself to concentrate, bring herself back to the here and now.

"Place her In my hands, our hands, and she is going to have to admit to herself, and others, that she is sick. I would want her to state it herself, in her own voice, that she is mentally ill. My intention would be to eventually progress her until she is ready to join one of Dr Ecclestone's experimental groups, I believed you have been shown around her facility."

"Oh yes, very impressive." She hoped that she wasn't giving away the state of numb shock that was slowly spreading through her being.

The facility had indeed been impressive but had filled her with trepidation, chilled her to the bone with a Gothic dismay worthy of Poe himself.

The woman went on with an ever-building fervour; there was no stopping her now. "With my guidance, my governance, she will readily come to admit to herself that she needs, so desperately needs, the security that only such an institutionalised and disciplined environment can offer her. The rigid routines, the conditioning, the isolation even the uniform, no matter how humiliating, and believe me, Anne knows all about humiliation."

Was this woman insane? Were they both insane? Mary found herself questioning reality, was this real? A dream? A subconscious representation of her darkest fantasies? Well perhaps it was.

"She is a brilliant intellect, don't get me wrong, but at the end of the day I'm not sure that even Anne herself really understands her own motivations at times. There are an awful lot of procedures in her establishment that seem to me to be more about humiliation than having any real therapeutic or scientific relevance.

But let's be quite clear about this, you have to imagine your stepdaughter basically imprisoned in a psychiatric ward, trapped in a regime that can do nothing other than break her completely. Are you really OK with that, do you really understand the implications and repercussions? Personally I think that is *exactly* what you'd like to see, am I right?"

Mary was numb, yet excited, embarrassingly so, she hoped it didn't show. Finally she nodded, dumbly, almost afraid to speak lest she should somehow incriminate herself.

First Impressions

The dark brown leather upholstery, darkened, softened and veined with age, yielded to accept her with the comfort and friendship of a childhood bed. That very comfort and warmth initiated from her a deep yawn, prompting her aunt to suggest that she might recline the seat. As she had to often in the past she demurred; despite the underlying feelings of unease and panic she customarily experienced away from the familiarity of the house she disliked just as much, if not more so, the disorientation and confusion of awakening at some destination or other with little no recollection of the journey having slept throughout. Of late, though, more often than not the latter had been her experience; that her doctor had recently begun to prescribe a stronger sedative played no small part in this and yet without it her agitation would have been so great as to preclude her crossing the threshold of the front door let alone that she might venture further abroad, even in the company of her aunt and even if cocooned within the car. That this particular trip was to be so long, was to terminate in a region of Britain unfamiliar to her and at an establishment the details of which were known to her in only the vaguest manner made her more determined than usual to remain sensible throughout.

The clinic was located in the West Country. That much she knew, Devon or Cornwall, she was uncertain which. Her doctor had been vague, or at least *she* had thought so but then again she could just as easily have missed or misunderstood something, either way she hadn't pressed the point for fear of appearing 'woolly headed', naive or both.

Chapter 2 | An Intertwining of Fates

After all, her doctor knew of the problems she was having, her inability to concentrate, her short attention span - they formed a large part of the diagnosis, embarrassed her immensely, and she was loath to appear any worse than she actually was, even to herself. Then again, denial was all part of it, something she had to face up to, admit to.

Despite her fear of an impending panic attack, her trepidation in the face of the journey ahead, a numb relaxation had begun to settle on her, calming and yet, in cleansing her mind of concern, granting a peculiar clarity of thought and a sharpening of her resolve while at the same time releasing her from her fear of failure in fulfilling that resolution. There was a warm sense of gratitude, gratitude for her aunt's insistence that she preface the excursion with a warm mug of cocoa and an extra diazepam pill and gratitude for the loving and merciful legacy of the latter. Softly, warmly, calmly, she sank lower in the seat's familiar and friendly embrace. The gravel of the short curving drive crunched under wheel and she watched as the lawn and neatly bedded roses drifted by, the procession ending with the passing of the two red brick pillars marking the interface between house and garden and the minor public road that ran past. They turned left passing rapidly along a canopy tunnel of curving and kissing treetops in the direction of the town centre; they would meet more major roads well before the latter's bustle and then would come the monotony of the motorway.

She knew this part of their route well, she could afford to shut her eyes for while, just for while, she could listen to the passing road through the soft drone of the engine she knew this road well enough to keep track, she could always look around from time to time... just let her eyes close, just for a while...

Whether through the sedative, the soft music floating from the CD player, the mature song of the classic Bentley's engine or through some combination she couldn't be sure but that she had fallen asleep, and a deep slumber at that, she could be certain; the glowing green hands on the walnut surrounded dashboard clock showed 12 o'clock, it was midnight, she had been asleep for over six hours! Her seat had been reclined at some point; it had been its restoration and the accompanying enforced posture change that had aroused her.

Awakened and startled she made a grab for the thick red tartan blanket that still partially covered her yet had slipped down to her lap, gathering it about her shoulders, not against the chill of the air but rather as a self-conscious reflex. The car was quite warm enough, there was no need for outerwear, for cardigans or coats; as her aunt was apt to say "you won't get the benefit when you get out". She was never allowed her cape in the car, it travelled occupying its own seat at the back in a neatly folded grey pile surmounted by her beribboned boater. In a logic-defying twist she was always offered the blanket and had ever gratefully accepted; even though seated within the protection of the car she little welcomed the public's gaze, even if incomplete and fleeting. This was especially the case on this trip, her aunt having insisted that her ' indoor dress' be the more comfortable option for such a long journey. Bad enough that she might be seen head and shoulders, ribbon-bowed plaited pigtails, gymslip yoke and school tie, but, although less likely observable from the outside, the frilled legs of her, near knee-length, bloomers peeped well below the hem of the pleated skirt when seated.

Strangely enough, despite the embarrassment she felt, there was nevertheless something reassuring about that uniform and her aunt's enforcement of it; true it sapped her confidence, seemed to dissolve her will, yet somehow it calmed her. She was hard-pressed to put her finger on it; perhaps it was the symbolism, of being under control, her life under guidance, discipline replacing decision making and lifting the responsibility of an awkward adulthood from her softly sculpted young shoulders. Whatever it was it soothed her and along with the comforting blanket and deep soft seat the outcome was forgone.

The gates lying ahead were an ornate insurmountable range of black spike-topped iron, floodlit from either side from where they were noticeably under the observation of a pair of closed-circuit security cameras. They were already smoothly gliding open as they approached, the car slowing to cruise through and doing so well before the gates had reached the limit of the travel such was their breadth and that of the grand driveway beyond.

Ahead lay a gravel road, for the term, driveway, really did not do justice. There was a tight curving bend to the left and then one to the right, the route meandering through a forest of tall pine backlit by glistening shafts of frosty moonlight. Somewhere in the distance a fox barked, clearly audible over the quiet engine's hum and the soft hiss of tires on gravel so fine as to be perhaps better described as coarse sand.

In due course the wood land opened out revealing the night sky to be of the densest black velvet, stained silver by the half-moon's smile and studded with diamond-sharp stars massed in a density of constellations that she had never before seen, certainly not in the city, not even in the countryside, not really; clearly they were a very long way from the nearest town or even village. Ahead lay a final straight section cutting across an open field of shimmering silver waves that suggested, as far as could be perceived in the moonlight, wheat balanced on the very edge of harvest. Only in the far distance was the pristine sky disturbed; the source of this sacrilegious pollution, in due course, revealed as the floodlit glare of a second set of gates every bit as imposing as the first but of a more modernistic functional appearance.

The flanking walls of dark stone were surmounted by brick and then in turn by an array of radially arranged iron security spikes, the whole being of perhaps 4 m in height. As before so did these gates swing open upon their approach but did so with an unhurried relaxed attitude requiring that they momentarily halt, granting the travellers a little time to absorb their surroundings before moving on. In contrast with the first set through which they had passed and that had seemed strangely un-remarked of by either name or notice, here there stood to either side a pair of large illuminated signboards proudly displaying an heraldic shield device, like some early-age logo, surrounded by an ornate arcing script of black edged gold lettering proclaiming: St Mary's retreat and private sanatorium.

Beyond that shifting forest of black steel bars lay the discreetly lit facade of the main building, as imposing as it was bizarre. Standing a fair four stories of red brick, much of it ornamental, the facade was intersected vertically at regular intervals by fluted, semi-circular, white marble pillars standing proud from the surrounding brickwork with Norman-arched stained-glass windows nestling between, each framed in carved barley sugar twist sandstone surrounds.

Chapter 2 | An Intertwining of Fates

Ivy clothed much of the facade, climbing pillars apparently willy-nilly and yet intentionally, having been carefully trained around each window and notable architectural feature. From beneath the gabled eaves gargoyles bled with menacing intent yet diligently kept guard, as at the upper corners of each window and above the main entrance. The latter, hidden in shadow and recessed back in a stepped stone-arched portico, symmetrically occupied the centre of the first floor and was reached by way of two flights of brick framed marble staircases that swept symmetrically up either side of the facade from the curving terminus of the driveway at ground-level. Their, still distant, impression was of some Victorian neo-Gothic folly, the whim of some long dead eccentric benefactor; a hospital for the needy, perhaps, built as much as an egotistical memorial as to fulfil any truly altruistic leaning.

The final 200 metres or so passed between neat hedges and conifers: A grand avenue of topiary that could only hint at the formal gardens beyond and around which they now skirted. Those symmetrical forms, so beloved of the 17th and 18th centuries, presently lay unseen and secret yet nary a car's length to either side; each radiating from an identically ornate fountain-centred fish pond and each nested, private and protected, safe from the eye of any new arrival or visitor.

Directly ahead and looming increasingly large, emerging slowly from within the shadows cast by the surmounting monumental stone staircase, double gates of dark oak began to dominate the ground-level façade. Lying central to the approaching building these lay beneath the curves of the twin marble staircases that arose from either side to meet at a pillar flanked terrace where upon opened out the grand doors of the main entrance.

The drive way took on a gentle decline, curving down to meet the gated archway at a point sufficiently lowered, the girl guessed, as to provide sufficient clearance for a coach and horses in days gone by. They came smoothly to a halt, the dark oak panels dew-glistening in the headlights and the whole taking on an unsettling impression of prison gates, a vision made all the more concrete by the opening of a door hidden inset within the left-hand gate revealing to the probing fan of light the figure of a woman dressed in the immaculate trim-belted and white piped navy blue dress of a hospital matron. Her appearance was particularly poignant to the girl, the woman's status instantly recognisable by comparison with her aunt's own uniform that she had seemed to have become so fond of wearing in recent times. Blonde hair was neatly pinned in an austere bun above a face perhaps best described as handsome rather than beautiful and possessed of an aspect at first worryingly stern but that quickly dissolved into a reassuringly welcoming smile, instantaneously shifting the scene far removed from the sinister overtones that had seemed so tangible only moments previously.

The woman disappeared back inside. The sharp slam of the door was immediately followed by the deeply-resonant hollow-trunked sound of a lock releasing. The panelled gates swung inwards admitting both car and occupants into a white flagstone courtyard centred on a golden floodlit fountain. The latter being in the form of a pair of affectionately-embracing and entangled angels, one with wings spread, the other with wings folded, each with one arm held erect, the two coming together overhead with intertwined fingers from where issued a golden umbrella of water reaching up perhaps a further metre or so in height.

They glided to a halt alongside a softly illuminated carved oak door, the uniformed woman, who had been following briskly behind, coming up alongside the passenger door as they did so. Behind them the gates, presumably electrically operated, had resumed their protective embrace leaving, upon the cutting of the engine, only the fountain's rainfall and a peaceful seclusion attainable only in such a privately enclosed world-space as this.

Leaning forward, ducking down a little to improve her view, the nervous passenger was looking up and around through the windscreen and side windows, cautiously relieved that this new world should be so safely swaddled and nested. The courtyard was flanked on all sides by four ivy clad stories rising cliff-like in brick and stone and overseen at the rear centre by a green-spired clock tower; the burnished copper of youth having long surrendered to verdigris in maturity.

The woman leant forward, opening the door while simultaneously offering the support of her arm, with an accompanying lost-friend smile and warm words of welcome. Apparently oblivious to the girl's floundering and embarrassed scrabbling for her cape on the back seat, she insistently yet gently ushered her from the car. Briskly she shepherded the flustered and still disorientated girl the short distance to the mediaeval styled arched door, adding voiced agreement to her aunt's view that, notwithstanding the night's chill, the few metres to be traversed did not warrant the added complication of outerwear so soon to be discarded, seemingly insensitive that the girl's motive might be other than to gain the additional warmth.

A couple of paces beyond the iron-furnished oaken door lay one of more modern design, realised in smoked glass, and beyond that, tastefully and extensively lit in softly subdued tones, lay an expanse of white marble tiled flooring a large proportion of which was taken up by a mosaic depicting the coat of arms that she had seen on the signs upon their approach but here including a Latin motto above and below: St Mary's asylum, 1858. That this latter came into view side-on confirmed the impression of their entrance having been by way of some minor side door. Rich oak panelling seemed to cover every surface bar floor and ceiling, they were within a balconied atrium of three stories surveyed all about by the eyes of rather officious portraiture - men and women of stature and of a bygone age their importance writ large in their grace and style.

To their right the party passed one wing of an impressive dark oak staircase, that swept majestically and symmetrically from either side of the hall, swathed in ruby red carpeting and guarded by two imposing oak carved griffins. This wooden alp, in actuality being situated to the rear of the space, presented a dramatic enough backdrop to greet any entering, more conventionally, through the main doors, yet was no less imposing when approached from their, more oblique, angle.

Straight ahead, positioned centrally in front of the grand staircase, the horseshoe desk both commanded the space and by dint of the computer screens, keyboards and telephones situated behind it, represented the only visible concession to modernity. Hanging directly above the latter, and of a curvature to match, a gently illuminated glass panel hung from discreet chains or wires, it proved impossible to discern which, this spelling out in glowing blue letters: Reception.

Despite the late hour two young women sat illuminated by the side light issuing from curved brass desk lamps.

Chapter 2 | An Intertwining of Fates

Each wore the light-blue dress typifying a British nurse's uniform, the details of which, though, spoke of an expensive exclusivity far removed from a typical hospital of the day. Both nurses had stood upon the party's approach, the careful detailed tailoring of their dresses being apparent even in that half light. Waists were neatly cinched by elasticated nurse's belts of the selfsame blue fastening by an elaborate silver buckle rather than by the usual simple clasp, long sleeves were terminated in neat white cuffs edged with blue piping, nurses caps of white were perched on neatly pinned hair and around the shoulders each wore a matching blue tippet against the chill of the night air, this being trimmed with white piping.

If not for the medical uniforms and a certain atmosphere of professional efficiency there was brought to mind the impression of a high-class hotel, a celebrity-ridden 'character' retreat of impeccable stately home or castle pedigree and suitably exclusive - mere wealth in itself would not suffice to give entry here.

That this establishment was, indeed, every bit as celebrity-ridden and exclusive as it appeared she knew from what the doctor had told her and yet the opulence of the interior, the imposing architecture without, the security precautions, all were far beyond the images that had been conjured in her mind's eye all those weeks before. A retreat for the rich and famous, those with problems real or imaginary, offering cosseting where necessary, pandering to foibles but nevertheless offering rehabilitation for those abusing, and abused by, various substances and all vouchsafed beyond the prying eyes and lenses of even the most determined paparazzo.

The girl could feel herself physically shrinking as they approached the desk; yet another two pairs of eyes now swept her up and down, were regarding her, appraising her, from her bizarrely high-heeled and silver buckled 'Mary-Janes' to her childishly beribboned and pigtailed hair. She could feel their eyes pausing and lingering around the fleetingly step-synchronised flashes of bloomer-flounces around her skirt hem, could feel her heavy heart further petrified, could feel the fireside-burning spreading further across her cheeks. One of the nurses, the dark eyed one, stifled a giggle, she was sure of it. The other looked up and smiled and then just as quickly looked away only to reface the approaching group with a sort of poorly controlled condescending poker face, the 'tell' visible as a twitching in the corners of her generously lipped mouth as if to give into a smile, even the slightest, would be to give away too much.

From behind her a woman's voice, cultured, educated, addressed her aunt. Words of greeting and other pleasantries were exchanged, then there were inquiries as to the ease or otherwise of their journey. Throughout there was the betrayal of a certain familiarity that she found surprising, although such surprise was reassuringly tempered by the inference that this familiarity had been mostly mediated through a third-party, being her doctor, and developed further through the various telephone arrangements that had had to be made. Quite why she should have been unsettled by this she couldn't say, it was something buried deep in her subconscious, some kind of primal alarm, some hunch that all was not quit right.

Then a note of concern: "We were expecting her to be somewhat older, her application stated that she is eighteen years and six months. Forgive my asking but there are strict lower age limits legally applicable to medical research subjects. How old *is* she precisely? I take it that you *can* confirm that she is over eighteen?"

"Yes of course I can, I have all of the legal documentation with me here; I always have her passport and identity card with me for safe keeping, she is so woolly headed she'd only go and lose them if it were left to her."

She couldn't help but be miffed at this inference not to mention being put out by the way the woman continually seemed to insist on directing all enquiries about her through her aunt, as if she were somehow too stupid to answer for herself.

"Oh, that's just fine", the woman was examining the proffered passport. "It's just that she looks so young, I guess it is the school uniform. One doesn't come across many girls of her age still in school uniform these days. So few schools even *have* a uniform nowadays and fewer still enforce it for their older pupils, how standards have slipped over the years." There came a subtle clearing of the throat, faintly indicative of embarrassment. "I'm not at all familiar with that particular uniform; it *is* a trifle unusual, if you don't me saying so. Where does she attend, somewhere quite exclusive one would imagine, is she a boarder?"

"Strictly speaking she left school two years ago but, what with her illness and the fraught family circumstances that I spoke to you about on the 'phone, we have had to postpone her university placement for the time being. As an interim measure I have been continuing her education at home, to a limited extent you must understand. She is not particularly gifted academically, personally I would question the wisdom behind her being offered a place to begin with but we are doing our best to bring her along, within her limitations of course."

"And the uniform?"

"At her psychiatrist's suggestion; she felt it would be of benefit to all concerned. She is of the belief that, in some such cases, the trauma, the suffering through which the girl has so recently passed and, in some senses, is still passing, may best be relieved by what she describes as 'total care'. Apparently the problem stems from modern society's insistence on the assumption of the mantle of adulthood at an ever decreasing age; not everyone is quite ready to grow up, are they sweetheart?" She turned to face the shrinking-violet girl, the last comment having clearly been aimed squarely at her.

There was a short teetering embarrassed pause before a tiny voice came with an uncertainty and hesitancy suggestive of one well below her biological age: "Y,yes, I,I mean n,no aunty."

The girl's aunt smiled back her approval before returning her focus to the uniformed woman walking alongside; reinforcement was important, she had always to be consistent. She went on: "With such cases she believes that discipline and restriction, in freeing the patient from the burden of choice, can, ironically, in the long-term be emancipating. In freeing her of the yoke of responsibility we are allowing her to reclaim a modicum of the carelessness of childhood, releasing her from the stranglehold of marketing manipulation, the slavery that is 'peer pressure' not to mention the mindless indenture to fashion one so often sees these days."

The matron was nodding enthusiastically. "And very good to see it is too! Please forgive me if I sounded critical in any way, I was merely intrigued. Believe me, I wholeheartedly agree with your decision. We get young women coming here from a variety of backgrounds and virtually all seem to share in common a particular attitude. It is clearly evident of the failure of modern society to place sufficient emphasis on standards of behaviour, decorum and discipline.

31

Not that they don't quickly show improvement once in our hands of course, but it is reassuring to come across a young lady so conspicuously kept under control, I feel I really must congratulate you. "

"Thank you"

Having reached the reception desk and acknowledge the nurses, both of whom greeted her with a smart "good evening, Matron" their guide turned to address then both, reclining back slightly against the desk front, her right forearm resting on the desktop for support.

"I think it will stand her in good stead when she comes under the research protocols in operation here. I'm not sure what the doctor has told you in this regard but the range of behavioural and psychological research projects carried out here involve quite exquisitely delicate experimental manipulations that can easily be disturbed by external influences.

We have to control against introducing any confounding variables that might mask or invalidate otherwise valuable results. We try to take into account, and control for, all foreseeable sources of 'noise' in the data, I'm sure you understand."

"Yes, of course."

The girl was looking lost now, she was not at all sure that *she* understood; her interest had ever been in the arts; painting, drawing, design and avant-garde dance were her world. Such terms as had just been used were totally nonsensical to her and had swept past her like the will-o'-the-wisp. Her aunt on the other hand was nodding with a smile of enlightened agreement.

The woman went on: "The basic framework is an extension of the so-called 'Stanford Experiment' but here the exploration is more keenly focused and targeted at just one side of the equation. The test subjects comprise a single group that we like to refer to as 'the patients', volunteers that have been recruited through a variety of paths. The staff on the other hand, in contrast to the Stanford protocol, are all professionals, screened and hand-picked by way of an entire battery of psychometric testing, interviews, personality profiling and, quite intrusive, personal background checks."

The girl shot her aunt a nervous sideways glance, the latter again nodding her knowing agreement, her continued smile buoying the girls trust, lifting the moment of uncertainty.

A pause had arisen whether by chance or by design, so as to encourage interrogation; it was duly filled by her aunt's softly-cultured tones and informed query: "I'm intrigued, what were your criteria?"

"Without betraying confidentiality I cannot go into much detail but suffice it to say that areas such as sexual predilection, ethical standpoint and moral framework were extensively probed. In addition we were looking for a natural propensity towards dominance in both working and personal relationships and, of course, a solid background in psychiatric nursing."

The girl was beginning to feel not a little afraid, what had she let herself in for? She was not at all sure she liked the sound of any of this, she again glanced nervously at her aunt and, seeing the latter's smile broadening still further, in her trusting way, decided that the two women were sharing a joke at her expense.

32

To say that they were sharing some amusement would not have been an untruth, that it was at her expense was doubly true, that it was a joke *per se* would depend on one's standpoint. Indeed her aunt had known something of all of this beforehand of course but she had wanted to hear it from the horse's mouth, so to speak. In her mind, her internal dialogue voiced what the matron had only been able to infer: They had assembled a hand-picked team of dominant lesbian sociopaths. They had placed, in a world designed around their darkest fantasies, a group of women totally lacking of conscience, morals and ethics yet skilled in manipulation and control and allowed them the total and unopposed control of a group of attractive adolescent girls. Of such material Gothic horrors are made, but *this* was a terror so beautifully crafted as to be considered no less than a work of art.

The issue of social compliance in this connection was still to be fully explored but this most definitely went far beyond the scope of the original Stanford experiment and it certainly wasn't going to be interrupted after a mere few days. Her thoughts were interrupted by Matron's continuance of her explanation.

"Of course within the basic scaffold small subgroups exist through which much of our work in such areas as the pathogenesis of phobias and the problems of institutionalisation in the long term mentally ill are carried out.

Tonight you can both stay in a guest rooms here in the main building." Then, turning to the girl with a warm smile of welcome: "Tomorrow you will be transferred to the experimental suite, a room is already for you." Returning her attention to the girl's aunt she went on: "The measurements you sent us looked to have been just fine. As I believe I explained in the letter I sent you, we require all our test subjects to wear a uniform. She can try on hers in the morning before you leave, we generally prefer the subjects to be in their uniform before entering the unit if at all possible." Her attention having once again swung back to the girl she continued: "Some of our subjects have had a problem with this part of the protocol in the past but you must try to understand, it really is a very necessary component. for one, it helps ensure that the staff treat all of the subjects equally. We find it reduces the problems associated with favouritism and bias, eliminates intra-group competition and aids group cohesion and identity.

They had begun walking again now, towards, then up, the imposing height of the broad winding staircase. The matron was still talking, although clearly now addressing the girls aunt: "Of course the other advantage inherent in our adoption of uniforms for both test subjects and staff is in highlighting the limits of social compliance when taken to an extreme extent, that is, in an environment wherein the distinction and contrast between two groups has been deliberately sharpened well beyond that ever encountered in the outside world.

All our staff members, Matron and the nurses, wear uniforms fairly typical of a medical institution such as this and that are generally accepted to endow and represent some level of authority. It must be said, though, that we have made *some* stylistic changes above and beyond that encountered in the usual day-to-day nursing uniforms specifically in order to enhance the authoritative attributes. By way of contrast, the uniform that has been developed for our test subjects, our patients as we like to think of them, has been designed and styled so as to strongly suggest, both to the wearer and those around them, an element of subservience."

Chapter 2 | An Intertwining of Fates

Somehow the girl, following behind the two women, had missed entirely the gist of this last statement. Tiredness had again overcome her and, despite her novel surroundings, she was finding herself trudging up the long flight through a fog of exhaustion and confusion. In this, at least, there was some mercy; she had been spared the anxiety that might otherwise so easily have her overcome her.

The hotel atmosphere, the 'feel', extended into and throughout the corridors. Dark oak doors lined either side, each numbered and richly decorated with the carefully carved counterparts of the Ivy that clung to the exterior, and each separated from the next by a series of, obviously original, oils and watercolours depicting various country scenes. Although her aunt was clearly taken by many of the works that they passed, the girl, on the other hand, found herself shying away from those depicting open panoramas and landscapes. She hated herself for it, felt faintly ridiculous that she should have let her agoraphobia get to this point, to get the better of her to such an extent she couldn't even bear to look at a painting.

Her room was situated next to her aunt's; there was a connecting door should she become upset at any point and both rooms were *en suite*. As always the more exclusive clients had to have their anonymity protected, there could be no wandering around in the corridors; the outside door to her room was to be locked until morning. Left alone she looked about her; the room was spacious yet not so large as to risk unnerving her. The pink satin covered four-poster called to her of the welcome of its luxuriant softness and she went to sit on its edge, the material's soft chill apparent through the thin fabric of her bloomers, her short skirt having ridden up. A long white satin nightdress was laid out across the bottom of the bed and on the floor a wicker laundry basket waited hungrily. She was alone, but that was a blessing, there were no longer the appraising laughing eyes and she could at last discard that ridiculous 'school' uniform that her aunt always insisted she wear.

She kept her shower short, a heavy tiredness still threatening to overcome her. Having dried herself she slipped the nightdress over her head, shimmying it down over her slender shoulders, a shiver of delight running down her spine at the cool caress of the fabric where it flowed languidly across her rapidly stiffening nipples. Despite everything, despite her customary appearance, she was a woman and a highly sensual one at that; a woman with a woman's needs.

Instinctively her hands reached behind her. Nimble fingers ran gingerly across and around the curvature of her buttocks where thin lines of tender wheal-raised flesh quivered at the juxtaposition of inflamed heat against the cold slippery touch of the fabric, inducing a sensual metamorphosis; the legacy of near-unbearable pain transformed as if by some cast spell. The raised edges of each wheal, a parallel band of three curving across and around each buttock cheek, stood out through the fine fabric, each being of perhaps one and a half times the width of a pencil, but certainly no greater. As she had once heard her aunt comment to one of her acquaintances with a particularly mortifying clarity; "...a thin cane is a flexible cane and a flexible cane is key to a more complete punishment", how true indeed. Either side of this band of chastisement she could make out less defined, less tender swellings of more historic origin. She traced each sensually to and fro; there it was again, that excitement, building. Each wheal was a reminder that she was under control, that her *life* was controlled, that *she* was controlled.

34

She was becoming breathless, had to stop, perhaps in bed, later, mustn't get caught; her aunt would be horrified, she didn't allow such things. That last thought itself, that she wasn't *allowed* the release she so desperately craved, that the decision wasn't hers, was almost enough in itself to push her over the top. Reluctantly she shifted her attention elsewhere; it would be safer later.

She explored the room further, taking care not to trip on the minor train of fabric that trailed behind her. Everything was there, television, radio, music centre, all of it top-flight equipment. By the bed an extra CD layer had been added and was connected to a pillow speaker much as she used at home. She had previously voiced concern that she might not be able to sleep without her doctor's relaxation recordings.

She did momentarily try the television, it had been so long, she could find nothing but static on any channel yet her tiredness blunted her disappointment. She settled down under the covers, turned on the CD player and clicked off the bedside lamp. Her doctor's familiar, cooing, voice drifted with her across the floating landscape of clouds, dreams and warm comfort. There would be some bad moments, they always were; sometimes there were fields, spiders scurried in those fields, sometimes crowds scurried like those spiders, crowds in streets, crowds in shops and market places. But mostly there would be a soft cocooning, small comforting and safe bedrooms, all girlish and cradled in safety. Home was safe, her room was safe. She would dream of being warm, safe and alone in her room, that was what the recording would ensure, what her doctor would ensure, that was why she needed it so much. Once she used to fear sleep, fear the dreams, but not any more, not once her recording was playing.

The morning bloomed brightly through the stained glass of the window, the multi-hued shafts segregating the room with an arbitrarily shifting kaleidoscopic colour coding. She stretched out, the space around her, the king-size bed, momentarily disconcerting. Something had roused her, of that much she was certain, quite what it had been she knew not. There was some residual half-dredged recollection of a ringing bell yet she could see no source and all was now quiet save a general hubbub background of birdsong and the occasional raucous call of what she took to be a peacock. There was a confused grogginess about her, a mental fog, she almost felt hung-over, almost, but not quite, that was not quite it; it was more a weary, heavy, wooliness. Where what she?

As if in answer a nurse floated in through the shimmering coloured haze, an apparition in blue and white proffering a breakfast of fantastic proportion and variety. Figs, mangoes and fresh yoghurt vied with steaming scrambled egg, bacon and black pudding for her attention and all laid out on the glass top of an ornately carved wooden tray.

Breakfasted and having attended to her usual morning ablutions she found herself at a loss as to how to progress. The laundry basket had long gone on its way and she realised that she had not brought her suitcase from the car the previous night. She had the nightdress they had provided her with but little else. Again an answer had come to her unspoken question. It was uncanny; *it was almost as if someone were reading her mind!*

Chapter 2 | An Intertwining of Fates

There were two sharp raps upon her door and then there was yet another nurse, this one accompanying a wheelchair and proffering a bottle-green quilted housecoat that she carried draped over one arm and that, even in that position, as practical as it undoubtedly was, appeared quite hideous through her adolescent eyes. With what rapidity that teenage sensibility was to be expanded and challenged further we can only guess at. Suffice it to say that in quick succession she was to learn of her aunt's unexpectedly early departure, necessitated by the pressure of business, her eminent transferral to the experimental unit and the hospital's ruling that all patients be transferred by wheelchair regardless of their apparent fortitude.

The pep-talk took up the time; she was fortunate indeed to get accepted on such a program, she was to both confront and overcome her limitations and then, with their help, she would undoubtedly be offered a place at a much more prestigious university, when the time came, than the one to which she was originally destined. Moreover she would be leaving financially secure, she would be far more advantageously placed than the average student.

They had seemed to have traversed the network of affluent richly decorated passageways in mere moments, they had reached the lift and with the bleeping acceptance of a multi-digit code, preceded by the turning of a key, they were inside, the doors gliding closed with the faintest of clicks. A key was inserted into a control panel and turned. There came the gentlest of movements, barely a shudder and then only initially, then faint droning hum. There seemed no perception of movement. Ascending? Descending? She had no idea.

The nurse had come to the close of her little presentation as they had arrived at the lift and now stood silently alongside the wheelchair, the girl having been left facing the rear wall, there being insufficient room to manoeuvre the chair around once the doors had shut. She tried looking back over her shoulder, oddly there appeared to be no floor indicator, in fact there appeared to be no indicator of any sort. The inside of the lift appear to be featureless apart from the keyhole in the control panel and even that lacked any sort of indication or markings. The floor was covered in a thick white carpet, the walls and ceiling were every bit as white but with the appearance of some softly padded plastic material or fabric. How she was to come to dread this monotony of white she had as yet had little conception.

The nurse had simply inserted a key and turned it clockwise, perhaps a quarter turn. There was something about the movement, a certain discontinuity encoded as little time-lapses of hesitation, that suggested a series of alternative orientations were available, perhaps representing different floors. She decided that it must be the case but it was impossible to be sure. For while she mused over the rationale behind such a poorly designed and ambiguous system, for how long she couldn't tell, she always seemed to be in such a fog these days, calm, true, but muddled. Time often seemed to ebb and flow around her these days, it went quickly, it went slowly. What had she been thinking about? What *was* it? It was so annoying; she couldn't quite recollect, something to do with the lift controls? She just couldn't quite recall ...

The door hissed open. A nurse seemed to emerged from the adjacent wall like a ghost, her white uniform blurring the boundary between woman and structure. To some degree she had expected the clinical whiteness, just not to this extent, not taken to such sense-distorting perfection.

36

To her left the gently curving reception desk hid yet another nurse, as equally white-camouflaged as the first and appearing to almost to float like some apparition, discorporate within the contrast-impoverished landscape that was her habitat.

Pleasantries were minimal, a clipboard was handed to the reception desk nurse, her soft peach complexion exaggerated by the framing of her nun-like headdress, and duly signed. With that, her escort departed.

The girl had gone to stand but was asked to stay seated. Moments later they were on the move, the reception desk nurse pushing, her companion taking up the lead, perhaps two paces ahead. All around a silence reigned beyond any she had ever heard, if such an observation could ever be sensible. It was silent yet not *quite* silent. As she became acclimatised so she became aware of the soft rustle of the nurses' dresses, the rhythmic swish of nylon-clad legs. Tiny, insignificant, details assumed greater stature and new worth. She was learning the importance of observation; in time such minutiae would become an obsession.

Ahead, the nurse's full hips swung with pendulum fascination within the closely-fitted confines of her skirt. But it was something else that held the girl's attention. It hung from the nurse's belt, the woman having placed a hand against her right hip to steady its swing; every bit as long and thin as her aunt's cane yet white and lacking even the few ridges and irregularities expected and accepted of the smoothest rattan. There was a perfection to the finish, a sheen that suggested some form of plastic or, perhaps, glass fibre had been employed in its manufacture; the lower section rippled with each step, despite the woman's steadying hand, displaying a whip-like behaviour suggestive of an extreme, serpentine, flexibility.

It certainly could not be as it appeared of course; such a thing would be illegal no matter what waivers she might have signed. Obviously there was some sort of legitimate function for such a device, although, try as she may, she was unable to fathom any likely medical scenario that would require a long thin whippy length of plastic rod. Then again, who suffered corporal punishment nowadays, let alone in an institutional environment?, It would be more than they, or anyone else for that matter, would dare do these days, surely.

And yet was she not, herself, an exception? Of course there always had to be the exception to prove the rule, wasn't that what they said? Perhaps she *was* that exception? Besides, had not even *she* had cause to question the legitimacy of her aunt's introduction of it into their relationship? Had she not, on more than one occasion, entertained the notion that, as unlikely as it seemed, her aunt perhaps had some covert motive, that some sort of illicit satisfaction was to be wrung from her wielding of her cane. Always, though, her conclusion had been the same: It had to be this way, it was the only thing that would work with her, help her, she had deserved it. It was 'tough love', but did it have to be quite *so* tough? Her aunt had the right and she accepted that fact yet hated herself for her own docile acceptance. Why did she always seem to end up defending her aunt's treatment of her? Why, even in her own mind, did she always have to come up with these constant excuses for her aunt's behaviour, not to mention her own submission? Somehow she couldn't quite fathom, perhaps she never would, it was just the way it was. If anything it was diagnostic of her illness and yet that notion, in itself, only served to underline her aunt's integrity and add truth to her words...

Again her thoughts were interrupted; they had arrived. Before them stood a white door. A door as unremarkable in its plainness as it was extraordinary in its delineation, or rather its lack of delineation previous to its swinging out from the wall. Few barriers guarded greater transitions than that to be experienced by one crossing that threshold. Ahead, and standing aside so as to give passage to the wheelchair in which the girl now sat so apprehensively, the nurse bent at the waist, sweeping her right arm arcing through the air in an over exaggerated, almost ironic, gesture, welcoming her new patient to her new world. One girl's world, for the next three months anyway.

A Funeral: In Finality a New Beginning?

"Was it the dreams again?" Real concern, Julia's voice was a beacon cutting through the mental fog of sleep.

Sweat soaked her through, saturated her bedding, the girl was shaking. The woman braced her with one arm around her shoulders while arranging the pillows, so as to support her back as she sat up, with the other. There was a mug of warm milk waiting by her bedside and the usual brace of green and gold capsules.

A dream, Just a dream?. Not *just* a dream, *that* dream, that nightmare, again. How often had she awoken from it now, just like today. Why did it have to be today of all days? Wasn't it the funeral today? Where was she?

Julia's presence was somehow confusing, although, as always, she was grateful for it and for Julia's smiling reassurance. Susan Stringer looked around, her mind heavy, slow; she was in her room at home. It was coming back to her, it *was* the day of the funeral, *that* was why Julia was here, she had been staying over for the last few days to help out with the arrangements. Oh God, Oh God! It was today, at 10 o'clock, she was shaking again, sweating profusely in panic. Julia passed her the capsules then held the mug up to her lips for her to wash them down, she would hear no argument.

The procession snaked up and down avenues lined with London Plane trees passing two-storey terraced houses little changed since their 1880s inception. This had been his origin, his making, her father; they passed the house in which he had been born, the two houses in which he had subsequently been brought up throughout the later phases of those early years and, finally, they passed his first school.

The estate had been very different then of course, a private estate owned by the Church and built originally to house 19th-century railway workers. Later Westminster council had purchased the entire estate -the lowest point in its history some would say, the area deteriorating to the point of becoming downright dangerous to be in, at least after dark. Later still, many of the homes had been sold off to the residents; the resulting upsurge in pride had since transformed the area. Baskets of flowers now decorated doorways, flower boxes brightened window sills from behind carefully painted ornate barley-sugar twist guard rails of black iron. The Queen's Park estate, nice enough, now, yet lacking the gentrification typified by Notting Hill, merely a canal's width and a couple of main roads distant and just as equivalently in the shadow of the swaggering sun-blotting giant that is Trellik Tower.

These houses, though, lacked the grand scale of Notting Hill, little more than two-up-two-down brick-built semi-cottages huddling behind tiny front gardens, many still sporting privet hedges, with a plaque of stone over the front door decorated with a monogram and the date of building. At each turn a pair of spired roofs identified the corner houses, providing a faintly churchlike character to the welcome and a preparation for the idiosyncratic architecture lying beyond.

And then they were pulling out onto the grey bleakness of the Harrow Road, its only saving graces being the opening up of the view to the canal and the continued survival of the local library building. A short drive through the early lunchtime traffic saw them soon passing under the pale cream stone arch, the expanse of All Souls Cemetery, Kensal Green, opening up to accept them.

Throughout it was as if she was floating dreamlike; somehow it just wasn't real, she felt detached, but mercifully so. There had been ample enough time to reflect, this was all for the best really, a merciful release for her father and relief from her torture; he had been an active man, he would not have dealt well with the infirmity, the debility. That last stroke had been devastating, the damage widespread; had he survived he would have been left totally dependent, a prisoner in his own body. This had been the severest of a series of four such episodes, each more crippling than the last, the first of which had struck him barely 6 months ago. His death had not been unexpected but, nevertheless, she had had no option other than to witness his deterioration and with that, despite Julia's support, her own.

Yet, in truth, without Julia's support she couldn't have got through it: it had been Julia who had suggested and arranged the counselling sessions that had helped so much, Julia who had suggested that she delay her university placement. And she had been right too; she could see what Susan couldn't, that she wasn't ready for it, wouldn't be ready for it for quite some time, that she would need time to convalesce. Julia had handled it all for her; she had written to the relevant people, obtained assurances that her place would be kept open. Yes Julia had been wonderful throughout, she would be forever grateful; the consultations with her private doctor would not have come cheap yet without Julia's insistence she wouldn't have even recognised that she *needed* help. Without Julia's persuasion she would never have adopted the relaxation techniques the doctor had recommended nor accepted the use of the sedatives she prescribed, no matter how mild, how gentle. She knew now that without these things and without the concerted support of these two women, Julia and her doctor, she would not have gotten even this far.

Her stepmother was the first to emerge from the leading limousine. Susan had opted to travel in the third, or rather she had had the decision made for her; Julia had made so many decisions for her over the last six months, she always seemed to know what was for the best. As always she was closely accompanied by the supportive Julia, she was kept well away from the upsetting sight of her stepmother and well back from the infinitely more upsetting sight of her father's coffin; Julia had been right again.

Then, with grim inevitability, it was her turn to step out, she did so unsteadily gripping Julia's arm for support, Julia in her turn momentarily entertaining the notion that she had the girl somewhat over-sedated. In the event, Susan's unsteady gait went virtually unnoticed as did her slightly insensible, stupefied expression, most eyes being focused on the graveside and the 'grieving' widow.

Chapter 2 | An Intertwining of Fates

True, the girl's stepmother glanced across from time to time but showed little concern nor interest. Julia was taking the greatest of care to guide the girl, holding her close with a comforting arm round the shoulders.

All along it had been Julia that had orchestrated Susan's support and treatment; she had been a nurse, she was professional, responsible, she had recognised that the gentle sedatives, originally prescribed for the girl, would become insufficient but she knew also that a girl as independent as Susan, or rather as Susan had been, would be apt to reject the sense of dependency that came with heavier sedation. As the girl's father's condition had deteriorated, as the girl had become more upset, more amenable to support, so she had gradually increased the dose.

It had always been clear to her that the girl was going to need greater support, particularly towards the end and especially on this day - she had been careful, systematically monitoring the efficacy of each increment and ensuring that the changes would remain virtually imperceptible to her patient. More recently, though, she had been able to introduce greater hikes in Susan's medication, the girl having become far less conscious of the effects. True, Susan had, on occasion, exhibited evidence of having suffered brief amnesic episodes and it was true that, of late, those episodes were becoming more frequent but Julia, with her usual diligence, had been monitoring the situation.

To Julia this was an acceptable side effect; it only affected a relatively short period, at the peak of the dose, before the effects of the drug began to wear off. The girl was clearly not aware of these lapses and in many ways it was seen as beneficial. Indeed, it had been expected; Julia had kept careful records, subtly testing the girl without her being aware, assaying the effect at each increment by way of carefully structured probing questioning and feeding back the data to the girl's doctor. She estimated that at the next increment there would be reached a consistency of amnesic episodes, in that such an episode would occur with each provision of the girl's medication. If this proved the case they would plateau the dose, it would be then left to Julia to modulate the dose so as to tailor the length of each amnesic period to their requirements, if not then the dose would be incremented once more.

The weather seemed to conspire with the mood, overcast yet allowing for enough irony as to, on occasion, paint the distant chapel with shifting shafts of bright gold. Above them and all around the horse chestnut canopy seemed to be prematurely mottled in reds and variegated golds, autumnal even though only, in truth, late August.

There was a silence around the graveyard, a peace beyond the senses, the silence of lichen and mould and dank fallen pre-autumn leaves. There was an odour too, one that she associated with such places, had done since she was at school, when she had spent many a summer's afternoon with friends wandering, sitting, sometimes smoking, and not always tobacco, doing anything in fact rather than suffer maths or domestic science. Such places then had seemed gifts of salvation but that smell had been ever present and now permeated throughout those memories; death, she supposed, although, in truth, more likely the odour of some plant favouring soil enriched by mechanisms upon which she would rather not ponder nor dwell.

There was something else hanging on the air, the canal perhaps? She couldn't be sure what it was only that there was an oily industrial legacy to it and that it carried a darkness with it that seemed to emanate from the skeletal and obsolescent form of the gas holder hovering in the distance, over the preacher's shoulder, the image floating mirage-like through the distorting haze of her mind. Its obsolescence seemed a commentary on a man's life, her father's life; decay was everywhere and, even if not immediately apparent, was waiting in the wings. The priest's words washed over her, she was devastated, beyond comfort, beyond faith or belief.

There was no release to be had here, not for her, nor was there future promise offered. Euphemisms could not give comfort; he was *not* 'asleep', he was *not* 'resting', he had *not* 'passed on'. Her father was dead! There, she had done it, she had thought the unthinkable, admitted that of which she was in most denial; that she was now alone in the world!

Yes there was her stepmother of course, but here was a woman of an age more suggestive of an older sister and possessed of a nature that the term 'grasping' barely did justice to. That woman's mere presence was sacrilege enough, that she should dare shed a tear, hypocritical, an insult at best!. "The bitch, the bitch" the words ran through her mind, were all she could think of; at least the hatred blunted her grief.

Susan was the last to attend the graveside. She tossed a solitary rose down onto her father's coffin and read for the last time the brass plate, his name, her family name, not that bitch's. The first earth was falling onto the pine as she turned away, somewhere a rook or two muttered a mourning croak. She broke down entirely, ran, stumblingly, to the arms so often her support in the past and more so now, more than ever before.

There was irony here, as there was irony everywhere about her; this woman was that bitch's best friend, was actually faintly related to her in some distant way, she gathered, and yet they were as different as chalk and cheese. Julia had this empathy, warm and genuine; it was almost as if she could read her mind - from the very start. Julia was the only one who had ever really understood her, the only one to have recognised her problems, who had recognised issues that she, herself, had been unaware of.

Their meeting had been accidental, fantastically so. It had come about with serendipity beyond explanation. She just happened to have been visiting the very day her father had first been taken ill. Her concern and support had been immediate and genuine; it had been Julia who had accompanied her to the hospital, not *that* bitch. No, not her; her stepmother had stayed behind, there had been important calls to make apparently, clearly more important to her than her father's well-being had ever been. Since that day their relationship might best be described as un-separable, yet not as friends *per se*, not really as equals; somehow there had never quite developed that familiarity. There had always been some distance reserved between them and yet that distance was welcome somehow.

Julia was like an elder aunt, a title that woman preferred and the use of which she encouraged. Not that she was particularly easygoing, far from it; it would be fair to say that she had a propensity to be overbearing, perhaps even controlling. It was just that the support and comfort she offered had become so much a part of Susan's life.

Chapter 2 | An Intertwining of Fates

Julia's insightful explanations could be as reassuring as the revelations were unsettling - she had been on the threshold of some kind of nervous breakdown, that much was clear to her now. It was also clear to her just how much she owed Julia, needed Julia; after all just how right had she been? Just *how* accurate her reading of the situation had been. The woman's insight had been quickly confirmed by professional diagnosis, once Susan's initial stubbornness had been overcome and she had finally deferred to Julia's persuasion to submit to a consultation.

The hearse and the limousines were pulling away now. She had been expected to take her place alongside her stepmother, at least for the return journey. Distraught beyond measure, despite the warm heavy-numbing effects of her pharmacological crutch, she would have nothing of it. She would not sit alongside that bitch; her furs, the designer black funereal accessories, brought bile to her throat.

'Aunt' Julia's invitation came as a godsend, a reaffirmation of faith. At that moment she would have agreed to anything other than having to return home with that bitch, anything, and to make matters worse the effects of the sedatives were beginning to wear off, she could sense the fear and panic returning. She needed Julia, aunt Julia.

There were provisos, of course there were; The woman lived alone, save for a house keeper, she was well used to her privacy, her 'own space' as she put it. There would have to be rules, limitations and restrictions but at least she would be outside of that bitch's sphere of influence. Besides the decision had been made, Julia had decided. As always Julia knew what was best for her and she clearly wasn't going to allow even the *contemplation* of refusal, nor any reconsideration.

"I'm not at all sure you should put yourself through any more of this, returning home right now would be unbearable for you, the pain would come flooding in, trust me, it would be all too familiar, too closely associated with your farther. You need space in which to mourn." The woman's arms were enfolding, guiding. Susan was in the limousine and heading off without ever having really regained her composure, it was *fait accompli*, as simple as that, all for her own good. The decision had been made; it had been tangible within that embrace. The decision had not truly been Susan's, when had it ever been?

CHAPTER 3

LIFE AT AUNT JULIA'S: NEUROSIS, FRUSTRATION, AN AUNT AND THREE STRIPES

She awoke with a start, something had awoken her yet there seemed nothing to account for the disturbance. For a while she seemed to be experiencing a strangely familiar disorientation; she lay lost, floating in a sort of confused and misguided *Déjà vu*. Her surroundings, the childish nursery-style wallpaper, floppy-eared bunnies, all pink and grey, the matching curtains and flounced bed cover, the children's glitter-star spangled mobile hanging over the bed, all were familiar and yet strange. She was home yet not *at* home. Three months it had been since her father's passing, three months of cosseted residence with her 'aunt'. Still there was this oddly disorientating atmosphere, a dream-like quality that accompanied each awakening and that she couldn't quite pin down nor shake off; the world around her, the safe yet narrow little world she shared with her therapist and her aunt, seemed in a constant state of flux. Forever familiar, reassuringly nostalgic, yet strange, isolated, forever strange, a waking-dream almost.

Not that Aunt Julia's home had been unfamiliar to her when she had moved in; many were the times over that terrible six months of her father's suffering that Susan had taken a break here. At first it had been just for the occasional weekend, providing her with a short, but nevertheless essential, respite from the constant worry, friction and stress of her home life. Gradually such visits had become a semi-regular part of her life, evolving and lengthening into vacations of, at first, a week and then of two weeks. Over these last three months, though, ever since the day of the funeral in fact, things had been different. She had taken up a semi-permanent residence with her aunt, not that she would have wanted to have imposed upon Julia,. Indeed such an accusation could hardly have been levied; the woman's invitation had been insistent to say the least, a refusal would never have been accepted nor had it ever been an option.

In all this time Susan had yet to return home; there was dread there. There were memories there that she just didn't have the strength to face, not yet. There had been experiences there that she had little enthusiasm to relive. And she didn't have to. She didn't have to face those things, relive those dark days. Aunt Julia would deal with it all, she had made that much clear; she wasn't going to *allow* Susan to face it. For her part, Susan didn't want any link with that time and, with aunt Julia's encouragement, she was trying her best to blank it out, all of it, at least for the time being.

She had thought about having some of her clothes and other personal belongings brought over but with her characteristic indecision and procrastination had still to do so.

Not that she would have had to have been personally involved; Julia had said from the start that she would be happy to organise it, yet somehow, for one reason or another, the opportunity never seemed to arise, the chore always seemed to get postponed. Then again, Julia had tended to discourage it and Susan's councillor, an acquaintance of Aunt Julia's, tended to concur. The consensus of opinion was that, for the immediate future, she cut herself off from anything and everything pertaining to her old life. For the immediate future isolation was to be her restorative, isolation would provided her with the space she required if she was to grow, if she was to progress beyond this point.

What with the hurried arrangements and the distressing occasion Susan had been unable to bring much with her; Julia had insisted that they depart immediately after the funeral and would broach no argument. After the first couple of weeks or so the few things that Susan had brought during her previous sojourns to Julia's home had become somewhat overdue at the laundry. The clothes she had arrived in, a her funeral outfit, had quickly been labelled as unsuitable and packed well away, Julia saying, quite rightly, that it was probably better they be out of sight and out of mind.

A temporary solution had been proposed in the shape of an old tennis dress. This was an oddly dated-looking A-line panelled style in white cotton that came with matching and daintily frilled white knickers and that was decorated over the left breast by embroidery work in green and gold thread. The latter formed what seemed to be some sort of badge consisting of a heraldic shield upon which was what appeared, bizarrely, to be a depiction of an open textbook crossed diagonally from either side by what looked like two traditional crook-handled school canes, the whole being surmounted by a Latin motto.

Some days she remained in her nightdress but to sit out in the garden or to attend the lessons Julia had organised for her, Julia having enlisted the help of a home tutor, it was always that old tennis dress. There was often talk of a shopping trip and the purchase of a new wardrobe for her, yet, somehow, it never seemed to quite materialise. Likewise the few things she had kept at Julia's never seemed to have found their way home from the laundry.

She never felt the need to question these developments, her life had just settled into a comfortable, easy, routine; in a way she felt too comfortable to question. Indeed, she was loath to talk about, or even think about, anything that might threaten to freshen the memory of the dark period that had gone before. Subconsciously she was doing anything possible to avoid thinking about that awful day, anxious to avoid any mention, any reminder, any thought or memory.

Similarly the developments in her social life, or rather the latter's deterioration, went un-remarked and engendered little concern. Her boyfriend had drifted away during the early days of her father's illness, it had been her own fault, she had spurned his concern then neglected their relationship and had finally driven him off. Then there were her circle of so called 'friends', many she had lost contact with when she had left school, true some had persisted and a couple had even kept in contact for a while in writing when she had first moved to aunt Julia's. Gradually, though, the correspondence had dropped off, the replies to her letters dwindled and, what was more the truth of the matter, she had lost interest in keeping contact.

Had she just become lazy or had the act of correspondence become too painful? Did it smack too much of linking to her past? She wasn't sure, but deep down inside she knew that, for her own good, she should avoid anything that threatened to link her mind with that awful period, and that included 'friends'.

In this belief she was aided and abetted by the words and deeds of both her therapist and Aunt Julia, although it has to be said that the sedative her therapist had prescribed, although mild, had had its part to play. This latter cushion was something on which Susan increasingly seemed to drift from day to day, seemingly floating aimlessly around the house like the white fluffy clouds that she sometimes felt were inhabiting her head. That the dose had been gradually and progressively incremented since its first prescription undoubtedly bore no little responsibility for this.

To the lay eye perhaps, a fly on the wall as it were, the girl would almost certainly have appeared over-sedated at this point. Indeed, it must be said that the entire situation, if viewed from afar, might likely have raised some eyebrows, perhaps engendered concern, in even the most dispassionate of observers. As a lay person one might well, and perhaps justifyingly, have raised the concern that the girl was becoming a little too dependent on both sedative and therapist. However, is it not often the case that the remote observer, being not privy to the full intricacies of the plot, as it were, and lacking the detailed insight of the professional, perhaps confused by the subtle and the complex motives involved, is prone to misunderstanding? How easy it is to misunderstand a situation taken at face value. Is it not prudent, under such circumstances, that one gives sway to the judgment of the learned professional? After all, who are we onlookers to judge what is, or is not, being done in the girl's best interest? Who are we, mere lay observers, to criticise the likes of the most eminent Dr Ecclestone?

Not that the developments surrounding Susan's life had stagnated; there had always been changes, never drastic but changes nonetheless and evolving over time. One example; Julia had always encourage the term 'aunt' be used of course, it seemed to engender trust, but gradually, over time, Susan's consistent use of this title seemed to assume a greater importance to the woman. Julia gradually became more insistent on its use. Now she wanted Susan to use it whenever she needed anything, whenever she was told to do anything - more and more often it felt to Susan as if she was being told, rather than requested, to do one thing or another. Likewise whenever she received anything the preferred expression of due gratitude was now always that suffixed with the term 'Aunt Julia'; "...a nice quiet and polite 'thank you Aunt Julia' is what I would prefer to hear" as Julia had said.

Thus it was this particular morning, but this morning was to be one of a sudden lurch, for certainly the terms ' shift' or change were insufficient, in her circumstance.

It had started uncharacteristically mild for early December in Surrey, even if set against the backdrop of a Britain held in the chaotic grip of increasingly wild and unpredictable shifting weather patterns - the legacy of global warming it was said. Not that such dire warnings held much relevance to Susan. She was shielded from such uncertainties, discouraged from unnecessary involvement in current affairs.

Television and radio were not exactly banned in this household just carefully vetted. Anything thought potentially worrying or upsetting or likely to become so, was banned, or so well discouraged as to effectively be so, music was to be classical and then of the softest, gentlest pieces available: Aunt Julia's dislike of 'loud music', by which she inferred almost anything in any modern idiom, was well-known.

As usual her early-morning cocoa arrived courtesy of Julia, the two sedative capsules rolling loosely around on the tray, their glistening green and black plastic coating catching the few rays of sunlight that had managed to sneak through the narrow gap in the curtains. The girl's eyes were bleary and thick with sleep, her mind sluggish, weighed down with the after-effects of the sleeping pills that had only recently been added to her regime. She sat up slowly, drowsily, uncertainly and shakily reached for the mug and the first of the capsules, the tray having been placed on her bedside cabinet. Then the shock:

"How many times do I have to remind you, how many? Thank you, Aunt Julia, that's all want to hear, thank you, Aunt Julia! How difficult can it be to just remember to be polite when someone has gone out of their way to look after you, when someone has been kind enough to wake you up with a lovely mug of cocoa?"

The mug seemed to throw itself out of her hand, dark golden-brown cocoa staining covers and carpet alike; Aunt Julia's voice had been piercing, her anger and irritation annunciated with every syllable. She had never known her aunt express anything like *impatience* before, let alone anger, and anger of such magnitude. It seemed so out of character, notwithstanding the woman's undeniably overbearing stance at times, but more than that, it seemed out of all proportion. And it was continuing unabated...

"Do I need to punish you like a child; is that what you'd like? I'll tell you this much; if things don't improve, and quickly, I think it might be better for all concerned if you were to return home!"

Susan was horrified; her aunt seemed to be almost shaking with anger.

Aunt Julia went on: "The least you could do is apologise, *what* should you say? Come on."

"I,I'm s,sorry, Aunt Julia"

"That's better!, Now, what *else* do we say?"

A pause and then, comprehension coming slowly: "Thank you, Aunt Julia."
In that moment a change had come, an irrevocable change in their relationship, no gradual shift in equilibrium, not the evolutionary drift of old, no, now there was a definite and deliberate intent to the proceedings.

For Susan's part, she was rattled; she had been threatened with being sent home and then there was this mention of 'punishment', what did it mean? Most of all, though, it was the thought of being sent away that most mortified her. On reflection, nothing else really mattered to quite the same extent, she needed her 'aunt', had come to depend on her, she needed to be here, needed to stay right here. Her inner voice succinctly summed it up: "Aunt Julia is the only one who can help, who *wants* to help".

But what if she could see into her aunt's mind, what then? What if she could see through her aunt's eyes, see the reason for her aunt's distant expression, share her fond memories - let alone her future plans - what then?

Would she still listen to her inner voice or would she, at last, begin to question herself, question her own beliefs? Would she, perhaps, question those thoughts, beliefs and ideas that seemed to be hers, and hers alone, and yet were so strangely alien? And behind her aunt's kindly, yet distant, gaze?...

The memory had come to Julia in an intrusive flash: It was a couple of years old now, this recollection, yet as clear as if it had been that very morning. She had gone to see Anne's, then new, house. She already knew at the time that her friend employed a young girl to help out around the home; previously a live-in nanny who, through some dispute or other, had fallen out with her employer and who Anne, being friend to both girl and employer, had felt obliged to put a roof over, as it were. Other than that the girl's name was Penny she had known little else about her friend's 'little helper' up until that day. Nor had she given the situation much consideration other than to wonder at how an arrangement, supposedly intended to be temporary, had come to persist for what was rapidly approaching two years; it had irritated her to think that her friend's hospitality might be exploited so.

She had known Anne for years, she should have known differently than to have thought that *she* would be the one to be exploited, far from it. Dr Anne Ecclestone always had good reason for everything she did; her talent for turning adversity and misfortune, even if not her own, to opportunity was the stuff of legend, gossiped over in tea rooms and common rooms across the campus.

On this particular day the adversity was some drama or other in the kitchen; a packet of peppercorns, it turned out, had been spilt across the floor. The misfortune was undisputedly penny's and the opportunity, as always, seized with both hands by Anne. For a moment there had seemed a danger of a tantrum on the girl's part, the spectre of an embarrassing domestic upheaval unveiling before a guest loomed large. That moment had been brief however. Indeed, the moment had been expertly pressed into service. The potential for embarrassment was not only circumvented but turned to advantage as visitor became witness; before her eyes Anne had amply demonstrated the effect of such training as had since been adopted by Julia herself and that she was presently bringing to bear on *her* charge.

It had been a moment of enlightenment; the use of psychological methods, even if subtle, in fact the more subtle, the more efficacious she was later to learn, could clearly provide a greater degree of influence over a girl then she would, at that point, have ever dreamed possible. Flexed in hands such as Anne's and wielded in the correct manner even the most rebellious of spirits could be curbed. Indeed, her enlightenment had grown with every moment; a few words, well chosen, can punish like the whip or reward as might the lover's caress, the harshest of chastisement juxtaposed with the sweetest of carrots.

This, most certainly, was not intended to replace physical chastisement, she had learnt, far from it. She could clearly recall how Penny had knelt before the two of them, brushing the peppercorns into a neat pile.

In her mind's eye she could still see Anne standing there in her black leather knee-length skirt and white satin blouse, hands on hips, the right flexing rhythmically at the wrist as she tapped the leather tab of the riding crop insistently against her skirt hem, her legs astride of the area wherein knelt the girl, looming over her. "Clear it up you stupid child. Now, get up, come on, quickly." Anne's voice revealing a harshness to its character that she had never before noticed.

With her pink nylon overall rustling with every movement the 'child' had risen to her feet. Despite having reached the age of majority, her 21st birthday having passed some two months previously, being addressed as 'child' had clearly been nothing new to her. "The ' child' addressed as such tends to behave as such"; the gospel according to Anne, by which she meant that in emphasising and implying a child's dependency she was also continuously underlining her own authority.

The obedience to the snapped command had been immediate and automatic even in front of a visitor, a witness such as Julia whom she had never before met and to whom the only 'first impression' *she* could ever hope to achieve was that of downtrodden skivvy. Though her burning cheeks had betrayed her humiliation there had been no hesitation, no hint of rebellion; all too often hesitation had been awarded a good half dozen swift cuts of Anne's thin cane or riding crop across that fat bottom of hers or, indeed, the equally painful cuts of expertly chosen words across that vulnerable mind. The girl was controlled in equal part by word and cane, as would, in time, be Susan; yes, it would take time, it couldn't be rushed, but now that she was certain, certain that she had her fully in her hands, it would be inevitable…

As we watch, scenes evolve to acts, intrigue and subplot evolve to history. As such, as a tale couched in past tense and with an admitted ambiguity of timeline, we can only gaze back at *fête accompli*. Surely then, we, as mere observers here, are absolved of all guilt; even to the point of allowing that we might entertain a certain secret voyeuristic delight. For there can be no greater distance, no greater divide, than that which spans even the most miniscule expanse of time.

Frustration is a Velvet Touch Conditioned by Word and Rattan

Exactly at what point in her stay it had started she couldn't quite say. Not that she hadn't sometimes done it, on occasion, before she had come here; what woman hasn't ever taken some solitary comfort? No, it wasn't that which was bothering her, it wasn't the sense of guilt, rather it was this uneasy sense of it being out of control. No, she couldn't quite say when it had started to become the way it was now. It certainly hadn't been in the first few days after her arrival, she would have been far too upset. No, it had just slowly crept up on her, insidiously.

It had started in the mornings, her aunt would bring her cocoa and with it her medication and, after waiting just long enough to supervise her taking the capsules, would take her leave to attend to her work. Generally, Susan would finish around half her drink, the full mug was way too much for her at that time of the morning, before reclining on her pillows once more and, reaching across to her aunt's old cassette player, settling back to enjoy one of her relaxation tapes. At some point she would always doze off to awaken perhaps an hour or so later; Aunt Julia never demanded that she rise any particular time of the day, believing that she best be left to relax as much as possible, the only proviso being that she be up and dressed by midday on the days that her aunt had arranged for her tutor or the doctor to visit.

It was when awakening from this doze, when she was at her most comfortable, that her fingers would begin their secret exploration, their gentle probing experimentation.

At first it had been as it always had, at home alone in her bedroom, yet it had been sweeter somehow, it had lacked the pangs of guilt. Gradually, though, it had changed, became more demanding, nagging, it would intrude on her thoughts through the day and she began to find it harder to concentrate. It was becoming more than a habit, more, even, than an obsession; it was becoming an addiction, it was consuming her. It was no longer the way it had been, it was if those tormenting digits were no longer hers; there was a rhythm and a tempo to their manipulative caresses that would be constant throughout, no faster nor slower. She seemed to be totally unable to either make their strokes more rapid or the stimulation more intense, there was just that excruciatingly slow rhythm. She would reach orgasm eventually, the resulting delayed release shattering in its intensity, but could do nothing to hasten its sweet absolve.

Many, many, such mornings passed filled with ever more lingering and teetering pleasure and with her ever less unable to break the gentle, lazy, swinging rhythm that her soft fingers dictated, no matter how tantalisingly and tremblingly close to release she came.

Each morning it seemed to go on longer, her orgasm towering ever higher, always hinting at ever greater delights beyond, the foothills ever steeper. Her fingers were learning their art well, becoming such beautifully tormenting torturers.

This day had been the most intense so far; left to her own devices she would have rushed at it, thrashed her way to completion well before this point. The sensational waves rippling through her, threatening to tear apart her very sanity, had reached a point beyond bearing long, long ago; in actuality some thirty minutes previously. Nevertheless she climbed inexorably towards her climax, slowly, oh so, so slowly. Her lips moved, softly sighing, then begging for release, then sighing once more, her body slithered with serpent-like undulations amongst sweat-soaked bedding. Still those fingers would not let her go.

They savoured their control, their sensitive silken tips had learnt too much of her desire to allow her release of her own free will; those fingers were far too educated now, they were not going to let her off so easily. It didn't matter what *she* wanted; those fingertips would only brush with just enough pressure and with just sufficiently rapid tempo so as to ensure that the promise remained and that the summit ever approached, came ever closer. They would provide for just enough to drive her on, but no more than that.

Then, right there, right at the summit, right at the edge, those fingers began to soften their caress, slow their tempo, maddeningly just when she needed it most, threatening to leave her stranded just short, so, so, close and then, and then... There was something pressing against her anus, then penetrating, a finger that now slowly, lazily, dragged across that sensitive and most private rosebud, the final straw had come...

Her other hand? Why had she done that? Her hand?

The spasms of orgasm were rippling through her still, her stomach muscles contracting rhythmically and uncontrollably. Dully, with the last vestiges of fading consciousness, she became aware of something rhythmically squeezing the index finger of her right hand, the hand that had rescued her; her anus, in its turn, with concerted spasm, was reporting back the details of its gratefully-delicious violation.

Her vagina repeatedly and uncontrollably sucked at the fingers of her left hand, their tips wrinkled and soaked in the clinging moisture of over an hour's expert stimulation and denial, moisture that was trickling thickly down to pool in globs on the already sweat-soaked sheets.

For a while she just lay there, she always did, but this time she was barely conscious, this time she had lost control, totally. Then, gradually, the wet discomfort forced it way through her floating afterglow, rudely dragging her back to the reality of what had just happened, showering her with consternation, whispering to her of the most hideous and humiliating repercussions. There had often been some dampness, some sweat to mingle with her guilt, but never anything like this.

Easing herself tackily from between the sheets, the duvet having long departed for the floor, peeling the cotton from her skin where her nightdress had ridden up into thick white satin folds around her midriff, she gained her feet unsteadily. Looking down, the true horror hit her, disgusting, mortifying; the bottom sheet in particular accused her, the staining obvious even given a most cursory glance. What if her aunt should see? Mrs Chartriss, the housekeeper, when she came to change the bedding, how could she miss it? What would she think it was? Worse, would she *know* what it was? Whichever the scenario, and one or the other was inevitable, the outcome was too hideous to contemplate; she would just die, surely she would.

An idea formed, she glanced over at the mantel clock, a marble and bronze art deco creation flanked on either side by kneeling supplicant female figures of voluptuous proportions. Aunt Julia would be in her study at this hour and her housekeeper would be collecting the groceries, she would have to be quick but as long as she was quiet she could go about her business unnoticed and unchallenged.

The first wash cycle had been underway for some time before Aunt Julia appeared at the top of the stairs. Despite the utility room being located in the basement and possessing a concrete floor the washing machine's rumble tended to propagate up through the structure. Susan had known that of course, she could sometimes make out the low hum in her room, but she had hoped that her aunt would be too engrossed in her work to notice or would ignore it, believing it to be simply her housekeeper at work. She had reckoned without her aunt's attention to detail and her almost obsessive supervision of her charge.

Aunt Julia smiled down at her. Her eyes signalled friendship yet there was a subtle component of scolding about her speech, almost playful yet with an overtone note of concern. Susan was left without doubt that she wouldn't get away with this again, but on this occasion, at least, the evidence had been successfully concealed. "What are you doing down there, sweetheart?"

Susan thought quickly or at least as nimbly as she could within the constraint of the ever-present hobble that was her medication. "I, I thought I should help out a little from time to time. It's just my night things, aunty." Why had she used that particular form of address, she never had before? She felt sheepish, the peculiarly childish form of address she had just absentmindedly used filled her with embarrassment; her cheeks began to burn and, cursing her propensity to blush, she attempted to correct herself, yet only succeeded in making matters worse. "I,I m,mean aun…"

50

"Sssh!, calm down, sweetheart" Aunt Julia's interjection, pointedly truncating her attempted correction, somehow magnified her awkwardness; Susan felt tongue-tied, small. "You know you don't have to do that. It is one of the reasons that I employ a housekeeper, you silly girl." The tone was gently scolding. "The reason that *you* are here is to convalesce. Remember what the doctor said? We want you to relax *totally* for a while, that's the whole point, to rest, to relax totally and I mean totally. You *know* you shouldn't be concerning yourself with *any* kind of work at the moment, not at this stage, sweetheart. You *know* how quickly you get tired; you're just not quite feeling yourself right now, are you?"

Aunt Julia had been slowly descending the steps throughout the scolding and now, having reached the front of the washing machine, momentarily glancing down at the settings, she placed an arm around her charge and began to gently guide her back up towards the main house. "Come along, honey, you're looking *very* tired. You look so flushed; I don't think you're feeling very well. You're really *not* feeling very well, are you, sweetheart?"

This last sentence, in truth, was not a question, not even hypothetically, it was more a statement of fact, almost an instruction. Her aunt never really *asked* her how she felt, she didn't seem to have to, it was as if she could read her mind. It was the same with her doctor. She guessed it was that insight what made her so good at her job, her diagnosis so complete. There were times, though, when it seemed as if she was being virtually *told* how she felt, how she *should* feel and yet, unaccountably, she always seemed to accept it. Deep down, she felt sure that it was true, that they were right about her, but she didn't want to have to admit it to herself. Surely, though, this morning's episode was evidence enough.

"It's quite nice out today, why not have a sit in the garden for a while?" They had reached the lounge wherein the late November sun played in autumnal pools of dark orange-brown across the parquet flooring and floor-length curtains floated away gently on the rustling breeze to either side of the part-open French-doors.

There was a slight chill to the air, although it was still far warmer than it had any right to be at this time of the year. As usual she had on the short tennis dress that her aunt had given her, she would have to face going home at some point, retrieve her own things, but for now it would have to do. Today, though, she would need to wear something over the top against that chill if she was to venture out. As always her aunt had the remedy close at hand; she held up the navy-blue quilted nylon housecoat by its shoulders for Susan to slip into.

Quite from where her aunt had procured this particular sartorial gem was something of a mystery. It had simply appeared on the coat hook at the back of her bedroom door a couple of weeks previously. It was a horrid thing, it really was, but at least it was of an adult appearance, albeit suited to a much older woman than Susan.

She slipped her arms back into the sleeves while her aunt held it aloft, the soft nylon quilt initially chilling her, belying the warmth it would soon provide and of which she would be grateful once out in the chill garden air. Much to Susan's annoyance and frustration Aunt Julia, coming around to the front, began to fasten the buttons for her. This was something her aunt was becoming more and more apt to do of late and that had, on more than one occasion, been the catalyst for no little friction between them.

Not that she wasn't grateful for her aunt's concern but, after all, she wasn't an invalid and it irritated her. Recently there had been times when she had begun to feel a little stifled, when it had felt to her as though her aunt was treating her as if she was mentally defective or something.

Together they walked out to greet the early afternoon sun, Aunt Julia clearly elated by the crisp early-winter beauty of the scene, Susan, a little less certain. The latter, despite the housekeeper's absence, remaining a little self-conscious as to her appearance while, at the same time, being glad of the extra warmth and grateful that at least that silly little tennis dress was now hidden from view.

After a few minutes stroll Julia returned her study, leaving her charge to her own devices. A folding garden chair waited, all softly padded and inviting, by the fish pond. Susan sat for a while listening to the little fountain's tinkling raindrop fall and watching the goldfish drift below the rippling surface, below the little flashes of sunlight that reflected off the surface like a myriad twinkling stars. As so many times before it was those rippling shifting star-spangled patterns of light that drew her attention, the fish below drifting outside her depth of field before, slowly, the glinting wavelet-born starlight itself drifted out of focus. She was all alone with that strangely pleasant, otherworldly, sensation that was so familiar to her now, as if she was drifting out of her body, as if she wasn't really there, not physically.

Thirty minutes had passed by the time Julia returned, now carrying her little tape player. Susan was sitting motionless, her wide eyes reflecting the water's shimmering surface in their own calm pools. Coming up behind the girl, the woman's long, delicate, fingers gently reached out to the nape of her neck, beginning a slow, rhythmic, longitudinal stroking action, up and down, up and down; there was no discernible response from her charge. Only when after some time there was still no response from the girl did she begin to speak:

"The pool is ever so relaxing, don't you think? You love watching the fish glide, back and forth, back and forth, below the ripples, but it is so, so, tiring trying to keep your eyes on the fish with those pretty ripples flowing across, so, so tiring. Look at the ripples, look at the lovely silvery light, look at the soft soothing ripples, they are *so* beautiful and yet so *tiring* to watch, so beautiful that you have to watch them, so tiring, so, *so* tiring that your eyes feel too tired even to look away. As each ripple passes the world around you seems more and more to drift away, more and more to drift out of focus. There are *only* the softly rippling pools of light, now. The only sound that you can hear now is my voice, growing sweeter, more lovely with each ripple that passes. My lovely, lovely, sweet voice, your aunty's voice, the voice of your aunty that you love and trust so, so, much. You do *so* love your aunty don't you?"

The voice flowed sweetly past, swirling and eddying around the girl with the slow motion ooze of molasses, a gentle inundation that softly swallowed her thoughts, ideas and beliefs in its insistently rising, sticky, tide. From somewhere Susan heard a new voice, her *own* voice, it was her own voice so she knew it must be true: "Yes, aunty, I do, *so* love you aunty, I love you ever so much."

"That *is* a good girl, you are *such* a good girl. Now, why not let your eyes close, just for a while, have a nice little nap, you *know* how *very* tired you are. That's it, let's rest those tired eyes. Those tired eyes are closing now, closing, closing."

With her left hand the woman reached around to ever so gently brush her fingers down across the girl's eyelids, the latter fluttering like butterfly wings before coming to settle over those pretty-pool eyes. Fairies lived in the ripples and swam through the fountain's rainbow-lit spray. Hand in hand they danced across her dreams, flickering and flittering about the pool, sprinkling in sleepy-dust all that came close, all who heard their whisper. Susan slept, the fountain-fairies' whispered lullaby now joined by the soft voice from the earphones. Julia returned to her study; the tape had an hour to run and she had much to get on with.

Susan dozed on in the winter sun, a blanket lying across her legs and lap draping down to her ankles to keep warm her legs below the housecoat's hem. From time to time Julia checked her charge from the study window; it was getting far too late in year for bare legs, she thought. She would have to sort something out for her, not tights though, definitely not tights, so unhygienic, it would have to be stockings. A shiver ran through her and, forcing the image from her mind with no little effort, she returned to her work.

The next few mornings found Susan more and more succumbing to temptation despite her resolution to desist and her growing sense of self-disgust. Again and again there came the torturous attention of those fingers, her own fingers, their seduction now perfected to the point of rendering nonsensical any pretence of self-control. Again there came the mortifying acknowledgement of the evidence of her misbehaviour, and again, and again.

She tried turning the bottom sheet over, then tried turning it the other way around. Perhaps tomorrow she could get it to the washing machine without anyone noticing. But tomorrow never came; always there seemed to be someone around, either her aunt of the housekeeper. Both ends became stained, then stained multiple times, the discoloration overlapping and darkening, and then...

It had happened. She had returned to her room after her shower, her mouth fell open aghast; her bed had been stripped. Her aunt or the housekeeper, it didn't matter who, whoever it was they couldn't have missed it, the telltale staining, the sinful odour.

All day she had done her best to avoid both women, at tea they were both present, at tea she self-consciously waited, weighed down by guilt and embarrassment, her cheeks shamefully burning. She waited for some comment, a knowing look perhaps, yet nothing was said nor were knowing glances exchanged. For a while there was relief, everything seemed to be normal, then gradually a new dimension of consternation began to open up; surely everything was *too* normal, one of them *must* have seen it, how could it have been missed?

She was glad when the evening finally drew to a close and she could return to the familiar comfort of her bed. Yawning, she pulled back the covers; no, nothing had been said, and for that she was grateful, but if she had thought that her indiscretions had gone unnoticed she was clearly mistaken and the extent of that naiveté was staring back at her. At first glance all had looked normal then with a double take it had hit her; a rubber mattress cover had taken the place of the bottom sheet.

A full week went by, still without comment, still all seemingly routine. For the first few days her embarrassment had augmented her self-control but then, gradually, the habit returned.

The rubber cover added to the humidity, kept her sweat around her and became slippery with her juices. If anything it added to the piquancy – more and more often she would awake to find her nightdress was as stained as her sheets had been. She had progressed to caressing herself through the fabric, the satin offering a subtle interface, prolonging still further the agony and ecstasy of it. Again she could do nothing to hide the fact, nothing that would assuage the mortification she felt, yet still nothing was said.

The nightdress would be whisked away to the laundry pile and returned, magically, to her pillow without comment, again, and again, and again. On the third or fourth such occasion though, still without discussion or recrimination, she found that her nightdress was now accompanied by a pair of short legged knickers, her mortification being completed by the discovery that the soft satin disguised beneath a latex inner lining. Nothing had been said, nothing needed to be said - the accusation was right there in her hands, embodied in the protective garment and as silent as it had been with the provision of the rubber bed cover. Unlike on the latter occasion though, she was granted no respite, not even temporarily. Quite the contrary; the drive, the ache, not only went unabated, it seemed to have intensified.

There was something about those knickers, the sensuous slippery softness of the satin, the intimately lubricated caress of the latex and, yes, the smell, even the smell. She couldn't keep her hands off herself; her fingers now drew out their delightful torture of her at night as much as in the morning. There were two, then three sessions daily until it was as much as she could do to think of anything else during the day other than to anticipate the hour at which she could again retire to the privacy of her room. Excuses soon came in many guises - she needed an afternoon nap, she had a headache - her ingenuity forever being stretched and taxed in her drive to return to the warmth and comfort of her rubber sheet and those knickers.

Time passed, the winter drew in more closely about them and despite the weather-man's predictions the garden was white with frost more often than not. As had been promised a shopping opportunity had finally materialised but Susan had turned it down; Aunt Julia had gone alone, Susan preferring the safety of home and the privacy of her room. The result had been somewhat disappointing as far as the girl was concerned, Aunt Julia returning with several pairs of stockings, a quite hideous button-through bottle green long-sleeved cardigan, that looked as if it belonged in some school somewhere, and an old-fashioned open-bottomed girdle that she was assured would be: "More comfortable then a suspender belt". Other than these additions to her wardrobe there had been little change to her routine.

There was still the silly little tennis dress, although now augmented by the cardigan and worn over the girdle and stockings ensemble, the latter, being of a long length and being teamed with short suspenders, remaining 'decent' even under the short dress. There were still the regular visits to the privacy of her room, such visits having grown in frequency as her torturers had refined their torment of her; more often than not in daylight hours she felt compelled to return to her aunt's company despite having failed to reach a satisfactory conclusion, the frustrated ache coming with her and taunting her with promises of later release.

That she no longer wore the matching tennis knickers below her dress aggravated her condition; *those* knickers, she had been told, had been packed away. Their replacement had been described as being more substantial and far more suitable in the chill of winter. Indeed the new knickers *were* more substantial; high wasted 'big knickers' they were of a shiny white nylon satin but, like her bedtime attire, they were lined in the finest, most clinging, latex. All day she could feel the intimate slipping and sliding of the soft rubber, she was now practically permanently wet, practically permanently aroused, living only for the return to the attention of her lover, tormentor and torturer.

Had time stood still or had an age passed in the blink of an eye? It amounted to the same thing; a full five seconds of incredulous open-mouthed and very pregnant silence, the gestation of outrage and anger stretched and morphed across a landscape ravaged and laid bare by sheer ice cold terror. The blood had crystallised in her veins even as the handle had turned, muscles had locked together in futile antagonistically shuddering knots. She had thought... she had thought what, exactly? What *had* she thought? That was just it, really; she had thought precisely nothing, nothing at all, *that* was the horror of it. Her thoughts, those perverted images flooding through her mind, all had gone into to a freeze-framed analysis of the most appalling clarity before petrifying to finally collapse in formless dunes of, of... nothing, absolutely nothing. The enormity of the situation had just been too much, too overwhelming; a temporary, yet, for all intents, total, mental collapse had been her only escape route.

Even with the partial recovery of her faculties there was still nothing she could do, her sense of helplessness now cruelly sharpened, her shame highlighted in the glare of her returning awareness. No, there was nothing she could do, there was only the horror, her body prone and splayed with hands still writhing around her crotch and, above her, her aunt's face, once ruddy with embarrassment now darkening with anger and twisted with undisguised disgust.

" Disgusting, disgusting. I,I,I don't know what to say, you *disgust* me. Are you a whore, a pervert, is that it?" The woman was livid, beside herself, the girl, terrified, mind still numb, could only manage a pathetic "n,n,n,no, I, I..." before being cut off by her aunt.

"For God's sake just shut up. I've never seen anything so disgusting in all my life. You filthy, filthy girl! It's a sin, what you're doing, don't you know that? A sin!" There came a pause, her aunt shaking with indignation, the girl trapped in a boiling cauldron of emotion from which even tears would not give release, for none would come, not even tears, the enormity was just too great.

Finally came the bombshell, Susan's world was engulfed in its own private Holocaust, hopes, dreams, all were put to the slaughter. A finger stabbed accusingly almost to the point of her nose, her aunt's face so close that she could feel the words as much as hear them: "You're out of here, now, right now! I can't have a thing like you in my home with your filthy perverted acts. I'm going to 'phone your stepmother right now, she can come over and pick you up right away and I'm going to damn well tell her what you have been doing here too!"

Somewhere in Susan's mind something cracked, crazing like a windshield under a bombardment of hail. "No! Please, please, please! I, I didn't mean to, p,please it, it's not my fault. I, I, it, it just happened"

Her aunt's anger was not appeased; if anything it seemed fuelled by the girl's pathetic whimpering. "What should I do then? Are you sick, should I call your doctor? Have you put away, put in a home? Yes, I wouldn't be surprised if that was what she suggested, after all she'd be the first to admit that you have not been responding well to treatment at home. You have become far worse of late haven't you?" Silence: the girl fidgeting awkwardly under the bed covers, having now tugged the duvet up under her chin, her aunt drawing an impatient breath. "I said; you have been far worse lately haven't you?" The woman tut-tutted loudly. "Haven't you?"

"Y,yes, Auntie, b,bbut I,I…" yet again the girl was cut off mid-sentence, left staggering, off balance, her aunt continuing with unabated anger.

"And just what you mean by 'it just happened'? Just what the hell is that supposed to mean? Don't you know what you're doing any more, is that what you're saying, that you can't even be responsible for your own actions any longer?"

"No, I, I mean yes, I, I m,mean I I'm n,not sure, I…"

"Yes, perhaps I *should* 'phone the doctor, maybe it *is* for the best if you end up being put away. I'm not sure *I* can help you any more."

"P,please don't, Auntie!. P,please! Anything, anything, anything, please!" Susan hearing her own whimpering voice in third-person disbelief as if through a distant dream or played back from some, long-forgotten, recording.

The woman, for her part, seemingly, by some supreme effort of will, having calmed herself, was clearly determined to press home the advantage. "But I have to do *something* about this, this… this misbehaviour. You are clearly sick, aren't you? Even you must see that now. This episode, it's yet another of your little problems coming to the fore. These problems you have, they're not normal, you must realise that, the doctor has explained that to you enough times, I have explained it to you. I think we have both shown great patience with you but still you won't admit it to yourself. If only you would only admit it to yourself it would be a start. After all if you were to contract flu you wouldn't hide it and certainly not from yourself, you would recognise it, get it treated. The problem is that you are sick *right now* and yet you are trying to hide it away from your self, to deny it. Why can't you just at least admit it to yourself, you *are* sick right now aren't you?"

"Y,y, yes auntie." Deep down this was costing Susan dearly, she felt as if she were offering up pieces of her soul and the shame burned hotly in her cheeks accordingly. Deeper still, a small but insistent voice whispered to her that they were right, Aunt Julia, the doctor, all of them, they were right.

The woman bristled once more. "What do you mean, yes? Yes you are unwell or yes you are in denial? I would have thought it was pretty obvious, even to you, that both are equally true, being noncommittal is helping no one"

"I,I I'm sick, auntie. P,please, I I, I am sick, p,please don't send me away. I,I'll do anything, please!"

"That's better, but it's still little excuse for what I caught you doing just now. What do you think your friends would say about you if I told them? What if I was to tell them that you lay there half the day interfering with yourself, masturbating?

What if I was to tell them that you had to have a rubber cover on your bed and that your nightdress was becoming so badly stained that you had to be made to wear rubber knickers to protect it? What do you think they would say about you then, don't you think they would call you a pervert?"

"I, I, I, I'm not s,su, I mean, I, I don't think..." the girl was completely flummoxed now, head spinning in confusion. Could it be, was it true, was it?

"Perhaps they already know, perhaps they could sense it about you, perhaps they could read it between the lines in your letters. Perhaps that is why none of them ever comes to visit you, why none of them even writes to you any more. When was the last time you had a reply from *any* of your letters?" No answer. "Well, when was it?"

"I, I, I c,can't remember, auntie."

"Well it's been a very long while I can tell you. Do you know what I think? I think they have found out about you in some way, I think they know what you do. Can you imagine what they have been saying about you behind your back, what do you think they call you now?" Another long silence, the girl quietly and slowly shaking her head in the negative, in disbelief. Another deep, impatient and exasperated breath was drawn in by the woman standing over her: "I asked you a question, I expect an answer. What do you think they call you behind your back? what do you think you *should* be called?" On her face she wore, still, that hot seething expression, below, flowing in the deepest, slowest, current she was being chillingly at her most calculating. She was only too well aware of the psychological havoc she was wreaking, of just how damaging this was becoming for the girl, but it had always been her intention to depart the girl's room accompanied by a large chunk of the latter's self esteem tucked away securely beneath her arm.

"I,I,,I'm not..."

"Come on, come on. do you think they call you a pervert, yes or no?"

"I,I, m,mean, y, I, s,surpose, b,but I..."

"I'll ask you once again; what do you think they call you, what do you think they *should* call you?" Now sharp and insistent.

"A, a, p,p,pervert, a,a,a auntie" Her voice had become the smallest it had ever been in her life, barely more than a whisper, but she had finally got it out.

"That's better, much better. Yes, a pervert, what you have been doing is a perversion, quite vile, so, yes they're quite right to call you that, it is the correct term for you don't you think?"

"Y,y,yes, Auntie"

"What is? What do you think I'm talking about, *what* is the correct term for someone like you, a dirty girl like you?"

"P,p, pervert, auntie"

"Say it properly girl, I want you to say it properly in a nice complete sentence, I want to be certain you understand. If I am to help you then you need to convince me that you fully understand what you are, what you have become and, more importantly, what should be done about it. At the moment, to be honest with you, I am at complete loss. Now, let's try again, what are you?"

"A, a. a, p,p..." haltingly, a horse, begrudging, whisper.

"No! Again! Start again and damn well apologise this time"

"I,I,I,I'm ssorry auntie. I,I,I,I'm a,a, p,p,pervert, auntie."

"So, the question still remains; what should we do with you? How can I justify having a pervert living with me? The trouble is you are all alone now, your father has passed away, God rest his soul, but at least he was spared the shame you would have brought on him. Your boyfriend left you, your old friends have deserted you, and I am loath to send you back to your stepmother but there may be no other choice. The doctor and I are the only friends you have at the moment, don't think I don't understand that, but how can I have you continue to live with me if you're going to behave in that way. Do you really think I should have to put up with having a pervert living under my roof?"

"N,no, auntie, I,I mean I,I,I,I'm ssorry, auntie. I,I'll n,never do it a,again, I promise, please, p,pplease!"

"But what *am* I supposed to do then? I have to do *something* for your own sake. You've seen the newspapers, read the headlines, perverts are punished, they get sent to prison"

"Y,yes b,but I'm n,n,not a..."

"Perversion is perversion, perverts are perverts. Don't you think perverts deserve to be punished?"

"Yy,yes, auntie, but. but..."

"Well then, you deserve to be punished, don't you?" No response. "I said don't you?"

"B,but I,didn't..."

"Enough! You've admitted you are a pervert, you have admitted that perverts deserve punishment, I just can't see what else I can do. How can I have you living under my roof like this, what if you were to do something in public, what if it was to get out, what you do, how you behave? It would reflect on all of us, myself, my housekeeper, even the doctor, all of us might be tarred with the same brush."

"But p,please don't s,s,send me away, auntie. P,please don't send me b.b,back home, please, p,please, I'll do anything, I p.promise. Punish me, I,I,I d,deserve to be p,p,punished, anything, but n,not by s,sending m,me away"

"But I just can't see what I can do, how the hell am I supposed to punish you in any way that is going to make any damn difference, in any way that is going to ensure that this kind of behaviour does not repeat itself under my roof. I can just imagine what the Victorians would have done with a girl like you. Yes it would've been easy for them, in their time, they knew exactly how to deal with dirty little girls with dirty little habits in their day. Yes, it's a shame but this is the 21st century and you are no little girl, not that that would have mattered to them, grown woman or not they would have tanned your behind, taken a cane to it. But there you have it, you are going to have to leave I am afraid. "

The girl's eyes were wide with panic: " No, no please, please p,p,punish me, I, I, don't mind how, really I don't."

"You stupid, stupid, girl what would you have me do, should I cane you like they would have done in the past, is that what you want?"

"I,I,I'm not sure, I..."

"Who ever gets caned nowadays? That's why the country is in the state it's in, no discipline, no backbone. That's why you are in the state *you're* in, and girls like you, you're all just becoming little sluts."

The outburst was explosive, it was meant to be. Suddenly Julia was reaching for the 'phone, then the receiver was in her hand and she was beginning to dial…who, who exactly? Did it really matter who? Not at all, not to her charge at any rate, a girl to whom to leave here, to live without her aunt, would be to die. No, it would be worse than dying.

"P,please, p,please, the c,cane, anything!"

"Too late for that now I'm afraid."

"No! No! P,please, please c,cane me, please cane me, please!" Still begging pathetically she made a grab for the receiver only for her aunt to parry her attempt with her other arm, sending the girl sprawling to land in a sobbing heap of flesh and satin; her tears had finally come through for her. Then, at her lowest ebb, through tear-blurred vision she watched as, almost as if in slow motion, Aunt Julia quietly replaced the receiver on its cradle.

"Right then, so be it, if it's the only way forward then it is the path we must follow, we must at least give it a chance." She stood gesticulating imperiously toward the right hand side of the bedroom. "Lie across the bed and hold up your nightdress and don't you dare move until I get back, I mean it!

Where it had materialized from she had little inkling, she knew only that it had taken mere moments for her aunt to return with it, swishing it through the air as she approached with the consummate ease of a well practised hand.

The cane was of rattan, not that such a detail was known to the girl nor would it have meant much to her had it been, but suffice it to say that it was of a traditional crook-handled appearance and supple in the extreme, being of a thickness comparable to that of her aunt's little finger, a remarkably dainty finger at that. Moments later and it had begun; her first caning, her first taste of corporal punishment of any form in fact. No ceremony was observed beyond a series of light preparatory taps on her right buttock cheek with the cane's tip so as to confirm the aim and then:

Thrrack! The latex of her knickers amplified the sound out of all proportion to the actual force of the impact. Yes, it stung, but it was not *so* bad.

THrrack! Harder this time, painfully stinging despite her knickers' intercedence.

THRRAACK! "Owww!" That one *really* stung, but it was bearable. It was the shame that was the hardest to bear, that and the humiliation of actually having *begged* to be caned.

Then it was over. Just the three strokes, quite mild and placed across the girl's knickers. Nevertheless Julia was satisfied with her work; sheer physical pain had never been part of the equation on this occasion, never part of her plan. That the girl had accepted punishment from her, had actually begged her to punish her, *that* was the point. Yes, physically there had been little to suffer but psychologically? Well, that was a different matter; the girl would always remember this, her first caning, and in time it would come to fill a disproportionate niche in her mindset. There would be many, many, more opportunities to reinforce that mindset from now on, she was going to see to it that there were.

And so it was to be: A little more than a week later she was caught again - there was no mention of any 'phone calls, there was no need, Aunt Julia had sufficient authority; she no longer had need for the augmentation of props.

Another three strokes were received across that tautly knicker-clad bottom with the appropriate expression of gratitude; in aunt Julia's new world all boons granted were to be greeted with a cheerful gratefulness and by a softly spoken "thank you, aunty".

That, shortly after and despite the expedient of punishment, there should occur a third and then a fourth such episode speaks volumes as to the magnitude and the urgency of the unnatural fevered urges that were increasingly holding the girl in their thrall. Indeed, she could no more resist the temptation then she could go without food and drink; to ignore it was to ignore the urge to breathe, the outcome as inevitable as holding one's breath. For Julia's part it was clear that she would have to *up the ante* if she was to fulfil her duty; three strokes were awarded on each occasion, much as before, but now delivered across the girl's bare buttocks.

For the following two weeks the girl's aunt had no option other than to await her privilege with patience and anticipation. The girl's willpower had surprised her; she had detected nothing untoward despite the girl's previous responses to suggestion. The fifth occasion, when it finally arose, well warranted the six strokes she awarded; the woman's generosity now extended to providing premium quality to match the hike in quantity.

At night, though! Ah! At night. At night all was safe, all around fast asleep. At night there were no witnesses, no doors bursting open. Not that she was free, not any more, far from it. Nor had there been any diminution of her torturer's skill, anything but; a subtle refinement had been introduced, albeit via a third party. She would approach her culmination, the sensations building slowly to their crescendo, completion, her release, would be little more than a breath away, and then, and then…

The sensational panorama would fade below a chilling fog-blanket of shuddering cold-sweating guilt. From somewhere deep in her subconscious a voice would whisper; " pervert, you're a pervert". Shame and humiliation would begin to bubble to the surface. Then there would arise the memory of her punishments, but this would drive her excitement in a way that fell just short of her grasp of understanding and explanation, yet ultimately would lead to further recriminations in her mind, further self-accusation of perversion. Her subconscious was guarded now; a sentinel stood, forever vigilant, just short of her escape. So, so close, but the way barred nevertheless. Sometimes, but only sometimes, she could overcome this barrier but such occasions were becoming rarer, one could almost say endangered.

Viewed from outside of her frame of reference, the girl's growing sexual repression would have been obvious, for those embroiled though, those embedded in the manipulative games of others, vision is, more often than not, impaired. Yet the question remains: Why?

Then there came the night-time incursion. Trapped, caught again, but the two of them at the door this time; Aunt Julia *and* her housekeeper, both in their nightdresses. How had this happened? Had she been *so* indiscreet, noisy perhaps? What had given her away? The caning was inevitable of course, that the correction was to be immediate, *that* was the shock. It was to be given in the middle of the night and to be witnessed; a new dimension had opened up before her and she didn't much like what she saw.

That it *had* to be so was obvious to the girl's aunt, was it not all summed up in that one term; correction? This was behavioural correction after all, behavioural modification, and as such it was important that it be administered so as to be as strongly associated as possible with the behaviour to be modified. That the girl's activities had been detected when she had been so close to her goal was more than pure chance also. Rather it was key to her aunt's agenda, as was the severity of the punishment she intended to inflict; it *had* to be a shock, driven deep into the girl's subconscious, there to remain for all time.

The girl was crying openly by the third stroke and begging by the fourth. By the sixth stroke she was utterly finished, having had to be held down by Julia's housekeeper from the penultimate.

She was given the news the very next day; her bed was to be moved into her aunt's bedroom, there would be room for it at the foot of her aunt's bed. She was still far too numb from the pain and humiliation of the caning of the previous night to object. But there was yet still more humiliation to endure; overhearing her aunt discussing the move with her housekeeper was particularly galling, the repeated references to 'the girl's lack of self control', the housekeeper's suggestions for 'further restricting the child's behaviour'. She would be able change for bed in her old room, she was to be allowed that much privacy at least, but then it was to be straight into her aunt's room to sleep and she would have to be quick about it too; she was not to be allowed time for any 'misbehaviour' to occur.

Now there was no hiding place; for a while, still, if she was very, very careful, she could get away with some surreptitious fumbling, but with very little satisfaction. Partially it was the stress engendered by her lack of privacy, partially it was the repression developing in her subconscious, and each wasted, frustrated, effort was only serving to nourish the latter's growth. Then, after a few nights of carefully covert, if frustrated, manipulations, something changed.

The bed, her bed, something had happened to it, a broken spring perhaps? She had no idea, she only knew that it now squeaked and quite loudly at that! Climbing under the covers, or even just perching on its edge, was now accompanied by harsh rusty-hinged creaking. The slightest movement during the night, even turning over let alone anything more untoward, was greeted by that telltale alarm. Many a disturbed night's sleep was suffered and shared by both women while she learnt to lie still in her sleep - but learn she eventually did. Her aunt knew that she would, the device was a great training aid, sleep deprivation a fine punishment; it was certainly training Susan. Not that Susan was to be relieved of the drive, the yearning that throbbed through her all her waking hours, but there was now a distinct conflict developing between desire and repression, between reward and repercussion - neurosis.

Pavlov had done it with his dogs, pared feeding behaviour with electric shocks -that was the conflict, they were driven by hunger yet feared punishment - in the end they had whimpered pathetically, postured submissively. Her technique with the girl was far more subtle of course but the conflict was just as real, the outcome inevitably comparable. Julia knew what she was doing; this was *her* world, *her* influential sphere, after all.

For Susan life progressed from that day forth as if a fork in the road had been taken, a misdirected turn along a track so well rutted as to allow no return.

61

There were days that almost, but never quite, approached normality. Such days, though, were gradually becoming the exception and in any case were interspersed with periods in which, at best, she felt as if she could do little right by her aunt and at worst were characterised by episodes perhaps best described as being of humiliating psychological cruelty. There were many more affectionate kisses from her aunt's rattan to be grateful for, but their gift was no longer restricted to an occasion of solitary sexual impropriety nor was the venue limited to the bedroom.

Day by day the infractions ruled as being 'caning offences' grew both in number and in their pettiness. She was caned for not addressing her aunt correctly, not being respectful to the housekeeper 'Miss to you, girl' and even, on one occasion, for having her pen and pencils in an incorrect order on her desk. She was caned over her desk, her aunt's desk, across the bed and, most humiliatingly of all, while lying across the housekeeper's lap, her aunt wielding the cane while the other woman quelled her struggles, holding both her arms up her back in a hammerlock with surprising strength, forcing her to remain double despite her protestations.

On more than one occasion she had thought about running away. She had made plans but, no matter how careful her preparation, she somehow just didn't seem able to go through with it when the time came. Partly it was the thought of leaving the house; it had been such a long time since she had last been outside, other than for her daily walk in the garden, and even then in the company of her aunt. Indeed, her doctor now paid house calls, three times per week, in order to 'spare her the stress and worry of travel' as her doctor put it.

She was right of course, the doctor, she was always right and so was Aunt Julia, that was part of the problem. There was always that sense of panic when she was outside, a dizzying sensation of being out of control. It was undeniably wrecking her life; it was one of the things that she was being treated for and this selfsame debility was barring her path to independence. Not that the treatment seemed to be working, at one point she had even entertained the notion that, somehow, it was all just making her worse.

She had voiced her concerns to her doctor on a couple of occasions, had even suggested that she stopped her treatment. The doctor had just seemed to have sidestepped the issue, changed the direction of their conversation. She couldn't quite recall how it had come about but somehow, on both occasions, she had found herself talking about her relationship with her father and the thoughts that had been running through her mind on the day of his funeral.

Of course it must all have been part of her underlying problem, she realised that now, her concerns were merely a way of distracting herself from issues she was too afraid to confront. The doctor had this way of getting inside her head, of understanding what she was trying to say, what she needed to say, even if she, herself, did not always know. She had ended up in tears on both occasions, had found herself actually begging the doctor to continue with her treatment. She had recognised then just how much she needed the support, both of her doctor and, unfortunately, of aunt Julia; therein hung her quandary. Giving up on her therapy really wasn't an option, at least not for the time being, and yet, at times, she really did feel the need to get away from her 'aunt', to regain some independence.

For one thing, and it was a really big thing, there was her inheritance to sort out and the family business. Her aunt was supposed to be handling all of the legal side for her but was she? How could she be sure? Her aunt was always reluctant to discuss it, usually citing her concern over the girl's ability to 'handle the pressure' in addition to all of her other 'problems'. But, then again, there was undoubtedly truth to her aunt's concerns; had not merely the act of bringing up the subject brought on one of her 'attacks' on more than one occasion? How often, after such a confrontation, had her doctor had cause to change her prescription, to increment her medication? She would have to confront her stepmother directly one day, that much she knew, but for now it would have to wait; the panic would come, that awful feeling of panic, pounding heart, sweaty, clammy palms, throbbing head, the room spinning dizzyingly. She'd give it another week. And she did; she gave it another week, then another, then another...

Then two things came at once, as such things often do. Firstly, Aunt Julia had announced that she was going to be out of the country, perhaps for as long as two to three months - no explanation had been given. Secondly, a flyer had fallen out from between the pages of the local newspaper as she had retrieved it from behind the front door. The paper had to be taken directly to her aunt of course, that was the rule; she was discouraged from flicking through it lest she should come across something that might worry or disturb her. The flyer, though, she tucked away in her knickers, the tennis dress being devoid of pockets, not knowing quite why.

Two totally unconnected events, occurring well within an hour of each other. Completely unconnected in their encounter and yet, for the second time within a year, two events, bound together through serendipity, were to completely change the direction of her life. The first, although at first sight offering her a way forward, taken in isolation would undoubtedly have been insufficient to really force her hand. Indeed almost immediately she was conjuring up scenarios whereby she might remain where she was; perhaps the housekeeper would be staying on, perhaps the doctor could visit more often, her home was relatively local even if her office was in the city. It had taken the flyer to press her. It had taken the flyer to bypass her customary indecisiveness, her reluctance to embrace change and her overwhelming yearning for stability.

There was something compelling about that flyer. It was just a call for volunteers for medical research, she had seen such adverts before, but it was strangely fascinating, she felt compelled to read it again and again. It offered her the chance of regaining some independence and yet, between the lines, was contradictorily suggestive of stability and support. At some level in her psyche it seemed to appeal to both her dependency and what was left of her independent spirit at the same time. An impossibly antagonistic concept to most, the mutual exclusivity glaring, yet oddly sensible, acceptable, even *desirable* to the girl who now sat reading it for, perhaps, the twentieth time.

Reassured by the faintly familiar patterning, embossed into the glossy paper and catching the light in rhythmic ripples, gently rocking to and fro, to and fro, she gazed from behind the safety of soulless glazed eyes, her thumb-sucking innocent comfort a gauge of her acceptance. A woman, corrupted, yet made innocent.

CHAPTER 4

INTERACTIONS: A LADY, A DOCTOR, AND A PROSPECTIVE EMPLOYEE?

A Historic Correspondence

It was an old correspondence; it had been kicking around her office for several months. Somehow it had found its way between the pages of a journal she had been using; she made a mental note to be more careful in future. The doctor read it through for the second time that day; it was not so much what it said, more what it alluded to.

"Alison has interviewed dozens of candidates. For what seems like months now she has been bemoaning the demise of the once traditional governess. Frankly I am not at all sure what her expectations truly are, whether they are ever likely to be fulfilled, even in principle. I blame myself in some ways for ever mentioning it but one tries one's best to help, even though it so often seems to rebound in one's direction. The fact is, I had thought that I had a good grasp of the scope of her aspirations in that direction, now I am not at all sure what she is after and I don't think that she really is. To be honest, I really don't think she quite understands the extent and limitations that were traditionally associated with the role. And the girl's age, she could be married! Probably should be too, perhaps that is her problem. It all seems a little ridiculous to me now, in the cold light of day."

The writer continued:

"... Apparently many of them have had one thing or another in their favour but none of them seems to have been quite what she was looking for, not that she really knows, exactly, what it is she is after, as I have said. In some way their views did not quite seem to fit in with her expectations, whatever they are, your guess is as good as mine..."

The bespectacled woman screwed up the letter, intending it for the waste basket, then, pausing to think, unfolded it again; it went into the shredder. It was better to avoid a paper-trail in today's atmosphere, not that there was anything particularly incriminating about the contents, at least to the casual reader.

She well understood the writer's consternation but was struck by the diverse facets, intricacies and coincidences woven between those lines. She knew the writer well but not so Alison of whom, up until recently, she had been only privy to hearsay. However she had understood enough to realise that the girl, of who's care there had been so much correspondence and concern, was of no familial relation whatsoever to this Alison Stringer. Oddly enough, though, the woman's only living relative appeared to be the writer's step daughter, Susan, of whom she was cousin. The selfsame Susan Stringer presently resident in this very institution, their latest recruit in fact, registered as a clinical research subject although yet to be assigned to a researcher.

But *this* woman, this *Alison* Stringer had never had children nor even married. She had been suspicious when she had first received the letter, not of the writer but of Alison Stringer herself. Much had occurred since that letter had been written though. She now had a better grasp of the influences in, and drives behind, Alison's life and relationships. The surprise was not so much the woman's sexual orientation, that much was written clearly between the lines of so much she had learnt, no, rather it was the type and enormity of the relationship in which she was so obviously embroiled. Her psychological profile indicated her to be possessed of one of the most dominant personalities that she had come across and suggested an almost sociopathic moral stance. More, coincidently and incredibly, she held a master's degree in behavioural psychology.

She wondered how Alison's quest had gone; she had heard no more mention of it. The woman's relationship with some young woman was of no concern of hers, how could *she* ever presume to be so judgmental. But to have denied an interest, whether professional or personal would have been hypocritical.

Was it really a governess that the woman had been after? Probably not, and if not, if her assumptions were correct, then the time might be right to make a suitably discreet, surreptitious, approach, she had the ideal candidate in mind. There might or might not be some opportunity inherent in the woman's relationship but there certainly seemed scope for the woman within her organisation.

She made another mental note; she would write as soon as she had some free time, perhaps at lunch, after the seminar. There was no risk, she knew too much about the woman for her ever to be able to blow the whistle and, besides, she was never wrong, she knew a good bet when she saw one; the woman would be an invaluable addition to the staff.

Idly she wondered just how much the woman knew of her cousin, Susan's, situation. Was she aware, was she perhaps involved in some way? She doubted that she was, certainly Julia had made no mention of meeting her at any point and Julia was always most diligent in her reporting.

"Well, we'll soon see" she remarked to no one in particular "let's have Julia make the first contact and we'll go on from there." Rising to leave her office for the morning rounds she couldn't resist a faint smile, the thought had struck her; how often life revealed these cyclical patterns, they seemed to underpin the whole concept that some people might term, fate.

Alison Stringer

Alison Stringer leaned back, interlocking her fingers comfortably behind her head she sighed deeply. This last candidate, the one she had interviewed this morning had come the closest. Without being too explicit she seemed to share many of her views and really appeared to grasp her requirements. She had said that she had heard of the position through a mutual friend. Alison had been surprised but a quick 'phone call had soon confirmed the woman's story. Julia Soames, what was it about that name? Something familiar, perhaps shared with some minor celebrity? Well, the woman, herself, had clearly realised that she was not absolutely *perfect* for the position but at least she understood the requirements.

Better still, she had been able to recommend a woman with whom she had had some dealings in the past and who, apparently, had a most admirable record of dealing with troublesome adolescent girls. Indeed the woman actually *specialised* in working with such young women. Apparently she was currently working for a Lady Marchment, based, she thought, in Gloucestershire or possibly Devon, but thought that something could possibly be worked out.

Miss Julia Soames had sauntered out with a cheery smile, promising to stay in touch and to set up a dialogue with her West Country acquaintance.

"Well, we'll see" Alison muttered to no one in particular; her dog looked up and she smiled at him, only to see the poodle yawn and stroll off out to the garden.

"Typical, no one listens" she muttered, involuntarily yawning and finding herself unexpectedly overtaken by fatigue.

"The power of suggestion" she thought to herself idly.

The Doctor

Dr Ecclestone leant back into the plush brown leather chair, the back semi-reclining in response. For while she just simply relaxed, her arms resting on the softly padded rests, her head supported comfortably by the headrest. Behind her the afternoon sun painted impressionistic clouds and shadowed ivy through the arched stained glass window. Before her those very same images danced in the white spaces between bookshelves and above dark oak panelling; the shadowed ivy animated by the late afternoon summer breeze brushing past its exterior counterpart.

The Technicolor display had begun its infiltration innocently enough, gently burnishing the gold-leaf titling and red leather binding of the psychology tomes, piled patiently awaiting her attention at the left of the dark mahogany desktop. Its advance had proceeded without response, crossing the leather guarded perimeter of the green blotter without incident. Now, though, its incursion threatened the large screen positioned just beyond the blotter, diamond patterns of light and shade and the reflections of bookshelves had begun to replace the uniformed girl knelt in prayer. With a sigh the psychologist leant forward to retrieve her glasses from where they lay on the blotter, her sumptuous executive chair moving with her.

Rising she turned towards the window, absentmindedly smoothing down her exclusively-styled knee length brown leather skirt. Her hand on the shutter she paused, taking in the ornate gardens laid out two floors below, watching appreciatively as two nurses traversed the bowling green-flat lawn, each wearing the clinic' s conventional light-blue long-sleeved uniform dress with its white cuffs and rounded white collar both trimmed with blue piping to match that of their white caps. She noted that, despite the late afternoon sunshine, both nurses were wearing a neatly buttoned long-sleeved navy blue cardigan over their dress, not any indication of the air's chill but rather a reflection of the strict standards enforced by the clinic's management. For a moment she found herself reflecting on the differences between a private clinic, such as this, and the public sector. The two women having now reached the path to the main entrance, directly below her window, she could make out the gold and red embroidery of the hospital insignia that she knew would be echoed on the dress beneath.

Not some shapeless public sector nurse's dress or, worse still, 'scrubs', but one carefully tailored, fitted and made to measure; the elasticated webbing belt more a detail of styling than of any real necessity to form.

With yet another sigh she pulled the hinged rosewood shutters across the ornate stone-surround window and returned to her work; the Sun's disruption reduced to a few surreptitiously intruding fingers slipping down between narrow slats to paint dusty mottled stripes of gold along the dark ruby silken edge of the Marian Dorn rug lying below.

There was something about one of the messages in her email that caught her attention, dragged her away from her notes. She opened it and her smile broadened; good she's coming, she thought. She couldn't refrain from reading the principle point out aloud. "She has been vetted and is amenable to the ideas behind our work here."

The doctor leaned forward, simultaneously and habitually repositioning her glasses with the fore finger of her right hand. Of the six white squares comprising the grid on the screen before her five were occupied by a vaguely humanoid green outline. One view had been selected and the window, having expanded out to occupy half the screen, was filled by the head and shoulders of a green-stripe attired girl. Her small snub nose and over-large soft blue eyes, framed within the confines of her green and white striped Victorian-styled bonnet, retained their prettiness despite the absence of eyebrows that bestowed a de-personalised doll-like appearance upon her. Her skin possessed the pallid complexion of one long hid from the sun; on close inspection one might just have made out the long-faded remnants of the freckles that had once bridged that pretty child-like nose yet did so no more. Her eyes were wide, innocent, yet more than innocent, expressionless and yet not quite, they had a doe-eyed glazed quality about them, a lack of any real focus as if deep in daydream. But there was something else there, despair? Not really, at least not in isolation. No, it was more a combination of defeat, resignation and hopelessness.

The girl's mouth full lipped and once known for its pout as much as for its come-hither flirtatiousness was now devoid of either; devoid of tone, the muscles totally relaxed, the pretty Cupid bow lips hung slightly parted, her jaw slack. Her lower lip attracted the light to glisten at its centre whereupon a small trickle of saliva was slowly growing and an elongating droplet threatened to join the fate of its predecessors as the glistening darkening rivulet flowing and pooling on the girl's dress front, just above the second button, at the point at which the fabric began to press out and forward around her breasts. There was no attempt to wipe her mouth nor the trickling dribble that was slowly working its way down her gracile chin. Nor had there been, as was attested to by her drool-stained bodice. Not that she seemed restrained in any way, either in a physical sense or by the restriction of discipline - neither struggle nor turmoil were evidenced in that face, merely a docile acceptance. A faint twitch of a smile quivered in the corners of the doctor's mouth, novice thespians, hovering uncertain in the wings as if awaiting some unseen prompt. Leaning forward, her slender fingers ran across the keyboard in a staccato burst of rattling plastic and the knitting-needle clack of long, expensively manicured, nails. On the screen the focus pulled back to a full-length shot, the image simultaneously expending to fill the screen.

She scribbled a few notes, some ideas, she felt inspired; Alison Stringer was coming, she was going to have to arrange a suitably impressive tour of the facilities and some sort of demonstration. By all accounts the woman was the key to a potentially interesting test subject; a broad demographic cross-section was essential to the work.

Alison's Arrival

The previous few weeks had seen Alison Stringer tied up with company affairs, business meetings and seminars; she really hadn't had time to think more on the subject of her 'little domestic problem'. Still, she had been surprised and delighted when the letter had appeared on her desk; it had been written in a rather regal but un-mistakenly feminine hand and on the finest and most expensive paper she had seen in a long time. She remembered thinking at the time how rare such attention to detail was in the modern world; there was something reminiscent of a past-gone age about it, a more cultured, refined, time, a time of standards and manners and of sharply-delineated social strata. These were things for which she hankered most; a return to a time wherein all had their station, aspirations were simple and limited and exemplary service was the norm, only to be expected.

She had brought the letter with her. She couldn't resist reading through it again, besides she had already worked her way through practically all of the day's papers and halfway through a paper back, that she had bought on impulse on the platform at Paddington, and there was still the taxi to come.

The first page was headed with a family crest and coat of arms and introduced Lady Marchment who then went on to explain that she had had some correspondence with Julia Soames and that she felt that she understood Alison's situation. She explained that she did, indeed, employ a governess for her two nieces and that the woman had proved highly efficacious in the performance of her duties. Her employment, however, was ongoing and would continue for the foreseeable future. Alison recalled how her heart had dropped somewhat; it had appeared as if her hopes were about to be dashed.

However, in the letter Lady Marchment went on to say that under the right circumstances, if Alison would have no objection to her stepdaughter taking up residence at her establishment, it might be possible for her governess to take charge of her alongside her nieces, both of whom were young women of around Alison's stepdaughter's age. Alison Stringer's spirits had soared, this sounded perfect, almost too good to be true; the girl would be out from under her feet at for a while, dissuaded from medalling further in her affairs and yet she would still wield control over her, albeit by proxy via a, presumably strict, governess.

Somehow it still all seemed too perfect, despite having since learnt more. It seemed that Lady Marchment's 'establishment' consisted of more than merely her place of residence; she ran a highly successful business, apparently some sort of health spa and retreat with a discreet but highly respected reputation amongst those to whom 'rehab' was as habitual as was their weakness. Then there was her philanthropic work; therein lay another story, clearly there was more to *that* than met the eye.

The final page was peculiarly enigmatic and vague. Without being critically explicit Lady Marchment had gone on with a caution; Alison should understand that Lady Marchment's nieces suffered certain behavioural and psychological issues that required an approach beyond the guidance usually included within a governess' remit. She went on to point out that the woman she employed was uniquely qualified to handle such problems but that she was uncertain as to whether her, rather unorthodox, approach would be appropriate for Alison's charge or, indeed, acceptable to Alison.

It appeared that Lady Marchmont had had spoken with the woman who, in her turn, had stated that she would be prepared to take on Alison's charge but had indicated that the girl would be required to undergo the selfsame treatment as her other charges so as not to disrupt the day-to-day running of the home. In closing Lady Marchmont had invited Alison to visit, to meet with her and her governess and to witness, first-hand, the efficacy of their regime.

Alison stringer carefully replaced the letter in its envelope and slipped it into her handbag; she might need to show it on arrival, she had heard that the security was pretty tight. The train was slowing now, the sloping platform apron passing the window. She piled the discarded newspapers at the rear of the table beneath the window and got to her feet, reaching across to retrieve her handbag from the adjacent seat she made her way to the end of the carriage, the door hissing open at her approach. They had said on the 'phone that a taxi would be waiting; a 20 minute ride and she would be able to see for herself.

Marion Marchment

The iron gates were imposing, standing perhaps 5 metres or more and being even more ornate than she had expected. Beyond, a gravel road meandered through pine forest before opening out on to manicured lawns and landscaped gardens and then finally the house itself.

She had expected, perhaps, a country mansion or large house and had pictured Palladian columns and wide staircases. Instead the buildings looming ahead possessed the neo-gothic architectural feel of a Victorian hospital or asylum.

Her taxi was met by the imposing figure of Lady Marion Marchment herself. Tall, aristocratically English yet with a certain Nordic air. With silver-blonde hair piled high above fine high-cheek-boned features, delicately contoured nose and piercing dark blue eyes she was 'power dressed' to an almost 1980s excess in a tight-skirted business suit, the whole screaming authority, authority, authority.

Her first surprise was the governess's youth she didn't look a day over 30. Somehow Alison had envisaged someone of more mature years. Her second surprise was the woman's mode of dress. Yes, she had expected someone smartly and formally attired certainly, perhaps something like a personal assistant, or even housekeeper. Other than for her youthful looks and her undeniable attractiveness the woman who stood before her was the perfect image of the strict hospital matron of old.

"I am afraid I do have to admit to having invited you down here under somewhat false pretences. Not that I can't be of assistance in the matter of… ahem… how shall we say… your 'step daughter', wasn't it? "

"Yes, but…"

"Not to worry, as I was saying, it's not that I can't be of assistance, quite the contrary. I have a greater empathy with your situation than you might imagine, but hear me out and I think you'll find that we, here, can very much be of assistance to you…and, perhaps, you to us. The 'false pretences' refer more to the situation pertaining to my two nieces. Again, I feel that I should qualify that admission before you get the wrong idea about me. The situation regarding their care is very much as I have described, the duplicity to which I refer, if duplicity it truly is, and you, yourself must be the judge here, is more tied up with exactly how one defines the term 'governess'."

"How so?"

"Well, to tell the truth, in engineering my particular tableau I have employed two 'governesses to fulfil different roles at different phases. The first was anything but conventional in her approach, but probably closest to what most would understand by the term. The second was, and is, even less so in approach and, I imagine, a million miles from what you would have expected. It is the first woman that I would recommend to you in the first instance but I would be surprised if you don't find the second part of the path I am about to outline to you even more appropriate for your 'step daughter' to follow, particularly if you were to have some personal involvement and input. As to my nieces' current governess, well, let me introduce Matron here."

More pleasantries were exchanged, Alison shaking hands with the navy-blue uniformed woman and, despite being a prospective employer, finding herself unable to shrug off the overbearing authority of the woman. Despite her usual confidence she felt intimidated; somehow she couldn't imagine instructing *this* woman, *this* woman clearly controlled others, it was obviously what she did.

They walked together into the main house, Marion Marchment continuing her monologue. "I think you will understand the reason for my somewhat surreptitious approach better once you have had a tour of our little…'facility'. I have to admit to having had you vetted and scrutinised quite closely. I must apologise for the intrusion into your privacy but much of the work that goes on here, behind the scenes shall we say, is sensitive and, to be honest, not without its risks. I'm sure you'll understand once you have been shown around. If you like what you see, and I am confident that you will, I'd like you to consider a proposition that I have been thinking of making.

To put it succinctly, with your, how shall we say, predilections, your nursing experience, your financial and domestic situations, I have come to the conclusion that you would make a valuable addition to our team, in more ways than one. I think you would find that the rewards would indeed be mutual; our work here, you will find, is capable of enriching your life in ways that you will have previously only dreamt about, I can assure you of that!"

A Prospective Employee

The clinic was of a far more modern appearance than she would ever have expected based on the building's exterior, indeed, the term 'high-tech' came to mind. She had been told something of what to expect; the patient accommodation was in the basement, accessible only by way of a lift, operated by a key, and a coded keypad entry system. The unit's layout and its design philosophy had been described in detail during the pep-talk, yet nothing that had been said had truly done it justice, truly prepared her for the initial impact; stunning was the only word for it. Alison stepped from the lift, her kitten-heels sinking into the thick white carpet and tripping her as she did so. The contrast with the wood panelled rooms of the main house above could hardly have been greater; walls floor, ceiling, everything was a clinical white. To her left was the reception area, the white plastic desk attended by a nurse who, in contrast to the nurses she had come across in the main house, was dressed entirely in white. The latter's uniform dress was teamed with a old-fashioned white headdress that entirely covered her hair and framed her face, producing a vaguely unsettling impression of some ghostly nun.

She was shown straight through to the clinic's experimental suite, passing by the ghostly nurse-nun and then through a set of double doors guarded by a six-digit security code. The passageway beyond continued the all white theme. As in the foyer the illumination was indirect, being by way of strip lights recessed into the tops of the walls so as to up-light the ceiling, producing a gentle, diffuse, shadow-free uniform glow over every surface. The effect was quite disorientating; Alison found it difficult to keep her eyes focused, difficult to judge the length of the corridor. It reminded her of an optical illusion she once saw demonstrated at a science fair as a child. It was quiet in the extreme, the acoustics totally dead, yet that silence was imperfect; from somewhere far off in the distance there came the rhythmic swoosh of surf on a shingle beach. There was an overwhelming feeling of peace that was really quite soothing, almost dream like, and yet she was not at all sure how long she would want to linger here.

She passed through yet another door. The room beyond came as a shock, in its way more disorientating than even the passageway's sensory distortion; there were windows here, there was daylight flooding the room. But weren't they in a basement? Windows? Daylight? How could this be?

The room was sparsely furnished, but clearly identifiable as a hospital ward. There were six hospital beds, three on each side. Between each bed lay an identical window, there being six in all; three were set in each side wall, two lay between beds and one was set to either side of the door. They gave the room a light airy feel yet did nothing to lessen the feeling of isolation that, increasingly, she was finding harder to ignore.

Each window was covered by a grille of criss-crossing white plastic mesh fitted flush to the wall. Intrigued she couldn't resist walking across to the nearest, situated to her right and immediately adjacent to the door through which they had just passed. Inquisitively pressing up against the unyielding plastic she could see nothing save shadows cast by what looked to be bars mounted on the exterior, the latter being the only feature to break the monotonous diffraction of daylight through white frosting of the glass.

Beside each bed was a simple white plastic chair which she quickly discovered to be fixed firmly to the floor, as it became clear, was all the furniture.

The room needed something, even some flowers would help, perhaps a television? Looking around it was obvious that there was nothing of the sort. It was pristine, that was the only word for it; if not for the neat pile of what she took to be night things sitting in the centre of each bed she would have sworn that the room was unused had she not been told otherwise. There was something else too, it had hit her as soon as she had entered, an odour, not the disinfectant twang one might have expected, although there *was* undeniably a hint, no it was something else, quite strong but not immediately recognisable.

To Alison it was obvious, once she had gotten over her initial surprise, that the windows had to be false. That she had felt the compulsion to look out through one of them, despite having the benefit of previous knowledge, was a gauge of how skilfully woven was the deception.

If the daylight was artificial then so too were the phases of night and day. The protocol had been outlined during her earlier briefing. The lighting was kept on 24-hours a day, it was only the light from the windows that was varied; six hours of light, six hours of dark. During the latter six hours of 'night' the girls were allowed three hours sleep. Mealtimes were once every four hours, upon waking, at 'midday' and one hour before bed. In this way each 24-hour period encompassed two sleep periods and two 'working days'. In reality, though, this was varied slightly such that the 'day' experienced by the girls was slowly rotating as related to the outside world. The stated purpose of this was simplicity itself; that there should be no reference to, or influence from, the outside world that might mask any experimental manipulation.

The nurse could sense Alison's uncertainty. "At the end of the day who can say for sure what aspects or factors may contribute to the development of a phobia. Here the only factors present are those that we can control for. Of course there are some sacrifices to be made, some loss of freedom to be suffered but the girls that come here, our volunteers, are better off in the long run I assure you."

For a moment Alison was at a loss; inside all was turmoil but not for the reason that the nurse had construed. Her younger cousin, Susan, was here somewhere, living under one of their regimes, undergoing some sort of treatment, but where, what were they doing to her? Would she be put in charge of her? Oh God! What if she were to be put in charge of Susan?

The nurse, on the other hand, had clearly decided that the woman needed further reassurance: "You have to understand; some of the girls we house here could be said to have been in moral danger; perhaps exposed to drug taking or in danger of drifting into crime or prostitution for example. They may not appreciate it nor have expected the cost, the discipline we enforce, but in the end our methods ensure that we have the nice compliant subjects we require for our studies and, I think, girls free from the degradations of modern society.

"Good docile psychiatric patients all?" Alison was only half joking, deep down she was looking for a response in the affirmative. She was to be disappointed, no response was forthcoming. She was not to be so easily put off, she was intrigued now; "So, this investigation I've heard so much about, the origin and propagation of phobias, have you made much progress?"

Now the nurse's eyes lit up noticeably, there could be no doubting that she was excited by her work, perhaps rather more than might have been justified by a conventional scientific interest All caution was thrown to the wind. "In certain subjects we have been able to induce quite severe agoraphobia, we have had *some* measure of success in all cases." She smiled as she continued "I'm sure you can appreciate how this can make a recalcitrant teenager easier to handle. We have been experimenting with associating a new phobia with a girl's existing phobia to produce these effects. In some subjects we have been begun to associate their phobias and panic attacks with certain decision-making tasks, this seems to have the potential to develop a really deep dependency on their carers."

Oh God! Oh God! Susan, living here, under the care and control of these people! She could think of little else. She knew for sure now; this place was for her, it was a living dream world, she would be working in the midst of her darkest fantasies. Now, if only she could arrange for her little friend to be sent here. The unfaithful little cow!

Together they walked the length of the ward and back conversing with ever greater enthusiasm, a rapport was building between them and with it a new world was opening up before Alison Stringer. The nurse had recognised a kindred spirit, she was proud at what she had achieved. Alison, for her part, was devouring greedily every detail, her practiced, observant, eyes scanning about her with equal avarice.

The room's centre was dominated by a long white plastic table with an attached bench seat running the entire length of one side. The nurse patted its top affectionately as they passed by. "For meal times", she stated as if in response to some unasked question. Seating positions were marked out by black numerals and letters printed on the tabletop. The same characters were echoed on the wall above each bed.

A small platform or table was affixed to the foot of each bed upon which stood a white plastic dish and object which, as a one-time nurse herself, Alison immediately recognised as a bedpan. But these were quite unlike any bedpans she had ever had experience of; certainly plastic was a common enough material these days, but *transparent* plastic used for a bedpan?

And there were other oddities and refinements; The seating area was located over the main body of the bedpan, as was conventional, but within the seating area their was a divider running across the bedpan body segregating the collecting area into a pair of cavities. It was obvious that the forward cavity was for collecting liquid waste while that to the rear of the divider was intended to collect solid waste. A graduation running up the centre of the divider could clearly be read from the outside and was obviously designed to allow for rapid and easy measurement of urine volume and, perhaps, estimation of stool size.

The nurse explained that some of the experimental work they carried out in this section involved manipulation of dietary constituents and that detailed examination of stools provided valuable feedback data. Indeed, in addition to the collection of samples, her daily duties routinely included filling in a record card for each girl with a detailed description of both her stools and urine.

Chapter 4 | Interactions…

Apparently Matron had set up a protocol to ease staff's workload. Each girl was required to inspect her own bedpan and to call out a standardised description when instructed. Matron had drawn up specific instructions as to how this was to be achieved; a specific formula to be recited each time, intended to simplify and standardise information gathering and recording. Upon Matron calling out a patient number the patient concerned had to describe her stools' colour, texture, aroma and shape, with each characteristic clearly enunciated and followed by "Matron" or "nurse" as appropriate; a little bit of discipline of which Matron was inordinately fond. This formula was scripted and compliance with it was strictly enforced.

"For example if I were to address patient 121A '121A, bedpan girl' I would expect her to hold out her bedpan in front of her, just below her chin, and recite: 'patient 121A, nurse' and then to go on to describe her stool's colour, texture, odour and size followed by her urine's colour and smell. In addition I always insist on the use of full sentences, it removes any possibility of ambiguity. For that reason the description is always reported in the form: 'my stools are soft, nurse' or 'my stools have a strong odour, nurse'. I imagine this probably seems unnecessarily humiliating to you but it does minimize mistakes and misunderstandings, besides I find a little humility often goes a long way in quieting the more quarrelsome individual." There was a glint in her eye at that last remark that did not pass Alison's notice.

This ritual, it turned out, had originated when it was decided to remove reading and writing materials from the unit. Up until that point the girls had, themselves, filled in their own record sheet each day. The removal of pens paper, books and magazines had, of course, been yet another way of tightening control over experimental conditions. By exerting closer control over the girls' experiences it was hoped to better control for the effects of external influences.

The humiliating scripted ritual had evolved under the loving, guiding, influence of Matron of course. In fact many of the more discipline-orientated aspects of the regime had been introduced since her appointment, usually under the guise of improving experimental control but, as far as Alison could make out, in reality often just for discipline's own sake. For example, although talking had never been allowed in the classroom or during group therapy sessions, *quiet* talking had been allowed on the ward. Matron's view was that this was too disrupting and could too easily influence experimental results. Now a strict rule of no talking between patients at *any* time had been introduced and, incredibly, was enforced by corporal punishment; the strap or the cane. Apparently even Lady Marchment had doubted that the introduction of corporal punishment could be achieved successfully, nevertheless that is exactly what Matron had achieved. A testament to her strategy of taking one small step at a time as much as to the power of her will.

This was always Matron's strategy; as a small erosion of freedom became accepted so it would be followed by the next step, some new but equally small and, in itself, insignificant imposition or restriction. This was a strategy Matron was rightly proud of; a *tour de force*, a veritable master-class in psychological manipulation. Now a girl could, and would, be punished for merely making eye contact with another patient; they were very carefully and continuously monitored and scrutinised for any attempt at communication or interaction.

Alison walked across to one of the beds, quickly realising, as she did she so, that she had identified the source of that odd, all permeating, aroma. It clicked in her mind, for the first time since walking in, a flash of recognition from her past nursing days, the gloves she had sometimes worn. The odour emanated from the beds and bedding; pillows mattresses and bedcovers, all had white latex rubber covers.

Alison picked up what appeared to be a nightdress and was surprised to find that it, also, was of white latex, soft and as fine as to be semi-transparent. The design looked rather childish, she thought; it had short puffed sleeves and little frills around the neck and hem, but was doubtless practical nonetheless. The dress fastened at the rear by a zipper and the skirt flared markedly from the narrow waist to what she estimated would be approximately mid-thigh on an average late-teen girl. Holding it up by the shoulders she could see that the bodice was thickened around the lower torso area, forming a figure-moulding combination of dress and foundation garment that would undoubtedly impose an exaggerated hourglass curvature on the wearer. She wondered as to why, what was obviously night attire, should have been designed so as to incorporate such stringent figure discipline.

Immediately below the neatly folded nightdress, equally neatly arranged, had lain a second garment and she now found herself examining what, incredibly, appeared to be a pair of incontinence knickers. These were also fabricated in white latex and were of a bloomer style, apparently designed to terminate just above a girl's knees. Both the buttock area and the legs were decorated by a series of frills of the same fabric and looked, to Alison's eye at least, rather cute, if rather babyish. In a slightly sinister twist, the thickened and slightly rigid waistband, upon further examination, she found to conceal a spring-steel band, embedded within the rubber, that emerged at the rear as a loop and eye arrangement clearly designed to provide for fastening although there appeared to be no obvious means of connecting ring to eye. Internally there was a series of straps or bands which, she quickly realised, were designed to retain the thick absorbent pad that she had found lying atop the pile.

The nurse explained that no personal belongings were allowed in the unit and that only clothing issued by the hospital was allowed to be worn.

These were quite obviously the girls' night things although the knickers, it turned out, did have a dual purpose, their being retained during the day if a girl was menstruating, the internal straps then pressed into service to secure a sanitary towel. At least this was the procedure for such contingencies in this group but there were four other such groups in total, she was told, each with their procedures in place dependent on their experimental requirements. Alison could not see how an experimental protocol could have any bearing on the arrangements made to deal with a girl's period and when pressed as to how these arrangement might differ, the nurse's example, something to do with girls having to wear a Kotex belt and towel under 'special' knickers, although tantalising was no more enlightening. Further details were not forthcoming.

The loop and eye fastening arrangement, it transpired, could accommodate a small padlock. Apparently there had, on occasion, been problems arising from the 'toiletry rules' in force and there had also been one or two awkward situations arising from girls using their bedpans outside of their designated toilet periods. This latter was potentially most problematic at night when it could disturb the sleep of others but had also caused disruption to classes and treatment sessions during the day.

To Alison this sounded more intriguing than ever, it seemed as if, throughout the tour, she was being fed tantalising crumb after tantalising crumb, each begging a question and each leading her further into their world. Now what was all this about 'toiletry rules' and what the hell was meant by 'toilet periods'? For once some sort of explanation was forthcoming; Matron made the rules here and it had been she that had introduced the concept of scheduled toilet periods, much as there were strictly scheduled mealtimes and sleep periods, and for much the same reason. As in many institutions, it was simply for the convenience of the staff, although in this particular institution, because of the nature of their experiments, such schedules and routines were more encompassing, closely controlled, enforced and adhered to, than in most.

The idea of routine times for meals and sleeping was nothing new to Alison of course, although she got the impression that these would probably be more strictly adhered to than elsewhere, but the idea of only allowing these young women to go to the toilet at certain times of the day, how did they manage that? How the hell could they enforce it? Did they lock the toilet door? Did they hide the bedpans? She had been only half-joking when she asked this one.

It was obvious that the nurse did not see any implied humour. "There are no toilets on this ward, Ms Stringer, we could take away their bedpans of course but we don't. Matron believes their continued presence is better for discipline."

That 'Matron' again, thought Alison, everything here seems to revolve around her. "Yes, but what happens, how does it work?"

The nurse went on: "It's very simple really, just as there is a wake-up bell, a mealtime bell, and the classroom bell, nothing unusual there, so there is a toilet-time bell. There are periods set aside for their toilet after breakfast, after lunch, after tea and after supper."

"But what happens at other times, what if one of them just needs to 'go', you could hardly just stop her could you? And what happens at night?"

"No, we certainly do not believe in trying to stop *anyone* going to the toilet at any time, day or night, although a member of staff might well say something to discourage it or, indeed, to encourage a girl who is doggedly holding on. You see, we believe in training here rather than simple proscription, that is our philosophy; it should all be part of a girl's discipline. In the daytime each girl has her bedpan at the side of her bed of course, in the classroom a bedpan is always kept available on a chair at the front of the class. However, outside of the designated toilet period the use of either is followed-up by three strokes of the cane. If, on the other hand, a girl fails to use her bedpan at the designated toilet time she is treated by the application of suppositories and / or diuretic drugs and laxatives, her compatriots then being obliged to remain seated on their bedpans until such a time as she has completed her ablutions."

"And at night?"

"There is usually little problem once a girl settles down but, as I have said, we have had one or two problems in the past with girls, new girls in particular, getting up at night to use their bedpans and disrupting the whole ward. To be efficacious punishment is best applied so as to be directly associated with the offence in the miscreant's mind, but obviously this would create a further disturbance. The locking waistband that you noticed on the incontinence pants simply and effectively enforces their use at night. If a girl should urinate in her knickers at night, and it does occasionally occur even with our long-stay residents, she is not punished but rather praise is given, as long as, that is, she has simply given in and done her toilet in her pants without fuss or complaint."

"Oh my God!" Right at that moment it was the only thing that came to mind; from the viewpoint of a patient a more apt exclamation could hardly have been invoked.

And then they reached the supply cupboard, the nurse had promised her a look at an example of the girls' day uniform. The area of wall immediately in front of them had little to differentiate it from any other part of the near featureless expanse of white other than for a faint vertical line and a key hole at around shoulder height. A key was duly offered up and jiggled into position, a deft turn and two regions of wall swung outwards, the cupboard doors becoming fully apparent for the first time, each being perhaps of a metre and a half in height and one meter across. Alison gave a poorly stifled gasp of surprise; it wasn't the row of little green white striped nylon dresses that rustled harshly together on their hangers, no, it was the pile of white garments stacked on the shelf to their left, the pile from which white leather straps of various diameters protruded and hung haphazardly.

She hadn't been sure quite *what* to expect but she certainly hadn't expected this! The last thing in the world she expected to see was a stack of straitjackets. Indeed she hadn't been absolutely sure what she was looking at initially, her mind repeatedly denying what her eyes were telling her. Not being an expert in the arena of psychiatric care she required further examination but despite what her common sense kept telling her, this only confirmed her initial impression; it was indeed a neatly stacked pile of straitjackets, at least from what she had seen at the movies and on television.

The prospect astounded yet somehow frightened and frilled her all at once. It sent a cold chill down her spine but also filled her with a burning excitement, an entire pantheon of emotions were colliding, the inertia making her head spin. Susan, in a straitjacket! She couldn't quite believe it, would it be possible? Perhaps even probable? Suddenly she wished she could be alone, private, *very* alone, to assuage the craving-ache that was building in her, nagging at her.

CHAPTER 5

INSTITUTIONALISATION (1): SUSAN: THE FIRST DAYS

Susan had arrived mid-afternoon. She had only brought with her one small suitcase but nevertheless the nurse on reception had said that it would have to be stored away for the time being. There having been something of a mix-up the room she was to have taken was not yet vacant and she had not yet been assigned to a research group. Apparently It could possibly be as long as two to three days before she could be entered into a study. Meanwhile, as she could hardly return home now, it would save time later if she could undergo some preliminary psychological tests. Unfortunately she would have to wait until one of the researchers was free but in the meantime she could go and take a shower and then she would be shown to a waiting room.

"Just leave your case here dear and go through with the nurse to the shower room". Susan only hesitated for a moment before the nurse, who had come in by a side door, was talking and, putting an arm around her shoulders, was firmly steering her towards a second door, immediately behind the receptionist.

"Come along dear, hurry along".

Susan, startled, found herself being led down a long white corridor. She had not really had had any chance to take in what was going on, it was all happening so quickly. She had certainly been taken aback by the tone of the nurse's voice. There was something about her, the no-nonsense attitude the air of authority. She had not expected to be spoken to like that, so brusquely. It was something she had never experienced before, never in her life; it had caught her by surprise, caught her off balance.

Having reached the door at the end of the corridor the nurse went ahead using a key selected from a bunch that hung from her belt. It had all happened so quickly, from speaking with the receptionist to being ushered out along the corridor. This was the first time that Susan had really taken in this nurse that had had the temerity to have spoken to her so brusquely, and that was now guiding her so authoritatively. She was taken by the contrast between the appearance of this woman and the nurse at the reception desk. The latter had been dressed in the conventional blue uniform dress of a modern hospital nurse. The women she was now trailing was wearing a calf-length white uniform dress with a white elasticated belt, from which a bunch of keys hung on a short chain giving her something of the air of a jailor or wardress. She had white high-heeled shoes and white stockings or tights, but most striking of all was the white headdress.

The latter completely covered her hair such that only her rather stern yet still rather beautiful face, as Susan was to later observe, was exposed. A rather old-fashioned looking headdress, Susan thought, like something from the 1950s. Turning slightly, so as to allow Susan passage, the nurse ushered the girl, again rather brusquely, through the door, allowing Susan her first really good look at her from the front, confirming her initial impression, from the women's head dress and authoritative manner, of a no-nonsense hospital matron, yet seemingly from another age.   The nurse or matron, as Susan was increasingly thinking of her as, was wearing a semi-transparent apron of PVC or, perhaps, a thin rubber, and of a rather old-fashioned looking bib and skirt design with her elasticated belt fastened over the top as it was a permanent part of her uniform.   Her dress, though, appeared to be of a more conventional material, perhaps polyester, Susan thought.

The room in which he now found herself was quite small perhaps 3 metres by 4 metres.   Somehow she had expected white tiled walls and perhaps a tiled floor, it was after all presumably a bathroom, shower room or some sort of changing room. Strangely the floor, and later she discovered, the walls, were layered with some sort of plastic material, fairly soft yet tough, apparently padded but presumably waterproof.   Safety precautions, she thought, typical of today's PC world, totally over the top.   She supposed that one was less likely to slip and if one did, one was less likely to be hurt one's self, but was it *really* necessary?   On her right, occupying most of the length of the wall, was a standard hospital examination couch, the only remarkable thing being that it was completely white, even the top, which, from her experience were generally of black or brown leather.   This, she was rapidly becoming aware, was something of a common theme. She had started to notice that everything in the room, absolutely everything, was white, not at all what she would have considered a practical choice of décor.

She could see that the couch had adjustable stirrups attached, it was obviously a gynaecological examination couch.   It had various wheels levers and controls and looked as if it could be adapted to many different formats and uses.   Strangest of all there appeared to be some sort of nozzle protruding up from the centre of the couch.   There was something rather unsettling and vaguely frightening about it all.

On the floor alongside the shower cubical was a white plastic basket to which the nurse was now gesticulating. "Come along girl, into the shower, you can put your things in the laundry basket for now.   You have a nice warm shower and I'll be back in a couple of minutes to see how you're getting on".   With that she turned on her heel and quickly left, closing the door behind her.

Susan felt uncertain, not sure what to do and yet somehow, for some reason, she felt swept along with the momentum.   The shower looked inviting at least; she *did* feel rather sticky after her journey.   Quickly she undressed, placing her clothing in the laundry basket as instructed, and entered the shower.

The cubicle was semicircular and quite small, occupying one corner of the room. It felt even smaller once the door had slid shut. The gently curved walls and door were manufactured in a transparent plastic, as translucent as window glass, and, despite being alone, she could not shake off a feeling of embarrassment that had started to manifest in her mind; she couldn't avoid feeling like some sort of exhibit, like something on display in a glass case for the amusement of the public. Yes, she was alone for now but before long the nurse would be coming back.

Chapter 5 | Institutionalisation (1) …

She didn't want to be seen like this, naked and on display. From inside the shower she briefly scanned the room, looking for a towel. Seeing nothing, she briefly considered getting out and re-dressing, even though already soaked.

At that moment the nurse returned carrying a small white towel which she left on the couch. Without pausing to speak and without so much as an acknowledgement of the naked, showering, girl she gathered up the laundry basket and was gone.

Susan Stringer was alone again and relieved to be so, at least to some extent. Quickly she climbed out of the shower and grabbed at the towel. She was immediately horrified to discover it was far too small to go all the way around her; it was more of the size that she might have used to wipe her face and hands over with rather than the bath towel she would have expected. Nevertheless she dried herself with it as best she could and, having done so, stood, holding it up in front of her lengthwise, trying to cover herself as much as possible and nervously awaiting the nurse's return. At least she wasn't cold; the room was comfortably heated, even the floor felt slightly warm under foot.

The nurse returned within two or three minutes of her finishing drying off.

"I've taken your old things to the laundry for cleaning. Where are the clothes you brought with you? You did bring a change of clothing I take it?"

"They're all in my suitcase..." Susan began, before abruptly being cut off mid sentence.

"Are you always so rude?"

"What?...I,I,I'm not sure what you mean" Susan was nervously stammering, suddenly finding herself in a state of total shock and, uncharacteristically for her, lost for words.

"My title is Matron, that is how I am addressed here and that is how *you* will address me. Now where is your suitcase girl?

"Th, th, the nurse, th the nurse in reception, sh, she said something about p,putting it in storage for the time b,being." That stammer, it was getting worse! What was wrong with her, why was she so nervous? The woman was being so bloody rude, just who did she think she was? She had to pull herself together, be more assertive; people like that, they just walk all over you if let them.

"Where are your manners girl. Have you forgotten already, you *stupid* girl?" The woman had actually shouted that time…and called her stupid!

"I am *always* addressed as Matron, always. I will *not* put up with rudeness, from *anybody*"

Susan suddenly found herself close to tears, her confidence seemed to be ebbing away from her, "S,s,sorry Matron". She couldn't believe that she was saying it, and with such deference. She was stammering again; she'd rarely stammered or stuttered in her life before but in under half an hour of arrival she was most definitely developing a nervous stammer.

The woman went on in her bullying tone, pressing home her advantage, keeping the girl off balance: "So you didn't think to get out a change of clothing first then?"

Susan just stood there, silent, dumbfounded.

"Well girl?"

"N, no I,I,I g,guess I didn't"

"What?" bellowed Matron.

"M,m,mm Matron" Susan was learning her manners.

At Susan's correction Matron's voice changed completely, magically. Suddenly she was speaking gently, softly. In fact her whole demeanour had changed; she was smiling. The contrast with the Matron of mere seconds before could not have been greater. "That's better, girl" she cooed, and then, hardening her voice once more, yet not to such an intimidating extent as before, she went on; "So why couldn't you have just gotten a change of clothing out before you left your case at reception?"

"I,I,I don't know, I,I,I didn't think...Matron." She had managed to get out the 'Matron' part in time, just.

"And why was that? *Are* you stupid, girl, is that what it is, is *that* your problem?"

Susan didn't know what to say, she was slowly descending into a state of complete shock, mental colapse, she just stood there trying not to cry, a last-ditch attempt not to show weakness.

"Well, girl? I am asking you a question, are you too stupid to understand?" Matron's voice was starting to harden still further.

"N,n,no I,I,I mean YYYes I,I,I'm ssorry Matron." Susan, despite herself and her resolutions, was beginning to gently cry.

Matron's voice immediately softened again, now taking on a soothing, insinuating, note of empathy. "That's a good girl, it's always best to admit to our mistakes and our limitations don't you think?

"Y,Yes, Matron"

"Good girl! " "Now, we will just have to get you sorted out the best we can. I won't be able to get to your suitcase for the time being and your uniform is not ready yet so I'll just have to get you some nightclothes from the hospital stores, not necessarily totally suitable but it will have to do for now." With that she turned and left, again closing the door behind her.

Susan found it difficult to gauge exactly how long she had been left there, alone. She surmised that It must have been close to half an hour, but it may well have been longer, before the door, bursting open without ceremony, had announced Matron's return. Susan had continued standing throughout, somehow reluctant to sit upon that rather sinister looking couch and not daring to venture out with her only covering being the small white towel that she still clutched about herself. She had been listening intently for the woman's return, in fact listening for *any* sign of life, but had received no forewarning of her imminent arrival. Now that she had started to think about it she realised that she hadn't been able to perceive any sound at all coming from outside the room; all around seemed in a state of utter silent, serene and Zen-like, calm.

She had had time to look around the room; there were no windows she noted and other than the sinister couch, that she had tried her hardest to ignore, and the shower cubicle, there was nothing really to look at. There was just the uniform whiteness of the floors, walls and ceiling. In fact she had started to find it more than a little disorientating; it was strangely difficult to judge distance or to concentrate on anything in particular, basically it was all rather boring, but excruciatingly so.

Matron was carrying a small pile of what at first appeared to be white plastic bags or sheeting but that, upon a second glance, Susan could clearly see were garments of some sort. Turning, Matron placed the pile down on the couch. Susan could see a clear plastic bag balanced on the top containing what appeared to be a thick wad of cotton wool or something similar.

"I'm afraid this is the best I could find and they only had incontinence bloomers in your size. It's all hospital issue don't forget and, as this is a psychiatric hospital, they tend to cater for patients with various problems, still, it will have to do for the time being. It's better than nothing at least, isn't it?"

Susan just stared at the pile. Matron appeared to be waiting for something. "Well, girl? Have your manners left you again? What do we *usually* say when somebody is kind enough to give us something?" Her voice had hardened in the way that Susan was already beginning to associate with being in trouble.

Susan bulked momentarily but then, with a supreme effort of will, she summoned up from somewhere a contrite; "t,t,thank you, mm Matron"

The woman smiled, the soft voice was back again. "Good girl." There was no patronising note to it but rather it was said as one might reward a dog under training. "You get dressed now like a good girl and I will be back in a couple of minutes." With that she turned and left, the door closing behind her and there came again that eerie silence, made all the more so by Susan's noted inability to hear Matrons footsteps receding, as she might ordinarily have expected.

Susan went straight to the pile, eager to cover herself up with anything. Without pausing to examine the contents she put the clear plastic bag to one side and went straight to the clothes. She quickly grabbed at what appeared to be a pair of knickers, lifting them up by their waistband; they were plastic! Thin white PVC! Lifting them higher allowed the legs to unfold revealing that they would be rather better described as bloomers. The legs appeared to be designed to come down to about knee-length and had an elasticated cuff at the bottom of each. The waistband was noticeably thickened and was also elasticated. Susan felt like crying again, she couldn't wear these, she just couldn't. However she felt sure that Matron would be coming back before long and she had to cover herself up with *something*; she wouldn't put it past this woman to make her walk out into the corridor with nothing on at all otherwise. Hurriedly she examined the inside; she wasn't at all sure which way round they were, having never come across such a style before. A label identified the back, stating in black lettering; *St Mary's, psychiatric wing: Incontinence bloomers, PVC, female.* Having determined back from front she hurriedly stepped into them. Pulling them up her legs she shivered at the unfamiliar feeling of the material. She had to carefully ease the leg cuffs over her knees, finding that they were quite tight but that, once in place, they were not unduly uncomfortable, being lined with a particularly soft rubber compound in that area, a provision designed to ensure a reliable watertight seal around the lower thighs as much as for comfort. It was only upon reaching this point in the proceedings that she noticed in the crotch area what appeared to be some sort of arrangement of straps. The purpose of these would have to remain an enigma; she certainly wasn't in the mood to puzzle over it and Matron could be back any moment.

Susan had to wiggle to pull the waistband into position and couldn't help but gasp slightly as the rear seam slipped between her buttocks. The shiny white plastic fabric sheathed her bottom like a second skin. It wasn't that the knickers were tight *per se*, just that they seemed to be moulded to her exact shape. Indeed, she had vaguely noticed when she had initially held them up that they seemed to be somehow, 'girl-shaped', even in the absence of a body to fill them.

Looking down she could now see that the legs ballooned out somewhat before finally terminating at those tight, secure, leg-cuffs; it almost seemed as if they had been *designed* to look ridiculous. She certainly *felt* ridiculous wearing them, she was starting to feel like crying again; if anything she felt more self-conscious then when she had been naked. In fact she felt that she might as well *be* naked, the white PVC shrouded her bottom with barely the slightest wrinkle to the fabric.

Moving about she found that was becoming aware of a slight puckering or invagination at the front where some of the fabric had pulled slightly into the outer lips of her vagina. She self-consciously plucked at the fabric at that point but to no avail. She began to realise that it was not so much due to the material pulling at the front as due to the actual shape of the knickers themselves; they seemed to have been designed to fit the female form as closely at the front as they did at the buttocks. Strangely, though, in complete contrast to the rest of the garment, just beyond the very rear of the gusset a sort of sack of excess material hung down loosely to swing between her legs, this originating from the area covering her anus. The worst thing of all, though, was the realisation of how distinctly contrasted was the dark triangular shadow of her pubic hair through the thin white fabric.

If she could have seen herself from behind, though, she would have been made even more self-conscious; her bottom had been moulded into two, almost perfect, white, shiny, hemispheres, albeit rendered pinkish where they were shaded by the flesh below. The cleft between was now exaggeratedly distinct and shadowed, broadened by the pull of the fabric, the back seam fitting so close as to be well nigh invisible other than at its very centre from which emerged the bladder-like swage of hanging excess fabric.

At least she wasn't naked, she thought, although she wasn't at all happy at the prospect of being seen in those knickers. She had always been a somewhat shy girl as regards her nakedness and her, not unsubstantial, feminine attributes but she was now gripped by a growing feeling of humiliation and shame the like of which she had never before experienced. She grabbed at the nightdress, wanting to cover her breasts but mostly wanting to cover those awful, embarrassing, knickers. The dress, she quickly realised, although white to match the knickers, appeared to be of a soft latex rubber rather than PVC. The design looked to be rather childish, with its short puffed sleeves and wide collar, reminiscent of a Victorian child's sailor suit, teamed with a short but full, circular skirt. As if to emphasise further the juvenile image, delicate frills decorated both the edge of the collar and the skirt's hem.

Ordinarily she wouldn't have dreamt of wearing such a thing but she seemed to have little choice. She felt sure, now, that Matron would very soon be returning and the atmosphere of the place, the way she had been treated and the way she had been spoken to had seemed to have undermined her confidence somewhat; she had been feeling less and less able to stand up for herself as time had gone by and now was at something of a low ebb.

She held it up by the shoulders, examining it with ever growing distaste. It was obvious that the dress fastened by way of a rear zip running from the skirt's waistband to the neck. It was supposed to be just a hospital-issue nightdress and yet it seemed to be so carefully tailored. The bodice was nipped toward the narrow waistband of the skirt, gently curving in at the sides. At the front the material protruded slightly at roughly the area at which it would cover the breasts. The whole garment looked almost as if it were already actually being worn, moulded to, and by, a womanly curvaceous form. Printed over the left breast area were the words: *St Mary's Hospital psychiatric wing*. Below this, boldly printed in much larger type, was: *43C*. She was somewhat at a loss to grasp what this latter designation might infer, it didn't seem to make much sense as a dress size and it certainly wasn't her bra size.

She was in something of a panic now, rushing to cover herself up before Matron returned. The zipper had been fabricated in a tough nylon and seemed rather stiff, she had to struggle but eventually managed to ease it down to the waist band. Stepping into the dress she pulled the waistband up her legs, having to wiggle her hips as she did so in order to ease it over them and up on to her waist. Bringing up the front of the dress, she noticed that the thin rubber fabric of the bodice was thickened and reinforced locally at the sides, just above the hips, in the form of a series of narrow vertical panels that curved inwards toward their mid-point and were reminiscent of the stays in a Victorian corset. The dress was thickened at the front just below the breasts whereupon the fabric was reinforced to form an integral pair of firmly supporting bra cups. Strictly speaking, these latter features might better have been described as half cups, the reinforced region falling well short of being sufficient to contain the entire breast, having merely been designed with function in mind; to support and elevate the breasts.

As she might put on any step-in dress she slipped her arms forward into the sleeves and pulled up the bodice frontage, lifting it up on to her shoulders, while, simultaneously, manoeuvring her arms further into the sleeves, shivering her shoulders and shrugging the bodice into place. Then… failure; her breasts had completely missed the waiting integral cups and, try as she might, she found herself unable to fit into the bodice. Easing her arms and shoulders from the bodice she tried again and again.

Trial and error eventually lead to the discovery that she could only fit into the bodice by positioning it with its shoulders and arm holes low down and with her arms directed at the ground, practically directly at her feet. She was then able to wriggle and shiver her way into the bodice, the reinforced, under-wired cups coming up from beneath her breasts as the bodice was lifted up to her shoulders, all at once gathering, lifting, separating and thrusting.

Her arms, having negotiated successfully the smooth, soft, powdered latex sleeves, she tugged at the puffed shoulders with each hand in turn, then with both hands, finding difficulty, still, in shrugging her shoulders into place. Her breasts, already elevated to a far greater extent than she had ever experienced from any bra, nevertheless still hindered her efforts. Reaching around to the rear she had managed to grasp the rather oversized zipper tag but found herself unable to pull it more than, perhaps, a quarter of the way up her back at best.

To fit the bodice onto her shoulders, she began to realise, would necessitate, and result in, the positioning of her breasts unnaturally, uncomfortably and ridiculously high. The dress just didn't fit. It couldn't be made to fit, even in principle, it was just ridiculous. It was not that the size was too small, although the fit was very snug, so much as it seemed to have either been badly designed or designed for some physiological freak of a woman. She was almost shaking in frustration; surely no natural woman could have the figure to match and fit the curves and profile imposed by this dress!

At this point her thoughts, her struggles, had been abruptly interrupted, the door bursting open, giving passage to the bustling and efficient personage of Matron. With practised appraising eye, rapid of thought, rapid of action, viewing the now blushing girl with no little satisfaction yet resisting all temptation to linger over the scene unveiling before her, Matron deftly manoeuvred around and behind the girl. Without word, pre-empting any objection by dint of her decisive and efficient action, she grasped the zipper, sharply displacing the girl's hand as she did so, and drew it smoothly upward, although with no little effort it must be said.

Even to the least observant onlooker that oversized thick nylon zipper tab would have been an obvious and outstanding feature. Now the rationale behind the design became clear. The purchase afforded allowed Matron to smoothly fasten the dress, despite the closeness of the fit, against the naturally-yielding curves of the girl's body, flattening the tummy, pulling in, moulding, sculpting her sides, refining her waist, narrowing and clinching. All at once teenage puppy fat was forced and shaped, squeezed and exuded into an exaggerated hourglass. In Matron's practised hands the strong white nylon zipper glided ever upward concealed as it went by the latex covering as the dress-back closed up. Reaching the girl's upper back Matron gave a final long, forceful, pull with her right hand whilst simultaneously tugging at the back of the collar with her left. One final sharp tug on the zipper tab closed the collar, the zipper snapping into its final resting place at the back of the girls neck, Matron at this point lifting the girls long blonde mane out of the way.

With these last actions the dress had finally been pulled up onto Susan's shoulders, simultaneously elevating her bust which by this point had assumed a somewhat unnatural inclination. Her breasts had been raised high, up and out from her body while being thrust forward into the dress's thin latex bodice, acquiring for all the world the appearance of two pink-white melons. The combination of the uplift provided by the integral bra cups, the almost total lack of confinement to the front and the upper sides of the breasts as well as the thin, elastic nature of the latex used at this region of the bodice conspired to leave her breasts grossly distended yet tightly and closely sheaved.

A particularly cruel observer might even have described the result as being not unlike two large inflated condoms or, perhaps, a pair of pink/white party balloons. Where the material was stretched around the breasts it had acquired a semi-translucent sheen, reflecting the light and, if anything, exaggerating still further their size. The effect from Susan's standpoint was anything *but* aesthetically pleasing, the realisation quickly dawning on her that the integral reinforced bra cups, although securely supporting and suspending, did so only from the underside up to a point just below the breast's lateral mid line, providing less coverage than a half cup bra and only slightly more than a balcony style might.

What was more, and this hadn't really been obvious upon first inspection, the reinforced portion of the cups consisted of two curved platforms of roughly a 'U' shaped cross-section and open fronted, the front portion consisting of the material of the dress itself without reinforcement of any kind. Susan could feel that the support extended, at most, a little more than two thirds of the length of her breasts, particularly now that they were thrust forward and out into the dress front and distended by their unnaturally high suspension.

There had to some mistake, surely, someone had provided the wrong size, that had to be it she thought. Her mind was in a turmoil, it wasn't so much that the bodice was tight *per se*, not that it was too small, that it didn't fit. No, if anything it was quite the opposite. It was almost as if the dress, like the knickers, had been carefully tailored to fit her every curve, but so, so perfectly. The result was to enhance and exaggerate her feminine attributes, but not in an attractive way, she realised, but rather to a ridiculous extent, a humiliating extent.

Throughout the dress the latex fabric seem to vary in both thickness and elasticity depending on its function at a given point; whether supporting, constricting or merely covering. In the region of the breast front, however, the material appeared to be particularly thin and highly elastic. Although excess material had been allowed for the swelling of the breasts at that point the fabric was nevertheless closely stretched around each breast, the darting of the material allowing each breast to be sharply delineated rather than the dress front merely stretching across both breasts. Even the outlined contours of her nipples were clearly visible through the thinly-stretched material, the white rubber tinged reddish-pink by their colouring, each surrounded by a noticeable circular region wherein the white latex had acquired a darker, brownish-pink, under-shade courtesy of her areolae.

Finally, growing more agitated by the moment, her anger mounting, she made her decision; she wasn't having any more of this, this, this treatment. She was a volunteer for heaven's sake! She had expected to be greeted with gratitude, to take part in simple experiments, simple psychological tests she had been told. Perhaps in-between, while waiting, she would be accommodated in something akin to a comfortable hotel room, watching television, reading books perhaps. But this? The way she had been treated since her arrival was nothing short of disgusting! There was no other word for it! Yet she felt hesitant somehow.

It was this place, the very way she had been spoken to and treated, and, yes, the way she was now dressed was part of it. All of this perhaps, it all seemed to be conspiring against her, to be sapping her self-confidence, keeping her off-balance and unable to regain her composure. This dress, they had described it as a nightdress, it was just ridiculous and she felt ridiculous in it. Couldn't they have just got the size right least?

She had always been proud of her large firm breasts, ever since at school, when she had been one of the first girls in her year to develop and flower. True, she had occasionally been self-conscious about their size. Like most teenage girls she had harboured a certain insecurity as regards her looks, despite her undeniable beauty, despite the continuous compliments; she had already caught the eye of many an eligible bachelor as well as, it must be said, that of certain less savoury characters.

Yes, she had, at times, been somewhat self-conscious about her rather precocious curvaceousness but had ever been confident of her attractiveness. Nevertheless the exaggerated prominence of her breasts in this dress, the translucent balloon-like sheaving, the deep shadowed valley between, these things now conspired against her, highlighting those insecurities, keenly heightening that teenage self-consciousness. For the first time in her life she found herself actually feeling ashamed of those once treasured feminine assets, indeed, of her very womanhood.

The Corridor: A Back Passage and a Downward Spiral

Matron leading the way, Susan following close behind with a nurse bringing up the rear, the trio moved out into the corridor, Susan guided, gently yet firmly, from behind by the nurse who had placed one hand on Susan's right shoulder as if to steer her. They turned left, heading away from the direction that Susan had initially entered from barely an hour before. As before, the corridor was both silent and white, white all around, in every direction, whether she looked to the left, to the right, up to the ceiling or down to her feet. These features, so notable to her upon her arrival, were now, now that some time had past (how long? She wasn't sure) even more remarkable. She found the white-monotony seemingly to have become even more disorientating; she felt certain that the corridor was, somehow, far longer than it had been. It was difficult, no, impossible, to judge distance; the all-white features viewed against the white background fooling the eye, manufacturing an optical illusion from every vista.

Her feet, now bare, appreciated the soft thick white carpeting as she was guided, without pause for reflection, along the passage. To the left they were passing regularly spaced, unmarked, unlabelled, white doors, each identical to that by which they had just exited the shower-room and each absolutely and utterly indistinguishable from the next. To her right, inset into the wall opposite each door, were windows through which daylight flooded, augmenting the shadow-less diffused illumination provided by the lighting system, the latter providing indirect, covert, illumination from a source within a recess at the point at which wall met ceiling. The windows, although quite large, being of approximately one metre long by half a metre high as far she could estimate, and being roughly at shoulder height to her, did little to relieve the general monotony. Each window, as in the shower room, was of frosted glass and was protected by a white grille mounted flush to the wall, the actual window itself, the glass, was inset, perhaps a quarter of a metre or so behind the protective grille.

Still somewhat wrong-footed but nevertheless having regained some composure, turning slightly to the nurse behind her, she inquired as to their destination, demanded to know what was going on. Her reward was simply a sharp admonishment, the nurse, simultaneously raising a finger to her lips, starkly stating: "Talking is not allowed in the corridors, it disturbs people from their work" and then, more softly, now guiding the girl with a hand beneath her elbow, "come along now dear, keep looking straight ahead if you don't mind".

The corridor, in fact, terminated just a few more doors along. Indeed, it was nothing like as long as it had initially appeared, its elongation being by way of a trick of the light; whether by accident or design she could have no inkling.

Chapter 5 | Institutionalisation (1) ...

Passing through an end door they were immediately confronted by a white barred gate that would not have looked out of place in a prison. Beyond the bars lay a small landing immediately across which was an obvious lift door, albeit white like the rest of the surroundings.

Matron unclipped the ring of keys from her belt. Quickly selecting the correct key she swung the gate open. Susan found herself ushered through before she had even had time to as much as *think* of objection; indeed she heard the soft click of the gate shutting and locking behind her as if in the far distance, as if in a daze, an almost dream-like state. Moments later and another key, lift doors slid open revealing a lift interior essentially identical to the scene outside, right down to the thick white carpet. Susan was ushered inside followed in quick succession by Matron and the nurse. The turn of Matron's key in the plastic control panel was followed in quick succession by the silently-smooth closing of the lift doors, an ever so gentle lurch and then a soft hum.

This was quietest, most gentle lift that Susan had ever been in, there had been so little initial sensation of movement that she could not be sure whether they were going up or down; if anything she thought they must be going down but there were no floor indicators and the only control was the single key and lock mechanism. The mechanical hum continued to fill the air yet still there was little, if any, discernible sense of movement in any dimension. In fact, had it not been for the humming Susan wouldn't have been at all sure that they *were* moving. She was starting to think that something must have gone wrong, surely the lift was stuck, malfunctioning! She was gradually becoming overwhelmed, drowning in a rushing swirling tide of panic; for as long as she could remember she had felt uncomfortable in enclosed spaces. She wanted to say something, ask something yet she felt intimidated, oppressed. It was building up within her, it was pent up but about to bound free; she was going to scream, she was...

With a barely discernible jolt the humming stopped, for a moment fulfilling her worst nightmares, then relief, the door floated across, opening in almost total silence, the faintest swish at most but discernable enough for all that. Certainly enough, together with the change in light level, to reassure of freedom even through tightly squeezed eyelids, enough to release the pumping pressure throbbing in her head, relax sweating clenched fists, unfurl cramping fingers and un-bed deeply palm-embedded fingernails.

Susan was ushered out, the nurse with one hand upon her shoulder urging her forward. Matron, following on close behind, removed her key from the control panel as she went, the lift door unnervingly, eerily, no, *supernaturally* gliding across behind her.

Susan quickly realised that her impression had indeed been correct; the lift had become stuck, they had gone nowhere, they were back on the same landing, facing the selfsame prison-like bars and the locked, barred security gate. Just beyond was the door to the corridor, through which they had only recently passed. As before Matron unlocked the gate, ushering them through and then on through the door beyond, back out into the corridor, the gate closing behind them, relocking with little more than a click, barely audible yet somehow all the more sinister for it. Matron again took the lead, the nurse at the rear guiding Susan as before, the group moving briskly back along the corridor.

88

Susan felt confused, why were now going back the way they had just come? Were they going to use the stairs? She couldn't recall passing a staircase on the way in, perhaps it was through one of the other doors. They were passing the doors again, now, of course, to their right, the windows now lying to their left.

Susan hadn't been aware to begin with of the way the unsupported extremity of each breast, perhaps a third of the artificially distended length of each torpedo appendage, bounced with each step. But as time had gone by, as the trio had progressed further, she had slowly become aware of a sensation in her nipples, not exactly an irritation, nor exactly a chafing of skin against fabric, at least not a simple, to and fro, motion, no, it was something entirely different, something disconcerting rather than uncomfortable. The elasticity of the latex endowed the fabric with a tendency to grip the nipples slightly, each bounce, each step, resulting in a gentle tugging, a soft and ever so subtle sliding and pulling motion. The awful truth dawned; that this sensation had so suddenly become apparent, that it was growing in intensity, was not entirely unconnected with the steady hardening and distending of her nipples, thrusting ever more insistently out into their elastic condom prisons.

The sensation, if truth be told, was not unpleasant, or rather wouldn't have been had the circumstances been different, more appropriate. As it was, the effect on the girl was disconcerting to say the least; the uncontrolled, and uncontrollable, response to enforced stimulation so readily and obviously apparent to even the most casual of observers, her hideously-growing embarrassment leading to further overt, and therefore embarrassing, physiological effects.

With cheeks turning the deepest of crimson she felt the blush spreading inexorably across her face, only too well aware how this response clearly signalled her shame and embarrassment. She was giving out the most blatant, overt, indication to all around her, all who might see her, of the humiliation she now endured. Her surroundings seemed to fade away, all she seemed to be able to think about was how she looked to the matron, the nurse, worse, how she would appear to anyone approaching their group, were someone to come from the opposite direction. The mere notion was mortifying, intensifying her blushing discomfiture still further.

She was suddenly glad of the silence, their isolation in the otherwise deserted corridor. At that moment Susan, although generally of a particularly gregarious disposition, did not think she could face anyone, not face-to-face. At least the nurse was behind her and the only thing she had to face in front of her was the white back of Matron's uniform, with its nipped in waist and tailored skirt, the latter outlining her broad hips before flaring out to gently swish against her stocking-clad calves, the soft rhythmic hiss almost the only sound to be heard, the swing of her skirt hem, to and fro, to and fro, almost hypnotic.

Suddenly a shock, more a revelation; the doors, there was something different about them! This couldn't be the same corridor after all, not the passage they had been in before. Each of *these* doors had a small sliding plate mounted at roughly head height, the design suggesting that it might perhaps be a cover for a spy hole. In addition, at about chest height, there was a removable plate upon which, in large black letters, was a number and a letter.

This latter plate or plaque appeared to be of plastic and to be held in a form of slide-in frame that was part of the door. The next door they came to had exactly the same features, and the next, and the next, each door with a different number and letter combination.

It was as they were passing one particular door, perhaps the fifth, that Susan had taken particular note. This door bore the number *43 A.* This had been particularly notable to her, partly because they had slowed down at that point and partly as it reminded her of the number printed on the nightdress she was wearing. It was obviously the same format, was it the same number? No, she felt sure it said '*43C*' on her nightdress.

Her thoughts were in turmoil, more so than ever, chaotically crashing around her head like marbles in an empty tin, and just about as useful to her right now. The only clear impressions that she'd formed, the only logical conclusions that she could reach, pointed to her now being in a different corridor. These doors were very different; "cell doors" she thought, prison-cell doors, that was what they looked like, that was the impression they gave her. The only time she had seen similar doors to these had been on a TV programme about a Victorian prison, or had it been about an asylum? She couldn't quite remember.

But the lift hadn't been working? If it had, if anything, she would have thought that they had been going down. But then…*that* would have meant they would have to be in the basement since they had initially started out on the ground floor. It didn't make sense, none of it did; the windows, the daylight coming in, they couldn't possibly be in the basement. Yet in the lift she had been certain that they hadn't been going *up*, absolutely certain. She had finally convinced herself that they hadn't been moving at all. But this was definitely a different corridor, albeit with identical decoration, the now all too familiar all-white theme; the same Zen silence ruled here too.

The next door they reached Matron stopped at. This door had no number, the plaque holder, vacant and waiting. The nurse, reaching into her uniform hip pocket, retrieved a white plastic plate with the number *43C* in bold black lettering. This Susan saw for the first time as, reaching past her, the nurse had slotted it into its holder. Almost simultaneously, Matron had unclipped her keys from her belt, and, having deftly selected the correct key, inserting it into the flush keyhole, the door swung open. Susan was hurriedly ushered over the threshold, the door's thickness and evident iron construction reinforcing her earlier impression of a cell door. Not that she was to be allowed the mental freedom to pursue this notion further; already she was being issued with instructions and dictates and, instinctively, she knew she'd best pay attention.

Home Sweet Home

Initially Susan hadn't actually, really, heard anything of her instruction. She was stunned. She stood looking around herself, around the room, although, what with the thick iron door, the lock and the spy hole, the description 'cell' came to mind, more than' room'. As in the shower-room earlier and the corridors she'd walked through, everything, but everything, was white. As she stood with her back to the, now closed, door she found herself facing a perfectly cuboid, near featureless, white, space.

The floor was covered wall-to-wall with the same thick white carpet that seemed ubiquitous throughout this part of the building. To the right was a typical hospital bed but realised all in white and, from appearances, possessing a padded frame. Looking immediately straight ahead she found herself gazing in some surprise at what appeared to be a child's combined desk and chair, positioned up against the centre of the end wall and apparently manufactured in some sort of white plastic. Immediately above the desk, just above the head height of an average seated adult, was a square window of white frosted glass with dimensions of around half a metre by half a metre. This, as with the windows she had seen in the corridors and in the shower room, was inset back into the wall by about a quarter of a metre and protected by a white plastic grille fitted flush to the wall. To the left of the desk, in the left corner facing out from the rear wall, was a toilet. No cistern was visible just the toilet bowl and seat, nor was there any obvious handle or other means of flushing apparent. Other than these items the room was bare, featureless and soulless. As she had observed in the corridors the lighting was provided both from the daylight let in by the window and by indirect artificial lighting, evidently emanating from a source hidden within a recess running around the edge of the ceiling and covered by a white diffuser, notably well out of reach.

Susan jumped; they had been talking to her, Matron and the nurse. She had been miles away, struggling with her thoughts, bemused by her surroundings, the rapidity with which her situation had been changing, the strange feeling, almost an acceptance, that somehow, in some way, her status had changed. Now Matron's sharp voice cut through, slicing deep into her thoughts, snapping her back into reality, or at least what passed for reality in this place, at this moment.

"*What* did I just say? You haven't heard a word that I or my nurse have said, have you?" she was making little attempt to hide her annoyance, her irritation. Susan felt as if she was walking through a dream (a nightmare?), staggered, aghast, she just stared ahead like a hypnotised rabbit, clubbed into submission by Matron's concussive delivery, her bullying insistence demanding an answer. She must answer, Susan knew, but what answer? What *had* been said? For around the third or fourth time already that day Susan found herself lost for words, near to tears. No not near, not any more, she *was* crying.

Susan, despite her resolve, was gently sobbing now. That this had any effect on Matron at all was beyond all the girl's expectations. As it was it *did* have an affect, an affect apparently beyond all reason. Matron's voice abruptly softened, assumed, once again, the strangely soothing, reassuring, almost singsong, tones that Susan had experienced previously in the shower-room.

The effect then, as now, had been similar; wrong-footed, the girl had been thrown off-balance, confused. This time, however, her equilibrium had been even further disturbed by the near-schizophrenic change in Matron's voice and manner. This time Matron's attitudinal turnabout had been even more pronounced, even more extreme; a smile, friendly almost maternal strayed across her face as she spoke. This time Susan could only gaze wide eyed through a soft-focus veil of tears as Matron reassuringly placed an arm around her shoulders, gently guiding her over to the small desk while, simultaneously, reiterating her earlier, missed, instructions, now in an odd, cooing, voice that was having a calming effect on the girl while, nevertheless, holding her full attention.

In fact Susan had barely been aware of being seated at the desk, despite having to wiggle her wide hips and bottom onto the low little seat, squeezing herself into the small space, the desk pressing up against her torso. She had found it impossible to concentrate, to compose her thoughts, yet she had found herself paying careful attention to what she was being told, to Matron's instructions. The woman's voice had seemed to fill the room, not by sheer volume, not by loudness, quite the opposite, yet that very softness, juxtaposed with the strange situation in which she now found herself, commanded her attention to the exclusion of all else. The room, her surroundings, seemingly faded away, she had felt herself becoming victim to a growing tunnel vision, a growing white tide had began to wash over her, clouding her senses...

Then she had been alone, they had left, the door closing behind them with the slightest, padded, thud. Her memories, their departing words, the only evidence that anyone else had ever been there in the room with her, such was her sense of isolation.

How long had it been? How long had she waited? She was alone now, alone with her thoughts, the silence almost deafening, a strange, intense silence she had never before experienced. But then again, it was not *quite* silent, not quite absolutely. There was something there, if she stayed still, listened hard, a far way sshhshwassh-shhwassshh, not initially obvious, barely audible. In fact it was not really audible at all if she fidgeted, the soft rustle of her PVC pants was enough to mask it. So she had sat still, listening intently. And she had done so for some time, becoming more and more desperate to hear something, anything, from outside.

The sound, when she had become aware of it, was like an old friend. It was familiar somehow, yet at odds with her current surroundings, disorientating. Gradually the image had formed, maturing in her mind's eye, materialising in a way reminiscent to the relief afforded by the image of a lost loved one, slowly emerging from the mist, or the path home, to safety, intermittently glimpsed between vague shadows and sporadically-shifting pools of moonlight. It had come to her in this way, not as a flash of inspiration, of recognition, but rather as an acceptance of faith, an unquestionable truth. It was the sound of surf on a shingle beach, far, far away. She hadn't really thought about it on her journey here, to the hospital, was it near the coast? The sea? She hadn't thought so and yet she could plainly hear the sea. She had begun to wonder about the beach. How far away could it be for her to be able to hear it, the surf, here in this room. Strangely, once that she had become aware of it, it seemed to have become easier to hear in some way.

She had begun to fidget somewhat, the PVC bloomers rustling with each movement as before and yet now without seeming to interfere with her perception of those faraway waves. Indeed, on the contrary, the rhythmic beach-surf sound now seemed to blot out that soft PVC whisper.

Her constant fidgeting finally broke through that surf-induced reverie. It was not that the seat was uncomfortable as such; indeed it had turned out to be far softer than it had looked and having the same spongy quality to it as did the desk top. She had wondered as to the utility of the latter, it would clearly be difficult for one to write on anything other than a hardback book on such a soft pliable surface. No it was not the seat itself, it was just that she had been gradually becoming aware of a new sensation, demanding her attention, an insistent urging.

It had finally been her full bladder that had pulled her out from the rhythmic surf and offered her back her freedom to reason, to think again. Susan had been sitting transfixed, staring at the blank wall, slack jawed, her mind filled with that unvarying, controlling, rhythm. She suddenly looked around, almost as if waking from the deepest of sleep. How long had they been away? Matron had said she would be back soon to take her to see one of the researchers, she was just to wait here for a short while until a staff member became available. She looked up, the window behind its white grille seizing her gaze. The frosted glass was now a black obsidian slab, appearing all the blacker for interrupting and intersecting the otherwise perfect white flow of the walls. In fact the window was the *only* interruption to that monotony; she couldn't really see the room's door as a separate entity within the wall behind her. The room was as light as ever but no longer had that day-glow from above the desk. It was night time; that much was obvious.

What had she said, that Matron woman? That something was wrong with the burglar alarm system in some of the rooms, yes, that was it. A 'malfunction' Matron said, but that it would probably be fine and in any case she would probably not have to wait too long. However she *had* appended the advice that it would be best if Susan would remain seated until sent for. Apparently the alarm used a motion detector and in some rooms, although it was automatically deactivated by the badges that the nurses wore and so was turned off while a nurse was present, it had an unfortunate habit of becoming reactivated. Apparently the security company had been called in and their engineer was trying to sort out the problem but it was a somewhat sophisticated system and the problem elusive.

Bloody ridiculous, she thought. She needed the loo and she needed it now, alarm or no alarm. Their bloody alarm would just have to go off wouldn't it!. Nevertheless, despite her resolve and irritation, she arose tentatively and with some trepidation, a concern that she would have been hard-pressed to put into words if called upon to describe her feelings, had anyone been interested. As it was, having risen she proceeded with all haste, finding her need greater than she had first perceived. This despite a certain stiffness of limbs, only be expected in one obliged to occupy such a cramped position, yet it must be remarked that, had she paused to consider, perhaps not such a stiffness as she might have expected given the circumstances and her perceived passage of time. Little more than one pace separated toilet pedestal from desk. With a growing urgency she tugged at her under things, scrambling, fumbling with growing panic, irritated at having to wriggle out of the close fitting PVC garment.

The lack of elasticity inherent in the fabric required her to fully drop the bloomers to her ankles in order to be seated, to continue with her ablutions, a necessity made all the greater by the low posture she was forced to adopt. The low pedestal, she found, required her to maintain an awkward stance, a low squat with knees and breasts in close proximity. Her privacy and isolation notwithstanding, the sweaty, musty, odour arising from her never regions, from her bloomers, brought the burning blush of earlier back to her cheeks anew.

The thick absorbent pad was now displaying a definite tinge of yellow, spreading slowly as she watched, testament both to the airtight efficiency of PVC, and of a momentary loss of control on her part. She squatted there in growing embarrassment and humiliation. Even though in private at present she dreaded the coming amplification of these feelings, these sensations, as inevitably her present situation became public, to be shared and discussed amongst others.

Having performed her very necessary ablutions, rising anew, somewhat stiffly, from her ungainly posture, she was immediately struck by two things: No toilet paper!, No handle! She could see no way to flush. Perhaps a hidden button in the wall, she felt around for this but to no avail, her fingers finding nothing but the smooth, soft, padding of the wall. She was not really in a state of *huge* consternation concerning these factors, having only urinated, it was more an irritation and an embarrassment not to be able to flush, to have even the faintest smell of urine diffusing throughout the room. It was not nearly as humiliating as the urine impregnated pad and the, now slightly fishy, odour emanating from her knickers. Having been completely unable to fathom as to how the flushing mechanism might be triggered she gave up in irritated resignation. Someone somewhere had slipped up, she thought, they had clearly given little idea or thought to feminine comfort.

The more pressing problem, one that was quickly becoming apparent upon redressing, was the absorbent pad fitted within her knickers; this now noticeably damp to the touch, yellow tinged and no longer exactly fresh to the nose. Yes, she wanted to pull up her knickers as quick as possible, wanted to hide the smell, but the thought of pulling up the garment with the wet pad inside was not exactly a welcome one. The only option, surely, would be to remove it, place it aside somewhere. So doing, she readjusted her knickers, the direct contact of the PVC with her most sensitive and private regions she now endured with some distaste.

She looked around for a suitable receptacle in which to dispose of the now soiled pad, rapidly coming to appreciate her special circumstances, not really expecting the provision of such a convenience. Finally she determined that to place the pad upon the edge of the toilet seat was the most expedient action, clearly she would be unable to flush it away and, besides, what with the small size of the toilet bowl she would not have been surprised if it had become blocked had she been able to. The yellowing pad, the only colour in the room really, seemed to mock her from its throne, to almost dominate the room.

That it would be one of the first things to be seen upon anyone entering the room played on her mind, she dreaded the humiliation of that moment to come, the inevitable moment, when Matron or the nurses would return.

Susan was beginning to feel quite awful; there was no other word for it. The pants, the bloomers, now devoid of their absorbent layer yet just as airtight, were very quickly beginning to feel hot, sticky. Her mood was not lightened by her tiredness; an overwhelmingly exhausted heaviness had started to descend upon her.

She moved over to where the bed lay, perhaps no more than three to four decent paces diagonally, certainly not much more. Two loud bleeps greeted her arrival. She startled momentarily then, shrugging her shoulders dismissively, began to examine the mattress, remarking to herself on the latex covering, the raised area of mattress that in effect functioned as the pillow, all latex covered, the bed frame of a hospital design but fabricated from some pliant, yet tough, white plastic, and superficially spongy to the touch.

Suddenly Susan jumped, practically leapt out of her skin, the sound had started, the noise, the alarm she realised, the sound she was to quickly come to think of as torture. Wheee-orrr! whee-orrr! An irritating rising and falling siren, loud, yes, not quite painful, not intense enough to cause hearing damage, just the most irritating, annoying, unrelenting sound she had ever heard. Like the gnat buzzing around one's ear at night, denying sleep, the tap that just won't stop dripping, only magnified a million times. She just couldn't think straight, quickly running through the entire gamut of variations available for ear protection but all to no avail. Hands over her ears, fingers in the ears, head on the pillow, head under the rubber bed covers, all failed. On and on it went, Susan growing increasingly desperate, it would drive her mad, she knew it would, just knew it! Just couldn't stand it!

Finally in resignation she got her feet again, hands-on ears, the siren, the alarm, her personal gnat, personal torturer buzzing around her head, worthy of some mythological Chinese water torture. In desperation she approached the door, or at least the apparent outline of the door, such being the level of camouflage of the doors tight flush fitting coupled with the white-on-white continuity of the room's scheme. With both fists she was punching, pounding, hitting out… but not thumping, for such a description would imply some worthwhile outcome, some sound to be heard above that incessant screaming cacophony. Even the slightest sound would have provided some satisfaction, some hope that someone might hear her, come to her, reset the alarm.

In this the walls and the door were not her allies. Having the same tough yet pliable surfaced that she had experienced earlier in the shower room they absorbed the impact of her hands, her clenched fists, with a sponginess clearly designed to avoid injury to patients who, disturbed perhaps, might be prone to self harm or simple accident. Whatever the intention, the result ensured that there would be very little in the way of sound production or effect to show for her efforts.

How long she continued with her futilely-padded cushioned hammering can only be guessed at, except to say that, finally exhausted and in despair, she half sat, half collapsed, at the desk, her elbows resting on the desktop sinking into the padded surface, hands still on ears, and, head thus supported, she gently cried.

95

Chapter 5 | Institutionalisation (1) …

Susan wasn't even clear in her own mind at what point it had ceased. The noise had stopped, she presumed that the alarm had reset or somebody had turned it off, if that was indeed possible. For a while it almost seemed as if she could still hear it, it took some time to realise that it was no longer jarring on her, that it no longer hammered upon her mind, no longer tapped against her head like the centre knuckle of some sadistic demented math teacher in the classroom from hell. She was no longer ensconced in her own little private torture chamber, the one she had begun to build for herself in her own mind. She was free to return to the peace and quiet, the overwhelming whiteness and silence of her new reality.

The rhythmic swirl of the tide was slowly becoming apparent again, filling the otherwise dead void-quiet of the room. At first she just sat there motionless, numbly, nerves jangling. Then, as she gradually regained her composure, she became aware of something else nagging at her; she was bored. Not the boredom of a long car journey or slow-moving film, a stodgy novel perhaps or some old classic, no, this was quite different. It was just so, so, quiet, mind numbingly quiet, mind numbingly boring. There was nothing to hear except the rhythmic sound of the surf, nothing to see but white, white-everything, white-everywhere. There *was* the frosted night-black window of course, but that sat behind a white grille and betrayed no detail.

At exactly what point the door behind her had opened she couldn't be sure. Certainly a nurse had entered, that she had been vaguely aware of, but the main thing, the thing that had brought her back to reality with such a jolt was the ringing of that bell. A bright, brash tintinnabulation; ding, ding, ding, ding, each perhaps a second apart and strangely seeming to emulate from all over the room at once.

Startled Susan had sat bolt upright. Mere moments later, before she even had time to look round, a white plastic bowl and spoon had been placed before her, quickly joined by a white plastic beaker full of what appeared to be milk. Looking up she saw her saviour had been a young nurse with pretty green eyes, Susan couldn't be sure but she somehow received the impression that the nurse was blonde although her hair was completely covered by her white headdress. She had a sweet soft, encouraging, voice, lilting, yet there was a note of authority there. "Come along sweetheart, its mealtime. You must be feeling very hungry after your journey." With that she turned and left. Susan was indeed hungry but was also full of questions. Why was she still waiting to be seen? What time was it? Why had the alarm gone off ? Would it go off again? Clearly her questions were going to have to wait.

The bowl before her appeared to contain a light-coloured porridge, almost as white as the bowl itself. The spoon was of a soft rubbery plastic, quite small, the kind of thing one might give a small child to eat with; another annoyance, another irritation. Hungrily she began to eat, irritated that the bell, the ringing that had announced the arrival of her meal, continued unabated. The porridge proved to be very nearly completely bland, nevertheless her hunger drove her on. She reached for the plastic beaker gulping down perhaps half its contents; it certainly looked like milk, yet it didn't seem to smell of anything in particular and, like the porridge, was practically tasteless.

She had finished her drink and had very *nearly* finished eating, grateful for any activity to ease the boredom of waiting. Then the ringing ceased...

96

Almost instantaneously the nurse, the same young nurse with the pretty eyes, reached around from behind Susan's chair, removing the bowl and the beaker and reaching back to retrieve the spoon that Susan had put down in her surprise. Again she hadn't heard the nurse enter. Susan turned, resolved to ask, nay demand, to know how much longer she needed to wait. Her reward was the rear view of the nurse exiting, the door closing behind her, locking with a soft click.

Susan had little option but to sit and wait, too worried now to investigate the room more fully for fear of triggering the alarm again. At least the nurse hadn't noticed the soiled pad on the toilet seat, or if she had at least she hadn't mentioned it. Again some time had passed, some unknown period, again Susan had been startled, a bell was ringing, but one of a different pitch, a different cadence, more rapid, more urgent than before. This time she *had* been aware that someone had entered the room behind her.

Moments later a hand appeared under her right elbow, gently yet firmly guiding her out of the seat, accompanied by a soft feminine, almost motherly, voice, gentle yet firmly authoritative. "Toilet time, sweetheart" was all that was said. Susan began to protest she didn't really need to go right now, not *right* now. But it was all happening too quickly, she was led to the toilet. She found herself facing two nurses. One she had met earlier, of large build, attractive of countenance, yet slightly masculine of frame. The other was new to her acquaintance, petite, very feminine. Both nurses were dressed in the now familiar white uniform and headdress. They stood looking at her, at the yellowed, soggy pad balanced upon the precipice of the toilet seat. For Susan's part, though, there was some relief to be had; the matron was conspicuous by her absence, small mercies she thought.

It happened quickly, so quickly. The petite nurse, who Susan could now see was wearing white latex gloves, stepped forward and, before Susan could do anything, grasped the waistband of her bloomers, pulling them with one swift, practised, movement, down to the girl's ankles. The larger, nurse simultaneously pressed down on Susan's shoulders, guiding her firmly down onto the toilet seat. Susan was in a state of shock, stunned by the rapidity of this new development she found herself unable to do more than just sit there, feeling humiliated.

The smaller nurse, the pretty petite one, turned and left the room, returning mere moments later, or so it seemed, with a white kidney shaped dish. She deftly plucked the soiled pad from where it still lay on the toilet seat, now between Susan's widely spread thighs, and placed it with some reverence, certainly somewhat beyond Susan's comprehension, in the dish, laying it out along the latter's length like some exhibit, as if some evidence to be presented at trial. Without further comment, other than a fleeting look of disgust that she had allowed to cross her pretty features, the nurse turned and left, taking her dish and with it Susan's soiled pad to some as yet unknown destination.

As always here, it was beginning to seem, Susan was to be left in the dark, unlike her physical reality, her environment, which, on the contrary, was bathed in perpetual light. Unchanging, eternal, infernal, white and bland to the point of distraction, to the point of screaming. Seated now, here, upon the toilet, in front of witnesses, under supervision, she just couldn't 'go', just couldn't do it. She couldn't have 'gone' even had she been as desperate to relieve herself as she had been earlier, not under supervision, not with the humiliation!

Chapter 5 | Institutionalisation (1) …

The larger of the two nurses remained standing in front of her with undisguised impatience, arms folded. In due course the bell ceased its ringing." Come along, up you get" a much harsher tone this time. Susan was only too glad to stand up. So doing, she bent to pull up her knickers, one hand reaching for the waistband. The knickers reached her knees, but no further; already a hand was beneath her right elbow urging her away from the toilet, causing her to waddle rather than walk, the girl struggling, still, with the recalcitrant garment. The petite young nurse had returned. From behind her came the unmistakable sound of the toilet flushing, she presumed automatically; no one was near it. The big-built nurse was leaving the room, the door shutting behind her, the younger nurse was standing at her elbow.

There followed a short intermission, beyond which there again came the ringing of a bell; different, more resonant, a deep rich somnolent gong-like bong, bong, bong, not particularly loud, buried, muffled as if from the bowels of the building and propagated through the very structure. It was almost felt as much as heard.

Susan was standing alongside the bed now, her cheeks rosy red with shame, struggling to pull her bloomers back up, struggling to cover herself, regain some dignity. The young, petite, nurse, the friendly nurse as Susan now thought of her, having led her over to the bed, was speaking quite softly "bedtime, sweetheart". Just this, nothing more, simultaneously leading Susan to stand at the bed head. Throughout her time here so far one thing that Susan had noted was the strangely silent nurses; they never seeming to speak to each other and only rarely to Susan, even then only the minimum required.

Upon re-entering the room the petite nurse, unseen by Susan, had placed a small white tray on the floor alongside the bed. Beside the tray she had placed a white plastic packet. Now reaching down, the nurse retrieved the packet, tearing it open and revealing the thick sanitary towel within, far thicker than the pad Susan had so recently removed. "Come on sweetheart, you'll feel far more comfortable with this". So saying, and to Susan's not inconsiderable chagrin, the nurse quickly bent, slipping the pad into the restraining straps in the gusset of the incontinence bloomers, still hanging around the girl's thighs. Having achieved this to her satisfaction and almost in the same movement, the nurse reached into the dish, retrieving a dampened pad of what appear to be cotton wool. This she quickly wiped this across Susan's genitals; practised, effortless, too quick for objection. There arose an immediate, if faint, aroma of disinfectant, Susan noting a slight stinging sensation. Standing back from her work, arms now folded with satisfaction, the nurse simply said "knickers up, sweetheart".

Although said sweetly, softly, there could be no doubt that this was an order. There was a note of unwavering authority in her voice, an authority that Susan was increasingly finding it difficult to stand up to, although on this occasion there was little incentive for defiance. A rosy-cheeked Susan tugged at her knickers for all she was worth, hips wriggling in effort, grateful for the covering provided, grateful to regain, at least in part, *some* privacy. Still, even with this relief there came the embarrassment, the humiliation, implicit in the wearing of such a garment. Now this embarrassment was magnified a thousand fold; this new, thicker, sanitary towel was anything *but* discrete.

This was little more than an adult diaper, Susan thought. What was worse, during this procedure she had again caught sight of the words printed on the label inside the back of her bloomers: *St Mary's psychiatric wing, incontinence bloomers, PVC, female.* Having been again reminded of what those words inferred, they now seemed more an accusation then a description.

The larger of the two nurses, the one Susan had earlier mentally labelled as being 'butch" had returned. She pulled back the duvet, sheaved in its rubber covering. Susan could see that the latter was attached to the bed by a system of white toggles and eyes, starting from a point about halfway along the mattress's length and continuing up to the point at which the ' pillow' was positioned. From the bed's foot to the point at which the eye and toggle system began it was not at all obvious at what point the mattress ended and the duvet/covering began, the mattress cover and duvet appearing to be one and the same.

Only for the second time today Susan needed no persuasion, no coercion; she was exhausted both physically and mentally. Without further instruction, needing little encouragement, she slipped between the rubber covers, no longer worried nor concerned as to her institutional surroundings; in some strange, indescribable, way she was feeling comforted by them. Mostly she just wanted her privacy back, despite the feeling of isolation, of boredom. And then there was the terrible, totally overwhelming exhaustion, this heavy tiredness that was overcoming her.

Satisfied that Susan was in bed the large nurse left the room again, the petite pretty nurse, the blonde, or so Susan had surmised, remaining behind. The nurse squatted, pulling the duvet up over the reclining girl's shoulders and attaching its edge to the bedside, working her way quickly up from the bed's midpoint to the girls shoulders, slipping each eye over its corresponding toggle and, with a deft twist of her dainty hand, securing the fastening; a strange analogue of the traditional tucking-in-of-the-patient that might be seen in any hospital. To Susan it felt firm rather than tight, restraining yet not frightening, the reassurance floating in the back of her mind that she could easily wiggle out if she so wanted. Yet it was also a reassuring swaddling, perhaps it had triggered a subconscious childhood memory, she wasn't sure, she knew only that she felt comforted.

Her task completed, the nurse half-sat on the edge of the bed. In the distance Susan could still hear the insistent bong, bong, bong of the slowly repeating, low, deeply resonant, gong-like bell. She could also still hear the surf on the beach, certain now that it was louder than ever before; the tide must have come in she thought, vaguely, sleepily. The nurse reached over, gently stroking Susan's forehead; "you try and get some sleep sweetheart, you looked *very* tired, *so* sleepy. I'm surprised you can keep your eyes open, they look *so* heavy, *so* tired".

The nurse was stroking Susan's brow, so motherly, so maternal, so unlike her stepmother. It had been one of the things that had originally attracted her here, to get away from that bitch, at least until she was ready to face university. Those soft sweet fingers stroked so gently, rhythmically, brushing Susan's brow with a caress as soft as her voice, her tone conversational yet soft:

"I often find I can hear the sound of the sea at night my room, it really helps me to relax, to get off to sleep. You can hear it from here too if you listen. It's *ever* so soothing. Just let your eyes close, just for a moment. Yes, that's it, *that's* a good girl. You can hear the surf clearer now, more distinctly, in and out, in and out.

It's really lovely, just the surf and my voice washing over your body, gently washing it out to sea, you can imagine floating in the sea, such soft fluffy cloudy lightness, in and out, in and out with the tide, and above just white fluffy clouds floating past. The tide is gently going in and out, in and out. You can hear the surf, the rhythm, each wave floating another light fluffy cloud by." The nurse's voice had gradually become more and more drawn out, monotone, the words becoming rhythmic, slowly synchronizing with the rhythm of her stroking hand and the sound of the surf. The soft gong-like bell had gradually faded away to nothing. Susan's eyes were closed now her breathing rhythmic, a heavy sleep enveloping her, cocooning her in her own private world of white fluffy clouds and soft lapping waves.

"That's a good girl, why not count the soft fluffy clouds as they drift by, that's a good girl, count the clouds while you listen to my voice, it's very important to you to keep count of the clouds, you mustn't lose count, that wouldn't be a good girl and you do so much want to be such a good girl, you do so much want to learn to be *such* a good girl. Counting the clouds is getting so tiring but you have to continue, only when you know how many there are will you be able to relax more fully, become a good girl, a good sleepy girl. If you listen, the surf is trying to help you, you can hear what the surf is saying, it is trying to speak to you , to help you. As it goes in and out, in and out it whispers each time, it is your friend, it is trying to help you get better, to get well, you can hear it now, listen it's just like a child's chant; a *good* girl is an *obedient* girl, a *good* girl asks no questions, that's what it is saying, your friend the surf, you can hear it can't you, yes of course you can, why not join in, repeat with the surf so that the surf can hear that you understand, that it can help you, be your friend, you want the surf to be your friend, you want the surf to be your friend so much, you need the surf, the sound of the surf, listen to the surf now, a good girl *is* an obedient girl, a good girl asks no questions. That's it, whisper it as the surf whispers it, in time, in rhythm with the surf, whisper it along with the surf: *A good girl is an obedient girl, a good girl asks no questions*."

Slowly Susan's lips began to move, the whisper, when it came, came in a slow slur as if from a drunk or the deeply somnolent: "*A good girl is an obedient girl, a good girl asks no questions*" the whisper hesitant, pausing, rhythmic, a rhythmic chant perfectly in time with the sound of the distant surf.

Bending over the sleeping, whispering, girl the nurse gently kissed her forehead "that's a good girl" she whispered. "You will always hear those words when you hear the surf, the lapping waves, whispering to you. Think of the surf as your friend, keeping you company when you're lonely. You will never be alone as long as there is the whispering surf, as long as you can hear those words that it whispers so beautifully, as long as you can whisper them back, letting the surf hear how much you love it, your friend. You love that whisper, love those words, want to strive to get well, strive to be a good girl, a good obedient girl."

The nurse rose, silently, leaving the sleeping girl, the rhythmic soft slurring whispering, the girl's lips moving in sync with the un-varying rhythmic sound of the surf, waves breaking upon a tropical shore, fluffy white clouds drifting above.

Susan awoke abruptly, startled, jolted awake by a sharp, shrill ringing. Her first thought of the day: another damn bell! Automatically she went to sit up, the tight elastic bed-cover springing her back down before she had risen more than a few degrees above the horizontal.

She lay still for a moment, disorientated yet safe in her rubber cocoon. The events of the previous day slowly returned in an almost hallucinogenic, kaleidoscopic, jumble. She closed her eyes again, for a moment, no more.

Suddenly she was no longer alone, a nurse was there, *her* nurse, she thought to herself for no particular reason. The petite, pretty, nurse back was beside her bed. Without speaking, not so much as a cheery 'good morning', she crouched, deftly releasing with practiced skill the bedcover's retaining toggles that had insured such a firm, comforting, swaddling throughout the night. As she went she simultaneously and unceremoniously swept aside the duvet with her free hand.

Susan was still feeling sleepy, uncharacteristically devoid of energy, deflated; a leaden heaviness afflicted her limbs, was weighing her down. Before she had even had time to even think, to gather her thoughts, the nurse was helping her to her feet, supporting her by a hand beneath her right elbow, an arm swiftly placed around her shoulders, reassuringly, supportively, aiding in the task of guiding the dazed girl across the room.

Susan, feeling hazy, lightheaded, was glad of the support, glad of the company, and now particularly glad of another fact; that damned bell had stopped. Just three paces, no more, and she found herself guided gently yet firmly down onto that seat again, at that desk. Up until now no word had been said, either way, but now came the nurse's soft west-country lilt, the authoritative tone almost subliminally buried. "That's a good girl. Come along; sit down like a good girl."

Susan was back sitting at that damn desk again; it seemed only moments ago that she had been sitting here, waiting. In front of her, on the desktop, were laid out the white bowl, the white beaker and, alongside the bowel, the childish white plastic spoon; her breakfast, Susan supposed. She glanced up at the nurse who, in her turn, shot back a reassuring, beaming, sugar-sweet smile, yet said nothing. Susan returned her gaze to her 'breakfast', the latter differing little, if at all, in appearance from her previous meal. A white milk-like drink filled the beaker, the bowl, containing some sort of porridge as per her previous meal, now appearing even whiter than before in the daylight glow that now issued from the white frosted-glass window above the desk, from just above her head.

For some reason, although hungry, Susan's attention had been drawn to that window. She had momentarily lost interest in the meal before her, the lack of any specific, discernible, aroma emanating from the latter, together with its uninspiring appearance, further facilitating that distraction.

Yes, there was definitely something about that window, or rather the featureless white-misted pane sited beyond the protective grille, beyond the obvious focal plane, that she had missed before. The realization came to her quite suddenly that that was *exactly* what it was about it; that the window was not *quite* featureless, not quite. For some reason she had become aware of a series of evenly spaced zones, barely perceptible shifts in light intensity, barely perceptible vertical bands wherein the frosting of the glass appeared slightly more opaque, a faint alternating pattern of light and dark. Bars! There are bars on the outside of this window! Perhaps on *all* the windows! The thought hit her; it really *was* a prison.

Despite the fact that she had just spent the night in a small room, as close to a prison cell as anything she could have imagined and behind a heavy locked door. Despite the security precautions she had witnessed, the locked barred security-gates regularly bisecting the corridors, the key operated lift. Despite all this, she hadn't felt trapped in any way nor locked in; she had trust, she *trusted* them. Until *this* moment, *this* realization, *this* revelation. Yes, she had decided that she didn't *like* the situation, that as so as soon as she had the chance to speak to someone in authority she would resign from the program, simply leave. But *now*...Now everything had changed; that realization, those bars on the window, somehow it affected her. Somehow the whole situation, her perception, had changed. In that instant she had become trapped as some misguided 19th-century naturalist might once have trapped a moth or butterfly in his capture bottle, its fate; to be suffocated by chloroform.

Somehow snapping out of it, Susan instinctively reached for the spoon where it lay beside the porridge bowl. Despite everything she was hungry, not so much by dint of an empty stomach, although her stomach did feel empty, rumbling, more driven by a desire for the taste and texture of food, for the mouth-feel. Stirring around in the pulpy, sludgy, mixture, feeling oddly fascinated, satisfied, by the resulting spirals, she lifted a dollop toward her mouth, tapping off the excess with her index finger, loose, runny dollops, splashing and splattering back into the bowl with a dull soft plop, looking for all the world like soggy, slushy, cardboard-like white papier maché.

Suddenly a break in the silence, in actuality more a slash then a break such was the severity. "What do you think you're doing, girl?" The nurse, that sweet nurse, but her voice had changed, it was sharp, cutting, startling. Shocked, jolted, Susan fumbled, dropping the spoon, the pulp spluttering onto the desktop, small globs sputtering across the front of the latex nightdress, across the tight balloon-globes of her breasts. The nurse continued in the same sharp vein: "Where are your manners? You don't just help yourself! Has anyone told you it is time to eat yet? Have I told you that your meal is ready, have I said that it's mealtime yet?"

Susan was taken aback, a response that was fast becoming almost habitual for her in this place. What madness *was* this? What was all this stuff about etiquette and manners? The food was just sitting there in front of her; of course she would expect to eat it, why would she expect to have to wait? What would be she be waiting for? It was obvious that the nurse was expecting an answer, was growing impatient. Reaching across the seated girl's shoulder and placing the spoon back beside the bowl she said sharply: "Well, girl, are you lost for words or just rude? I asked you a question". Susan had descended into her, now customary, state of shock. Her self-confidence suddenly deserting her she frantically searched around for something to say. What *should* she say? Again she found herself stammering, something she had rarely done before coming here. "I,I,I I'm not sure" was all she could manage.

Susan could sense that the nurse was getting more irritated, it was all in the voice; she just knew that her friendly nurse was no longer smiling. The woman went on: "You're not sure? Not sure of what? Not sure whether anyone told you to start eating or not sure what to say? Well, you *could* start by apologizing. Now, come along and be a good girl, you know what to say, I'm sure."

Towards the end of this latter sentence the nurse's voice had softened, the phrase 'be a good girl' being particularly delicately enunciated.

Despite a deep sense of humiliation Susan found herself saying sorry, more, to her chagrin, Susan had remembered to use the correct address, good manners were *so* important. "I,I I'm sorry nurse" she stammered, feeling the now all-too-familiar blush spread across her cheeks as she did so.

Yet again a startle, a jolt, a shock; words interrupted, the silence between abruptly, rudely filled by an intrusive ding, ding ,ding. Already there was a certain familiarity, last night's meal wasn't it? Instinctively Susan began to turn, to look around, only to be again interrupted, finding the spoon placed in her hand, the nurse having again leant across from behind. The nurse's voice, now coloured by the return of her soft, soothing, coaxing tone; "come along sweetheart, eat up, it's mealtime, I'm sure you must be *very* hungry". A strange singsong tone, notably odd, yet to Susan strangely familiar, even reassuring. "That's a good girl" the nurse continued.

As before the porridge was desperately bland, the texture pulpy, almost nonexistent and, lacking any real 'mouth feel', was not truly satisfying. The drink too was utterly bland, neither warm nor cold, a good description being' tepid'. In actuality it was all at room temperature and, like everything else in her new, but rapidly more familiar, environment, perfectly comfortable, perfectly nice, just so, so boring.

Susan ate quickly, she was indeed hungry, not a real deep down rumbling-stomach-hunger, indeed she was feeling somewhat bloated if she was to be honest, fats becoming aware of a new need, a rapidly growing urgency now vying for her attention. No, it was not this deep-seated type of hunger, it was more a case of her *appetite* requiring satisfaction, the need to *taste* something, *chew* something, that was the desire, her drive, now.

Throughout the proceedings the bell continued its insistent ring, the nurse twittering on behind her. What was it with this woman? Susan, thought to herself, would she never shut up?. Susan, eating, try to ignore, to shut out, the irritating bell and the nurse's equally insistent chatter: "That's it, eat up, it's nice, that's it, you *are* a good girl, *such* a good girl"

The bowl's bottom had begun to show between glutinous globs of porridge, although difficult for Susan to truly perceive, the lack of contrast between bowl and porridge, the near-white upon pure white, conspiring to fool the eye. Susan, scooping up what was possibly the penultimate spoonful was yet again interrupted; the most abrupt of silences had descended, the bell having ceased its ring. Seemingly simultaneously the nurse picked up the bowl, spoon and beaker and was gone. Susan was left to swallow the last mouthful alone, dumbfounded.

The urge, this new urgency, was growing now more and more demanding of her attention. Instinctively she grasped at her abdomen, gritted her teeth. She had been holding back, worried about their stupid alarm system, despite herself, despite being certain that the engineers must have fixed the problem by now. A sharply-stabbing pain had her squeezing out from behind the cramped desk and sidestepping crablike across to the waiting toilet, levering herself up, precariously balancing against the desk corner with her right hand while simultaneously tugging at those hideous knickers with her left.

It was with the greatest of relief that her weight slumped heavily down. The plastic ring that constituted the seat momentarily deformed under the impact, her fleshy buttocks similarly moulding, morphing, to match. Her bowel movement initiated in this selfsame moment, her knickers simultaneously slipping to their final resting place, washing around her ankles in a PVC pool, the elasticated waistband now a plastic hobble.

In her urgency the double beep had gone unheeded. Indeed there had not been any problem with the alarm system when she had previously used the loo. Only when she had moved to the side of the room, by the bed, had the alarm been set off. Besides she had assumed that the fault had by now been corrected. Certainly the nurse that had brought in her breakfast had not reiterated anything of the warnings given the day before. Now, however, her mistake, her erroneous assumption, was obvious but the knowledge was of little use to her now, it had come too late. Wheeeee whoooo! Wheeeee whooooo! Susan could do nothing about it now, just try to block it out, try to ignore it, concentrate on finishing, getting back to her seat, back to the desk. It would reset eventually if she were back at her desk, this much she knew, but for now she was trapped, crouching low on this ridiculous little pedestal, arms wrapped around her middle in a self-hugging display of abdominal cramping and the efficacy of hospital laxatives.

She felt out of control, she was just going and going. Diarrhoea! The thought cut across her mind in a demeaning wave of humiliating horror. The implications, the repercussions, passed in front of her eyes as if a procession, a tableau of ever-increasing humbling humiliation played out to an accompaniment of wailing siren and low, embarrassingly-rumbling toiletry resonance. The aroma, now filling the room to remain well after the event, would be waiting to point the accusing finger.

A new problem, a disaster in fact: Where had the bloody toilet paper gone? Susan was sure that one of the nurses, one of the pair that had visited the previous evening, had brought with her a toilet roll. Yes! She had! Susan had taken careful note, had been relieved. She had intended to demand one, make a fuss about it and so she had been relieved to spot a roll had been brought in. It was that butch looking nurse, Susan recalled, she had had it in her left hand when they had come in, she had stood there fiddling with it while Susan was on the loo. Where was the bloody thing now? Not that there were too many places where anything could hide, could be misplaced, not in that tiny sparsely furnished little room. There had definitely been one brought in, but there was certainly nothing approximating to toilet paper anywhere in the room now. Surely they hadn't taken it with them when they left? Why would they? It didn't make any sense. Nothing did, not here! There was nothing she could use, no paper, no wipes, nothing of any description and the problem was far worse than before.

Desperately she tried to make sense of it all, tried to weigh up her options, find a solution. All the time with that bloody insistent alarm nagged at her, wheeeee-whooooo, wheeeee-whooooo! It cut through her concentration, it jammed her thoughts, it forced impulsive action. Anything just to get cleaned up, get back to that bloody little desk and it's ridiculously small childish plastic seat. Anything to get that bloody noise to stop!!...Anything!!!

Again the removable absorbent incontinence towel in her knickers came to her aid. She was glad now of the increased thickness, the bulk, of this new pad, the very features that had been the source of so much consternation. It was only with the greatest of care that she was able to achieve anything close to the standard of personal hygiene she deemed acceptable. Both sides of the towel had had to be utilised, the girl desperately trying to concentrate on avoiding contact with her fingers, contact with that loathsome brown slime, throughout desperately trying to block out that constant banshee-wailing.

There had been no choice this time but to dispose of the used towel in the toilet. Even as she had done so she had been aware, at some level, of the trouble to come; the nagging foreboding, the likely repercussions, worried away at her. Why oh why couldn't she just flush it away, remove the evidence, both visual and olfactory? The aroma, now conspicuous in its pungency, invading every corner, seemed to mock her in her impotent attempts to clean up. On the other hand, she dreaded the actual moment of flushing, dreaded the outcome; she was absolutely certain the toilet was going to become blocked, and then what? What would happen then, when it *did* flush?

Susan Stringer sat, waited, what else was there to do here? Alone, isolated, she began to contemplate the undoubted uniqueness of her situation before finding that she had drifted away yet again, had lost track of time and of her train of thought, her musings, for the time being, forgotten.

In fact her situation was far from being unique. If, for the incredulous, evidence be required it may be said that such evidence resided close at hand. Close, that is, from the perspective of the reader, those of us gifted the privilege to change the scene at will.

CHAPTER 6

INSTITUTIONALISATION (2) :
30C: THE GIRL NEXT-DOOR

Geographically less than two metres away, albeit separated from her by the half metre thick soundproofed dividing wall, her circumstances were shared. Behind the door of the very next room, if she could have seen past it, the merest glance at patient 30C, sitting at an identical desk, would have been evidence enough both of shared circumstances and of the consequences of those circumstances.

At this particular instance 30C, once Lavinia Vitesse, is having her hair 'styled'. Already Matron's shears have been put to good use, before the girl had had her shower. The bottom two and a half to three centimetres of each pigtail has been cleaved away, taking with it the ribbon bow that had tied it in a single clean action, the shears slicing clean through each braid in turn. This is the third such 'styling session' that this girl has undergone in her six months of residency and, having learned the wisdom of docile acceptance, she sat quietly throughout the cutting and while her remaining hair had been carefully un-braided and combed through. Then it had been off to the shower.

Now she sits unresisting as Matron tightly braids each side before tying off each pigtail with the regulation bottle-green and white ribbon. Standing back to admire her handiwork she simultaneously retrieves a tiny plastic bottle from her dress pocket and, pausing only to make a couple of slight, and frankly, obsessive, adjustments to the bows, applies two or three drops of the clear fluid to the centre of each, 'just in case'.

"Stand up, girl, let's take a look at you". The girl stands, slowly rising to her full height, wincing as she does so, the rubber knickers momentarily adhering to the soft skin of her buttocks before slowly peeling away and in so doing drawing her attention to the throbbing, raised, cane lines that lay beneath.

With eyes of violet and hair of a natural black gently-waved sheen she looks the picture of a young Elisabeth Tailor, perhaps of around the era of 'National Velvet', stretched to fit a taller frame. Despite her almost 19 years and generously full-breasted figure the illusion of a rather precocious girl of the age of a 'National Velvet' era Tailor as been carried into reality by her uniform. That she is actually taller than Matron seems to amplify her awkwardness rather than aid her confidence, further adding to that illusion. She stands demurely with hands crossed in front of her skirt and head bowed while Matron fits the little Victorian-style bonnet onto her head, securing it by way of its broad matching ribbon, tying the latter, with some fastidiousness, into a neat, yet oversized, bow beneath the girl's chin. Again Matron stands back, admiring, appraising, her work as might an artist. Slowly, then, she circles the girl, her gaze systematically sweeping up and down the vision before her. Her work in its entirety, from the patent-look plastic bottle-green Mary Janes to the crown of the green and white striped bonnet.

Stocking seams are examined and found straight, suspenders sufficiently tautened. Posture is checked and confirmed sufficiently submissive. The head is held sufficiently bowed, the hands are correctly positioned in front of the skirt, hands crossed with palms turned outward; the latter gesture of surrender necessitating a pronounced stoop.

Returning again to the girl's rear Matron pauses before bending slightly and lifting the girl's skirt from the hem, pinching the latter delicately between the thumb and forefinger of her right hand. Her left hand now explores around and across each latex-smooth globe in turn, ensuring no ripple, however slight, should Interrupt the doll-like moulded perfection so expertly rubber-sculpted from that rather over-fat bottom. Sensitive, tactile, fingertips appraise the raised, thin, cane welts running across each cheek before reluctantly shifting to trace the centre seam from the waistband down to the point at which it becomes camouflaged by shadow, the point at which it plunges deep into that gluteal-cleft valley. Matron's index finger pursues the thickened rubber line with an inappropriately languid sensuality along the artificially defined separation between buttock-cheeks that are held parted almost as if by an unseen human hand. She feels around the exaggerated indentation that marks the puckering of the fabric into the girl's grommet-lined anus, feels around the gently raised periphery of the grommet's exterior. Journeying further along the shadowed valley she encounters the change in texture that announces the transition to the transparent gusset area whereupon the seam diverges to follow two opposing ovoid paths, accommodating the polythene intimacy of the so called 'examination window'.

"Bend please sweetheart" Matron sounds slightly breathless, although none are present to bear critical witness nor to comment save for a browbeaten girl too mortified, too lost in her self-conscious embarrassment to notice.

"Bend, girl" she says again, starkly, more forcefully this time. The girl is startled almost as if awoken from a deep sleep, she bends to grip her ankles, straight legged, knees locked. Matron's finger continues along its exploratory route, ring finger and forefinger now providing companionship as Matron's hand follows the contours of the girls outer lips through the thin supple plastic, noting the warmth, the girl's core heat, the central soft yielding of fabric confirming the requisite closeness of fit, that the central puckering is determined by her most intimate of contours.

For a few fleeting moments, fingers guiltily tarry, gliding as might a sculptor's hands turned to moulding and refining a masterpiece, working to ease nature's imperfections from the man-made perfection of transparency. Feminine-lubricated fabric slips effortlessly this way and that; starlight-spangled bubbles are gradually smoothed from their expanding viscous pearlescent pool.

For a few brief moments of *our* reality *their* time is stretched and deformed, becoming an indefinite temporal expanse wherein dance both protagonists in a common emotional entanglement of indistinct boundary.

That the girl's response is purely physiological matters not to her. That it is merely a simple reflex to mechanical stimulation, albeit enhanced and amplified in juxtaposition to her enforced denial, is beside the point; such knowledge cannot but fail to defend against the embarrassment and humiliation that this loss of control engenders.

107

That it should come at the hands of another woman only serves to exaggerate and de-rationalise the experience, fear and guilt adding to the piquancy of the mix, physiological excitement surging into a confusing mêlée of arousal.

Matron, too, has her guilty secrets to disguise, her excitement to be denied. If truth be told, her charge's visible arousal, but perhaps more telling, the girl's obvious psychological discomfiture in the face of that involuntary response, urges Matron onward, ever onward. She is now being driven towards a crisis of her own, the resolution of which is available elsewhere but will, of necessity, have to be delayed. She will need all her strength of will and determination, to hold out, but she knows only too well the importance of self control if she is to succeed here.

For those few brief moments, then, they are locked, the two of them, in a wild turmoil of positive feedback, the response of one fuelling the excitement of the other, before at last Matron's professional inner voice breaks through, her returning sense of self control coming as a relief.

Her other side too, Matron's submerged darker side, is to some degree glad of some respite; it would be too soon, too easy, there is the preparation, the training, to savour, the anticipation. Yes, there is the anticipation, the sweetest confection, yet how fragile the line of segregation beyond which, and in close proximity, lies the potential for frustration. Not that such philosophical considerations are ever to be granted more than theoretical status in Matron's domain; a harvest, sufficiently staggered, ensures a constancy of sustenance. Later she can, and will, partake of the wine of freshly ripened fruit, slake that peculiarly guilty thirst of hers in the company of one of her other charges, one of the ' long-term' girls.

Yes, she will extract the tribute due her, born of previous endeavour, fruit of previous exertions of her self-control. She will drink her fill and, even while doing so, in her mind she will be refining her gambit as regards the present situation, anticipating the future crop.

She is going to have to wait but it will be well worth it. In a room much as this one, or perhaps in her office, she will reach her Nirvana of excitement, of physical satisfaction, while her mind, wandering free of any shackles of sensibility or ethical consideration, will reach an equally satisfying psychological completion; exploring the dark recesses of her imagination, laying out new rules, new regulations, developing new regimes, fermenting sweeter still that delicious taste of anticipation that she loves so much.

For now she has obligations to fulfil here, duties to carry out that provide for a different and more immediate form of satisfaction; no less satisfying in its own way nevertheless it is a very different form of satisfaction to that which awaits her elsewhere but for which she will have to wait just a little longer.

The School Room Recollections (1): Introduction

The fact is, patient 30C hadn't always *been* patient 30C. Up until a few days ago she had been patient 30S. A minor change in nomenclature, certainly, a single letter, not much, one might think, but a troublesome change nevertheless. It was problematic for the clinic, a new nightdress had had to be ordered, printed with the hospital badge and the all-important patient number. It was troublesome too for the girl herself who had had to sit carefully unpicking the embroidered letter ' S' of the patient number emblazoned on the breast pocket of her uniform dress before, equally carefully, embroidering the new letter, a task particularly bruising of the girl's spirit. Yes, a single letter, in itself a small thing, but signifying a change in classification of great import to this girl's comfort.

How long ago had it been, a month? She had been selected to join the 'school group', thus the classification letter 'S' on her badge. The school group, she had been led to understand, was a long-running investigation into comparative education techniques and teaching methods. More specifically it was an investigation into the way that different teaching methods influenced learning outcome and was presently examining the efficacy of the old-fashioned rote-learning technique. She had been told she would be sharing a dormitory with other girls and living under a traditional boarding school regime. After the time she had spent alone in her room she had been excited, it sounded fun, although rather strange to be effectively going back to school at her age, being of just over nineteen years of age. Most of all she was to be with other girls, no more waiting, no more sitting alone,. How long had it been? She had no idea. They wouldn't have told her, she knew that, even if she had had the courage to ask, even had she been *allowed* to ask.

She hadn't been sure what to expect, there had been several corridors and a trip in the lift, then at the end of a particularly long corridor a door had been unlocked, the usual white door. Behind this lay a large room but first a locked barred metal grille had had to be navigated. Another one of matrons keys had jangled from the large ring that hung from a clip on her belt and the prison-like grille had opened allowing them entry into what turned out to be a large bright white circular room.

Straight ahead of her, on the far side of the room lay another white door, the centre of the room was dominated by a large circular white table, the top having a perimeter of gently rounded contour. An attached bench seat ran around its circumference, the whole being of white moulded plastic. On both sides of the room, equidistantly spaced around the circular wall and arranged radially, were six hospital beds, three on each side, the room being delineated by way of the two centrally opposing doorways. Each bed was furnished with its own narrow plastic topped table mounted on a bracket across the foot but with the facility of being positionable at any point along the bed's length.

The room's walls were intersected at regular intervals by a curved window, of perhaps half a metre in length, set back into a recess in the wall between each bed and beneath which resided a small plastic chair of the type with which she had become so familiar.

She was disappointed to see the usual frosted glass had been used and in addition, despite the claimed boarding school theme, the usual institutional white plastic grilles were in evidence covering each of the windows.

The reason for the rather cheerful brightness of this room had quickly become apparent to her, in addition to the windows around each wall the high domed ceiling consisted of a series of glass panes, the latter inducing in the girl the perception of having walked into some sort of conservatory or greenhouse. What was more, she could hear rain pitter-pattering against those panes, quite loudly too.

She had been disappointed upon looking up to find the whole ceiling covered with a white grille at the point at which the dome extended upwards from the top of the walls. Beyond the grille she could see nothing of the rain, just a defuse white light issuing through frosted glass, almost formless except for, and she had had to stare for quite some time to really be sure, what appeared to be the shadows of bars mounted on the outside. Hurriedly she had shifted her gaze to the side windows and, having got her eye in as it were, she had been able to confirm that the telltale shadows were indeed present there also. She had quickly come to the conclusion that she was now in some sort of outbuilding, linked to the main building by the corridor through which she had arrived, yet what a strange construction indeed. In her mind's eye she had tried to picture the external view and had come to the conclusion that it must look like a cage that someone had built a wall around and then had put windows in. There were bars across those windows and obviously running across the roof too and then there was the locked grille that they had had to negotiate on entry.

She had often been unsettled by the security precautions that she had encountered since her arrival, previsions that at times had seemed to her to be more appropriate in some high security prison. She had come to the conclusion that it was the legacy of the building's late-Victorian incarnation as an insane asylum, although she had at times wondered at the inconvenience endured by the staff. Whether it had been for financial reasons or to satisfy some desire of the owner's, the decision to retain the original features to the extent that they had clearly involved considerable inconvenience to all concerned.

There was something about this room that, from her first impression, had impacted upon her and that she could not easily sweep aside. Whether it had been the realisation that she would be continually seeing that prison-like locked grille or the eerie sterile atmosphere of that rotunda of hospital beds, whatever it had been it had sent a cold sinister shiver down her back.

Still soaking up the atmosphere her gaze had returned skyward; clearly it had been such an amazing sight, so unexpected, as to have failed initially to register with her. In the very centre of the room, suspended perhaps half a metre below the centre of the ceiling grille, and thus centred directly overhead of what she would later discover to be the dining table, was a mirror ball of the type one might once have expected to encounter in a dance hall but of perhaps half again the diameter.

A nurse dressed in the usual white uniform had appeared from the other door, the door without a security grille, and had stood, with her hands on her hips regarding her with an appraising eye.

110

Matron had introduced the woman as the dormitory mistress, and had told the girl that from that moment on the rather stern looking, stoutly built, middle-aged woman would be taking charge of her and that she should consider herself now 'at school' and as such under boarding school discipline. Without another word of explanation Matron had turned and left, keys jangling as she let herself past the security grille and out through the door beyond.

The woman had been quite brusque and the shocked girl, already staggered by her new surroundings, had been unable to regain her balance and composure. There was something about this woman's voice, a quality that she shared with Matron and that had the power to crush dissent even before any dissenting thought had had time to form. The girl had instantly felt powerless and dominated as the woman had recited the rules, regulations and restrictions under which this regime operated and to which she was now subject.

First and foremost; the ' no talking' rule was retained in the dormitory, the girl had felt her soul begin to collapse at this news, she had previously been told to expect the ' no talking' rule to be in affect in the classroom but she felt stunned at this revelation, by the realisation that she was to be with, and surrounded by, a group of girls of around her own age and yet be expected not to converse, to somehow ignore them. The woman had gone on to outline the rest of the regime, the bells at mealtimes, sleep time and toilet time were retained here but in addition there was another bell that sounded at lesson time, the school bell, and at that time all girls had to line up at that door at the room's end, the classroom door.

There was apparently a small shower room appended but insufficient space had been available when the unit had been set up to install toilets. This revelation had left her head spinning, she felt faint and a little sick as the dormitory mistress had casually gone on to outline the rules governing the issue and usage of bedpans. The woman had led her over to a bed at this point to illustrate her talk by indicating the chair alongside that was fixed against the back wall and upon which sat a bedpan. Not *just* a bedpan, although that would have been bad enough, as it was she had almost fainted; it was transparent, made from Lucite or some other translucent plastic. This bed, she had realised, was to be her bed, for up on the wall above the white plastic coated and metal framed bed-head was a large square glossy white plastic sign with, in large bold black letters, 30S. A similar sign adorned the wall behind each bed, the only decoration on the otherwise pristinely antiseptic white curved walls. It had come as a shock, that this was to be her bed, but the really major shock had come with the realisation that she was looking at *her* bedpan, her *transparent* bedpan, her only toiletry relief.

The rules and regulations had just seemed to go on and on. Some, specific to the regime, were new to her and many had seemed extraordinarily petty, other requirements and restrictions required little or no adjustment on her part. Of the latter, the news that her uniform was to be retained largely unchanged had come as a particular blow. She had expected, hoped for, even prayed for, a more conventional attire, perhaps even receiving her own clothes back. The thought of yet more pairs of eyes appraising her appearance, even if of those similarly attired, had only served to deepen her despondency.

The dormitory mistress had gone on to explain how, from the inception of the clinic and the decision to include in the over-all protocol a uniform for all test subjects, a great deal of effort had been expended to ensure that the conceived design be suitable for a large range of tasks and regimes. Susan's crestfallen expression must have spoken volumes as the dormitory mistress, with eyes sparkling, had been stimulated to enthuse further as to the practicality of the nylon fabric, expounding her opinion as to just why their green and white striped dresses were so eminently appropriate in the classroom while being just as suitable for the workhouse. This latter point had been somewhat lost on the girl and, as she never heard mention of it again, she remained as ignorant now as she had been puzzled then.

With an effort she dragged herself back to the present, there was no longer any pretence that this was anything but a punishment. There was to be no continuance of their previous charades; no excuses regarding the limited availability of accommodation nor problematic alarm systems nor legacy security precautions.

Matron had put it to her straight enough; she had been taken out of the school program after just one month, just one month served of her contract to take part in three months of experimentation. No, the time she had waited before selection, the time spent confined to this very room, or one very much like it, would *not* be taken into account, her contract had been very clear on that point. Now after just one month her place on that particular program had had to be filled by another subject and she was going to have to wait her turn to re-join, it would be at least a month before a vacancy would become due but ultimately her re-selection eligibility was to be based on Matron's recommendation or otherwise.

Nor would this time count towards her three months of obligation and Matron had every intention of ensuring that she did, indeed, fulfil that obligation. Indeed Matron would ensure that she spent *at least* another two months of her life undergoing that exquisitely crushing discipline and enduring those, quite literally, mind numbing lessons. Until that time she had been placed exclusively under Matron's care and had soon been made keenly aware that the longevity of that care was Matron's decision and Matron's decision alone.

She had spoken out of turn, stuttering out a question, a rare breaking of the no talking rule, desperate to know just how long she had been in residence, the answer had underlined her circumstances in bold: "It will certainly be another month now, sweetheart" had come Matron's response. The girl had begged, actually dropped to her knees clasping her hands in prayer-like fashion. Matron had pondered momentarily then had turned as if to leave the room. Behind her the girl had remained kneeling, head swimming. Another month, now there would be two months spent in this room! Another month just for talking?

That she had accepted this pronouncement, this judgment, as a prisoner might expect and accept an extension of sentence, that she didn't even pause, even for a moment, to question Matron's authority, *their* authority, their legal right to keep her locked away, imprisoned, had no little to do with having had previously spent three months in this room followed by three months in the schoolroom.

Yes, as judged out there, out there in that other world, the outside world, she had undergone three months of schoolroom training, three months of strict boarding-school discipline, obedience training and behaviour modification therapy sessions. Here, in *this* reality, in *her* reality, one month had passed, just as the one month she had previously spent in this room, waiting, had seen three such hurry past in that nearby, yet distant, realm of 'the outside'.

The girl's entreaty had neither fallen on deaf ears nor been entirely unexpected. Half out of the door Matron had paused, stroking her cheek with the middle finger of her left hand, the half opened door occupying her right, as if pondering some new thought, some flash of inspiration. Half turning to face her charge, an exasperated expression displayed on her rounded features, seeming to take pity on the girl, she almost apologetically explained how she had to issue *some* sort of punishment, how rules were important to the smooth running of any institution, why rules could not be allowed to be broken willy-nilly. "What am I supposed to do, spank you like a little girl, cane you?" she had added, as if absentmindedly narrating a passing thought. In response the kneeling girl had placed her fingertips on her shoulders, fulfilling the schoolroom-taught protocol demanded of one requesting a boon or permission.

"Yes, 30C?"

"P,p,p , please mm, Matron, pp please a, a, another p, punishment, pleeese."

Matron had by now fully re-entered the room, re-closing the door behind her, and stood imperious with hands on hips before the girl. After due consideration, the seriousness of the situation having demanded a lengthy period of soul-searching on Matron's part, she had outlined an alternative path of punishment. The girl had listened intently, numbly, humbly and then had had to ask ' nicely' for her punishment, reciting the number of strokes of the cane; Matron had said only the cane would do. She had had to kneel there begging for the cane then describing how she would count each stroke and thank Matron for it and declaring that she understood that, if for any reason the punishment was interrupted before the sixth and final stroke, if she should lose count, forget to thank Matron for a stroke or fail to remain bending, then the caning would begin again afresh.

Matron had explained how, after three such restarts, the punishment would have to resume the next day and so on until such a time that she should have successfully received the full six strokes. Matron had added a final proviso; if after three days the punishment had not been successfully delivered then the original punishment of an extra month spent in her room, and thus an extra month in this institution, would stand. The girl had had to confirm, verbally, that she understood that by accepting this caning she was also accepting the condition that any future punishment would be by way of six strokes of Matron's cane with exactly the same conditions in force. If after three days the punishment had not been successfully taken, yet another time extension of one-month would be imposed.

Today was her third day. She had been confident that first day, confident that she had made the right choice; six strokes of the cane and then it would be over, how bad could it be?

Back to Her Future: Matron's Cane

True she hadn't considered the humiliation aspect, hadn't factored in the effect, hadn't expected to have felt so crushed, so weakened, as she had done when the moment had come for her to bend over the desk, for Matron to release the lock that fastened the waistband of her bloomers and to ease them down to hang around her knees. Yet even then she had retained *some* confidence. She had tried to focus her mind on a different situation, tried to blank out not only the thought of what was to come but also any thoughts of the scene she was presently presenting, the view greeting Matron of that soiled pad in her knickers, the rise in odour released as the trapped warm air escaped from its rubber prison.

Try as she might she could not escape her surroundings. For one there was the protocol to remember, counting the strokes, thanking Matron. Secondly each attempt seemed only to lead to memories of the schoolroom, of the classroom, the lessons, the pointless rote learning of alternative and deliberately incorrect multiplication tables. 'One times three equals four, two times three equals five, three times three equals eleven, four times three equals...'

CRACK!. The pain had ripped through her schoolroom daydream and yet was bearable, she had never been caned at any time in her life, in fact never subject to any form of physical chastisement, now she felt cheered, it was bearable, she could get through this! ...

CRACK!. Another stroke, yet still bearable. "Stand up, girl, fingertips on shoulders ".

Puzzled, she had obeyed the order, only then had the realisation taken hold; she had forgotten to count, forgotten to thank Matron after each stroke. "Yes, girl, I can see that you have remembered now, a bit late though sweetheart. Now bend back over the desk and we'll start again."

CRACK... this time she had remembered. "Three, t t t thank you m,Matron".

Matron's voice had come to her lemon-acid sharp: "Stupid girl, I said we'll start again, that meant from scratch. What should you have said?"

The girl had barely been able to answer; her stoic facade had all but collapsed. "Ow o one, mmmm Matron."

"And where's your gratitude girl, your manners? One what, girl?"

"Ww o o one th thank yyo you mmm Matron". Patient 30C had begun to gently sob not so much from the pain but rather in sorrow, in mourning for her failing, nay, dead, fortitude.

Inwardly Matron had smiled, had welcomed this development, outwardly she maintained her professional detachment, her determination to continue going even so far as to comfort the sobbing girl. An arm around the girl's shoulders she had reassured her that she would be able to get through it, this time she would get through it. Simultaneously she had eased the girl back down into position, across that desk.

CRACK! " Wo, wo, one, t th thank you m, Matron."

CRACK!, Slightly harder this time, a pink wheal raising in response, but still bearable, just; "T,two th th t, thank yy, you m, Ma Matron."

CRACK!, even harder this time, a distinct raised red wheal developing across both rounded cheeks, dead centre, yet it had still been bearable, the thought had run through her head, she could do this, could still get through this, she still had hope: "Th, th, three th, th, thank you m,m,m Matron."

CRACK!, another wheal had been painted in vivid rose red across those, once pristine, snow-white globes, perhaps a thumb's width down from the previous. "Thh ff, four, t, th ,th thank y,yo, you m, Matron."

There had come two or three taps with the cane, dummy runs almost, that in hind sight she would later reflect signalled the last time she had truly believed that she might get through it. Sssshwwsssh CRACK!, the shock, a blinding flash momentarily replaced the desk, the entire room. Her reaction had been instinctive, a reflex, she had been totally unprepared for the whip of the cane up, under and across the sensitive overhang of her buttocks, a cane possessed of peerless flexibility, wielded in the hands of an artist and unerringly whipped across the valley whereupon upper thighs swell out into foothills of flesh. Whipped indeed, no mere cane stroke, this. This had been a cane wielded as whip, nothing less, and the product of such handicraft had stood screaming, possessed by uncontrollable weeping, both hands gripping red, swollen, throbbing globes of whipped girl-flesh.

As conscious thought had slowly returned the overwhelming, dominant, thought obsessing her mind was that she had failed. Seven strokes of the cane and still she had failed.

Today was her third day. The second day had started with a canning straight from bed. On both the first and second attempts she had so nearly made it through, jumping up on the fourth stroke of the first attempt and again on the fifth stroke of the second. The third and final attempt to suffer her punishment floundered on only the third stroke upon the receipt of which emotion and pain had conspired to rob her of the ability to express due gratitude to her corrector.

Yes, today was her third day, her last day if she was to avoid an extra month spent confined to this room, yet, perversely, her burden had now accumulated additional weight. The realisation of the existence of a previously unsuspected dimension now amplified her tribulation. Today she had not been caned immediately upon rising, as previously, but rather had been given leave to perform her ablutions first, even to having had showered. She had been shaved, but this was a normal part of the routine upon showering. She had then been dressed in the full uniform, the corselet, stockings, the dress, everything.

Of more significance, and of the worst kind, she had been given a pair of those awful 'examination pants' with their transparent close fitting gusset. Not that the sense of exposure was foremost in her mind at that moment, those knickers would surely be coming down all too soon, no, it was the implication that was so bothersome. The only time ' examination pants' had to be worn was for a doctor's visit. True, no differentiation was made between internal exam, psychological appraisal, counselling session or, indeed, dental hygiene session, the fact was, whatever the reason, a doctors visit necessitated the wearing of that most foul and hated garment. Although this she found most irksome and unnecessarily humiliating, the implications here ran deeper still.

Any doctor's visit would surely result in the observation of the evidence of her punishment, she had felt the raised welts through the thin fabric and knew that the associated discoloration would be clearly visible, contrasted beneath the white rubber, under even the most cursory of examinations; clearly then Matron's actions were condoned at some level in the hierarchy. This had been the shock revelation; Matron was not just exploiting a petty position of power to satisfy some perverted urge, clearly corporal punishment was an accepted part of the regime and Matron wielded real power. How could this be? Had she been manipulated into accepting this, asking for it even begging for it, or would it have been instigated anyway at some point? Was it preordained, pre planned? Secondly, and even more dispiritingly, came the realisation of the unlikelihood of enlisting any ally in her complaint.

The door swung open, admitting the tall graceful figure of Dr Ecclestone. The girl's huge violet eyes widened further still in surprise and shock, a response that registered with the good doctor who, for her part, was regarding her patient with interest, appraising her facial expression, the subtle nervous tick under the left eye, reading the girls posture, her body language, as one might read the most intimate and private of diaries. Her voice, as reassuring as ever, seemed inappropriate and almost surreal under the circumstances. "Nothing to worry about sweetheart, we have a counselling session scheduled for this session but I thought it best, under the circumstances, that the mountain come to Muhammad as it were." Then, looking at Matron, she went on: "It has been decided that all activities, scheduled or otherwise, be carried out in the confines of her room for the foreseeable future".

Matron momentarily looked concerned; "well, she showered earlier, doctor, just along the corridor."

"That's fine for today but for the foreseeable future her shower visits are to be a curtailed. Her regular shaving is to be continued of course, but *in situ*, and I'm afraid it is to be a sponge-bath-only routine for her from now on"

"Yes doctor."

"She is to be kept up to date with her schoolwork. Learning tasks will be delivered and it has been decided that you should be responsible for supervising and enforcing her school work quotas in the first instance. I realise that you already have quite a full schedule, do you think you'll be all right with shouldering the extra responsibility this will entail?"

"Oh yes, doctor, I'll be only too happy to oblige" Matrons smile did indeed convey her genuine enthusiasm, pleasure and anticipation for the task ahead.

"Fine, then I'll convey your acceptance. There are one or two other refinements we need to go over but in general she is to be confined to her room at all times, all doctor's visits, whether medical or psychological, are to take place here in her room and, as I have said, the continuance of her school work is to be strictly enforced."

From behind her glasses the doctor's intelligent piercing blue eyes scanned the room as, if searching for inspiration or perhaps merely an *aide memoir* , before finally her attention focused upon the little toilet pedestal. "The toilet in here doesn't seem have a cover at present."

"No doctor."

"I would be obliged if you could arrange to have one fitted as soon as possible, preferably later today, and also if you would be so kind as to inform the other members of staff that it is to be kept locked at all times."

"Yes doctor, that shouldn't be a problem, I'll have one fitted as soon as you have finished with her." Matron, glancing over at the girl, could clearly read from the latter's reddening cheeks her charge's comprehension of the implications of this conversation.

The doctor went on: "A bed pan is being sent over from the school room later today. Apparently she is quite habituated to its use and, as concerns have been voiced as to the effects on her of her treatment here, I thought it best for all concerned if we could retain, or at least simulate, as many aspects of the school-room regime as possible during her stay here. I have assured the school-room group that she will be returned to them suitably quietened and chastened but more importantly that they will be able to seamlessly continue with their training of her from the point that they left off".

Throughout Matron had listened intently. Nodding in agreement from time to time she had been scribbling notes, as the doctor spoke, into a little white plastic covered notebook that had emerged from the left hip pocket of her dress to a discordant, key-jangling, accompaniment, her hand having brushed aside the jailer's key-ring that swung across her hip from her belt on that side.

The girl, for her part, had done as much as humanly possible to maintain her pose, to refrain from glancing at either woman, knowing surely that neither woman could fail to pick up on it should she succumb. Head hung bowed she was effectively blinkered by her bonnet, extending as it did almost five centimetres out from her face. The disembodied conversation had bounced to and fro ping-pong fashion while she had gazed down numbly, consciously focusing her attention on the irregular pools of light reflecting off of her glossy bottle green Mary-Jane shoes, an occasional ripple of light and shade betraying one or other speaker' s gesticulation. She had been taught in the schoolroom to suppress the normal human reflex of turning to look in the direction of speech, taught too to resist the temptations of conversation, to avoid eye contact. Yet it was at the mention of the schoolroom that she had been tested the most, leaving her shuffling awkwardly and embarrassedly in response to their mentioning of her schoolwork, her future return to the schoolroom so that they might "continue with their training of her" and their casual discussion of her 'habituation to the use of her bedpan'.

In her perusal of the room Dr Ecclestone had seemed to have somehow overlooked Matron's cane lying diagonally across the narrow bed, or at least she had not acknowledged its presence. Now she pointedly looked towards it. There came a muffled "hrghrrmh" as Matron cleared her throat: "I can come back later, doctor, if you want to get her counselling session underway".

For a moment the girl experienced a butterfly-winged wave of relief, perhaps the doctor didn't know, had Matron been caught out? Then she was brought crashing down with the full grey force of the storm.

"No, no, Matron, it's fine, I'm happy enough to wait and I'm sure she would prefer to get it over with" then, looking directly at the girl yet being still out of the girl's field of view, " wouldn't you, sweetheart?", …No answer came.

"30C, answer the doctor, sweetheart" Matron was using her softest, most coaxing, tones.

The girl, now known only as 30C, knew what was expected of her, she had been taught in the schoolroom, questions were to be answered promptly, one did not hesitate, one did not think about the answer, one answered yes or no, simply that, no less and certainly, no more. "Yyy yes, mm,m Matron" came the soft reply at last...

For a split-second a whistling hiss had filled the silence, SSHSWTHRRACK! Then a banshee shriek, AAAAGHH!

She was on her feet, hands desperately kneading buttocks initially angrily wasp-stung then numb with shock but now developing a detailing to the pain much as a photographic negative might slowly emerge in the darkroom, a clarification to the agony, a screaming agony quite literally.

She had waited in position bent over the desk, outwardly a study in determination, inwardly a growing dread nibbled then gnawed away at that determination. The cane, crook handled, lay casually across the back of the desk filling her field of view, dominating her, the curved handle of yellowed rattan touching her nose as if to hold her there. Behind her the conversation had continued, she had taken the placing of the cane there, across the desk, her careful positioning, to be the prelude to the caning but the conversation had just continued. And so she had waited, bent from the waist, chin resting on the padded desktop, hands placed behind the back of her neck, legs straddling the attached seat and each adjacent to its corresponding desk support, those knickers, the examination pants, stretched to their limit to contain those overripe buttocks, her imagination involuntarily filling with the image of her most intimate secrets freshly shaved and obscenely displayed through that transparent plastic gusset panel. Perhaps she had imagined the retention of her knickers to be an ameliorating factor, that they might blunt the sharpness of the sting, then again perhaps she had the intelligence to realise that Matron would never allow such an amelioration if it were significant yet might allow some *slight* amelioration if it were to be offset by an element of humiliation of great enough magnitude. As she fervently wished for a return to the conditions of her previous canings, bare bottomed and without the benefit of witnesses, we can conclude the latter to be of the greater truth and be appreciative of Matrons enlightened understanding of a young woman's sensibilities and vulnerabilities.

A hand, Matron's hand, the girl had recognised the cuff and sleeve of the woman's uniform, had retrieved the cane. The girl had tensed, expecting the first stroke's imminence. Nothing happened, behind her the conversation had restarted, no mention of the upcoming event, not even a casual comment aimed to humiliate and degrade. It was as if she wasn't there, they were apparently discussing another patient, another girl; there was mention of legal papers, something to do with drawing up a 'statement of change of status', of having the girl become a voluntary psychiatric patient, of the need to arrange power of attorney.

118

Then there had been a moment of silence, unexpectedly mid-conversation. Behind her, unseen by her but fully witnessed with approval by the good doctor, Matron had flexed the cane between her hands forming a full circle, a measure of its extreme suppleness, a suppleness that comes from the careful preparation of selected rattan kept steeped in brine solution. This cane had little in common with that which had been used previously, this was a very special cane kept for a very special and specific purpose.

Then the stroke had whipped in, and now, standing sobbing, hands brought up to her face in shame, she knew, the girl knew, suddenly she had only two more chances to avoid the threatened one-month extension.

The previous canings had been bearable, at least initially, and had gradually got harder, but this… The first stroke, had shocked her, had been harder and unimaginably more painful than even the hardest strokes of her previous canings.

"What do you think you are doing, girl? Get back down at once"

The sobbing wretch remained standing, rounded, defeated, shoulders heaving up and down with each staccato-sobbing breath. Distraught tears oozed freshly-squeezed between fine, graceful fingers, emotion ravaged trembling hands cupped defensively in an attempt to hide the shame etched across her pretty, pain-contorted features. Behind her Matron stood coolly with her customary businesslike hands on hips posture, her cane, hanging as casual as a handbag from the fingers of her left hand, forming an acute angle with her skirt.

Matron was clearly unmoved by the girl's histrionics, neither sympathetic nor angry. She merely observed the scene with a casual detachment and a cool air of authority that well disguised the seething melee below. "Well, that's another chance gone, you have got just two chances left now and you won't even have that many if you don't get back down across that desk right now, this instant!" She had spoken softly, gently, but with a voice gradually hardening until the emphasis on '*This instant*' practically qualified as a bellow.

Still no response was forthcoming, save for a particularly deep and shoulder-shuddering sobbing intake of breath and a rubbery shifting of weight, the girl's knees momentarily threatening to give way to a knock-kneed collapse, still straddling, as she was, the seat.

"I'm going to count to five then you had better be back over that desk or you are down to your last chance, I mean it!" Now Matron had moved up close behind the shaking girl, her voice taking on an intimidating barking. "One, two, three, four…"

With a last defeated shuddering 'sob' the girl flopped her torso down atop the desk, her chin coming to rest close to the rear, simultaneously and involuntarily running her hands defensively back over her buttocks. Matron's voice instantly adopted its soft and coaxing 'reward' tone: "That's better, sweetheart, now let's get those hands back where they belong, back behind your neck". Stiffly, reluctantly, the girl obeyed. "That's a *good* girl", Matron's 'rewarding' voice again; she took great care in emphasising to her staff the importance of consistency in conditioning a girl and took equal care herself to ensure that she never failed to positively reinforce a desired behaviour with a praising word or an approving smile.

For a few moments, long, long, moments, silence again reigned, then finally: "Well, what have you forgotten?"

It was obvious to the girl that Matron was referring to the previous stroke, she knew the rules, true she had failed to keep position and so the punishment had to start from scratch but she still was obliged to express her gratitude for a correction, otherwise this chance, her penultimate chance, was also forfeit. At least now she had had a long enough respite to have regained some small crumb of composure but was it going to be enough? "Th, th, th-sob--thhank yy you, sob,sob-mmm Matron" she at last managed, breaking down into open crying, the effort, the huge, huge effort of will had cost her the loss of the little composure she had managed to regain. She had broken down into a series of gasping sobs, tears now flowing unrestrained, her hands nonetheless remaining with fingers interlocked behind her neck. As an option, staunching the flow by way of tightly squeezed eyelids was easily and quickly dealt with; there were rules covering such contingencies and Matron was nothing if not most diligent in the application and enforcement of regulations.

"Keep your eyes open, girl" the instruction sharply spat, Matron's 'punishment' voice. "What do you think you are doing? You do not tense your bottom, you *know* that, I am going to count to three and that fat bottom of yours had better be relaxed". Another regulation had been unconsciously contravened and that contravention was going to be dealt with. "One, two, three". Before her the proffered bottom visibly relaxed its tone, the owner receiving her reward, Matron's praising words, "that's a good girl", and a subtle, slight, yet cumulative, deepening of her training.

Satisfied that another contravention had been dealt with, Matron slashed in the first stroke of 30C's penultimate chance. As with the previous stroke it landed expertly plumb between two of the many raised, angry, welts that ran in parallel-lines across those otherwise virgin white globes, the legacy of canings bravely endured over the previous two days. Somehow the girl maintained her posture although crying quite openly now and quite loudly. From some deep down reserve she managed to summon the superhuman effort of will to stagger and stammer through the humiliating formula of quantification and gratitude.

SssSSHHWISSH-cCRRACK! The second stroke, again plumb centre between the pre-existing welts. "AAAGHHH!" again her posture was somehow maintained but the girl was clearly losing control, desperately fighting to catch her breath, practically crying like a baby now yet still struggling to gain sufficient control to recite the necessary formula, aware of Matrons surfacing impatience.

"Come along now, come on, I'm going to count to three between strokes from now on and I want to hear that my efforts are appreciated. One, two, three."

Matron's little speech, and the few moments that she had allowed the girl beforehand, had granted the girl a little extra time that she put to good use; "tt, thr, thr, three, th, thank yyyy you, sob, sob, sob, mmma...". ThhrrraaacK!

The third stroke had slashed in its venomous kiss straight through her stammering sobbing recital. AAAAARRGGHHEEEEEE! The scream had the doctor cover her ears, her eyes though, as those of Matron, devoured the scene with the gourmet appreciation of the true connoisseur.

"One, two..." the woman was dispassionately counting away the seconds, cane raised, the smoothly curved handle held just above shoulder height.

"Ffff, ffour, th thh thank yyyou m, mm ,Ma... ThhrrRAAACCKK!, so, so, hard, the hardest, whippiest yet, the girl shot bolt upright, a long silent pause hung in the air expectantly, perhaps for eternity, and then was razor-slashed through, the girl's cry a lost-soul banshee wail.

The knees went first, fat fleshy rubber coated white and red striped buttocks slumped blancmange-like down onto the little seat, only to just as rapidly re-launch as the impact reignited the cane's acid sting. Then, symmetry denied her, her left leg failing completely, she began to twist to one side, doubling up, both hands scrambling wildly over burning buttocks, before finally dropping down again, this time toppling over to the left and half-sliding half-slumping, side first, onto the carpet. Taking up a semi foetal position, hands manically gripping her buttocks, she lay crying, an embryonic writhing tadpole wreck of a girl. From their vantage point to the rear both women noted the yellow-green colouration spreading across the transparent gusset-panel of the girl's knickers, exchanging knowing and satisfied smiles.

Involuntary urination was an excellent outcome as far as Matron was concerned, it had occurred at the perfect moment. She had quite deliberately allowed the occasional lapse throughout this caning, had allowed a little extra time here and there for the girl to regain some self-control, she had wanted the girl to experience a significant number of hard strokes throughout this penultimate session, to at least approach the requisite six strokes, perhaps even believe that she was going to be able to take it.

She could make the girl get up now, make her get back over the desk for her final chance. With the doctor's help she could bodily *drag* her over the desk if need be. One, maybe two, strokes would be all she would be able to take. But that was not part of Matron's plan, she wanted the girl to undergo a few more strokes yet, and she knew now that she could afford to allow the girl some respite, some recovery time. The girl would be only too well aware of that unfortunate occurrence, it was going to be far harder for her to conjure up the fortitude to successfully get through six more strokes. She now had the weight of that additional humiliation to bear, the loss of her self-respect and of her dignity. She was going to feel crushed. It was going to be almost too easy but she would have to take care to ensure that the girl got close to the target. She was confident that, with care, she could end it, the whole punishment on the fifth stroke, take the girl right up to the finish line then trip her.

She had always been confident of course, Matron; she had had the necessary documentation already drawn up. She could have simply announced that the girl, having failed her alternative punishment, would be staying an extra month. No that would not be good enough for Matron's purposes, she would have the girl sign documentation clearly stating that not only was she requesting, for that was how Matron had worded it, to continue to reside in the institution, another term Matron liked to use, for an additional month but that, should any study she be involved in require a longer term of residency, she agreed to her residency being extended as necessary up to a total time of... as agreed by... and countersigned by...

This part was designed to be written up by hand at a later date as and when necessary. This was the part she knew the girl was going to object to, Matron wanted it that way, it was the reason for taking her right up to the finish line. Of course the girl was going to have a problem with it, after all it was effectively open-ended, it allowed Matron a free hand. She could, and fully intended to, extend the girl's time as a punishment as suited her. Nevertheless the girl *would* sign it.

Not that Matron was unfair. She wouldn't extend the girl's residency without good reason and she would always offer an alternative punishment. Of course the girl would have to ask nicely for her caning, to be carried out under Matron's carefully developed set of conditions, and it would be unlikely that she would ask for the alternative too many times before she came to accept the reality of her situation: that she was a free woman no longer.

Forfeit were the choices and decisions she had, as we all have at one time or another, taken for granted. Forfeit was the world of her peers, their star-lit universe of hopes, dreams and aspirations, the world of clubs, cars, holidays and boyfriends. That the latter was of particularly urgent concern to this girl was obvious to all those under whose care she now resided, all whose well-trained eyes that could read well the signs. The unabated gnawing, aching, frustration that had so often afflicted her over the previous months had not gone unrecognised nor had her carers remained unaffected. Quite the contrary; her condition had been shared by Matron with an empathy bordering on the masochistic.

No it is safe to say that her carers were fully cognisant of her concerns; never had isolation and privacy been so divorced and never with such carefully crafted deliberation. Yes she would come to accept that time was punishment and punishment, time and that Matron was the sole arbiter. How long she would stay would depend on how well she 'behaved' and Matron was of the opinion that a girl's behaviour was never a static thing but was, rather, to be considered a work-in-progress, to be moulded and remoulded, to be continuously refined.

After all she was a 'special girl', this one, one of three such girls in residence of which she now had two under her personal care, the third girl undergoing long-term schoolroom training, having been transferred almost two years previously. Yes, she was going to have to accept that she was under Matron's care now, her behaviour would be judged by comparison across an infinitely deformable landscape of stimuli, response times and magnitudes.

Matron considered herself a fair woman; punishment was easily avoidable by obedience after all. Yet outside of the context of the institution one would have been unable to avoid questioning the fairness of passing judgment set against such a subjective elastic scale as Matron's perception of perfection.

Only the most un-empathic of observers could fail to have *some* sympathy for the girl. After all it would be difficult to avoid the conclusion that, ultimately, the girl was going to remain in residence until such a time that Matron might decide other wise. That she was a 'special girl' was one thing but that she was a highly attractive 'special girl' was another factor entirely and a factor that had a great deal to do with Matron's perception of 'good behaviour'. Punishment was time and Matron would see to it that time was most definitely punishment.

And it was time, right now, time to recommence writing the last chapter of farce, it was time to cynically dangle the last knot of the girl's increasingly fantastical and frayed lifeline.

"Get up, come on, get back into position, girl. This is your last chance, six strokes and I want you to get through them all, now come on, don't let yourself down in front of the doctor. It's bad enough that you're crying like a little girl in front of her and you've wet yourself. You are a grown woman, I shouldn't have to treat you like a child, even if you do look like one."

"Urrgh!, aargh! ,hmmhf - sob, sob" the only response was a pitiful unintelligible mewing and a tightening of her curled foetal position, arms now wrapped round knees and pulling ever tighter, ironically resulting in an even greater degree of shameful exposure, the transparent gusset panel of her knickers stretching itself ever closer about her contours and the yellow-green staining, previously confined to that area, spreading thinly beneath the diaphanous white latex covering of her buttocks.

Dr Ecclestone watched concerned, concerned not so much for the girl's emotional state but rather that the punishment should continue without further delay. This was the perfect moment, the window of maximum psychological impact. The good doctor had come to a rapid decision. In an instant she was half-squatting half-kneeling behind the curled girl, propping herself with one stocking-clad knee sinking into the soft white carpet, her white coat opening to reveal the awkwardness of her manoeuvre to be on account of her tight knee-length black leather skirt that had now ridden up to mid thigh. She reached a motherly arm around the sobbing girl's shoulders gently coaxing her up to rise, comforting and coaxing without the slightest hint of cynicism, even though such dispassionate cynicism might well be clear to those of us voyeuristically viewing these events, even if only in our mind's eye.

She could trust Dr Ecclestone; the girl knew it with a certainty born of almost religious fervour. In Dr Ecclestone she had a friend and she had so few friends, Julia, ' her' nurse... who else?

"Come on sweetheart, you can get through this, you have to, you need to. If you were to give up now you would not only be letting yourself down you know, you would be letting me down, you would be letting down all those who have been helping you, all those who have ever helped you. I really thought you would have made the most of this chance. The people here are very selective in their choice of subjects. I had to be very persuasive to get you in but I thought that taking part in the work they are doing here would be your best chance to prove yourself. I thought that it would allow you the time and space that you needed in order to improve yourself, to circumvent all those silly phobias and compulsions before they left you reduced to a mental cripple. If you disappoint me now, disappoint yourself, you will never forgive yourself."

The doctor was at her most persuasive, her phrasing carefully structured, her words carefully chosen with subtle emphasis on those plucked from her menu of trigger words. The psychology was flawless if manipulative but, most of all, effective. With the doctor's help the girl was rising, unsteadily on rubbery limbs, shaking, incoherent, but rising nevertheless.

With Matron's aid and the girl's own efforts, the doctor gently guided the girl back into position, all the while her whispered words of encouragement continued, relentlessly following the same vein.

If her body was exhibiting sensible coordinated coherent control the same could not be said for her thoughts. In Dr Ecclestone she had faith; Dr Ecclestone would get her through this, she knew she would, she couldn't disappoint Dr Ecclestone, she had been a disappointment to everyone for so long, that much she understood now, could feel in her soul. She couldn't disappoint Dr Ecclestone, she *so* wanted to be a good girl, ever so much. She had to please Dr Ecclestone if she was to become a good girl, if she was to get well again. She had to please Dr Ecclestone, see the smile that would say ' you *are* a good girl'. A churning, chaotic, upheaval of determination, faith and ideas, few of which she could personally, truly, lay claim to, liberally sprinkled with implanted trigger phrases. Indeed one could question to what extent those quivering rubber coated curves were actually inhabited by Lavinia Vitesse at all at that moment.

She was back across that desk, legs again spread astride its polished-white plastic seat. Once again white suspenders, stretched over-tight, bit down, dimpling thigh-tops only slightly less pure in hue. Once again already closely-fitted knickers tightened their grip further still; unnaturally-parted buttocks found again even *that* cleavage augmented. The crotch-moulding transparent windowed gusset panel, now displaying its feminine wares through a contrast-enhancing film of green and yellow, again made its appearance from behind its uniform-skirt-curtain of green and white striped nylon. The latter summarily flipped-up on this occasion by the hand of the doctor herself.

Behind her, an uneasy silence had formed, expanding between the two professionals and filling with a crackling energy, unseen, unheard, yet threatening to overwhelm that very professionalism on so many levels, not all of which might necessarily be understandable by most in terms of overt sexuality yet deeply steeped in sensuality nonetheless.

Whereas the doctor, possessed of character icy in self control, bobbed easily above such temptation, Matron, for all her maturity was beginning to flounder. For a few hart-pounding moments that urine stained gusset filled her rapidly tunnelling vision, her head throbbed with blood engorged vessels before embarking on a helium-light spiralling ascent into faint. If anything the girl's intimacy, that Clingfilm-enwrapped fig, was possessed of a new succulence, a greater more intensely-beautiful symmetry than ever before, not so much in spite of that, still spreading, staining as enhanced by that piquant marinade.

To Matron's educated eye even the most subtle hint of the girl's inner lips added a delicious quality to the scene. The latter subtle indeed, marked only by the addition of a faint, clouded, mottling of thin pink shadow within the yellow sea, and then only at the very-most intrusive deaths of the plastic's puckered invagination, whereupon the outer lips were parted, albeit barely.

As a women Matron, of course, well understood any woman's reluctance to be subject to the intimacy of inspection invited by those knickers; perhaps even more than most, for had she not been their designer, at least in principle. Yet before her was not displayed the unsightly, even ugly, vision as might be disclosed by many forced into this position.

124

That the girl was ashamed to be so displayed was without doubt. That she had lost control, emptied her bladder, that the event had been, and remained, so devoid of privacy undoubtedly multiplied, geometrically, that shame. For all this, though, although possessed of no little satisfaction, still Matron was troubled.

Her mind was fevered, beads of sweat had formed upon her brow, her usually perfectly presented white uniform dress showed signs of a 'glow' as much due to repressed excitement as to the exertion of the canning.

She toyed with the cane, flexing it repeatedly between her hands, watching the tinted slivers of light shift up and down its length as she did so, repeatedly forming near circles with the brine soaked supple rattan. The girl was still beautiful. Too beautiful to truly know shame? Real shame? Was she really as ashamed as she ought to be, really aware of the shame of her own femininity? There was something burning, lustfully deeply buried yet rapidly percolating up through Matron's psyche, through the manifold filtering strata of denial, threatening to expose her, her motivations, the real 'Her'. A mirror to the shame endured by the girl bent before her, it finally surfaced bringing with it the deep conviction that such beauty, that lay prostrate before her, required, nay, insisted on punishment. The girl *had* to be punished for that beauty denied to so many, the many so ashamed as to enlist the surgeons knife in their quest to be 'tidied up down there'. For this she had to be punished, yes, but a particular punishment, a suitable punishment.

She looked down at the implement she held; not for this, for the imminent punishment yes, undoubtedly so, but not for this. The punishment for this would of necessity be a delayed one, such a particular and peculiar punishment would take time to develop.

The girl would be punished for this, she would see to it, not in the immediate future though; not that the girl couldn't be grommeted, she had already been anally grommeted, after all, fitted with an anal dilator, and a similar device for permanent vaginal dilation was available. Indeed several girls had been vaginally grommeted and there was a precedent for grommeting a girl in both orifices, although it had only been applied to two girls so far. No it was not that; this girl, this so perfect girl with that so perfect fig deserved the best. Perfection took time. The new design, her design, all those carefully thought out refinements, the girl deserved nothing less. The drawings had already passed final approval and had been submitted to a very reliable manufacturer of medical appliances. There would be a delay, perhaps of several weeks, but it would be well worth the wait and there was a certain *Je ne sais quoi* to the anticipation. She had incorporated all of her appreciation of the sensibilities and sensitivities of womanhood into the new device ensuring that it would distort as much as display, enhance and contrast. It would transpose beauty for blemish, both stimulate and deny. It had taken time, much time, to evolve, even in her fertile mind, but the final design was as unique in its completeness as an intimate feminine prophylactic device as it was a triumph in its parallel application as a subtle specialist feminine punishment.

Matron raised her cane and paused, anticipating the consequences both immanent and longer term. Ordinarily it would be the former, the rippling of the flesh, the cry, the reddening and swelling rattan- patterned imprint. With this girl it was definitely the latter, filling her imagination with a myriad images, sounds and possibilities.

125

THRRRAAAACCK! Anticipation, beyond bearing, having tightened her like a spring she paused no longer, her tension had been released, yes, but she had managed to control it, barely. The first stroke in the last of a series of nine such canings. Hard, certainly, hardest, no; she had delivered harder and would do so again, much, much, harder before she was finished with the girl. Hard enough to send home the message, light enough to be born with hope. Most of all she wanted the girl to retain a modicum of hope.

The girl cried out loudly but then the stroke was counted and Matron duly thanked, much to the latter's relief.

SSSSSHHRRAAACCCK! Harder yet still precise enough to land on an increasingly rare and precious virgin plot, quickly growing a swollen banked reddened groove, slowly merging into its elder, parallel, neighbours residing either side.

The girl's shriek was piercing, but yet again she managed the required formula albeit brokenly, weeping openly and continuously, knuckles whitening as she clenched her fingers into fists, although still behind her neck, in the effort to keep them there, to stay in position. The urge was to protect her bottom or even to grip the back edge of the desk, if only that was allowed, if only she could hold on to something, anchor herself just concentrate on that. Matron would never give margin for such instinctive response, there would be insufficient evidence of her charge's total submission and she required nothing less.

Accordingly the girl was admonished, told to unclench those fists. Hands had to stay behind the neck with fingertips touching and elbows held smartly out to the sides. As before she had to be reminded to relax her bottom, although clenched cheeks *per se* would not be possible wearing those knickers, the latter being *designed* to part and enhance the gluteal cleft, tightening of the muscles could be observed easily and could be dealt with, by forfeit, extra strokes or extra time. Matron suggested yet another month; the effect was immediate.

Again Matron raised her cane; in her minds eye the grommet was already *in situ*, the girl's outer lips gaping and slipping in pearlescent, yellow-tinted slime against the transparent plastic gusset with every movement and, at the gusset's lower apex, a prominent thimble like structure announcing the position of the integral reinforced clitoral hood. Matron's imagination conjured up in anticipated empathy, the sensation of dozens of tiny slivers of the softest, finest latex; the infuriating lining she had designed for the hood, each sliver a tiny golden fairy-kiss of promise. No satisfaction just promise and the merest hint of promise at that, an unresolved disappointment of a promise, the subtlest of hints, a subtlety she knew most women would rather live without yet it was a subtlety that she would ensure this *particular* girl would very much live with, day in, day out.

SSSWWSSSHSCCRRAAACK! Whipped in this time in a curving arc that had the pliable switch fairly bent double in mid flight.

"AAAARRRGH!", the scream deafening , the fourth stroke had crossed few previous wounds, but those it had were prompted to add their pent up fire, they wanted to break the girl and break her now.

126

That Matron intended to break the girl was without doubt, but not yet, not now, slowly over time, break her slowly over weeks, months, even years but break her thoroughly, permanently, break her beyond the repair of even the finest counselling.

It had been too hard, too hard too soon. What had she been thinking of? The girl had half risen, sprung with shock from the desk top, she was rising still. No! no, No!. she had misjudged the stroke horribly. "No!" Her shout urgent, almost to the point of betraying panic, a sharp pressed palm between the shoulder blades had the girl slumping down defeated.

To Matrons relief a broken-breathed sobbing babble started up, the formula bubbling out near incoherently "Th, Thh, Thhffff four, th th, thank yyyyouu mmmm mi, mis, mistress."

"I am addressed as Matron, you stupid girl, *Matron!*" There was no reply, just an outbreak of uncontrollable weeping. The girl's school room training had broken through: In her desperation and confusion she had lost herself, used the term of respect demanded of her dormitory mistress.

Three months of 'yes mistress', 'no mistress' in the dormitory 'yes Madam', ' no Madam' in the classroom had not passed by without affect. Three months in which she had said little else save for the parrot fashion recitation of multiplication tables and the minimal answers required by interrogation during her counselling sessions and even then, more often than not, she had been limited to one word answers. Three months surrounded by girls of around her own age, as far as she had been able to estimate, although one most definitely was possessed of a somewhat more mature figure, and yet three months without conversation. Her mind drifted back…

The School Room Recollections (2): Pigtails and Bonnets

She still had no idea of who they were, the other five girls there, they were all pigtails and bonnets, blank faced, doll-like and uniformed. Hair was always black, hers was natural but most, if not all, of the other girls had had theirs dyed. She had seen them having it done on ' hair day'; they all had to stand in line and await their turn behind the large white medical chair-cum-table apparatus that also doubled as the gynaecological examination couch. A white uniformed nurse would efficiently take her shears to each pigtail in turn, chopping through each just above the ribbon bow before un-platting each side in turn and roughly combing through. The seated girl would then be obliged to lean forward and down, her head partially disappearing into the specifically designed curved plastic sink were upon her hair would be washed and the dye applied from a plain white plastic squeezy-bottle. While the dye did its work the nurse would busy herself with other ritualistic tasks. The electric razor came first, humming across one eyebrow and then the other. Next came the eyelash clippers, eyelashes were kept short, then her finger nails would be clipped. Then it was feet up in the stirrups and the application of the speculum for the internal exam, the nurse's latex-gloved index-finger and thumb often appearing to tarry somewhat more than necessary around the clitoral area, eliciting more than one sigh of unresolved passion.

Finally there would come the intimate shaving. The entire pubic area would be carefully gone over in fine detail before the stirrups would be adjusted until the girls feet were practically either side of her ears and her anal area gone over, the nurse carefully edging around the large rubber grommet that occupied and rendered permanently dilated a girl's anus.

All this intimacy she had seen of these girls and they of her, yet she had no idea of their names or they of hers. Individuality was a precious thing and she had tried to make mental notes of the letters and numbers on their uniforms and any individual characteristics she could ascertain. The latter was usually reduced to differences of stature, gate and of figure, although all of their figures appeared grossly distorted by their uniforms and, other than when exercising, all of the girls had a tendency to a shuffling waddle, herself included; the thick pad-lined incontinence bloomers saw to that.

Even getting to 'know' her 'colleagues' to *that* extent involved a certain element of risk. Talking of course was punishable but equally punishable was making eye contact, in fact attempting any form of communication was punishable. It would probably be a greater truth to say that communication *would* have been punishable, had any one of them dared. And she would have dared, once she would have, but the other five girls had all been there far, far, too long by the time she had been sent there; all had been very obviously broken by the regime. Their timidly downcast eyes never seemed to leave their shuffling shoes, heads bowed as if in permanent penitence, hands crossed in front of rustling nylon button-through skirts, palms outermost in the obligatory, stooping, 'submissive posture' they took up whenever moving around and that was, itself, enforced by threat of punishment...

Her Future's Return: Breaking Point

Yes, yes, this stroke then, one more stroke, she most definitely wasn't going to be able to take it, one more stroke and the girl would be hers. Matron was flexing that cane of hers again, proudly trialling it's pliability, the result of careful preparatory brine pickling. She ran a appraising eye over the feminine curves presented before her; the next time she was bent for the cane she wouldn't be so proud of that rear of hers. She was far, far *too* proud of that fig of hers, shameless, but not for too much longer. The next time she was bent over she was going to feel very different, Oh yes, with her vaginal grommet fitted, the new design, she was going to feel very different, not one of the lucky ones any longer, no, not any longer! No matter how 'tidy' nature had left her 'down there' she was to be ' tidy' no longer. A suitable punishment indeed for one of her beauty, one possessed of such a sinful vanity.

And then there was the frustration to be considered, the girl was going to have to learn to deal with the frustration. In all probability, given a long enough time, the opportunity, the privacy and the boredom, the girl would most likely become habituated to stimulating her breasts and nipples. And the girl was going to *have* sufficient time, she would see to it. The boredom was ever-present of course and there was about to be an upping of that tedium. The privacy was only apparent of course, the girl was never out of the view of at least one of the several sub-miniature cameras that recorded her every move from their hidden spy holes.

The girl's open fronted corselet combined with her button-through dress provided for easy access as well as resulting in a certain amount of enforced stimulation; the girl could not have failed to notice how even quite slight movement tended to result in her dress's nylon fabric brushing to and fro across her nipples and areola. It was her constant temptation in her long hours of boredom, just as was that short skirt, not that she could achieve much now that she was in locked incontinence bloomers, although she had been observed on more than one occasion surreptitiously rubbing herself in the crotch area, absentmindedly manipulating the absorbent pad within against her intimacy.

A certain amount of such play was tolerated; indeed it was encouraged, at a subliminal level, by the aforementioned features of their clothing, and sometimes even by subtle verbal suggestions. But such behaviour was only ever encouraged so that it might controlled, so that it might provide something that could later be taken away, later denied them. The new prophylactic device was designed to do both, to give a little yet deny completeness.

Denied her previous absentminded relief yet possessed of the diabolical urging of a thousand tiny demonic digits new habits would, in the fullness of time, undoubtedly manifest and would be dealt with. Time was plentiful now, time enough for such habits to take possession, to tighten their grip. There would be no intervention until such a time that a compulsion of a level comparable to addiction had developed. Such a pathological condition would require treatment of course; there would be a modicum of piercing work, the fitting of the rubber nipple caps, and the job would be done, the girl's little toys will have been wrapped up and packed away.

CCCCRRRAAACK!!! The fifth stroke, quite deliberately landed diagonally across the purple and red tracks of the myriad previous strokes. Three days and each well beyond any semblance of six of the best; this legacy of pain came all at once; the pain of each stroke was again alive and reinvigorated...

And then it was the morning, or at least the wake-up bell. She was alone in her cell, for that was undoubtedly what it was, all it could ever have been called really, her cell. In front of her stretched two months of 'special isolation', whatever that meant. At *least* two months, that was what Matron had said, she had put the emphasis on '*at least*'. The threat was quite overt, an additional month had been already added to her time but it was quite clear that Matron would be happy enough to go through the whole procedure all over again should she 'step out of line in the slightest'.

She had endured nine separate canings spread over three days but she had fainted on that last stroke, the fifth stroke, she had failed. With all that she had been through she was still to have to face that extra month and it was to be spent undergoing some sort of psychological punishment designed with her 'reorientation' in mind. Matron would ensure that upon her return to the school-room her 'school room training would recommence where it had left off' and would be rendered 'twice as effective' by the treatment she was about to undergo.

Her more immediate concern was with the document that Matron was going to be bringing for her to sign at some point. She had been told the wording, the thing was open-ended, how could she be expected to sign something like that?

Such a document, clearly designed to empower, in the hands of someone like Matron? But was she not already in Matron's hands? Her punishment was to be the imposition of extra time, one month for each indiscretion or discipline breach. Alternatively she could opt to receive six strokes of the cane but under Matron's rigorous rules, rules that had clearly been designed to ensure the imposition of extra time regardless. Matron had said discipline was going to be very strict; indeed in the coming months she was to learn that there was only one way to be certain of avoiding punishment in one form or another; total obedience and absolute submission to Matrons will.

She was going to have to sign that document at some point, what choice did she have? Repeated canings, month after month under lock and key undergoing, what? Some sort of punishment, some sort of therapy or treatment? What would it do to her, month after month of whatever it was they were going to do to her? What would she be like at the end of it. What was she going to be like when they finally returned her to the school room? And then what? After yet more time in the school room, what was she going to be like? What was to become of her?

The School Room Recollections (3): Punishment-Rhymes

Those other girls, how long had they been kept there, in the school room? She had been horrified at the sight of them, the way they were; timid, cowering, shuffling dolls. She had looked up from her bowl one mealtime, dared to look up from the lukewarm milk-white porridge, the girl opposite her across the circular white plastic table had coughed, causing her to straighten up and for the first time her eyes had met with those of another ' patient'.

Just for a fleeting moment she had gazed into the girl's huge pretty brown almond shaped eyes, and yet they were dead eyes, the eyes of a cow, of some domesticated and tamed animal; a sleepwalker, there was no recognition there. And then, just momentarily, a flicker of something recognisable, of emotion, it was fear, sheer terror, a mortal, soul-endangering fear. And then she had looked down, but not before a single tear had tracked its way down to her cheek.

Punishment had come swiftly to them both; "patient 30S, patient 16S come here at once". Both girls had been startled, both girls had hesitated, albeit momentarily, and both girls were immediately reprimanded; "I said now! Patient 30S and patient 16S come here now, you stupid, stupid, girls". The other girl, 16S, as was stated on her uniform, began to weep openly like a spanked child, almost as if punishment had already been dealt her.

For Lavinia, patient 30S, this was the first mention of the term 'punishment' that she had heard since her arrival. In reality, though, she had been routinely and frequently, if covertly, subject to a form of punishment and, indeed, reward by means of the subtle expedient of the approving, friendly and reassuring smiles of the nurses or the withholding of the same. Making a point of ignoring a patient, while bustling about their room, particularly when a patient was being kept under such isolated circumstances, made for a wonderfully effective punishment.

A beaming, warm, smile of approval greeting a patient who, perhaps merely by accident of chance, was exhibiting some sign of a more submissive disposition made for an equally wonderful reward. Together and consistently adopted and repeated across all staff members the two extremes of expression formed the basis of a very subtle yet powerful form of operant conditioning.

The old Lavinia, the Lavinia that hadn't been through the hands of the manipulative, dominating and controlling Julia and her psychiatrist friend, the Lavinia who had yet to undergo repeated and unrelenting hypnotherapy, the Lavinia that wasn't yet buried beneath layers of post-hypnotic key phrases, who had not yet been subject to the controlling conditioning of those smiling nurses, *that* Lavinia would have stood up, shouted the woman down.

This Lavinia, this patient 30S with her almost totally debilitating stammer, her crippling agoraphobia, her equally crippling and worsening pathological indecisiveness, this patient salivating uncontrollably to the sound of a particular bell and whose bowels would empty to the sound of another, this patient stood, head bowed submissively and apologetically, hands neatly folded in front of her skirt, awaiting her punishment. How many smiles had it taken to refine and compel that submissive posture, that stance that spoke of such deliciously total surrender.

"No eye contact, girl, you know rules! What did you think you were doing 30S? You'll be talking next, or trying to, although I doubt anyone would want to listen to that irritating stammer of yours for too long. And you, 16S, you should know better, you have been punished before, talking without permission wasn't it?"

The responding voice had been small, timid and respectful. "Y,yes mmm, mistress, I'm ssorry mmm mistress"

The woman had turned her attention back to Lavinia, no more words, just her eyes boring into her. Lavinia felt as if she was to faint, her knees had become rubber, the room about her shrinking, tightening around her, the dormitory mistress's face filling the final tunnel of her vision. Finally she had managed a pathetically bleated; "I,I,I ,Im'm sssory m,m,mmmistress."

She hadn't known what to expect from the term 'punishment', she hadn't expected any form of corporal punishment, not in this day and age, and besides they were all volunteers weren't they? Not that corporal punishment was used, or even required, to control the girls in the school room, although both Matron and Dr Ecclestone were of a mind to introduce its practice at some later date, not as a form of control in itself but rather as a measure of that control.

Three doors inhabited the wall at the rear of the classroom, two to the left of the whiteboard and one to its right. Of the two doors to the left one door led to the examination room with its gynaecological couch, the other door, to the extreme left, led to an office style interview room wherein, throughout the day, patients, for such they were always referred to as, would be taken one at a time for one-to-one counselling sessions, hypnotherapy sessions and/or behaviour modification therapy, to return to their desk sometime later. The door on the right she had never seen open let alone been inside, that situation was soon to be remedied.

The dormitory mistress would always have a nurse present at mealtimes and both women now escorted the two miscreants through that very door.

Meal time had been suspended at the very moment of the infringement, food remained uneaten, the girls returned to the classroom; all were punished, that was always the way here, it was intended to instil a sense of social responsibility and guilt. They waited, obediently seated, silently at their desks, all upright, all heads turned toward the front, eyes dully gazing out from within the shadows of the extended blinker-like surrounds of their green and white striped bonnets. Four pairs of hands were positioned with fingertips touching puffball shoulders.

Behind that right hand door all was white and all was padded. The nurse had gone back into the classroom, presumably to rummage through one of the built-in cupboards, meanwhile the two girls had had to strip down to their underwear, neatly folding their uniform dresses, the sound of rustling nylon filling the air in the teeny room, before handing them to the mistress. Both girls were told to remove their bonnets and stand with their hands on their heads. The nurse had quickly returned from her errand carrying what appeared to be a pile of canvas sheets.

With the two girls standing, hands on heads dressed in their corselets stockings and rubber bloomers, and with both women now present there was hardly any floor space available for the nurse to put down her load, instead she divided her burden in two, passing half to the mistress. For the first time Lavinia could make out some detail amongst those shapeless folds of canvas. There were straps of some kind, and sleeves. And then it had hit her: straitjackets, *they were straitjackets*. Yes, indeed they were straitjackets and quickly indeed the two miscreants were enrobed in the same.

They were told to sit on the floor, as thickly padded as the walls, as their shoes were removed. Again the nurse had left the room, returning, with only the slightest delay, carrying what Lavinia was later to learn were medical restraints, each consisting of two padded leather cuffs linked by a short, strong, leather strap. These were quickly affixed to each girl's ankles.

The dormitory mistress had looked down on the two of them with satisfaction, there were to be no words of explanation just a simple instruction: " No talking". With those words both nurse and mistress departed, the closing door sealing the room as completely as to appear to practically evaporate, becoming part of a seamless continuous padded wall. With the two girls seated against the back wall there was little spare space and Lavinia soon discovered it was not possible to fully stretch out, nor could she topple over, her right shoulder was touching the right wall and her left shoulder was only a very short distance, perhaps two hand-widths, from the other girl's.

From the point of view of the independent observer the instruction not to talk would have been an interesting one. It would, of course, have been possible for the two girls to have been gagged; clearly such a contingency had no part to play in this particular stratagem.

The fact was they had been incarcerated in order that they might be trained; they had been told not to talk and, even though they were alone and unsupervised, they would not talk. Patient 16S had already been far too well-trained to dare talk without permission. In her turn Lavinia, patient 30S, would be discouraged by the presence of her deeply trained and unresponsive companion.

Additionally Lavinia would be only too aware that it was she who had caused them both to be punished and it would be she who would be to blame if any further disobedience on her part was to result in her compatriot's increased suffering; Indeed by this mechanism the most immense psychological pressure was being brought to bear on Lavinia to conform.

And then the nursery rhyme had begun; 'Boys and girls come out to play' apparently performed on a child's xylophone. The affect on her companion had been immediate; within the space of a few notes she had begun franticly struggling in her straitjacket, rocking back and forth until, totally distraught, she had broken down completely, becoming a spasm-racked wreck of uncontrollable weeping.

Had Lavinia recognised earlier the implications, the pertinence, of the events unfolding before her then surely she too would have been struggling, both physically and mentally; the concern and sympathy she had felt for the girl might well have been inwardly transferred. For, in witnessing the girl's reaction, had she not been gifted a view across time, a window into her own future? And yet such foresight, when recognised as such, was only to serve to bolster that dreadful inevitability. The presence of an example of their finished product, as it were, could only serve to ensure the correct moulding of their next; that had always been their intent, her 'carers', that was the reason for the double incarceration, the rational behind the punishment of the innocent along with the guilty.

In time, an unknowable time, the chiming had been displaced by an entirely different timbre, the pitch and cadence instantly familiar; simultaneously two stomachs rumbled, two mouths salivated, two girls were consumed with gnawing hunger. Within perhaps half a dozen chimes of the 'meal bell' the door had sprung open, seemingly as an apparition manifesting within the wall itself, to admit a sweetly smiling nurse carrying a white plastic tray upon which sat the familiar white plastic bowls and beakers, two of each, the door being carefully closed behind her by an unseen hand.

The nurse had manoeuvred herself to kneel in front of the girls and midway between the two pairs of bent knees. Sitting back on her heels and with the tray balanced upon her plastic-apron covered lap she proceeded to spoon feed both girls, offering a spoonful to first one girl and then the other, always smiling, occasionally speaking but only ever as reinforcement; "that's a good girl, eat up, you must be very hungry". Outside, the other girls would have been seated around the circular table, as at every meal time.

Both bowls having been emptied the nurse had held a plastic beaker up to each girl's lips in turn until such had been drained in each case and the girl's thirst quenched. Only at that point did the 'meal bell' cease. Despite the vastly expanded length of time it had taken to manually feed the two girls, as compared to the standard mealtime, the bell had sounded throughout. Only later was Lavinia to mull over the implications of this latter point; that the bells they heard in their room must issue forth from some source dedicated to that room, rather than from some source centralised throughout the institution. In addition she came to realise that for the clinic to go to such trouble and then to so carefully synchronise such events implied some function of great import to them.

She had had a broad and wide ranging education and was possessed of a general knowledge more thorough and detailed than most; the work of Pavlov and the term, conditioning, were not totally unfamiliar to her. They were being conditioned for some reason, all of them, and *she* had been, she realised, for some time, since her arrival in fact. She had determined at that that point that she would fight it, ignore the bells, but deep inside that part of her had already been defeated, did she not hunger at the sound of the 'meal bell', did she not give way to weariness at the sound of the ' sleep bell'?

They had sat there in silence since the nurse's departure, Lavinia having begun to mull over more of the practicalities, or rather the impracticalities, of their incarceration. Her stomach was full and it would all have to go *somewhere*; that was just nature. As it was she had had that awful anal grommet device fitted; even on that deeply, softly, padded floor she was aware of its presence, the anal dilator. She was always aware of its presence; occasional bouts of 'wind' now consisted of a softer and less violent release but one that was uncontrolled and continuing, the legacy of which was detectable with any shifting of weight or movement that might cause a momentary displacement of the leg cuffs of her knickers and that had become a faint but ever present companion. That, even in the absence of a major bowel movement, the earliest, more watery, products of digestion would be trickling into her absorbent pad was beyond doubt; the sticky-warm sensation had already begun to spread across her lower buttocks.

Then it had happened; somewhere a bell had started to toll, the other patient, 16S, was grimacing with the physical pain of her cramping stomach and the psychological pain of the shame of it. Lavinia, despite her recently developed determination of defiance, had felt her bloomers filling around her buttocks and thighs, the device holding open her anus denying her even that last vestige of control. Both girls had simultaneously began weeping with a despair known only to the utterly and totally defeated and had been weeping still when the nurse had arrived.

The straitjacket's crotch strap had to be released first to allow the nurse to reach up under the canvas and unlock, with the requirement of no little dexterity, the waistband securing the bloomers. Removing the restrained from the girl's ankles allowed the bloomers to be removed and unceremoniously dumped in the waiting bucket. A second nurse had entered and, with the difficulty expected of such close confines, rolled the girl over onto her side to allow a wet sponge thorough and unimpeded access. Lavinia could see that, not unsurprisingly, the girls anus was grossly dilated by the rubber-doughnut that constituted the anal grommet and for the first time she really understood how she herself now appeared, viewed from that angle. But there had been something else, when they had turned her over, her vaginal lips were equally stretched and distorted, the resulting gaping maw apparently surrounded by a sprung rubber-lined ovoid. This region had had to have special attention lavished in order to remove the risk of infection due to the ingress of her bodily waste. One of the nurses had then retrieved a oval black rubber plate device that, it had turned out, was designed to clamp over the poor girl's medically-corrupted vagina, effectively sealing it off from any further ingress.

The second nurse had been working on the girl at the same region, and upon completion of her task a short length of flexible white tubing protruded out from between the girl's legs, this latter being routed through an orifice provided in the rubber plate prior to its being fitted in position. The girl was now sealed from infection and successfully catheterised. A strong smell of disinfectant had filled the air and then she was re-robed in a fresh pair of bloomers. The latter having been locked back in place, the crotch strap was refastened and her ankles were placed back in restraints. In due course Lavinia too had been dealt with in a similar manner, albeit without the complication of catheterisation, and the two girls again left to their isolation. And then the nursery rhyme resumed its charming, chiming, song.

Mealtimes had come and gone without number, bloomers, now fitted over diapers, were filled and consequently changed. The 'sleep bell' would sound, promising respite, yet, shortly after, the nursery rhyme would restart its gentle jangling, both girls jolted awake by its resumption then dozing intermittently, all the while those few notes sounding, over and over and over through to the next mealtime. In time both girls had become indistinguishable in their desperation, in their weeping, both girls struggling within their confining bondage, the secure unrelenting swaddling-womb of their straitjackets, at each resumption of that once innocent but now so, so, terrible, song. Bodies writhed and twisted over and over, heads repeatedly thumped against walls and floor, with all the consequence of impact with the softest of feather pillows. Screams rendered throats so raw as to reduce to practically inaudible pathetic mewing any further protestations.

Only upon their thrashings becoming so wild as to threaten injury from the clashing of heads had more stringent restraint been called for; the addition of a simple leather leash, of a suitable length, between collar ring and ankle restraints enforcing the adoption of a safely-passive, if still writhing, foetal position. Thus restrained they had remained lying on the floor of their padded cell for a further week; not that the concept of a week would have meant anything to either girl by that stage. A further week of spoon feedings, diaper changes and, at least partial, sleep deprivation, and all of it to the constant accompaniment of a simple child's song, gently tinkling in their ears and through their minds.

There had been a time, a short period early on in their confinement, when for while all had gone quiet, peaceful silence had reigned. Lavinia had been cheered, filled with jubilation and renewed defiance. She had been buoyed by the knowledge that she had defeated them, that she had pulled through the ordeal unscathed and defeated them. A girlish giggling had, at length, evolved into a room-filling raucous laughter, initially unrecognized even by its originator. Yet it *was* her laughter, a strangely perverted laughter, one adorned with a hysterical, maniacal, edge; a laughter that, occurring within earshot of any rational observer, would surely have prompted the gravest of doubts be cast on the applicability of the term 'unscathed'. Indeed, to the more experienced ear, it would have spoken more of a woman driven close to her breaking point.

And then the laughter had subsided; again silence had reigned, that essential painful silence encountered so rarely in one's everyday experience and inhabiting so few terrestrial environments save such a room as that within which they had been confined. All had become deathly silent…

135

Silent, that is, save for the gentle sobbing of the girl known as patient 16S.

It had been an act of sympathy and concern as much as of defiance: "A, a, ar, aaar, are, yyyy y,ou, O,O,O OK" Her almost incoherent stammering barely audible even in that numbing silence. The response had been a voice wracked and stifled with the most primal, most phobic dread.

"N, , n,n,no, ppp, p,pleassse, nn,n,no."

Such had been the limit of their discourse; so soon had those vibrant xylophone notes begun singing their soft song of soul-torturing sweetness, so soon had that despair returned, so soon had she known the simple fact that she would never again disobey, never again disobey *anyone*, ever, ever again.

And yet she had. She had disobeyed, her present predicament was evidence enough of that. Not that it had been an act of defiance; rather it had been an act of desperation.

That particular event had occurred sometime after her obedient renaissance, her eventual release from the madness of that terrible confinement. How long after she had no inkling, for time's streaming had so long ago become clouded to her. From time to time she had observed the issue of new clean stockings to girls who had, by dint of carelessness, laddered theirs. True they had been verbally admonished and with expert humiliation, true too they had had to apologise in a particularly pathetic manner.

All she had wanted was a pair of clean stockings; other than for a fresh incontinence towel they wore the same clothes day after day. It was true that they were allowed to clean the inside of their bloomers with a damp sponge and also that they were obliged to wipe over the outside of their dresses in a similar manner. *Externally* their uniforms had to be kept looking pristine, the presence of stains and other marks were punishable, but there were no actual laundry facilities provided. In contrast, their bodies had had to be kept spotless: Showers were taken twice per day, before the first classroom session and again before the second classroom session. Before bed, each girl was cleaned intimately with soap and water by a nurse. There were regular internal inspections, thorough gynaecological examinations, equally regular enema sessions and full colonic irrigation.

Therein lay the irony: their bodies had to be pristine, inside and out, and there was an obsessive emphasis on feminine cleanliness, enforced by regular and repeated lectures and films on feminine hygiene. Yet, having showered, each girl was awaited by her uniform saturated with stale, albeit dried, sweat and permeated-through by her personal odour.

For Lavinia it was her stockings that were most problematic for her. Not that she had had previous experience of problems in that particular area but, what with those awful plastic shoes and not being allowed to wash her stockings, she had become more and more self-conscious of the odour originating from her feet, or rather from those stockings. Finally she had quite deliberately laddered both, but the deliberation of the act had been witnessed.

It had been the *deliberation* of that act that had brought her back here to this room and that had morphed patient 30S into patient 30C.

That one wilful act had resulted in the spirit-crushing series of canings she had experienced over the previous three days and had effectively placed her even more distant from the control of her affairs. She was now in the hands of a woman committed to distancing her ever further from that control, a woman committed to ensuring that she should come more firmly under the influence of the institution in which she was presently incarcerated, albeit voluntarily. She was in the hands of a woman to whom satisfaction was a distant land, an unknown quantity, a woman determined to bring her ever more securely under the institution's control. A woman who, two short hours earlier, had turned away from the slumped and fainted girl with the satisfaction of a job well done and had left to seek a reward commensurate to such an effort, to relieve, or rather to have relieved, the unique pent-up tension that only came with the caning of an attractive woman's bottom.

While her patient slumbered, having been revived by dint of the application of smelling salts and having been helped into her night things by Dr Ecclestone aided by a nurse, Matron had returned to her office. Not her room in the secure wing that she used for patient interviews but rather the comfortable oak panelled suite of rooms in the main building that comprised her office proper, a smaller room, branching off, which served as her secretary's office and an even smaller room that, in its turn, branched off of that. She had sunk back into her luxurious black leather reclining chair, the late afternoon sun rendering shafts of glittering golden starlight from fine dust hanging in the air. For a while she had pondered and then, reaching under the calf-length skirt of her uniform dress she had shimmied the full 1950s-style black satin knickers that she favoured over her plump thighs and down her smooth nylon-stockinged legs before standing, stepping out and kicking the discarded garment casually under her desk. From the top right-hand drawer of her desk she retrieved a dog leash of black leather and without further hesitation had stepped into her secretary's office.

The dividing door between secretary and mistress was like a portal in time. Without lay Matron's world; oak panelled, yes, large 19th-century oak desk, yes, but all else modern, all facilities, computer, filing system, coffee maker, it was all there. Within, the secretary's office was like a scene from a Dickens novel. First of all there was the gloom, there was a window but it was kept shuttered and those shutters locked; young women today were so easily distracted, could so often be found filing their nails, gazing out of windows and daydreaming at sunsets. Matron would have none of it, nor of young women wasting their time with mobile phones, surfing the 'net', nor sending e-mails to friends. There were no such distractions in this office; the girl sat on a small low wooden chair carefully recording a beautiful copperplate hand into a large leather bound ledger laid out on the plain brown desk before her, the brass curve stemmed desk lamp at its rear the only illumination.

Back in her own, plush, office Matron had slumped again back into her soft recliner. Having given the leash a sharp tug and feeling the girl's hot cheeks against her inner thighs she let her long skirt drop down over the girl's head and back. Leaning back she had placed her hands behind her head in relaxed satisfaction and let her tired eyes fall shut; all the better to savour her girl's lapping prehensile tongue.

She had two hours to savour this; in two hours her patient would be awakened to begin her 'day'. In her mind's eye she mulled over her patient's new regime, some part of which she had already put in motion. Other facets would require further refinement; such refinements as were presently developing, growing in concert with the tension, passion and excitement flowering from that hot breath, that much practised, much honed, obediently lapping tongue.

The girls sleep periods were to be of two hours repeated every four hours with a meal upon waking followed by her toilet, a sponge wash carried out by a nurse and being put into her uniform of course. 'Being put into' was to be the operative term here, in that that a suitably apt fraction of her punishment was to be the withdrawal of the privilege of dressing herself.

But now, with her pleasure rapidly approaching its crescendo, her right hand reached under her skirt to pull the bobbing head closer, the signal understood by the dominated girl as requiring the full penetration of her tongue into that orifice and the gentle nibbling of her mistress' clitoris with her lips. The ideas were pouring in, flooding her mind, structuring ever stricter, ever more subtle, training regimes. With Matron's gasping orgasm patient 30c's putative obedience-training regime received its final touches of masterstroke and flourish.

In her room, seated, waiting at her desk, patient 30C spontaneously, spuriously, giggled, an insane giggle? She couldn't be sure but she though it just might be, she certainly couldn't discount the notion, how could she?

In the schoolroom her erstwhile colleagues and peers were suffering their own delicious torment. Dr Ecclestone had considered the changes for some time but these things required consideration and clearance. The change most obvious to the girls, the most immediate change, was the appearance of the dormitory mistress with an addition to her uniform; hanging from a loop on the left-hand side of her nurse's belt and aligned directly opposite her ring of keys was a leather strap, or more accurately, a two-tongued tawse. The assistant nurse also sported the same accessory and upon entry to the classroom a new addition was seen hanging conspicuously alongside the whiteboard, a long, thin, rattan cane: corporal punishment had been summarily introduced.

Most traumatic, however, had been the second change and, unlike the introduction of the new punishment regime, this was discussed with them, or rather lectured to them as it was to be, as all things, an imposition rather than a choice. Dr Ecclestone had addressed them in the classroom.

From that day on, in addition to wearing their patient number on their uniform, they were to have an identification mark placed on their body, to be precise it was to occupy the right buttock cheek. It was explained to them that this was to by way of tattooing and was to be a bold and indelible representation of their patient number. They were simply told that, as it was to be indelible and therefore permanent, there were ethical considerations and human rights issues that would have to be tackled. In order to overcome any such objections they would be required to sign a waiver declaring their acceptance.

Many an eye nervously strayed across to the punishment room's door before returning to the paper before them, a blank sheet initially, for they were required to write out in full and in their finest copperplate hand the waiver as dictated to them by Dr Ecclestone herself.

Three times they had had to restart; each time a single girl, although a different girl on each occasion, had made an error and so they had all had to start afresh, the partially completed papers being collected in and torn up on each occasion. Finally, on the fourth attempt, the completed waivers awaited only signatures from those nervously shaking hands; waivers worded not so much as to give permission as to actually request the provision of an identification mark, respectfully asking in an almost pleading tone, stating how important it was to their feeling part of an institution, of really *belonging* to an institution.

The wording had been carefully thought through to drive home the humiliation of their situation and to further build on the foundation of learned-helplessness that Dr Ecclestone had skilfully engineered for her girls. There were one or two hesitations certainly, one or two pairs of eyes drifting back to the punishment room door, to that newly hanging rattan. Then, slowly, shakily, came the signatures; to many the names, their own names, appearing strange, unfamiliar, after so long a redundancy.

The actual tattooing was to be carried out in the dormitory. The five girls had had their knickers taken down and each told to bend over the back of her bed and wait. Medical restraints were placed between ankles and bed legs enforcing an exposed wide leg stance. Similar restraints were placed between wrists and bed rails and finally a strap around the waist secured the latter to the bed's foot rail.

A nurse carried out the tattooing, the tool being applied through a stencil template. As each girl was completed so she was let up. Only after the second girl's tattoo had been completed had the first began to weep, not from the pain, which had been negligible at most, but rather from the sight of that girl's buttock cheek and the knowledge of the disfigurement of her own body.

She had, they all had, expected the number and the letter, but not *this*, not *this* amount, not *this* size not *this* bold. The words were bold indeed and of the densest, blackest, ink:

St Mary's Hospital, psychiatric wing
Patient 16S

The number, the patient number, itself being around four centimetres high, the whole having been applied at a 45° angle covered the majority of the buttock cheek. *And it was there for life!!* She could never wear a bikini again, would never be able to let anyone so much as *glimpse* her buttocks again! It said she was a patient, it said she had been a patient in a psychiatric hospital; it would *always* say she had been a patient in a psychiatric hospital. She was broken, utterly broken and one by one the others joined her, as Dr Ecclestone had known they would.

Unbeknown to the girls in some ways they had been fortunate; Dr Ecclestone had been toying with the idea of reproducing the hospital badge and patient number, as appeared on their uniforms, as a tattoo across the left breast, coinciding with its position on their dresses' breast pocket. True, the two loci were not necessarily mutually exclusive but for now, at least, she was satisfied with the effect, she would allow a little time, allow them to regain some composure and then it would be 'knickers up and back into the classroom' but it was to be a new classroom from now on and how much more galling for them now?

Now to bare their buttocks to receive the cane, as they were going to have to, would also be to bare those humiliating black characters.

"Okay, come along, girls, knickers up and back into the classroom. There's nothing to cry about, you are all institutional girls, you are in an institution and you *belong* in this institution, don't you girls?"... A sullen, shuffling, sniffling, silence... "Don't you, girls?" More insistently this time.

"Yes doctor." Finally came the requisite response; five voices in monotonal automata unison.

CHAPTER 7

A WHITE LABYRINTHINE PROMENADE AND AN INTERVIEW WITH A DOCTOR

Susan Stringer was awake, if 'awake' one could truly define this state, this existence, the mindless monotony of the world in which she now found herself ensconced, this safe constrained realm of restriction, regulation and control. Awake-asleep, conscious-unconscious, these were relative terms lacking any true delineation; categorisation, classification and definition blurred, smeared beneath the thumb of institutional rigour. Today was to be different, though, totally different, somehow she could tell.

Today she had been roused in the usual manner it was true, the harsh ' wake-up' bell, as always, ringing in her ears, eyes opening to be greeted by the frost-white desert expanse that was her room. Today was different, today it was Matron herself performing the morning ritual. Today it was Matron who released the toggles securing the bed covers, today it was Matron who helped a still weary, unsteady, Susan to her feet, who guided her over to the desk.

One might view the replacement of one nurse with another or of a nurse by a matron unworthy of comment. Indeed at most one might, if one was to place oneself in Susan's position, expect to view such a change as insignificant, unremarkable. One might expect that the otherwise rigid adherence to the unchanging morning ritual of the hospital's regime would render such a detail subtle at most. However, few are those who have experienced Susan's little world, the timeless, featureless, cocooned existence that she now floated through. Few are those who have experienced her almost dreamlike state, the boredom induced daydreaming, the jarring insult of those demanding bells, the meaningless and pointless rituals and routines. It would probably be fair to say that only those who have shared Susan's environment, or one very similar, could hope to understand the importance of the minutest of changes. It would also be fair to say that all those who could claim such experience could be counted on two hands and could be found under the roof of this very institution, in the rooms adjacent to hers in the 'long-term' dormitory ward or the 'workhouse' suite.

A second nurse had come in, one that she had not seen before, and together with Matron half helped, half harried, Susan to her desk. The meal, her breakfast, awaited her as always. As ever, the white bowl of identically-white porridge, the white plastic beaker with the milky white tasteless drink, the white spoon.

The bell started, the mealtime bell, simultaneously Susan reached for the spoon and began eating. She had waited for the bell to ring, she hadn't really thought about it, realised it, but nevertheless she had waited for the meal bell. She no longer automatically reached for the spoon, not without permission from the bell.

Behind her she heard the rustle of Matron's uniform dress and then matron's voice coming, softly, "that's a good girl 43C, you're *very* hungry, I'm sure you are." Simultaneously she felt matron's fingers softly and soothingly stroke the back of her neck.

Susan, between mouthfuls, answered "yes Matron" and was immediately annoyed with herself, humiliated to find herself answering so automatically. She felt utterly ridiculous and irritated at her own acceptance of the silly, petty regime and routine. She just felt so tired, so heavy, so muddled, woolly headed. She was finding it increasingly difficult to think straight, difficult to protest, to put together an argument, to demand the right to see someone in charge, demand to leave.

They had no *right* to keep here like this, she was a volunteer, not a prisoner, not some psychiatric patient to be kept locked up. What was going on? When was she going to meet one of the researchers or one of the doctors. It just went on and on, every day some excuse, some delay, she would have to wait a just a little longer in this room, sitting at this desk, doing nothing. Why couldn't she go out? Not that she could, not dressed like this. Then again why did she have to remain dressed like this? She thought it was just temporary, just until they had sorted out somewhere to put her case, her belongings and the things she had brought with her, just until they found her a proper room and allocated her to a research project. Why *couldn't* she have her own clothes back?

So many questions, buzzing around in her head like angry bees, questions coming and going, trains of thought coming then ending sharply, interrupted by the insistent ding, ding of that bloody bell. What else had been said to her? She tried to remember, she went over all that had been said upon her arrival, all that had been said to her since…How many days? She couldn't quite work it out, each day seemed the same, no one event stood out in a mind since arriving, it was difficult to think back, to differentiate one day from the next. She went through his routine in her mind *every* day, over and over, sometimes all day, it was difficult to tell.

Why couldn't she have something to read? Just a magazine or newspaper would do. Why oh why couldn't she have her things, her clothes at least? What was that she had overheard Matron saying on the first day, the day she had arrived, something about her uniform not being ready? What did that mean? What bloody uniform? Why would she need to wear a uniform? What was that all about? Perhaps something *would* happen today; she could tell something was *very* different about today, yes! Yes! Something different was going to happen today!

Susan was jolted out of her internal frenzy of questions, the bell had stopped and with it, again irritatingly automatically, Susan found she had stopped eating, put down the spoon, and was sitting smartly upright with her hands resting on the desktop palms upwards, as was Matron's rule, while the meal things were removed.

How she hated herself for this compliance and particularly for her own mindlessness, her own blind obedience to these stupid rules. What was happening to her? What were they doing to her? It was going to damage her in some way, she felt sure, if she were to stay here much longer, it was going to damage her mind, break her personality. That was it, she was sure, that *must* be it. They were trying to break her in some way. No, no, she had to calm down, that was ridiculous, what would it be for? Why would they be doing it? Why to her? No, it was ridiculous, *wasn't it?*

142

Chapter 7 | A White Labyrinthine Promenade …

The answer to any bar Susan herself, and possibly, Alison, her close cousin, would have been obvious. It would certainly have been so to anyone who knew Susan's stepmother, even in passing let alone any lucky enough to be within her confidence. It would have been just as obvious to any fortunate enough to have been privy to even the earliest negotiations that had taken place all those months earlier. Negotiations and discussions between stepmother and prospective, and soon to be most influential, stepdaughter's newest best friend, Dr Samantha Ecclestone.

Susan knew she had to pull herself together, Matron was talking, that was what was important, she had to listen to Matron, pay attention, Matron was important. It was not that she wasn't listening, deep down inside she wouldn't dare not to, it was just that sometimes words just seemed to wash over her, she just felt so tired, so, so…fuzzy, yes, that was it, fuzzy.

The last few mornings had found Susan progressively more reluctant to leave her bed. She had been feeling leaden, slow witted. She had been finding it difficult to concentrate of late, indeed difficult to think about anything at all for any length of time without finding that she had, presumably, drifted off in some way. Daydreaming? She couldn't be certain, could never quite remember *what* she had been thinking about. Of late, more and more often she had found herself jolted back to reality by one event or another. Mealtimes, toilet times, bedtimes, came and went, each heralded by its individual bell. Each time it felt as if she had just been jolted awake, as if she had drifted away for a moment, just for a moment though. Surely she had only just had her last meal, surely it had only been a few minutes ago that she had last used the toilet, almost visibly shrinking under the humiliation of a nurse's supervising and appraising eye, how long had it been? She just couldn't quite remember. Susan would find herself blinking, sitting at the desk, presented with a meal, seemingly only minutes since the last. Her hunger, though, spoke to her of a different reality, a far longer period, a period that Susan was increasingly and, worryingly, less aware of.

She had seemed to have faded away, become lost in her own little world, outside of time, outside of the tedium of her surroundings. Her world? How much of it was really hers? Why could she not remember what she had been thinking about mere moments previously, those daydreams? Had she been sleeping? She could remember the sound of the surf, how sometimes she imagined it spoke to her, that they conversed like old friends. Occasionally she found herself reciting something, a kind of mantra recited in a sing-song voice like some half remembered nursery rhyme. It was something to do with being a good girl, but she couldn't quite recall what, it left her as a half remembered and rapidly fading dream. And as is oft the way with dreams, the more one reaches forth, the more they recede, just fade away.

The day's first meal consumed, Susan waited. Bells rang and stopped,' toilet time' came and went, Susan, as always, unable to perform in the full glare of witness, under appraising eye, finally allowed to return to her seat, her dire need remaining unresolved. She waited, expectantly but with an ignorant expectance. Something was going to happen today, she felt sure. Still she waited. Bells rang and stopped, a meal, the second since waking, eaten, more tasteless, mulchy, porridge…More waiting…waiting…waiting…

Stomach cramping, her need urgent, still she waited, holding on as long as humanly possible, if only the toilet bell would ring, right now she felt, she *knew*, she wouldn't care how many nurses were lined up, watching, her, how unbearable the humiliation.

Bleep, bleep! The double bleep greeting her first step from her desk warned of the certain and impending disaster. The wailing alarm easily outraced her bowel movement and for an instant she didn't care. The sheer relief! Then the realisation: She had triggered the alarm, she had to get back to her seat, sit still, let it reset, just had to, couldn't stand it. Susan, mind befuddled by sedative and sound, desperate to get back to her seat, desperate to do *anything* that might bring silence.

She had no expectancy of the usual comfort most take for granted, they always took the wipes with them when they left, the nurses. Why? Why, did they always have to do that? Susan had no idea, just acceptance. She did the best she could under the circumstances, the best she could to clean herself up. All that was available was the absorbent pad in her knickers, it had worked before but it seemed doubtful that it would be sufficient this time. The result of her best efforts, the soiled towel, was stuffed down the toilet for what else could she do? Disgusted by the smell, the sight, she was desperate to be rid of it; clearly, leaving the pad on the edge of the toilet seat, as before, was not something to be contemplated on *this* occasion. This was far, far worse, far more humiliating. If only she could flush it, if only that damned alarm would stop she could think clearly. But would it flush away in any case? The toilet bowl seemed so small and, now in water, the already bulky towel was swelling. It was going to block up, she knew it, when it *did* flush it was going to overflow!

It was with shaking head that she eased up her knickers, resignation overcoming her. She wasn't entirely clean, she had done the best, but she wasn't entirely clean, she felt sure she wasn't. Yet what else could she do? She felt the PVC cling tackily to her skin as she moved. Slipping, slimily, against peach-like buttocks, lubricated now, the seam sliding to and fro wetly between those cheeks, running back and forth across her anus with each movement as she wiggled back into her seat. She was back at that desk but now each fidget, each shift of weight was accompanied by a reminder of that filthy lubrication, a reminder of her shame- and of the deeper shame to come.

How long? She knew not. In its own time, unhurriedly, the alarm ceased its torturous wailing, in itself an eternity. And then there was only the physical discomfort, the mental anguish. Now devoid of their absorbent pad, deprived of absorbency, the impermeable plastic knickers had become practically awash with sweat, feminine secretions and much worse. Susan was only too aware of the steadily building heat, the slippery moisture, the clingy, sweaty, slime-caress of slick PVC against her most tender regions and the attendant itching. The thick towel, the pad, had made her feel like some diapered child or incontinent retard, that much was true, but right now she was ready to quite literally *beg* for a new knicker-liner. She no longer cared how bulky it was, how it made her feel. This period, then, this fidgeting, itching, time spent squirming wetly upon her seat, this was her second eternity.

How long? She knew not and then cared not; Matron had arrived. With her was the nice nurse, Susan's nurse, the lovely nurse. Within moments of their entering the bell had started, the 'toilet bell', and Susan found herself positioned, with back to the little toilet pedestal, facing both Matron and the nurse. The nurse was carrying a white plastic tray upon which Susan could see a white kidney-shaped dish, a pair of smallish white plastic screw top containers, perhaps of around 250mL, a roll of toilet tissue and, right at the front, a trio of what Susan recognised as suppositories. Matron, standing hands on hips: "Toilet time, knickers down".

They must have seen the toilet, the mess, Susan thought. They must have. The blockage! Yet they were clearly expecting her to relieve herself. What would happen? The bell would stop and the damn thing would flush, automatically, she thought. And then what? It was going to flood everywhere, she just knew it.

She felt like crying, felt like a naughty child. It was with some difficulty, then, that she regained at least some semblance of composure, consciously and continuously reminding herself that she was no child, that she was an eighteen-year-old woman, or at least that was how she wanted to think of herself.

It should be said that she had begun to question even this. Just how mature, how independent, was she, was anyone, really, at eighteen? After all, they were treating her like a child and she was feeling like a child. Why couldn't she stand up for herself? Why couldn't she just stand her ground, demand to see someone in charge, tell them she just wasn't going to put up with this any longer? Somehow she just couldn't, she knew it, hated herself for it. If only she had more confidence.

Not so very mature, not so independent after all, she thought to herself, then buried this thought behind a facade of carefully constructed denial, the repository of all teenage insecurities and anxieties. That this fortification was crumbling, was presently being expertly dismantled brick by brick, stone by stone, was undeniable.

A White Labyrinthine Promenade

She had been thinking of running out, retracing the passageway back the way they had originally brought her. She could backtrack from the shower room, after all that had been quite close to the main entrance. But had it been before or after they had passed through the first of the security grilles? She couldn't quite recollect.

All this struggle, all this conjecture and all for nought. It was all academic; such an opportunity was obviously not going to be presented her. She was clearly being led in the entirely opposite direction from that by which she had originally arrived.

Having reached the end of the corridor the nurse walking ahead of them opened a door to their right, revealing yet another of those locked security gates beyond which, she could see, lay another long white and almost featureless passageway, windows on the left, cell-like doors to the right.

A key was produced from the bunch hanging from the nurse's belt. Swiftly the gate was unlocked, the party passing through, the gate swinging shut with a faint click behind them as they went. Susan, trying to take in as much as possible of her surroundings, to orientated her self, swiftly noted that at no time had she had ever seen any sign of a staircase.

As far she could tell the only access to the floor they were on, whichever floor that might be, was by way of the lift. That lift required a key to operate it, the knowledge of some sort of security code and, in any case, was at this moment separated from her by two long corridors and now by not one but *two* locked, barred, penitentiary-styled security grilles. The thought struck her; they were leading her ever deeper into the complex, ever further from the outside world, her old life, ever further from reality, *her* reality. This was *their* reality, this institution, and she was becoming more deeply embedded, mired, in its ensnaring machinations with every step.

Beyond that first security grille they made several subsequent right turns, certainly more than four, one after another, each at the far end of an apparently identical passageway, totally white, totally straight, a sort of man-made whiteout that invalidated any judgment of distance. At the end of *every* corridor, it seemed, was a door through which waited a similar prison-like security gate. Each of these subsequent gates had been unlocked by Matron, taking up her most appropriate guise as jailer, the nurse having been relegated to the trio's rear. Each gate, in turn, had shut behind them, locking automatically with a faint click, as they proceeded through, Matron at the front, girl following, nurse bringing up the rear: corridor after corridor, door after door, gate after gate, on and on, seemingly forever.

Always a right turn, or so it seemed, never a left. How could this be? It didn't make sense. Susan was losing track, she knew she was; her impression was of a pointless tour around the sides of a square or oblong floor-plan. She tried to be logical, surely they would have come back to where they had started from, maybe they had, more than once; she had no idea it just all looked the same.

Susan was desperately trying to hang on to the tiniest thread of logic, her mind wheeling, churning and scratching for any morsel of understanding, of explanation. There could only be one explanation, she must be mistaken, must have missed a turn they had made somewhere. Yes that was it, it had to be, a turn to the left, probably more than one in fact, that she couldn't quite remember for the some reason. She had become confused somewhere; it was her own failing, her own fault, her weakness or rather *one* of her weaknesses, her inability to concentrate.

How she wrestled with this thought, the implication that she could be so easily confused, could forget which way they had turned, *so* quickly, *so* completely. She struggled with the denial, that her memory could be *so* unreliable; there had to be some other explanation. In her mind's eye she backtracked through all the twists and turns they had made since leaving her room, desperately searching for the 'lost left', the change of direction she had not accounted for, all the time struggling to keep track of the number of passageways traversed, the number of corners turned, security grilles negotiated. Surely, if she hadn't made a mistake then, on more than one occasion, they must have passed her room and the other rooms in that corridor, those rooms with the numbers on the doors, the groups of numbers and letters like those on *her* room's door, like those printed on her nightdress over her left breast. Yet she'd scrutinised each door they'd passed, yes there were many doors that had the holders, the holders that held the plates that in turn displayed the room numbers, yet none of those holders were occupied, none of the doors had the numbers and letters that might denote occupation.

In time her constant perusal appeared to irritate the nurse walking behind her, presumably because she would occasionally and momentarily pause to take stock. From time to time, from behind, there came a gentle urging push, the nurse's hands resting momentarily on her shoulders and, whenever Susan appeared to hesitate too long, a sharp rebuke, "come along, look straight ahead girl", and then, as she continued on her way, there would come a much gentler, "that's a good girl".

Then something different; Matron had stopped at a door that was, as far as Susan could judge, about halfway along a corridor, although under the strange 'whiteout' conditions the only thing she *could* be certain of was that they were not at the corridor's end.

Susan had been lost in thought, had almost walked into Matron's back. She had become totally preoccupied with self-doubt, troubled over her loss of trust in her own memory. So many times recently she had found herself losing track of days, of time. Thinking back she couldn't seem to differentiate one day from the next. This inner doubt had been growing of late but if pressed she would have had to admit that, as with so many of her problems, she couldn't quite seem to recall exactly when or where she had first started to feel this way, had first started to lose confidence in herself to such an extent.

The door was on their right and, as with all the doors she had seen lining these corridors, it was illuminated by the light from the window directly opposed to it on their left. Susan hadn't even glanced at the windows they had passed, expecting, now, the disappointing, featureless, white frosted, expanse snuggled behind the protective covering of the ubiquitous white plastic grille. This window was no different nor did this door differ in any significant way from any of the others they had passed. All she could say for sure, from her experience so far, was that, whatever lay beyond, it wasn't a room such as she had been staying in; there was no plate holder for the room number or identification number or whatever it was. It was just a plain white door, lying practically flush to the wall with but a single key hole, in which Matron was presently turning a key. Beyond that blemish it was as pristine as artic snow, almost part of the wall and lacking even the conventionality of a handle. Without comment Matron walked through, holding the door for Susan, the latter urged through in her turn by the nurse to her rear.

They were in yet another corridor, as white as all the others, but this time there were no windows to be seen on either side, just doors. Behind her Susan heard the door close, a barely audible click confirming its automatic relocking. At the far end of the corridor, on the right, she could see a row of five small white plastic chairs, low child-sized chairs of the type she had spent so long sitting on in her room, at that desk. Opposite this seating area was a white door.

"Sit down, that's a good girl" the nurse's patronising tone came from over her shoulder. Matron gestured so as to offer her the centre seat, the chair directly opposite the door. Awkwardly, the small seat seemingly so far down as to be little higher than a footstool, Susan seated herself as best she could, wiggling her mature curves past its arms and down onto the seat.

She was immediately struck by the embarrassing exposure imposed by her posture, the short skirt of her nightdress having ridden up revealing the semitransparent crotch of the PVC knickers.

The low seating position resulted in her knees being somewhat higher than her bottom precluding the maintenance of anything *like* a ladylike disposition, her knees tending to swing outward as if they had a mind of their own, as if working in collusion to deepen her embarrassment. She realised that anyone coming out of the room opposite would immediately be greeted by a clear and unflattering view of what, quite frankly, any girl or woman of her age would prefer to keep hidden.

With that insight came shame and with that shame an unknowing premonition; a glimpse of a future wherein she was destined to become enlightened to the truth of Matron's oft-used descriptive term 'examination knickers'. The doubtful delights of the latter, at least, she had been spared on this occasion; but the time would come. Oh yes, the time would come and Matron would see to it that it would be not long in coming.

More sitting, more waiting. The nurse had left the way they had come, disappearing out through the door at the end of the corridor. Matron now stood with her back against the wall, on Susan's left at the end of the row of chairs. On Susan's right were two chairs then a small gap of perhaps two or three chair's widths before the blank white end wall of the passage.

Left to her own devices again Susan's mind began to wander, it was difficult to keep focused on anything in particular under these circumstances, there had been nothing to see, nothing to hear, nothing to do, for such a long time, how long? How long? She had been determined to get something done about it, demand to speak to someone in charge, this was her chance, she would sit here, practise in her mind exactly what she was going to say. It was just…well, she just didn't seem able to keep her mind focused, kept drifting back to worrying about her problems, her confusion of late.

Her main problem, she thought, was herself; she lacked self-confidence, that's what it was. She had been reluctant to admit it, even to herself, before, before she had come here. Indeed, once she would not have acknowledged even the faintest *possibility* that she had any problems, not psychological problems, not mental problems. But now, well, now…It was just that, with all the time she had had on her hands since her arrival, all that time with nothing to do but sit and reflect, she had become somehow more aware of her failings. Perhaps, she thought, she had never *truly* been *quite* well; the panic attacks, the agoraphobic attacks, her occasional stammer, perhaps all had been getting worse and she just hadn't noticed. Had she really been in denial all this time? How could she have been so blind, so deluded? It just didn't quite make sense and what was more, she couldn't quite remember when it had all started. When had she first become aware?

Her immediate concern now, though, was that, with all this self reflection, self flagellation almost, she was becoming agitated and the more she worried, the more she struggled with her failing recall, wrestled with her self-questioning doubt, the more she could feel that panic rise.

A panic attack, just moments away, the cold sweat forming: This was her own fault, what had aunt Julia said, the others, the nurse, Dr Ecclestone? She was to avoid anxiety, avoid getting into this state of mind, this constant questioning, constant agonizing over decisions. She had to breath deeply, think of nothing, let herself drift away, that's what she had been told. It was best to avoid situations she couldn't face up to, difficult decisions, open spaces, crowds…

Neither Sense nor Sensibility (A Girl in a Wheelchair)

The door immediately confronting her, *that* door, had opened; Susan was startled to find herself practically face to face with a girl. In truth, from Susan's lowly-seated perspective this did involve the somewhat rapid elevation of her focus; she had found herself, embarrassingly, facing the girl's crotch.

The wheelchair had emerged before Susan had quite registered that the door had opened. A white-uniformed nurse pushed from behind, carefully manoeuvring it across the threshold while, behind her in the room, a bespectacled, white coated, woman could just be seen standing to one side, holding open the door. For a moment Susan found herself at a loss to interpret what she was seeing.

Of the wheelchair itself there is little to relate except to say that it was entirely white, from the wheels, the spokes, the rims, to the curved moulded headrest. The colour scheme extended to the handles at the rear with which the nurse was expertly navigating the turn into the narrow corridor.

It is true that, upon careful consideration, the more observant might have noted one or two small additions, specialised characteristics, that might have seemed to differentiate it from the average work-a-day hospital wheelchair but even these, the various medical restraint anchor points, were quite discreet, particularly, as now, when not in use and in any case were not necessarily inappropriate in the context of a psychiatric hospital.

It is perhaps of no surprise, then, that Susan should not have considered it particularly noteworthy. Aesthetically, the most outstanding features were those *in absentia*, the *lack* of chrome trimmings, the usual black handle grips, perhaps black or grey tyres. Its occupant on the other hand, the girl, was a different matter entirely. At a casual glance, superficially childlike and yet there was her size, the overt voluptuous maturity of her figure, almost exaggeratedly womanly, feminine curves, maturely developed curving hips filling the seat, knees pressed out against armrests, a notably defined clinched waistline above which the aggressive high-breasted melon-thrust spoke of artificial suspension taken to an ridiculous extreme.

Indeed, for most observers this latter observation would have most rapidly and aptly crystallised, for surely even the most insensitive would have been hard-pressed to deny the inspiration to ridicule. But then there was the childish dress and yet even this juxtaposed with certain idioms of more mature fashion, inappropriate on a girl that Susan, after due consideration, considered might be perhaps in her late teens or early twenties at best. The image was perhaps overly mature, perhaps inappropriately sexual under these circumstances and strangely anachronistic, like some left-over from a bygone age, while, all the time, remaining undeniably institutional.

For Susan's part, It must be said that her first impressions had been somewhat coloured by her unusual vantage point. In fact her very first sight had been of the view up the girl's short skirt; tan stockings, old-fashioned, broad white, suspenders contrasting strongly against the dark welts and, plainly visible beneath the sheen of the thin white PVC or latex, Susan could not be certain, bloomer legs. Beyond even that, she had momentarily glimpsed, even while shifting her embarrassed gaze, the shiny, pearl-white fabric of a tightly stretched crotch panel, a distinct shadowed valley marking the puckered invagination at its centre.

Hurriedly looking up, her gaze had momentarily met the girl's eyes, a fleeting, truncated contact, terminated almost as quickly as made. The girl, in her turn, equally rapidly, had averted her gaze, a spreading shy flush painting her rounded and well fed cheeks an apple red even as the tingling burning sensation washing across the surface of Susan's skin had informed of her own mirroring complexion.

In that moment, despite its brevity, Susan had received the impression of blue eyes, the contact too fleeting to be certain, and an impression, too, of something else, something disturbing, something missing. Yes, that was what it was, something that was missing from that gaze, something that had been announced by its absence, even in that fleeting moment. Those eyes, the windows of the soul, yet that was exactly what they lacked, what was missing, sparkle, soul, life; it had been a gaze as blank as the frosted corridor windows, a gaze reflecting the institutional white walls and carpets. The way that girl's gaze had shifted, so automatically, so rapidly, as one might turn from unbearable horror as in terror, this Susan had found the most disturbing. The girl had seemed terrified of making eye contact as if, perhaps, suffering some dark, debilitating, extremity of shyness, deeply withdrawn perhaps, surely indicative of some sort of psychological imbalance.

Recovering somewhat from her initial surprise and embarrassment Susan hungrily ran her eyes over the seated figure before her; there was more here than that all-pervading whiteness, there was relief to be had here, relief from the crippling white monotonous numbness about her.

Before her sat an apparition very *unlike* everything else, an islet of green and white, of shadow, of black and of tan and, yes, even blue, the blue of the sky of the sea she cared not which. Perhaps she hadn't realised just how much the bland institutional surroundings had affected her but now she could barely control herself, control the hunger, she was devouring greedily every small detail of the image before her, a girl in a wheelchair, a psychiatric patient, a sad sight, an institutionalised girl in a wheelchair in an institutional dress, the most important, most interesting thing she had ever seen in her life.

Susan was desperately trying to take in, to note, every detail as if her life depended on some future, accurate, recall of this instant. Before her the girl sat passively, her nurse awkwardly manoeuvring the wheelchair into the corridor. From beneath a plain, green and white striped, bonnet, that would not have seemed amiss if detailed in some dark Dickensian tome, emerged two tightly plaited, glossy, jet-black, pigtails. The tightness of the platting and the shortness of the latter conspired to produce an awkward lie, each pigtail tending to an angle away from the side of the girl's head before curving upwards just before the point at which a broad ribbon held the end in a peculiarly oversized green and white striped bow. Light fell playfully about those ribbons, forming pools, whirls and shimmers wherever the fabric curved and folded, the sheen suggestive of a man-made fabric, washable, practical and institutional. The colour, pattern and sheen were echoed throughout the girl's bonnet and dress, suggesting the same fabric had been used for both and again reflecting the institutional emphasis on the twin values of practicality and cheapness.

Whatever the thinking that lay behind this costume, it was clear that little concession had been made to the sensibilities of the wearer. The only concession to style, if one could call it that, was the large, rounded, collar, an extravagance of fabric presented in a rather farcical oversized travesty of a 'Peter Pan' style being perhaps most reminiscent of a 19th-century, child's, sailor suit.

In the context of a private hospital, one might perhaps be hard-pressed to justify such detailing of styling, let alone the bonnet, as purely functional. One might argue, also, that the embroidery on the left breast pocket was an equally unlikely extravagance, although this at least might *just* have been justified on the grounds of organisational practicalities and identification. This latter stated: *St Mary's, psychiatric wing* in a large, curling, coal-black, script across the top of the pocket, immediately below which, and occupying most of the centre of the pocket, was embroidered, *24 C,* in large black block characters.

Stylistically the dress itself seemed to Susan to encompass some features of a school uniform summer dress she had once seen in an old photograph, something worn by girls from a private and very exclusive boarding school in some far off, bygone age. Other features, the fabric, the glassy buttons, the cut, the belt, the latter being of a similar fabric to the dress and fastening at the front with two buttons, were more at home on a 1960s dress-style overall, the like of which she had once seen on television, featuring in an old programme about a prison somewhere, she seemed to remember, and even then worn by a group of older women inmates.

On reflection, she decided, that was *exactly* what it looked like, a prison uniform, yet, again, not quite, sort of mid-way between a prison uniform and a very strict, very old-fashioned, school uniform. Indeed, a more institutional garb it would be difficult to imagine. Throughout the dress was striped, bottle green and white. The sleeves were long with buttoned cuffs, the shoulders were slightly puffed and of a style that in a far-off time might have been described as mutton chop. The bodice was close fitting, noticeably so, and, belying its institutional origins, could easily have been tailor-made for the girl such was the closeness of the fit; not tight exactly, just apparently well-tailored and closely-fitted to the figure.

Even to the unpractised eye it would have been obvious that the girl's underwear included some sort of foundation garment, perhaps a corset, some sort of surgical corset Susan decided. Yes that would make sense, the only really plausible explanation in fact.

This latter observation was consistent with the most glaring oddity, one that strangely Susan had initially missed in the hurried, embarrassed, shifting of her gaze. Now, having recovered somewhat and systematically, almost analytically, perusing the sight before her, Susan's eyes finally alighted upon the leg callipers. As if to confirm the girls obvious disability, ugly, old-fashioned looking and reminiscent of pictures Susan had once seen of polio victims in the 1930s, these fitted from the girl's ankles right up to a point just beyond the girl's knees and included a hinge at the knee joint.

Her gaze following on down to the girl's feet Susan saw that the girl was wearing fairly conventional footwear, conventional that is had she been a girl of around ten years old rather than in her late teens or early twenties.

Chapter 7 | A White Labyrinthine Promenade ...

Bottle green patent 'Mary Janes', the colour to match the dress, had been realised in a rather cheap looking glossy, reflective material, perhaps plastic, Susan thought, and again were suggestive of an institutional emphasis on practicality. The shoes fastened with a T-bar strap arrangement, most typical of a child's school shoe, by way of a contrasting white buckle that, again, was of an appearance suggesting plastic of some description.

And then she was gone, but not before Susan had made one final observation. The wheelchair turning away, its occupant had turned her head, subtly, ever so slightly, to shyly glance at Susan with eyes at the extreme of their leftward travel. Again the two girls' eyes had met for a split second, Susan registering...what exactly? Fear? Pleading? Susan was sure only in that it had been disturbing. And then...

"24C, what do you think you're doing girl?" The girl's nurse had spoken so unexpectedly sharply, so, angrily, that Susan had almost leapt out of her seat. By way of extreme contrast, and equally startling for that, the girl's voice, when it came, was tiny, as if in apology for its own existence, the reply barely audible, just barely understandable, a stammering muffled babble. "O,o,o, orrriiy u,u, urtth". It was with some difficulty, and even then only with hindsight, that Susan was able to interpret "sorry nurse".

There were no answers to be had here, just more questions to ponder. The girl was surely retarded or disturbed in some way and was equally clearly disabled, so why were they treating her in that manner? Why had they dressed her like that, in that ridiculous manner? Did that nurse really have to speak to her like that, all the girl had done was glance over? And that look in her eyes, that strange brew of fear and pleading, what did it all mean? Then they were gone, girl, wheelchair and nurse disappearing through the door at the corridor's end, Susan looking after, watching the door closing behind them.

With their departure had ended, abruptly, Susan's train of thought, or rather she had had the thread cut for her. There had come a sharp, rude, interruption: "43C, what do you think you're doing, girl? It has got nothing to do with you! Look straight ahead. The doctor will see you in a moment and she won't want you wasting her time so you had better pay attention." Matron's voice, as always, had been authoritative, commanding. Without thinking Susan had turned away, had returned her attention to the door before her and, as so often recently, her unquestioning compliance and both annoyed and humiliated her.

She waited, her irritation rapidly approaching rage, her complexion florid with an almost irrational mix of anger and embarrassment. Matron had spoken to her in exactly the same way as that nurse had addressed the retarded girl. It hadn't be necessary then and it was unnecessary now, completely unnecessary, what was worse was that she had done exactly as she had been told, what was wrong with her? They were talking to her as if she was a naughty schoolgirl and she was going along with it with little hesitation and even less protest.

Then the door, the doctor's door she was soon to discover, opened again... "43C, up you get", Matron again. Just for a moment, rising stiffly from the little chair, Susan felt like turning and lashing out yet found herself walking towards the waiting doctor as if in a dream, or should that be nightmare?

152

The nurse was guiding her with an arm around her shoulders, a semi-hug that seemed to instantly calm her and yet, simultaneously, sap her will still further, if such had been possible at that moment.

The Futility of the Familiar

All the way here, well certainly from the point at which they had arrived at that door in the outside corridor, when she had believed it to be of the doctor's room, before she had realised that it actually led to yet another corridor, *this* corridor in fact, her determination had been growing with every step. She was determined, now more than ever, that she was going to get something done about this, her treatment. This was it, this was her chance, she was going to damn well complain, get something done about the staff and their attitude towards her, get something done about Matron in particular. Most of all she was going to get out of here, resign from the programme, from whatever experiment she was supposed to take part in, no matter how simple, how non-intrusive they might promise them to be, no matter how friendly and 'nice' the researchers might turn out.

Now she tried to gather her resolve, prepare for the argument ahead. If anything the way she had just been spoken to, the way she had just seen that disabled and retarded girl treated, had made her more determined than ever. She just didn't want to know any more, she was going to go home, even if it did mean spending the next few months with her bloody stepmother! Anything would be better than this. A few months living with her stepmother and then she would be off to university, albeit without the funding that she would have acquired had she stayed the course here, taken part in their damned study. She knew, now, that she just couldn't stand it any longer, she just couldn't. Besides anything else there was the sheer bloody boredom for one thing and those bloody bells, over and over, and being treated like some disturbed child in an asylum or something...

... Why had she burst into tears? Why? She wasn't quite sure; it had just happened, that was all, just as the door had been opened, just as the white coated woman had stood aside to grant her access, just as the friendly smile had spread across her face, the simultaneous gesture of invitation made, that invitation coloured with an almost tangible air of authority.

Susan had been struck by the woman's large dark eyes glinting, sparkling, behind her white rimmed glasses. A white headdress adorned her head in a manner similar to that of the nurses; her hair was covered in its entirety bar one small wisp, revealing the doctor as a brunette, lying nonchalantly across her forehead and curling just above the fine aquiline nose. It had not been the sight of the doctor *per se* though. No, it had been the room beyond. Not that there was anything particularly sinister about it, quite the contrary; it was largely bare, sparsely furnished at best, an almost sensorially barren white desert.

White, everything was white; white carpet, white walls. An imposing white desk dominated the room's centre behind which lay a large, white, high-back chair. Beyond the latter a white frosted-glass window crouched back behind the usual white plastic grille and filled the space with its ethereal mist of light. No there was nothing unusual, remarkable nor outstanding, about this room. But that was just *it*, deep down, subconsciously, she had been expecting... what? What exactly?

There might have been a desk of antique mahogany, oak panelling, shelves of learned tomes, their leather bindings glowing in reds and browns? There could have been golden sunlight flooding through a window, the view beyond stunningly-framed; the hospital grounds, the trees and grass, the greens and the blues? Some colour? That was it! Some colour, something to look at, something to think about. Anything! Anything! Anything but this, this…monotony.

Deep down Susan could sense that further disappointments, further defeats, were destined today. A dark realisation, a slow creeping thin dread, the certainty crashing down on her, squeezing the spirit from her, to run like juice from an overripe peach, and this even before she stood behind the small white plastic child's chair cringing before that huge oversized desk, even before Matrons firm guiding hand pressed down upon her right shoulder, even before she had been firmly guided down onto that lowly seat, the doctor simultaneously gesturing a wordless invitation to be seated. Surely before long only the husk would remain to show where a vivacious young woman had once flowered.

Susan found herself sat low before the doctor's looming white desk, its top now only little below her head height. She was now obliged to look up in order to face the doctor, who, having taken her seat on the far side, now regarded her with dark, appraising, eyes across the white featureless expanse. Susan, ungainly-seated, could feel her confidence draining from her like the finest silver-sand through gnarled and twisted arthritic fingers. The low chair enforced the assumption of the exposed posture with which she was becoming all-too-familiar; knees high and spread wide, the near-transparent crotch of her PVC knickers stretched tightly and forming a window into her, not so private, world of humiliation, her brief latex nightdress riding up to the very top of her thighs. Even the absorbent pad of her usual incontinence bloomers would have been welcomed now, even that oppressive diaper-humiliation would have been preferable to this awful feeling of utter exposure.

The thin, moulding, plastic covering, emphasising rather than concealing, was worse in some ways than even total nudity would have been. Indeed, nudity would at least have allowed her a natural figure, a natural, normal, bust line, not this freakish melon-breasted appearance; the blatant distended rock-hard thimbles of her nipples, pressing out into the thinly stretched latex fabric, the pink, gently-throbbing, breast fronts, her areolae, as flushed as her cheeks, gifting a fine rose-painted embellishment to her humiliation. Looking up at the doctor, her self-confidence ebbing away with the outgoing tide, the surf dragging back and forth her hopes and dreams, little by little denuding the shore, she felt the tears come again, a gentle almost silent sob. Before us emotion whirls and eddies where soon there will be only featureless sea.

She was aware that the door had been closed behind her, she was also aware of the continued presence of both the nurse and Matron close-by. She had expected to have been left alone with the doctor, at least at some point in the proceedings. With the benefit of privacy, and in confidence, she felt she might just have retained enough resolve to speak up, complain about her treatment, complain about Matron's attitude, her domineering bullying. This scenario she had rehearsed in her internal dialogue, the speech practised until reduced to a series of clearly and cleverly worked out sound-bites.

154

Now, though, with the continued presence of her nemesis, she was discovering her resolution to be a little too dependent on her setting of the scene, her silence now as much testament to a lack of contingency as to psychological disadvantage. And so she sat passively, waiting, flanked by the standing, imposing, figures of both nurse and Matron while, before her, the doctor sitting back, relaxed, confident, conversed with her staff, looking past her, through her, as if invisible, transparent and of no account.

The doctor's attitude was clearly transmitted and equally clearly received; she was talking *about* her not *to* her. "So, this must be 43C, I understand there have been issues regarding compliance, more specifically, problems with sample collection?" Periodically the woman glanced down at her notes, adjusted her glasses and turned pages beyond Susan's view; the occasional glimpse of the blank underside of a document her only reward for the diligence of her gaze.

"Yes doctor" Matron's voice, contrite and yet as authoritative as, even here, even in this other intimidating woman's presence. "She has repeatedly failed to provide faecal samples in particular, at least at the requisite times." She went on "… and today, for the second time, she has managed to block the toilet".

The doctor interjected, clearly irritated: "How so?".

"The same way as last time, by stuffing her incontinence towel down it. Of course when it flushed it overflowed, flooded everywhere, a complete mess I'm afraid."

The doctor visibly bristled, then, sighing resignedly. "Perhaps there are behavioural or psychological problems present. What happens at toilet time, do we get *any* samples?" If anything, if at all possible, the doctor was displaying even less acknowledgement of Susan's presence. Behind her, out of her eye line, Matron shrugged slightly and, otherwise maintaining her professional detached demeanour, she continued with her report:

"Generally at toilet time she either can't or simply won't perform, although she has managed to provide a few samples of her urine."

The doctor leant forward slightly in her chair, interlocking her fingers together a she did so. "Well, it must be said that we have experienced difficulties throughout this study with the scheduling of sample collection, partly arising from the requirement to collect samples at fixed intervals but, with most patients, it seems to have been the supervised toilet use that has been the major issue." She went on: "Have you explained to her that close medical supervision is absolutely essential if we are to ensure that the experimental protocols are adhered to correctly, that the samples are collected regularly, at the correct intervals and under the correct conditions."

"Yes doctor I have. I can understand her reluctance to perform her toilet under supervision but behaviour such as she has exhibited today I can only describe as wilful disobedience. I can't help but wonder whether she is really suitable for this study, I get the impression that it is not what she expected. Indeed, I get the feeling that she would rather leave the study altogether."

Susan could hardly believe what he was hearing. Firstly, surely anyone would object to being watched while using the toilet. Secondly, Matron was blatantly lying, nothing had been explained to her in any sense let alone anything pertaining to experimental protocols and sample collection.

She had only been told that she would have to wait for a few days before joining a study group and being interviewed by the researchers. That would have been the point at which she would have expected to have been told about experimental protocol, perhaps be given consent forms to sign, that sort of thing. Thirdly, and most surprisingly, Matron appeared to be conspiring to send her home, exactly what she wanted most. Susan felt excitement building, a childish excitement, the-night-before-Christmas. Strangely, she felt almost like giggling, elated, they were going to send her home!

A lot of what was said from that point on had washed over her but now she saw the doctor, stooping slightly, retrieve something from a desk drawer, she heard the faint soft swish of the drawer gliding on its nylon runners, and a white kidney-shaped dish was placed on the desktop before her. Susan sniffed, she couldn't help herself but there was suddenly a pungent odour in the air and her senses were keen, acute, having been ironically sharpened by the dullness of routine. She felt herself blush deeply at the recognition, that is to say, deeper, as throughout a hot flustered flush had continuously occupied her teary countenance. The odour had come as a slap around that pretty face; even from her low position she could see enough to recognise the yellow-brown stained and bloated form of her incontinence pad from earlier in the day.

The doctor glanced down at it then looked up, still staring straight through the transparent girl before her. "I have examined her stools indirectly on both occasions that this has happened. This is her latest issue, retrieved by maintenance, and with quite some complaint I might add. It looks to me as if simple constipation may be her problem, at least to some degree." She glanced down at her notes before continuing: "I see that she has only passed stools on these two occasions so far which tends to confirm my suspicions. The smell is quite diagnostic too, the pungency, quite offensive". At this the doctor gave a sniff.

If it had at all been possible Susan would have surely blushed deeper still, as it was all she could do was shift her weight and fidget awkwardly. Despite herself, despite her most stoic attempts at re-composure, she found herself gently weeping again. Behind her, on her right, she heard a soft voice, the nurse's voice; "shh, it's all right child". Susan became aware of soft fingers gently stroking the nape of her neck, softly, rhythmically. This, the first acknowledgement since she had walked into that room that she even existed, somehow it only seemed to be making things worse; she had been trying to compose herself, to pluck up the courage to speak out, but now even this train of thought was being rhythmically broken, the thread being taken from her with each stroke of those gentle fingers. Soothing, reassuring, yes, of course, yet seemingly robbing her of rational thought. She was gradually relaxing now, finding it easier to let her eyes close, the heavy lids already drooping, so easy to float along with the stream, just sit and listen, wait to be *told* what to do. She wouldn't have to decide, wouldn't have to make a decision, wouldn't have to face up to her lack of courage, her lack of self-confidence, she could just be a good girl. After all that Matron had had to say the doctor was clearly going to send her home anyway, she could just relax, drift away... The conversation continued around her like an enveloping cloud of drowsily droning honey bees on a summer's afternoon, just voices, discussing her, discussing her future.

Somehow, Susan pulled herself back into the present, back into the room, forced herself to address her situation. Something had jarred on her numbed senses: The doctor was talking.

"... I noticed a rather diagnostic odour in connection with the urine soaked towel that she produced earlier also. I believe you have voiced concerns that she may have a vaginal infection, Matron?"

"Yes, doctor."

The doctor scribbled something on a notepad before continuing: "Well, I'll examine her in a moment anyway, but nevertheless I think it best that she be started on suppositories for her constipation and I will prescribe a vaginal suppository douche as a precaution. I have seen infection show up as a complication of long-term wearing of incontinence pants in some patients, a necessary evil I'm afraid."

What was all this about? Why did she need suppositories, they were about to send her home, surely they were? The doctor was still speaking "... I believe her uniform has arrived, Matron?"

"Yes doctor, I have to apologise but apparently there were some complications, something to do with her measurements, I gather she has put a bit of weight on since she was measured, mostly around the buttocks and the bosom by the looks of things, anyway, Mrs Simmons has had to let out the bodice and let down the skirt hem slightly. She said she'd rather that than let out the seams so as to retain a good snug fit around the girl's hips. A slightly larger corselet has also had to be ordered, adding to the delay. The delivery arrived only just before her appointment was due so I'm afraid there was just not time enough to get her changed in time, sorry doctor."

"Yes, yes, quite understandable, Matron, but I'd like you to make sure she is put in uniform as soon as she is returned to her room"

"Yes, of course, doctor."

Susan was just stunned, her mind reeling, what was all this stuff about uniforms again? What uniform? What were they talking about?, What the point of any of it, she was going home, wasn't she?

For the first time the doctor's gaze met Susan's although she was still obviously addressing her staff, at least at this point. "I don't think we need send her home *just* yet, I doubt she really wants to give up this opportunity." There came a slight pause and then, now definitely addressing the girl: "... do you sweetheart?"

This was Susan's chance and yet she felt lost for words, she grasped for a sentence but before she could say anything the doctor went on, her attention now fully returned to her staff: "I don't think we need give up on her just yet, from my experience, once we have her in uniform compliance will come more naturally to her. Of course I will continue to monitor her progress but, depending on the reports I receive, I am considering her suitability to join the 'strict-education' group or possibly even the 'workhouse' group."

What?? Susan had heard enough, what was this?. This was it, she had to make a stand now. She wanted no more of this nonsense. "Now look here!" Well that at least was how she had intended her first strike to sound; somehow it was not quite how those present perceived it.

"P,p,ppplease dddoctor I,I I wwwant, I wwwant t, t,to ggggo hhhh..." She trailed off, couldn't quite get it out, was stopped in her stuttering tracks, startled, as, without even the slightest acknowledgement, without comment, the doctor rose and, turning on her heel, left the room by a side door that Susan had not been aware of up until now. In short, she was left sitting literally dumbfounded and open-mouthed. A voice came from over her left shoulder, sharp, penetrating, snapping her out of her dumb confusion; Matron's voice. "Up you get, girl" Matron, clearly irritated, her words delivered with punishing venom.

The First Blizzard of Eternal Winter; the Journey Home

The final fragments, the remnants of failed resolve, tumbled with fresh tears to be felt physically as might the last shards of the pane shattered by some pebble, carelessly tossed, seemingly without forethought yet damaging just the same. She started to stand yet felt faint, the snowdrift carpet rising up to greet the white clouded ceiling forming a sudden, unexpected and uncertain, horizon. Caring arms had rescued her, her fall averted by nurse and Matron both.

She was in the short corridor now, just outside the doctor's office, where for so long she had waited, where she had encountered that strange girl in the wheelchair. A jangle of keys and she was back in the main corridor, Matron leading the way, the nurse to the rear, close behind Susan and positioned slightly to one side so as to guide the still softly weeping girl with a comforting arm about her shoulders.

"Shhh, shhh, hush child" the nurse's eternally softly spoken West-Country lilt. So soon it had begun its soft velveteen bandaging, layer upon layer of the soft draping fabric protectively, malignly, enwrapping her wounds, swaddling her thoughts...and doing... *what* else to her?

It was doing *something*, that singsong voice, something she shouldn't allow, something she should try hard to fight; she knew that now, she *felt* that now. But then a long gentle finger languidly wandered down the nape of her neck, then again, then again, and again.

They were still walking and yet she was no more able to maintain a logical train of thought then she had in the doctor's office, a thought would form, a thread would be followed and then... there would come that gentle touch and she'd have to start over, start afresh. "It's all right; you will soon be back in your little room all nice, safe and sound. You've just been a silly girl, that's all, such a *silly* girl ".

Until that point the only sound had been the rhythmic swish of Matron's uniform skirt swinging to and fro against her nylon-stockinged calves. Now Susan found her gaze fixed on that hem, found it strangely fascinating, the white hem rocking to and fro, to and fro, juxtaposed against those tan seamed stockings. That was just it, the contrast; here was something more than just white upon white upon white. And then there was that finger, trailing its innocent path from hairline to collar and over again, innocent and yet so perfectly synchronised to the roll of those well shaped buttocks before her, the swing of that skirt hem. Once commanding little more than a cursory glance or, at most, an appreciation of a shapely feminine figure or of a well formed calf, to Susan or indeed any denizen of the clinic this was tantamount to sensory overload, totally fascinating, *hypnotic*.

Now the spell had been partially broken, although Susan's gaze was still glassy, unshifting, locked, held in part now by little glints and flashes of tiny, yet intense, shooting stars of colour. Greens, reds, blues, all originating from a simple button fastening a nurse's uniform cuff, flashes of light from just above the dainty, well manicured, hand. The nurse's arm now hung around the girl's shoulder, quite casually from a first glance and yet in truth there was some design to this positioning. Had not similar care been lavished upon the multi-faceted design of the button itself. Faceted, as were its matching siblings, one upon the other cuff, one fastening her collar at her throat and one positioned as the last button of her skirt at the hem, to reflect light in diamond-bright-rainbow hues. The face of the nurse's fob watch and the clasps upon her belt had had a similar treatment; each reflected light with every movement, each circulated a swirling, gyrating kaleidoscopic pattern of the purest laser-like hues. Only that buttoned cuff mattered here though, they walked, the nurse talked on, ever so gently, and equally gently that dainty hand and cuff rolled to and fro, to and fro, an exquisite swathe of colour reflecting rhythmically in the corner of the girl's eye.

"Yes a *very* silly girl, aren't you?"

"B,b,bbbut." Susan managed a rather pathetic attempt to interject, still wanting answers despite forever being told not to ask questions, desperately trying to put together some sort of logical argument, even if restricted to her own internal dialogue, desperately trying to think past the soothing interruptions of those insistently caressing fingers, the fiery flashes of light that more and more locked her gaze.

"No talking!" Matron's voice sharply rebuked her, the woman deeming it unnecessary to turn around to address her charge; such was her confidence in her command.

The nurse whispered now, more gently than ever, her breath sweetly playing around the girl's ear, prompting a shiver to run down her spine: "Now, now, there you go again. You know the rules here by now, 43C." The nurse went on almost as if she had not heard Matron, as if Susan and she were the only ones present. "I know Matron was annoyed with you but it's really not her fault you know, the doctor is so *very* insistent on the experimental protocol being followed to the letter. It *is* very important, any disturbance could invalidate the results obtained from the various experiments; you wouldn't want that would you 43C? You wouldn't want to let everyone down? Because that's what you would be doing, you know. You wouldn't want to let *me* down, now would you?"

Somehow Susan knew she was supposed to answer: "N,n no n nurse". Her reward came instantly as one must always reward obedience if one is training *any* animal let alone a young woman:

"That's a good girl". The nurse went on gently: "You see controls are very important in scientific studies and part of the precautions taken against different conflicting effects is to ensure that the subjects are all treated exactly the same way and that there are no outside influences. *That* is why we have the no-talking rule and that stipulation includes only ever *answering* questions, you do not *ask* questions, ever. You do not speak unless spoken to first, it's very simple, you know the rules don't you 43C?" Again Susan knew to answer. "Y yes n nurse" And again came her reward. "That's such a good girl; you *are* being a good girl."

159

"Have you noticed how your stammer isn't nearly so bad when you're being a good girl, sweetheart?

"Yes, nurse"

"Oh you *are* being a good girl, *such* a good girl. You trust me, sweetheart, you believe in me, you *have* to trust and believe in your nurse. All good girls should. You know that, don't you?"

"Yyes nurse". Susan could say nothing else, couldn't concentrate at all now, all she knew was that they were walking steadily down a corridor that went on forever, a beautiful and eternally white corridor, her gaze locked by the swinging hem to the front and the flashing swirling rainbow orbiting in her peripheral vision. Beautiful and fascinating words filled her mind, the nurse's kind words. Such *kind* words, so kind, so *gorgeous* that that they, themselves, as if through some twisted synesthesia, were striped and spangled with intensely stroboscopic, throbbing, colours. Words shaded by ever-shifting rotating spoked patterns, reminiscent of the beautiful face of the nurse's fob-watch at bedtime. Always she would be soothed off to a fluffy deep sleep by the nurse's kind words and her pretty fob watch with nary a murmur of resistance.

"You know the rules, 43C", she again insisted, "don't you?"

Susan heard a voice reply as if in a dream: "Yes nurse", only vaguely aware that it was her own, let alone stammer-free.

"You broke the rules by speaking to the doctor, it made you very unhappy, it has made Matron very unhappy and it has made *me* very unhappy, your nurse, your lovely, lovely nurse.

You don't *want* to be unhappy, you are so eager to please and yet you have failed, you have broken the rules and it's making you so, so unhappy, bringing on one of your panic attacks, you don't want that to happen, do you sweetheart?"

"No nurse, ppp please hhhelp mmme" Susan was becoming increasingly agitated; there was that growing feeling of panic again. One of her 'attacks' was coming on, she knew it but there was nothing she could do about it. Then there came the helplessness, then the awful, utter, despair; she needed help, desperately needed help…

"Shhh, it's all right, I'm here, your nurse is here, your lovely, lovely nurse is here with you. We are almost at your room now, you will feel safe in your room, but to really, really make everything better again, for you to really feel better, you must apologise to Matron and me, particularly to Matron. You must tell her how sorry you are otherwise your panic attack will just worsen again and then you would have to decide what to do and you know how hard you find it to make decisions. It makes you feel so panicky to have to make decisions. Remember the waves of panic you used to feel trying to decide what to wear, staring at your wardrobe, the room starting to spin? That is why you have to do as you're told, say what you have to say, wear what we are going to give you to wear, you know that is true don't you sweetheart?"

"Yes nurse."

"You are such a good, good girl".

Matron's key lightly jangled, a door opened and they were back in her room. She was all safe and sound, tucked up in her little cell.

CHAPTER 8

A GIRL ON A SCREEN: MEMORIES OF A FUTURE'S PAST

The girl on the screen was standing in near knee-length bloomers, the broad elasticated leg cuffs, the frilled decoration above, immediately identifying the latest, improved, incarnation of latex incontinence pants. Her arms were held straight and angled out from her sides, her dress hem, daintily pinched between finger and thumb of each hand as if mid way through some royal curtsy, was held out perpendicular to the belted waistband, the skirt's fabric held practically parallel to the floor. Those erstwhile thespians had gotten their cue - the smile flowered and matured, the eyes twinkled, the slender fingers typed some more.

A string of text ran across the bottom of the screen superimposed in yellow on top of the image:

Patient 08C, Age: 18 yrs 10 mnths, Current Exp: Obedience-training, Exp Time 3 mnths 2 wks 5 dys, Total Residency 2 yrs 1 mnth 3 dys. Status: volunteer test subject with guardian's waiver, Change of status: signed request to transfer to voluntary psychiatric patient status dated... signed preliminary power of attorney dated... Guardian has power of attorney until aged 21 contact guardian for all decisions.

Dr Anne Ecclestone was pondering, her chin resting on her hands and her elbows, in their turn, propped up on the desk; at just over two years not the longest-term test subject she had in residence but by far the youngest at entry, strictly speaking though she was no longer a test subject, hadn't been since... The doctor performed some nimble mental arithmetic: Three days, the girl had signed herself in as a voluntary psychiatric patient just three days after her eighteenth birthday. Ordinarily a voluntary psychiatric patient's status would be reviewed on a regular basis but her guardian had been granted power of attorney until the girls twenty-first birthday which effectively meant that the girl had agreed that she was presently not fit to make decisions pertaining to her own affairs.

In this particular case, then, the *voluntary* descriptor was somewhat illusory; until she reached the age of twenty-one the girl's guardian would decide whether or not her case should be reviewed. The woman, in her turn, had passed on the responsibility. She had signed a waiver effectively placing any such decisions in the hands of the clinic and so of Dr Ecclestone herself. The girl was now incarcerated as effectively as if she had been 'sectioned' under the mental health act, as if she were *compulsory* psychiatric patient.

The doctor gazed at the screen seemingly fascinated; the girl had been in her hands for just over twenty five months and she had her for another, what... very nearly two years and ten months wasn't it? By her twenty-first birthday, then, she will have been resident for the best part of five years.

Five years of her young life spent socially isolated while others of her age would be forming relationships, travelling, experimenting with new fashions, going out to clubs. A great sacrifice, true, but the insights into the effects of long-term institutionalisation that were emerging were invaluable.

Such a study as this had never been her intention at the outset; her primary interest had been, and remained, the genesis and propagation of phobias. The unique aspect offered had been the ability, in some cases, to test her hypotheses in ways that, in any other setting, would have been deemed unethical. But, at the end of the day, without her patron, Lady Marchment, there would be no such research or at least none as fruitful; she would be forever hobbled by misguided ethics committees and short-sighted deans.

After all, Lady Marion Marchment's company owned and ran the private nursing home wherein her office resided. Both personally and through her company she had a stated interest in the factors leading to the institutionalisation of long-stay patients. She held the purse strings and very much called the tune; the funding had come with the proviso that her area of interest should be investigated as much as the doctor's own. Indeed it was to be the primary concern in the development of the framework of the unit and all other research would have to be carried out within this framework and protocol structure.

Marion Marchment's approach was similar to that of Dr Ecclestone's indeed they had quickly developed a working relationship between them that was far closer than mere patron and employee. Marion's approach was very much hands-on, she was very much more than a titled rich businesswoman; did she not hold a degree in psychology from the prestigious Stanford University, California.

The two women had closely collaborated in the development of the clinic's experimental protocols. Many of the elements introduced in order to eliminate experimental variables, the strictly controlled and unvarying routine, the bells, indeed those elements that most seemed *guaranteed* to lead to the institutionalisation of patients, were of Lady Marchment's specialised input.

The presence of certain ' special' long-term patients, though, had led her to consider investigating certain other aspects that would be difficult or impossible, by dint of ethical considerations, to study otherwise. There was the effects of long-term imprisonment on cognitive function and free will; who would consider the girl currently on the screen before her as anything other than imprisoned? Any pretence of volunteer status had long since passed. Then there were the effects of the psychologically impoverished environment, the dehumanising and behaviour-modifying effects of the uniforms; the nurses standing tall and authoritative, empowered by *their* uniform, the subjects reduced, weighed down, by the humiliation of theirs. She had seen some dramatic effects in that area. Even the most charismatic of newcomer found herself unable to appear anything but compliant, submissive; within days that charisma was merely an ember, within weeks self-confidence had crumbled, all but forgotten; the remnants of self-respect and vanity were left there only that they might be punished away.

She looked again at the record laid out before her. Five years of the girl's life; incarcerated behind bars and under strict discipline, uniformed, conditioned and trained. Dr Ecclestone felt sure she would have no option other than to recommend a further extension of the girl's residency.

She wondered as to the girl's IQ, she was loath to administer a standard test as such would constitute, almost by definition, a high degree of mental stimulation thus invalidating one of the principal elements of the protocol. Intuitively she felt sure that the sensorially impoverished surroundings, the social isolation, not to mention the work they had done with her in the months she had spent in the confines of the 'schoolroom', would have dulled her mind to the tune of several IQ points. She made another of her little mental memos to herself; she would have to develop a way to assess these patients indirectly in some way.

Up on the screen there was a sudden flurry of movement, the girl, startled, the glazed eyes refocusing and shifting. She dropped her skirt and, turning away, performed two steps towards the desk at the far end of the room before dropping to her knees, throwing her arms forwards and burying her nose into the carpet in a classically-prostrate exhibition of supplication. The rounded globes of the girl's bottom now faced out from the screen, her skirt having ridden up, the smoothly curving white latex surrendering to a pink-tinted gloss wherever the restraint of her arrogantly out-swelling cheeks most tested the elasticity. The latter curved out tantalisingly from beneath its decoration of white frills, the cheeks widely spread by a central outward swelling that curved downwards to thicken and hang noticeably between the girl's parted legs, this being the external manifestation of the bloomer's integral absorbent pad. That such a precaution was necessary was confirmed by an irregular darkening, a brown-yellow spreading decolouration around the area of her anus and running down between her lower buttock cheeks, and a similar yellow-green tinting of the latex between her legs. The whole was framed attractively by the green and white striping of the girl's skirt and set off by the silver glint of the metal D-clip that hung on the outside of each leg-cuff.

She had been watching the girl's progress with interest and no little satisfaction. Her thoughts ran quickly to be echoed in the journal lying before her; the girl had needed two punishment sessions but had obeyed every instruction given her over the last two hours, she noted. From this point on two of her four waking hours were to be devoted to obedience training, the other two hours were to be devoted to rote learning. There would be interruptions only for meals, toilet, and sleep, the latter to be limited to two hours in every six. Her hypnotherapy sessions at bedtimes were to continue but otherwise members of staff were not to speak to her, she was to be kept in total social isolation other than experiencing her training. She was not to be allowed to dress or undress herself at any time, she was to be washed and cleaned by staff members. The cover on her toilet was to be kept locked, she was to be allowed to use a bedpan but only in the allotted periods and then only under strict supervision, after which she was to be cleaned up by a member of staff.

The instructions were to be sharpened up, the time allowed for hesitation reduced. The punishing nursery rhyme would play many, many times.

Chapter 8 | A Girl on a Screen …

As Dr Ecclestone had often remarked to Matron: "Hesitation, however brief, implies forethought and forethought implies some element of choice. Choice has no part to play in true obedience."

The initial month was to be flexible, extendible: the goal was first to achieve obedience without hesitation, without thought and then, as a next step, to withdraw the vocal commands leaving her controlled merely by a series of tones.

Was such as this, then, to be to be *Lavinia's* fate? Was *this* to be the life of Lavinia Vitesse, her world, for the next month, perhaps longer? Yes, perhaps longer. How long? What was to going to become of her? So *many* questions, such *delicious* possibilities.

But what of the new girl? What of our Susan?

Memories of the Future's Past

Susan sat her desk and waited, there was little else she could do under the circumstances; the ongoing problem with the alarm system had seen to that. The engineers had yet to localise the fault, she had been told, in the meantime the problem had seemed to have been getting gradually worse.

At one time she had been able to get to the little toilet pedestal or even the bed, just about, without setting off the alarm. Then, for a while, she could stand and move around in the immediate vicinity of the desk and chair, although moving further than half a meter or so from that area was met with the familiar brace of warning beeps. More recently she had found herself pretty much confined to the chair but now even that confinement could not, in itself, guarantee freedom from that hated banshee wailing; she had meant to lean back, to place her hands behind her head in relaxation. Then there had come the familiar and dreaded beeps. A little experimentation had quickly informed her that she was now obliged to keep both hands on the desktop if she was to avoid the alarm's torture. Irritated by this new restriction and yet accepting of it all the same she could do little but use the time to reflect on her situation, mull over the new developments and the events of the previous day, if day was truly the correct nomenclature; more accurate terminology might have been: 'the events previous to her most recent sleep period'.

Her recollection was pretty vague at best; her return to her room; *her* room? Was it? *Why* was it her room? At what point exactly had she started to consider it *her* room? The swirl of thought jumbled, tumbled around her blurred memories. Yes the outbound journey was pretty clear in her mind, if strangely labyrinthine. True she was not really certain where she had been, at least not in relation to her room, not in terms of absolute direction, of bearings. Truth be told, if pressed she would have been unable to point out the direction in which lay the doctor's room but she could at least clearly recollect going there.

And then, of course there was that particularly vivid recollection, the image indelible; that girl, the strange girl in the wheelchair. She recalled the feeling of compassion, of pity, the unease, those strangely elusive, pleading, eyes. Then there had been the doctor, the tall dominating figure, in recollection, seemingly filling the entire scene. There was the huge desk, and that feeling, the feeling that, retrospectively in her minds eye, she was experiencing again; the notion of becoming Alice, Alice-in-Wonderland, Alice-Through-The-Looking-Glass.

164

Chapter 8 | A Girl on a Screen …

That was *exactly* it, a shrunken Alice, the room seeming to grow the doctor, the furniture, looming-large above. There had been a sensation of not quite really 'being', a sense of insignificance and of utter impotence.

Then, she remembered, she had had to make a decision. Yes, she knew she wanted to go home it was just that she had to decide exactly what to say, exactly when to say it. Why should that have been so difficult? Why was it always so difficult? She recalled now how she had finally interrupted the doctor, in retrospect rudely. Why had she been so rude? It was rude to interrupt, she knew that, but she had had to say *something*, try to make her point, make her stand. She had kept putting off the moment, just couldn't decide what to do. She knew, now, it had been a bad decision, the wrong moment; she must have been rude, why else had the doctor walked out, she must have offended her. Why oh why had she been *so* rude?

All she had wanted was the chance to speak, they were ignoring her, she needed to say something, to stand up for herself, and they were just ignoring her as if she didn't exist, surely they were in the wrong for that, not her. Something about this last thought chilled her; there was a kind of dread attached to such thoughts. In her mind's eye she saw Matron standing with hands on hips, her nurse, the doctor, all accusing. No, no it was *her* fault, all her own fault; it had been rude of her. Matron had said that she was ignorant of decorum and etiquette and she was right. Now she would have to wait again, wait until the doctor had time to see her again.

It was obvious that there had been some sort of mix up somewhere, the way she was being treated was clearly evidence, but then again there had been all that talk about collecting samples. Surly the doctor must know that she is an experimental subject, a volunteer, not some mental patient to be kept locked up. It was equally obvious that she needed to speak to someone in charge, but who, if not this doctor, and how long would she have to wait now? Anger rose quickly in her only to be just as quickly replaced by tears of frustration, then tears of despair.

Recovering her composure she continued with her self analysis, only to find further frustration, her memory growing hazy at the point of the doctor's departure. One of her panic attacks, she felt sure. At what point in her life had *they* first started to manifest? Somehow she couldn't quite recall, they just seemed to have crept up on her; perhaps they had been stealthily and surreptitiously, taunting her for years, interrupting, interfering with her life, her plans.

It had needed a specialist to recognise it, to point it out, although, of course, it had been Aunt Julia who had first suspected there was a problem. It had needed Dr Ecclestone to diagnose it fully, it had been Dr Ecclestone who had first enabled Susan to recognise it in herself, admit to it. This was important, she knew. It was important to recognise one's problems, one's limitations, if one was to confront them, that was what Dr Ecclestone had said. What had she called it? Agoraphobia? Yes, that was it, agoraphobia-linked panic attacks. She said it was probably behind her tendency to indecisiveness and, what was more, unless she confronted it, admitted to it, and this was important, it could, and would, get worse, become debilitating, ultimately leave her housebound. She remembered how frightened she had been at this prognosis. Now this dread was back, along with the certainty that her attacks were indeed becoming worse, and more frequent.

Susan spurred herself on; somehow retracing her steps back to her room in her minds eye was important to her in dealing with this new fear, this dread of the truth of Dr Ecclestone prognosis. Yes, she could remember quite clearly being let back into her room; she again bristled at this thought, her acceptance of this grotty institutional room. In truth Matron had merely unlocked the door and, tellingly one may think, the girl had walked in when bidden without protest or hesitation and had taken her seat at Matron's brusque order: "Sit up straight, girl, hands flat on your desk, palms up".

Susan could clearly recall the feeling of humiliation that had accompanied her obedience. She recalled, too, glancing across at the toilet, to where the ruined carpet lay or rather should have lain. Nothing but the purest white; no stain, no odour. How had they got it cleaned up so thoroughly and so rapidly. A different room? Yes, a different room, had to be, she had thought dully to herself, as if it really didn't matter any more. She certainly couldn't tell one way or another. Everything was the same, was always the same, nothing ever changed here. She had sat waiting for a while, not knowing, never knowing, how long but she remembered that it couldn't have been *very* long; she hadn't drifted away, off into her customary land of daydream.

And then came the moment that was burnt into her memory more thoroughly even than even her encounter with the wheelchair-girl had been; they had dressed her in that awful uniform for the first time. Matron's return had been signalled by the faint dull thud of the door behind her. Before she knew it she had found herself back out in the corridor again, just two doors along this time. Strangely this was a plain door, there was just a keyhole, no reference number, or whatever it was, as there was on her door and the doors on either side of hers, come to that there wasn't even a plate holder. That was what had seemed so strange for she felt sure, had made a mental note of the fact, that all the doors in this corridor were like hers; either numbered or at least having the plate holder for a number, and for that reason she had assumed that all the neighbouring rooms were residential. She couldn't have been mistaken she was sure and yet moments later and with the flourish of a key Matron had ushered her into a shower-room, she had recognized it instantly as the shower room from her first day at the clinic. Now, in hindsight, she knew it couldn't have been. How could it? There had been the ride in that lift, the walk through the corridors, more than one set of security grilles to be negotiated. No, no she was on a different floor. Still, it was disorientating, the two shower rooms were not just similar they were totally and utterly identical.

There were a couple of differences, though more procedural than architectural. Yes there was the white laundry basket as before and as before she was bidden to fill it with her soiled clothing but the apparel that had begun to pile in rubbery glossy folds of pearl-white had been a strange sight indeed, not the fashionable attire of the young lady in her late teens that had arrived, how long ago?. And then there was that smell, certainly absent on that first day. On the examination couch had lain a white plastic suit-bag that fastened up the centre with a stout zipper that Matron had struggled with as Susan showered.

The first glimpse of green and white fabric had initiated an unconscious groan from the girl, her heart falling as apparel, somehow even less appropriate than that which now lay discarded, had been carefully, neatly, *fetishistically*, arranged. Matron had turned on her heel and left then, taking with her the laundry basket. Susan had been left alone, the terse order issued in parting ringing in her ears: "I want you dressed by the time I get back". She had stood dumfounded, defensively hugging the tiny white towel around her as if to shield her person, her individuality, from the violation threatened by the items laid out before her. She remembered only too clearly how she had felt surveying that scene, the dismay, the dread, a particular dread being reserved for the ugly green and white striped dress taking centre stage.

She had done the best she could, there was little choice with her discarded things gone and they in themselves symbolised their own peculiar brand of torment. Throughout she had felt as if she was swallowing her pride with each fastening, hands shaking, and then there was the unfamiliarity of some of the items.

Matron had returned and, although Susan feared the worst, did not seem particularly upset that she had made such little progress, rather she had seemed pleased to find that Susan was getting on with it, perhaps expecting a more rebellious reaction then a pout and a quiet tear.

Yes, she remembered clearly how quickly, with Matron's aid, she had been dressed in that awful uniform for the first time then led back out into the corridor for the short walk to her room, head hung, weighed down by that awful feeling of defeat. She remembered being ushered back into her room, back to the desk, yet again, but now in that damn uniform. How different it had felt, how different it felt now, so final somehow, she felt crushed, something had been taken from her, something had been broken inside her. They had broken some part of her in that action, simply by putting her in that uniform.

No memory had ever been clearer than this, at any time in her life, the way she had felt, the thoughts that had run through her mind, new thoughts, intrusive thoughts, crushing thoughts. She had sat there, at that desk, in that uniform, the locks, the bars, the security grillees and barred windows, all these things had suddenly seemed to have taken on a new significance. And then her thoughts had been interrupted, although not entirely unexpectedly, merely the clockwork institutional routine continuing on unabated around her and careless of her mental turmoil. The usual mealtime bell had rung, the usual mealtime routine, then more waiting, more time to think, finally the ringing of the sleep-time bell had been gratefully welcomed, the comfortable constancy of routine embraced now with both arms. She recalled how she had yawned, exhausted, ready for sleep. She recalled too the disconcerting changes, changes introduced so gently, changes, she now accepted, that would soon become an invariant part of her routine. And she was comforted by that thought.

Now of course there was the uniform, the undressing, each item to be folded neatly and in a particular and specific way. And then there were the prescribed glycerine suppositories, the burden of this task falling to her nurse. Finally having to change into the latex nightgown now came almost as a respite. The hospital incontinence-bloomers with their thick sanitary towel, despite the humiliation inherent in their nature, now brought with them their own friendly brand of warm familiarity.

She had felt safe, reassured, the memory of these feelings particularly clear in her mind. The sleep time bell had continued throughout, of course, and she had found that she could hardly keep her eyes open, gratefully slipping down beneath the covers, her nurse leaning over her, the nurse's soft lilting voice, the light, the heavenly colours glinting off those buttons on her uniform, the nurse's fob watch gently swinging to-and-fro, to-and-fro, to-and-fro...

Now it was morning, or, at least, wake-up time. The wake-up bell had slapped her awake, it felt different today, it *was* different today. For one thing there were the physical aspects, her arms, down by her sides, now entirely useless to her. A refinement "well suited for noncompliant patients." She clearly recalled Matron remarking so to the nurse when she had brought in the new bloomers. These were of rubber rather than the PVC of her previous pair, thicker, larger and with longer legs; now the elasticated leg-cuffs rested just above her knees. She remembered her initial reaction to their appearance, being somewhat bizarrely decorated around each leg cuff with three rows of frills as if appearance was somehow important; a stylistic element hopelessly out of place on such an obviously functional garment and anything but cheering for the patient.

Of course the rationale behind this latter element would have been quite clear to any privileged enough to have observed the scene, any privileged enough to have shared in the amusement so clearly externalised in the smile that had spread across Matron's, otherwise stern, countenance. Indeed, it must be said that, despite her usual professional detachment, the nurse too, had been unable to quite fully conceal a certain patronising aspect that had intruded into her, otherwise familiar, sweet smile, betraying a secret, some might say inappropriate, pleasure, that ran far beyond any legitimate professional satisfaction.

The waistband was far thicker than that of her previous pair, being of over a centimetre in thickness. It was broad too, perhaps of a full three centimetres in depth. It had been clear to the girl, from the moment that Matron had held them out for her to step into, that both the waistband and, indeed, the body of the knickers themselves were semi-rigid. A reinforced stiffened framework was embedded throughout the rubber fabric, the most obvious feature being the rounded reinforced centre seam, perhaps as thick as a rather slender index finger, which ran from the lower edge of the waistband at the rear in a smooth curve down to the crotch area were upon it ran off into two opposing arcs, neatly delineating an ovoid space of roughly the size and shape of the average female genitalia, before again becoming one at the front of the crotch area and sweeping smoothly up to join with the lower edge of the waistband at the front.

Internally the most outstanding features apart from the elasticated straps which Susan had seen before, of course, and knew functioned to retain the sanitary towel, were two inwardly directed crooks in the centre seam, each forming a shape not unlike a knuckle on a tightly bent finger and resulting in the indentation of the seam by around two centimetres at roughly the position of the anus and by approximately three centimetres at the front of the ovoid crotch panel at the point at which the two curving oval sides rejoined to continue the central seam, this latter feature imparting a semi-conical shape to the invagination.

168

Having stepped into them the function of these latter features became abundantly clear as Matron, having retrieved a thick pad from a white box she had previously positioned on the bed, squatted to fit a large thick sanitary towel. This towel, being far thicker and longer than the one that had been used with her previous knickers, was held in place both by the straps to the front and rear and by locating onto the two centre seam invaginations, the towel or pad being of a semi moulded design and indented at these points. Looking down as she bent to pull up her knickers Susan's impression was that of some medical rubberised and padded variation on the mediaeval chastity belt; assurance of propriety being one such function, it must be said, that the garment did indeed share with its mythical mediaeval counterpart.

As with her previous knickers, as with these, the bloomer styling was retained, the usual loose bloomer-style legs hanging baggily from the semi-moulded body before terminating in broad, frilled, elasticated leg-cuffs. Susan had found that she had to wiggle her hips in order to ease the waistband up and over. As she had done so she had let out a little, involuntary, gasp of surprise and consternation; the indented pad and seam pressed up against her anus and outer vaginal lips constraining her in her efforts to slip the waistband over the final curve of her upper hips.

There had come an irritated 'tut' from behind her and she had found herself aided; the nurse reaching around her, giving a smooth but firm pull on both sides of the waistband while simultaneously clicking shut the integral spring-loaded lock and catch mechanism at the rear as the waistband slipped into its final resting place, slightly constricting and clinching the centre of the girls waist.

Susan remembered clearly the sensation of personal violation, those knuckle-like features and the moulded absorbent pad had penetrated her anus and the outer lips of her vagina. She had seen Matron apply a clear gel to the indented regions of the pad and had assumed, correctly, that it was some sort of medicated cream, she had now learnt of another of its functions, that of lubricant.

The nurse had stood back to admire her handiwork from the rear, to run her fingers across the slight thickening at the rear of the waistband wherein it accommodated the lock. The tiny keyhole was clearly visible at the point at which the waist band nestled in at the small of the girls back. An almost perfect fit, she observed, not tight, just firm; fitting close enough it to prevent removal yet not so tight as to cause undue discomfort to the patient. Susan could recall this point only too well; it was the point at which she had first become aware that something was dangling free, swinging loosely against the sides of her knees. She remembered looking down, wondering, noticing for the first time that some sort of white nylon clip was hanging from the outside of each leg cuff. The closest thing in her experience to these, the first thought that came into her mind, was of the type of snap-clip that one might find used to attach a dog's lead to its collar. Moments later and Susan had been enlightened to both the function of these clips and, for the first time, the relevance of the metal-lined eye residing in each wrist cuff of her nightdress.

The nurse, reaching forward from behind her, had quickly guided each of the girl's hands down by her sides, her wrists coming level with those leg-cuffs, and, moments later, each clip was neatly located in the eye of the corresponding nightdress wrist cuff.

A quick and simple device, but effective enough, for all that, to deter even the most determined patient from interfering with her incontinence arrangements. True this enforced a slightly stooped posture when standing but this was of little or no consequence to the comfort of the patient once in her bed, requiring only a partial adoption of the foetal position for perfect comfort. In any case Matron took the view that practicality took precedence in these matters; whether a patient be disturbed, incontinent or both, or indeed, as in this case, was undergoing long-term suppository or enema treatment, her primary concern was for the welfare of the patient, *visa vie* the hazard to health posed by any inappropriate contact with various bodily products. A secondary concern was the maintenance and care of hospital property of course. Both of these concerns could be dealt with by the simple expedients of ensuring the use of carefully designed sanitary wear and, of course, taking the appropriate measures to ensure that a patient didn't get her fingers where they had no right to be. Matron had seen, in the past, the way in which an 'accident' could trigger the most irrational behaviour, even in the psychological stable. If free to tamper the patient would likely only exacerbated the situation.

The girl's waking hours would be a different matter of course, these precautions then complicated by the emphasis placed by the sponsors on decorum and the weight they attributed to matters of appearance and standards of dress. Indeed, Matron herself had been closely involved with the design of the subject's uniforms and, under her guidance and influence, the uniform that had evolved allowed for, and was able to accommodate, a wide range of medical contingencies, feminine hygiene issues and, of course, humiliation possibilities.

CHAPTER 9

TEMPUS FUGIT, QUI BONO?

Yet again the bell had quite literally dragged her awake, how many times now, how many mornings? Certainty was impossible here, many things were.

Once she would have reached out dreamily to flop a drowsy hand upon the 'snooze button', before could returning to the escape of sleep, at least temporarily. Silencing the alarm, turning over, dozing, these were not options here, not here, not in *this* place. The bell rang, a nurse arrived, one got out of bed, it was as simple as that, an unchanging ritual.

Her nurse was at her bedside again, as always, bending, releasing the toggles with her left hand while pulling back the cover with her right. Susan, still heavy with sleep and yawning deeply, began to uncurl from her semi-foetal sleeping position. She stretched out in an automatic preliminary to sitting up, her legs straightening with a satisfying tensing of muscles, her arms though finding their path prematurely terminated by an elastic tug on each wrist accompanied by a squeezing-pull on each thigh, the restriction somehow unexpected despite...how many encounters?. The recollection of her bloomers' anti tamper mechanism, of her helplessness, came next, it always did; the awful realisation of dependency shaking her awake with all the vigorous efficacy of a bucket of ice cold water thrown full in the face.

Yes, changes had been made all right; new rituals had become accustomed, new procedures, new sensations, had been encountered and were novel no longer, yet not customary either. Currently it was primarily the aspect of sensation that concerned the girl. This was something genuinely new. There was the abdominal aching for one thing, the cramping of stomach muscles, bowels knotting. Then there came the screaming urgency. Now, having been helped up, sitting on the edge of the mattress, arms still resting uselessly against her rubber-sheaved thighs, there was another sensation, if anything even more unsettling.

She could recall distinctly how, as a toddler, she used to mess around in the little field behind her home. A particular occasion now came to mind; It had been a hot day and she had pulled off all her clothes, she remembered how she had stumbled, fallen backwards to end up sitting in a warm fresh cow pat, she clearly remembered the sensation, the smell, *the revulsion*. The sensation had come to her as a shock as she had sat up, the warm, sticky, dampness so reminiscent of something familiar and yet just out of reach, just out of reach until the resurrection of this once faded, once vague, memory.

Her emotions kicked in slowly at first. Initially there was the undefined feeling of revulsion, then disgust as the realization sunk in, as the memory sharpened, as comparisons were made and confirmed. Finely there was the panic, arising not so much from the here and now as from the memory itself; to be more specific it was the memory of the field, of the open sky. Somehow this part of the scene was the vaguest, the least certain, yet the more she thought about it the more she tried to put it from her mind, she wanted it to recede. It was the open space itself, it was the panic. She had been, and was now becoming, dizzy with panic. It was a *pursuing* panic; it was close behind, catching her, gaining on the present, encroaching on the here and now, invading the safety of her room.

She stood up, shot to her feet in fact, almost tumbling forward as her wrist cuffs tugged against their fastening at her thighs, her mind now in a turmoil of revulsion, dread and panic. She wanted those knickers off now, right now, had to get them off. She struggled blindly, her first reaction, to tug down the offending knickers, thwarted both by the attachment of the nightdress wrist cuffs to the bloomers' leg cuffs and by the latter's firmly locked waistband.

The startled nurse ceased her preparations, turning to see her charge's struggles, as she danced around semi-stooped. A look of amusement momentarily crossed the pretty nurse's face before subsiding below the carefully rehearsed façade of professional and authoritative detachment; with elbows wing-flapping out from her sides with effort the girl, her charge, looked for all the world like some deformed and demented captive rubber butterfly.

Nurse Gerstein: The Bedside Manner Doth the Nurse Make

The girl was becoming irrational, wild eyed, the nurse hid her smile, now was the time to act, to gain control. "Stop that – now!" The voice, penetrating, with razor-sharp tongue. "Stop that, at once!". It had taken a second, repeated, command, to cut through but cut through it had, yanking the girl back from the impending panic attack as a hand might drag a half drowned waif from the icy waters of an oily-dark pool.

Her nurse had regained control and she was grateful. The nurse, for her part, had to admit to a certain sense of relief. She placed a calming arm around the girls shoulders, drawing her close, simultaneously guiding the girl's head with her other hand to come to rest, side on, upon her cushioning breasts.

The glint of the nurse's fob watch had caught Susan's eye almost immediately: There were reds and blues and greens, all flickering in synchrony with the rise and fall of the nurse's white-uniformed bust and pulsating with every breath. Already she felt herself relaxing, watching the fascinatingly smoothly gliding path of the little silver-sparkling second hand across the swirling spiral-patterned facets of the face.

Not for the first time she idly, dully, wondered at the lack of minute and hour hands. For a moment, but just for a moment, she thought about the first time she had noticed. How she had tried to get close enough, how she had tried to read the time from the nurse's watches, when time really mattered. It all seemed so very long ago now. It didn't really matter, not at all, not if she could just relax. If she relaxed she would feel just wonderful.

It was so, so, wonderful not to have to worry about time, about things, things to do, decisions to be made, wonderful just to be told what to do, when to do it, not have to worry about it.

The sweeping hand continued along its arc, crossing counter-revolving digits as if to further invalidate the utility of the time piece, the entire watch face with its glinting swirling vivid-hued facets having begun to rotate in opposition in response to the discreet operation of a hidden button.

The nurse let her hand slowly raise so as to better cradle the glassy-eyed girl's head while allowing her fingers to gently stroke the girl's right temple, adding the comforting familiarity of this caress to her equally comforting words and suggestions. The light, reflecting multihued from the faceted cuff button of her uniform would add to the spell; this was the way she had been training the girl, the way she trained all her patients. She looked down at the entranced girl's face, smiling to herself; it had been so easy to train this girl, she had been so well prepared by Dr Ecclestone before she had come here, it had been easy, almost too easy for her taste.

She had trained the girl first to the special buttons she wore on her, otherwise quite standard, nurse's uniform, had trained her to feel relaxed, feel herself giving in, just at the mere sight of her uniform. She had trained the girl to find her eyes attracted to the flash of those buttons and to her belt buckle. Finally she had introduced the use of her watch, at first subtly, guiding the girl's eyes to it after an initial induction utilising her uniform buttons or belt buckle. The girl had responded well throughout that initial period; it had been simplicity itself to convince her of the belief that the relaxation she so craved could only be found in the lovely rainbow-shifting pinwheel patterns of light reflected from the face of the nurse's fob-watch she wore pined to her dress.

That time had passed now, now at bedtime she simply unclipped the watch and held it in front of the girl's eyes, compliance requiring only that she command the girl in an authoritative tone, whispering a post-hypnotic key phrase. The mere sight of her, in her nurse's uniform, the special faceted glinting buttons, was now enough to subdue any sense of defiance that the girl might still harbour, leaving her weak and susceptible.

For Susan's part the nurse's uniform, the very special uniform of her nurse, seemed so totally fascinating. The other nurses too, even Matron, the sight of them in their uniforms, even the standard nurses uniforms, there was something about it, about them, they all looked so authoritative, her very being, her will, seemed to crumbled to dust. She just felt *so* insignificant in comparison, was so insignificant, so small. Susan drooled, gazing glassy-eyed like some wide eyed living-doll in her nurse's arms, totally unconcerned about the whispered suggestions chiselling away at the very foundations of her soul.

Every Silver Lining Has a Cloud

Now came one of the less appealing aspects to her work, "every silver lining has a cloud on the horizon" as she liked to say. The girl hadn't actually had an 'accident' *per se*, this she could tell from experience , but the suppositories that had been prescribed contained a stool softener in addition to the laxative component and so it was only to be expected that there would have been a certain amount of what ,in medical parlance, was euphemistically described as 'passive anal leakage'.

The, much larger, vaginal-douche suppository, of course, would have completely dissolved by now, encouraged by the trapped heat in those sweaty, all encompassing knickers and the resulting soft gel, in its designed oozing, would have added its contribution. The latter, being, of necessity, gel-like and being too viscous to be have been absorbed by the towel, would have pooled; its efficacy as a douche, although undoubted, could lead to particularly unpleasant results at times.

Nurse Gerstein could well imagine the disconcerting sensation the girl was presently experiencing and both understood and expected the girl's panic, especially in combination with the, still unfamiliar, anti-tamper precautions. In truth she would have been disappointed otherwise and knew well how to deal with this situation, particularly with this girl, a girl who had been so obviously well and expertly prepared prior to her admission.

Now that the girl had been calmed the retaining clips could be removed from her nightdress' wrist-cuffs. So freed from her unaccustomed restraint, Susan had further regained her composure, as the woman knew, from experience, she would. The nurse had placed the diaper pail next to the toilet in preparation, alongside a one metre square white plastic sheet, the latter positioned so as to protect the carpet, 'just in case'. The nurse quickly guided the girl across to the site of her preparations, positioning her patient to stand in the protective sheet's centre.

The tiny key fitted smoothly enough, a half turn at the rear of the waistband was all it took and the sprung steel embrace relaxed, the girls knickers being left secured only by the garment's inherent rubbery elasticity. The girl was clearly having difficulty standing still, from time to time clutching at her abdomen as spasmodic cramps rippled through her, the urgency growing with every passing second. Nurse Gerstein didn't have long, she could tell from the girl's face, she had to put aside her distaste, work quickly now. Without further ado she whisked the knickers to the floor, simultaneously tapping each of the girl's ankles in turn with her foot in what she hoped was an obvious signal to step out, all the time trying to ignore the obnoxious odour now beginning to permeate the room, a semi-medicated fishy-faecal aroma that was, as far as nurse Gerstein could tell from her experience, peculiarly unique to this institution, not quite enough to make one retch but very unpleasant all the same.

Indeed the magnitude of this latter unpleasantness could now be read upon the girl herself, bright red cheeks hotly hidden behind cupped hands, an attempt to hide the deep shame and soul shattering humiliation, an attempt doomed to fail, her lips moving in a sobbing half whispered stammering: "ppplease".

Quiet and subdued the sound may well have been, yet not so quiet as to have been missed by Nurse Gerstein and serving only to attract the latter's attention to her charge's reaction. Sharply:

"No talking girl." Then, more softly, gently almost soothingly: "Come along now, you know the rules about talking. Now, take your hands away from your face, come along girl, that's it, hands down by your sides".

The camera was tiny, well hidden, but it picked out every detail, every nuance of expression on the bright red, shame etched face of the squirming teenager. A secret prearranged signal from nurse Gerstein and the toilet bell tolled. "On the toilet, now!" Susan required no second order this time, she almost threw herself down onto the low-slung toilet seat in desperation, her body's response to the impact-spreading of her buttocks across that miniature almost child sized toilet pan was as immediate as it was explosive.

Nurse Gerstein stood in front of the squatting girl, arms folded across her ample bosom. A smile of satisfaction momentarily flickered across her face; as much as she sought to deny it its existence nevertheless, for a fleeting moment, her emotion had betrayed her, had made public her darkest recesses. True there was more work to be done, preparations to be made, but time management was not her primary concern here; after all, was this not all part of the treatment, the supervision? She could deal with the girl's soiled undergarments later.

In the fullness of time the bell ceased its ringing, silence once again reigned. Susan looked up feeling exhausted, she wasn't at *all* sure that she was finished, she felt as if, perhaps, there was more to come but she had been told to stand up. She had little desire to remain squatting and squirming in front of this woman in any case.

The nurse having stood over her throughout, no more than a metre to the front, watching intently, taking notes, she had been glad of that bell, the ringing offered at least *some* camouflage, some cover, for the more embarrassing noises that accompany such a traditionally private function. Now again silently-exposed she was keenly aware of the few terminating plops and other sounds as she regained her feet once more. The smell was worse now of course, now that she had stood clear of the pedestal, an even greater intensity of burning spread across her face, she felt literally blinded by shame now; she hardly knew where she was.

Behind her she heard the toilet flush, automatically, the sound offering some token of relief in the knowledge that the source of her shame, or at least part of it, had now been removed from her room. Before her, though, as the nurse stood to one side, more shame awaited; she was greeted by the sight of her discarded soiled knickers and sanitary towel where they lay heaped on the plastic sheet.

The nurse, without comment, held out a small, wide necked, bottle, a sample bottle. It had been proffered her at the start of her ablutions along with the instruction to hold it under the flow of her first urine. Blinded then, both by shame and the pain of her convulsing bowels, she had pushed the nurse's hand aside. Now it was being proffered again. Susan, standing semi-naked, her never regions only partially hidden by the short flared skirt of the latex nightdress, felt crushed; it was obvious that the intention was for her to urinate into this bottle as she stood there, in front of the nurse and, worse still, with the nurse holding the bottle for her.

Chapter 9 | Tempus Fugit, Qui Bono?

The latter intent had been made clear to her by the fact that the nurse had freshly donned a pair of white latex examination gloves. Deep down, subconsciously, she registered, correctly, that this part of the proceedings was by way of a kind of punishment, a punishment for her lack of compliance.

"We must have a urine sample in here" The nurse sounded angry, but only momentarily then her voice softened, adopting her usual coaxing tone. "It's okay this time, sweetheart, but next time you must hold it in the flow of your first urination of the day, it really is quite important you know. We don't want to upset Matron, now do we?" So saying the nurse stooped slightly, holding the bottle in position.

Try as she might Susan was unable to produce more than a few drops. Strangely, the nurse didn't seem overly irritated by this, merely turning away momentarily to seal the bottle and place it in its holder on her tray, her voice remaining soft as she did so: "We'll see how well you get on next time, perhaps it would be easier for you if I were to recommend catheterisation".

Turning around from her tray she held out a small square white cotton pad, perhaps of six centimetres on a side. "We need a stool sample, sweetheart, it's easiest if I just take an anal swab before you wipe your bottom" Now Susan realised there was another reason for the nurse to be wearing those latex gloves. She shuddered inwardly at the nurse's next words. "Bend over and grasp your ankles, sweetheart".

Susan's initial, unsurprising, reluctance was quickly met with a sharp rebuke. "Come along, it doesn't hurt, just a quick wipe and it's done and over with". Not for a moment had Susan even begun to consider that it would hurt, at least not physically, but her pride, her modesty, these were different matters entirely.

This further delay was not unexpected and nurse Gerstein had an ace up her sleeve, a contingency solution used many times before. She began to gather her things as if to leave, making a rather obvious and theatrical point of packing away the toilet roll in so doing. Susan's concern must have been immediately obvious. "Well, sweetheart, I have to take it away with me when I leave you know, it's the rule, it's not my fault, I don't make the rules you know."

Susan didn't know what do, finally she opened her mouth as if to apologise, to plead. "I,I I" was all she managed before the look of anger crossed the nurse's face and a sharp rebuke was issued. "No talking, girl, did I ask you anything, did I ask you a question?"

"N n no, n, nurse."

"Then what do you say, girl."

"I'm so s s ssorry n, nnurse" Susan stammered out, remembering the correct form of apology. The nurse smiled again, Susan felt glad.

"That's a good girl, sweetheart. Now, would you like one more chance, for being such a good girl, for apologising properly?"

"Y,y yes p p please n, nurse." Susan sniffed a bit at this, unable to stifle a wayward tear.

"Bend over and grasp your ankles please. Come on, quick as you can."

Susan did as she was told. The swabbing, as promised, taking mere moments, yet taking some part of her with it, some fragment of her essential 'self'.

176

"I take it you're capable of wiping your own bottom when you're finished?" So saying she passed Susan a few meagre sheets of toilet paper.

"Yess n nurse, thank yy you nnnurse" Susan had begun to straighten up but a firm hand, pressing down between her shoulder blades, halted her part way.

"I want you to stay in position and do it" Susan was left gripping her left ankle with her left hand while reaching back between her legs, grasping the paper sheets and scrubbing away at the mess with her right.

All the while she was inwardly cringing at the scene she was providing. Outwardly her sobs were reward enough indeed for Nurse Gerstein's efforts in breaking her. She had failed again, failed to deprive the nurse of the satisfaction of a reaction, failed to hold back those tears, tears only supplementing the crushing misery of the humiliation bearing down on her.

At last Susan was allowed to straighten up. At first there was relief, then came further mortification; she was instructed to hold out the soiled paper for inspection. This had been a spur-of-the-moment refinement on the part of Nurse Gerstein but, having surveyed and appraised the effect on the girl, she quickly made a mental note to retain this procedure as a permanent part of the girl's regime.

She reached out to the girl, the offer of a motherly embrace gratefully accepted, her voice calming, soothing. With murmuring praising words she reassured, even as, with practiced eye, she surveyed the damage, inwardly basking in the glow of satisfaction that comes from the knowledge of a job well done.

Outwardly her smile beamed friendly reassurance, the promise of support written across those finally defined Nordic features, every inch the supportive nurse. Inwardly she smiled too, a different kind of smile, a smile that, had the girl been privy to it, would have sent ice to chill her soul. It was a smile of extreme satisfaction, a satisfaction that, although Saffron Gerstein herself would have consciously denied it, bordered on the sexual. Perhaps it not just bordered, perhaps to the subconscious Saffron Gerstein this *was* sexual satisfaction. Whatever its nature, there was little denying the building sense of excitement that ran through her as she viewed her charge; the girl's natural shyness, her guarded modesty, her readiness to tears so soon. Yes, this was the way forward with this girl.

She held the girl close, embracing her as her mind feverishly began to sketch out her report and recommendations. Catheterisation? Definitely and, perhaps later, she might recommend anal and vaginal dilating grommets be fitted.

Outside, her calm exterior remained steady, detached, but internally, well, that was a different matter. Internally Saffron Gerstein was on fire, the excitement reaching fever pitch as she imagined the effect on her charge of having to wear a pair of examination knickers once she had had a vaginal dilator fitted.

Turning away, leaving the girl standing, she squatted to retrieve the swollen, soiled, pad, quickly dumping it with some distaste into the diaper bucket, whereupon its safe arrival was confirmed both by the heavy squelching-wet thud and the attendant malodorous reminder of its nature.

Susan cringed inwardly, surely death would be preferable to this, if only she would just drop down dead, or the floor would open up to swallow her or perhaps, just perhaps, she would wake up, surely this had to be a nightmare. If it was then, perhaps she was destined never to be woken up.

Chapter 9 | Tempus Fugit, Qui Bono?

The nurse moved over to the bed carrying with her the white tray, with its various sample containers and packets, and the small white plastic diaper pail. Now Susan was again confronted by the sight of those hated knickers, squatting there before her on the plastic mat, semi-crumpled yet retaining enough structure as to almost appear occupied, as if possessed of their own life-force.

Matron surged through the door with such rapidity that Susan barely glimpsed the corridor beyond before the familiar low soft thump signalled its closing. Susan noted she had heard no key, no fumbling, no clicks, in fact nothing that suggested the unlocking of a door.

She had noticed these things before and was beginning to wonder if perhaps the door remained unlocked while there were staff present. From time to time the notion would come to her that perhaps she could just dash past, simply just run out. The answer was always the same of course, where would she run *to*?

She knew that the doors at both ends of the corridor outside concealed behind them a grille of steel bars running floor-to-ceiling with passage only possible via a locked and very secure gate. Furthermore she knew that beyond lay other featureless corridors, more steel security grilles with locked and barred gates and finally of course, should she even find it, even if she knew in which direction to head, there was the elevator, itself key-operated and, effectively, yet another secure, impenetrable barrier.

There were windows, yes, but each of those was protected by a tough security grille and beyond that, beyond the frosted glass, on the outside, perhaps glinting under a golden sun, there were bars; after all, had she not seen their shadows?.

Yes it was only too clear that she was not to leave until someone, somewhere, decided it was time for her to leave and only then.

True, she had never heard the sound of a key in the lock, not at any time, but she had decided that this was likely due to the thickness of the door, the padding, or soundproofing For whatever the reason she could assume that her door was kept securely locked at all times. Matron would never allow such a lapse in security. Whether it be from the habit of dealing with disturbed patients in locked wards or whether because, perhaps, they shared facilities and accommodation with actual psychiatric patients in some part of a secure psychiatric wing, she didn't know.

The latter case seemed more likely and in some ways was a preferable scenario, providing successful explanation for both the security arrangements and the presence of that girl in the wheelchair. The thought was comforting in a way, helping to assuage that disturbing image that had burned in her mind since she had met the girl. Yes, that was the best explanation, the easiest, most comforting explanation; the security arrangements could be explained, and yet there was the disturbing belief that she, herself, had somehow become misidentified, perhaps through some sort of clerical error, as one of the patients.

The tight security insured she would be safe of course but did nothing to relieve her growing sense of imprisonment. That uniform, the way it made her feel, the way it seemed to amplify the feeling of oppression, of imprisonment: She had been numbered, depersonalised, locked away behind bars, dressed in what to all intents and purposes was a prison uniform.

178

Matron stooped to pick up the discarded knickers then, holding them out in front of Susan, allowed a carefully crafted expression of revulsion to cross her face. "Come along, girl; let's get those knickers back on"

Susan's reluctance was easy to read causing Matron, wrinkling her nose in disgust, to exclaim: "Phew, well I suppose they *are* somewhat unpleasant. You can give them a quick wipe over with a piece of toilet paper first, if you must, but better get a move on. We really must get on now, the doctor wants to see you again just as soon as you are showered and dressed". She continued, now with a note of threat colouring her voice "…or you can choose to go without knickers, if you are that sort of girl, it's up to you".

There was to be another break in routine! She was to see the doctor again and so soon! She had feared that many days, even weeks, might pass, had been warned that the doctor was a very busy lady. In Susan's breast a childish excitement was blossoming into life. This must be my nurse's doing, she thought, referring of course to nurse Gerstein in the ignorance of any other nomenclature outside of that of simply 'nurse'.

Deep inside, Susan felt a welling gratitude to her nurse, an emotion that in magnitude was vastly out of proportion to any favour given, even had any real favour been bestowed. In that moment mere gratitude was rapidly approaching an intensity akin to love, love for the support and comfort that nurse Gerstein offered her, love of her nurse's approving smile.

Only momentarily did she ever wonder as to the woman's name; the staff only ever used titles, never names. It was supposed to keep relationships impersonal and professional and she had been told to expect it. 'Controlling for experimental variables' they had called it, but there was no doubt that it added to the staff member's air of authority as well as the atmosphere of respect and discipline. Staff had their titles and patients had their patient-numbers; how soon she had come to accept that.

Her nurse had been so understanding of the problems she had had during her visit to the doctor. She had explained the situation, explained that she could try and arrange another visit early on but that it would be necessary to appease Matron. It was Matron that had the final say after all.

Once back in her room Susan had had to make a deep and very humiliating apology to Matron. Her nurse had told her exactly how her apology had to be delivered, what to say, how to say it, even how she should stand when delivering it. Her nurse had stood with hands on hips watching as Susan had delivered the humiliating formula. She had beamed her attractive, approving and reassuring smile across to Susan as the girl had stood, red-faced, mumbling through her apology with submissively bowed head and hands folded neatly across each other, the latter positioned in front of her skirt and just below her uniform-dress's belt.

It had been a deeply humiliating experience, an experience of utter defeat, and yet the girl did not, could not, blame her nurse. It was Matron and the regime that was to blame. When her nurse spoke sharply to her it was only because she had to.

She stood quietly now. She accepted the proffered toilet paper from Matron and, squatting down, momentarily glancing up, nervously risking eye contact with her smiling nurse, she gingerly began to wipe the residue of a sweaty night from within the foul-smelling knickers.

179

Familiarity was beginning to ease the weight of defeat from her shoulders; acceptance eased the burden. She did the best she could with the meagre pad of paper but was anything but satisfied with the results of her efforts. There remained, still, that smell, a fishy-urine perfume that clung to the rubber as if one with the fabric itself. Urged on by an impatient Matron she stepped into the bloomers tugging, wriggling, as she had before.

There was an inevitability of compliance, perhaps it was the notion of being led around the hospital without knickers, exposed in that abbreviated nightdress, perhaps, subconsciously, she was simply beginning to accept that here, in this place, compliance was simply inevitable.

Whatever the force, it was enough to overcome the revulsion and abhorrence she felt at having to pull back on her soiled, smelly, knickers. No aid was on offer this time and the waistband was allowed to remain unfastened, short of her waist proper, her knickers not much more than three quarters of the way up.

It was in this state of semi-undress and while still struggling that she was ushered from her room, out along the corridor, holding up her knickers as best she could but in so doing unavoidably raising the hem of the short nightdress. This, then, was her quandary; let her knickers fall around her ankles, suffer the shame of that smell, permit the public sight of the soiling, or childishly bumble along holding up her nightdress as if to say; "look, mummy I've been a good girl, I'm all dry".

They had turned left out of her room and she had guessed their destination correctly; they were at the door she now knew led to the shower room. Lovely!, she was going to be allowed another shower, lovely! Lovely!

What Nice New Knickers You Have

The knickers were obscene there was no other word for it, just obscene. She was desperate for something to cover her exposure, certainly, but these things? The bloomers had been bad enough and she had feared and half expected to have been handed back the soiled pair that she only recently had taken off, but these things? Examination pants, apparently, at least that's what it had sounded like when Matron had sent the nurse out:

"She is scheduled for a doctor's visit and exam so she is going to need a pair of 'examination pants', if you'd be so kind nurse?"

"Yes of course, Matron". With that the nurse had left, returning with brisk efficiency in what had seemed mere moments, perhaps less than a minute, with a teeny pair of white, brief, knickers, so obviously the wrong size, obviously a hurried mistake. And yet Matron had taken no notice, passing them to Susan without comment other than a terse "come along, get your knickers on, we don't want to have to stare at what's between *your* legs all day".

That was not the *worst* part however, *this* was the worst part, it was only now, having pushed her feet through the leg holes that she realised that the swathe of stretchy white rubber that she was presently edging up between her calves was interrupted by a transparent panel. The gusset was formed from a different material, highly elastic and translucent polythene; *completely* translucent! She just couldn't believe it; the whole gusset was transparent and evidently intended to achieve a close fit. They were just obscene; there was no other word for it.

180

With some minimal procedural modification Susan's showering had progressed much as previously. Although naturally reluctant she had had no other option than to accept Matron's aid in divesting herself of her nightwear. For one thing there was that rear zip, she already knew from experience that she was unable to release, unaided, the catch that secured it at the rear of her collar. Secondly she knew only too well how the build up of her sweat during the night resulted in the rubber dress acquiring a tackiness, adding further complication to her frustration.

Having had, through practical necessity, to turn her back to Matron so as to facilitate the latter's aid, she had shrugged the latex dress from her shoulders, slipped the bodice down off her arms and, with a fluid motion, wriggled her hips clear of the skirt. She had allowed both nightdress and knickers to fall to the floor and had simultaneously stepped smartly out both and into the shower cubicle as one action.

In as much as her strategy had been to maintain her modesty as always she had been frustrated, architectural design working hand-in-hand with Matron's regime conspired to ensure the complete opposite. The cubicle offered little privacy and in any case her action had earned her a sharp admonishment that had her stepping out and stooping embarrassingly to retrieve her carelessly discarded accoutrement. Such casual slovenliness was out of the question here.

Not only had she been obliged to neatly fold her garments but obliged to do so within the constraints of a series of dictates that included the stipulation that her knickers were to be first turned inside out before being folded in such a way that the gusset was presented uppermost, this latter lesson seemed to have been the sole *reson d'etre* for having had to re-don her soiled knickers for a journey that could not have exceeded fifty metres. She had had to pile her things, with knickers to the top, before placing them in a small white plastic lattice work laundry basket that squatted on the examination couch against the opposite wall. Then had come the obligatory humiliating apology.

Finally she had been left alone to luxuriate in the shower's warm spray, Matron having exited with the laundry basket. True no soap was provided but the water had a soapy feel and, although there was an accompanying medicated aroma, was pleasant enough. Her revelry had been curtailed all too soon, the sounding of a bell coinciding with the cutting off of the spray, a new development to be sure but beyond her control and as such accepted without further thought.

There had been barely enough time to dry herself before a nurse had entered carrying the now familiar suit bag. Susan had tightly griped the tiny towel around herself as the nurse had busied herself in near silence. Only the swish of uniform against stocking-clad calves, the hiss of the suit bag zip and the nylon rustle of the emerging green and white dress betrayed her efficient presence. Totally ignored, Susan had been left feeling invisible and yet moments later, as now, she would have welcomed a return to such an inconsequential state for it was at that point that Matron had come striding in. With her return and her subsequent, almost casual, instruction to the nurse, the sequence of events leading up to Susan's present state of mental anguish had been triggered.

The nurse had quickly exited in compliance to her instruction and, with that, Matron's focus had turned to her charge.

Chapter 9 | Tempus Fugit, Qui Bono?

As she had on the previous occasion, without a word, Matron turned to retrieve the corselet from its resting place on the couch, turning back to face Susan as a single smooth movement. She held out the garment for Susan to place her arms through the broad shoulder straps.

The girl had done as bidden noting how the light glinted silvery off the corselet's shaped elastane abdomen and side panels, thankful for even this, albeit momentary, relief of the monotony of white.

The stockings had come next, light coffee tanned, seamed and fully fashioned. Under different circumstances she might have considered them quite sexy, if old-fashioned; as it was the effect was of burlesque, but not in a good way. As she had been previously instructed she had adjusted the suspenders, ensuring that the dark stocking welts nestled high on her thighs, little more than a hand's breadth from her crotch, and, more importantly, that the seams were straight, absolutely straight.

Matron, by now, had retrieved the dress; Susan had heard its characteristic rustle and knew without looking that Matron was holding it up by its shoulders behind her, impatiently waiting for her to reach her arms back into the long-sleeved frock. She shivered as Matron lifted the dress up onto her shoulders from behind her; the nylon fabric had a chill to it that she knew would shortly be replaced by a sticky warmth, the fabric having had been chosen more for its hard wearing practicality than personal comfort.

Matron had buttoned her cuffs for her, Susan being left to deal with the others. There was a sequence that had to be followed rigidly: The collar button came first so as not to be forgotten, the top button was to be kept fastened at all times, then she had to work down the front of the dress to the hem at mid-thigh, last of all were the two buttons that fastened the belt at the front.

It was when drawing the dress about her and beginning to fasten the first buttons that she had first noticed the smell. Not pungent yet noticeable nevertheless, the smell of BO, familiar, her own sweat from the previous day, the day before that and the day before that. She had been horrified, the nylon made the dress sweaty in its wearing, she had assumed they would have expected that, that the dress would have been laundered, at least at some point, or another dress provided. But now pulling up her knickers, those obscene knickers, right now such fastidiousness was the last thing on her mind.

She determined not to show any reaction. If their selection had been erroneous was it any fault of hers? If, on the other hand, and as she suspected, a deliberate hand had been at play, for how else could one come to understand their failure to comprehend such an obviously hopeless inadequacy of proportions if not deliberately so?, then the motive was surely their amusement and she would not provide for their entertainment. She determined, there and then, that she would pull those ridiculous knickers on no matter if they tore in the process; if they ripped, they ripped and rip they surely would.

For the first part, failure greeted her yet again, she felt the burning heat spread across her cheeks, her face reddening beyond that explainable by exertion and far in excess of that justifiable by ambient temperature.

For the second part too there was failure, the hoped-for rending of fabric and splitting of seams did *not* occur, indeed the elasticity inherent in both the rubber body and the polythene-like transparent gusset proved to be nothing short of miraculous. The garment easily stretched and deformed to accommodate her curves, testament to the skill of material scientists, synthetic chemists, and indeed the garment's designers.

She discovered, to her incredulity, that the waistband could actually be pulled right up onto her waist line and, indeed, was designed to do so, the knickers' waistband being designed in such a way as to grip on to a matching strip of rubber located for this very purpose encircling her corselet's narrowest dimension at its nipped-in waist and so ensuring a continuing snug fit.

Knickers in place Susan hurriedly dropped her skirt, tugging at the abbreviated hem, her imagination enough to inform her of the sight that might greet the casual observer should that skirt ride up. The lunar hemispheres of her bottom were delineated in an independent dance of pink/white latex, the centre seam sunken below view and evidenced only as the secretive darkly-cleft canyon between. A front view would likely reveal her private outer lips, moulded and detailed below the puckered transparent gusset, already glistening with the starlight of intimate moisture droplets. Should such a view become public, as surely was destined when seated on any of those low plastic, childhood-chairs that seemed to constitute the majority of the furnishings, at least as far as Susan's use was concerned, she would be, was going to be, devastated.

Thus attired and in defeated frame of mind a nervous, self-consciously uniformed Susan was led back to her room, twice earning reprimand for her skirt-tugging in the space of the fifty metres or so of traversed corridor.

Seated back at her desk, all sweating, itching, knickers and fidgety bottomed, she waited. The meal bell came and went with its ritualistic inevitability and the equally ritualistic consumption of porridge and slaking of thirst. Starving taste buds strained in effort yet again and, as always, went unsatisfied; salvation forever out of reach.

But at least now there was a reason - she knew now *why* she waited, they had informed her. She had knowledge and was cheered by that - any knowledge. Was not knowledge power, in a way? Even here? Perhaps, in a way. Was she again to be the arbiter of her own fate, was she to be handed back her freedom?

Today she felt lucky; today she *knew* she was lucky the nurse had told her so. She really was a very lucky girl indeed. The nurse had explained to her just how lucky she was and her heart was filled to overflowing with gratitude for her good fortune. This was to be her second visit to the doctor, a second bite at the cherry as it were. The doctor was a very busy woman and she might ordinarily have had to wait for anything up to a fortnight for a second appointment; a second appointment with in such a short space of time was virtually unprecedented.

If she was to be honest with herself she wasn't *really* sure if she should be feeling quite *that* lucky. True, without a consultation and pending the outcome of certain 'tests' and a 'personality appraisal' it would be impossible for her to be assigned to an experimental group but participation in their ridiculous studies no longer held any appeal for her. What she wanted, what she really wanted, was to go home.

183

Chapter 9 | Tempus Fugit, Qui Bono?

In fact, even less than that would suffice; even a book or newspaper would be freedom enough. She no longer had care for any financial reward; indeed, the sight of a breakfast cereal packet or the ingredient-list on a toothpaste tube would be sufficiently satisfactory in that respect. Furthermore, having not as yet actually taken part in any study she had been told that they were presently unable to begin to credit her for any payment. The latter point she really hadn't appreciated. The application forms and supporting literature had been awfully complicated; Aunt Julia had dealt with the majority and she had merely signed where her aunt had indicated.

That, despite having been here for... how long?... Did it matter?... Despite having been treated like dirt, or at best like some prison inmate, she had yet to earn a bean had come as a bombshell that had laid into her with heart-crushing effect. It had brought her down with all the brutality of some thug-guard's weighted nightstick. And she was supposed to believe herself fortunate?

Yet she *did* feel fortunate, somehow couldn't help herself. There was much more to it now of course; surely she had already failed practically every test of eligibility there could be. After all, they seemed forever to be berating her, forever criticising what they quaintly termed her 'manners', her 'behaviour', whatever they meant by that. Was it so unreasonable to inquire as to what was going on?

But what *was* going on? Why had they not just sent her home as unsuitable? Perhaps she was too ill to use, but why then the interview? Was it her mental state? Was she sick, mentally ill? Was she too *ill* to send home, was that why she had to see the doctor, did she belong here, in a hospital?

CHAPTER 10

COIFFURE, RIBBONS & BOWS: CANED BEFORE THE PANEL

Any Second Opinions?

Time had passed; they were at a door, the same door as last time? She didn't think so; it was off a side-passage, as before, but there was a notable absence of a seated waiting area. There was, of course, this time, no disturbingly wheelchair-bound apparition upon whom to displace her pity; she was free to indulge her self-pity to her heart's content, yet only within the limits bounded by her ignorance. After all how did she differ, in truth and unbeknownst to her, from that piteous sight other than by way of the absence of ugly word-stumbling orthodontic appliances, the restraint of leg braces and, of course, time, yes, perhaps time. Perhaps she was fortuitous after all; she was presently ignorant of the constraints that might be wrought by cruel whim in the guise of medical necessity.

The questions had been innocuous enough, at least initially, just the expected routine stuff, demanding little in the way of mental effort. In fact she had hardly been aware of her mumbled responses; several times matron had had to demand that she speak up. Her mind had frozen over the instant she had entered that room. It had not been the oak panelling nor the shelves weighted with dark reddish-brown leather bound volumes, their learned import advertised in gold leaf on their hand-tooled spines. Not entirely. Neither was it the, nigh room-spanning, fourteen-seater satinwood-inlaid red-mahogany board-room table, nor the row of red-leather upholstered carved oak chairs behind, high-backed, crested, throne-like and regal. Rather it was the panel seated in waiting. The panel under whose inquisitive scrutiny she was presently shrivelling and shrinking, her personality withering like some drying bloom under the penetrating glare of the desert sun.

More precisely it was that panel's composition to which her mortification most owed its genesis. Not that she had had any expectation of facing a panel, of course she hadn't; she had expected a white coated doctor, a single doctor, moreover, a woman doctor and in a bland modernistic plastic-white office. Before her that expected woman doctor did indeed sit yet accompanied closely to her left by a young blonde man in his mid-twenties or at most his early thirties with gold-wire rimmed glasses and dressed in a sharp smoke grey suit.

They sat together at the centre of the table as if king and queen, flanked on either side and at a greater divide by two much older men, both perhaps in their mid-sixties, one bald but for a grey horseshoe remnant of hair and the other sporting a badly dyed salt-and-pepper comb-over.

Both elderly gentleman were somewhat rotund, the one to the left of the table, to Susan's point of view, appearing the largest of the two, his girth exaggerated by dint of his ill-fitting waistcoat, the other, to Susan's right, seemingly less so, for which the flattery of a well-tailored suit jacket was owed a debt of gratitude. To her left she was regarded through wire rimmed half-moon spectacles perched halfway down a beak-like nose, to her right through more modern black framed glasses and intermittent puffs of pipe smoke. Both sported ruddy cheeks that tended to purple in the irregular fields of uneven thread-vein weave that were characteristic of regular and heavy whisky drinkers.

The younger man, seated directly across from her, she might have quite gone for had circumstances been different, perhaps if encountered in a bar or club. As it was his attractiveness only served to reinforce, by way of contrast, her own present self-perceived dowdiness, dressed as she was in that demeaning and frankly odorous prison uniform.

All three men were red-faced and plainly not through any environmental effect, the two elderly men were noticeably perspiring, breathing hard, almost slavering, their excitement quite overt! The pipe smoker in particular was becoming agitated, repeatedly tapping his pipe on the table's edge, a nervous tic afflicting the right-hand corner of his thin-lipped mouth. This latter gentleman lent further and further forward with each question, his eyes unmoving and locked on her crotch as if a toad taking aim at some scurrying insect, an impression made all the more concrete by his sporadic lascivious licking of his lips. His rubbernecked craning seemed somehow to increase in proportion to the depths of intimacy dredged by the interrogation.

The girl fidgeted on her low plastic perch, much to the unintentional provocation of her admirers, each wiggle only adding to her rancour and their titillation. She tugged at her skirt hem, the latter ruched up around her stocking tops and suspenders, only to be sharply told to sit still and, finally, to be instructed to place her hands on her head - Matron having become exasperated by her constant shifting in her seat. She tried in vain to bring her knees together, the resulting fluttering of her thighs only succeeding in drawing still greater attention, if such could have been possible, to that sweat-steamed, ovoid, polythene window lying between.

How much more humiliating would it have been for her had she known the truth of the situation, that from a medical or psychological standpoint only two of her inquisitors had any qualifying right to be there. There was the woman doctor, of course and then there was the young man, the one with all the questions, a qualified psychologist in his own right but drafted in merely to add piquancy and to sharpen the edge of the more personal, more probing inquiries - that they might cut deeper, scar more vividly. The two elderly gentlemen were much trusted guests; paying handsomely for the privilege but trusted guests nonetheless. One was a reverend, the other a QC, it matters not which was which, it mattered even less to the girl; that they were male and that they were present was quite enough. As to what delights they had purchased for their outrageous outlay, beyond the obvious voyeuristic delights we can only surmise.

186

Gradually the questioning had delved deeper and deeper, they wanted to know all about her boyfriends, her sexual proclivities, her sexual orientation. Whenever she was reluctant in her replies they shifted subject, probing her relationship with her father, how she had felt during his illness, what had been going through her mind as they had been lowering his coffin. She would quickly be reduced to tears and they would have to give her a few moments to compose herself and then again they would shift their focus. Did she masturbate? How often? Had she ever thought of it as a problem? All the time they were making notes, each participant having in front of them an identical buff cardboard folder, its contents spread out in a rough semicircle.

At first she wouldn't, couldn't, answer at all. Always the focus would change back to her relationship with her father; always there would be the tears and then the return to those embarrassing personal and sexual matters. There were questions about her toiletry habits, about feminine hygiene, her periods. Did she use tampons? Had she ever used a sanitary towel? Did she menstruate regularly? Was the flow heavy or light? Was there any odour, if so did she find it offensive? Gradually she began to answer even these intimate queries albeit haltingly and between mortified sobs but they were never satisfied; always there would be a return to those sexual questions.

In particular they seemed obsessed with masturbation; they wanted to know everything. Did she ever? How often? Where would she do it? How did she do it? What did she think about? What did she fantasise about? These were questions she just couldn't answer, the shame was just too great, but failure to answer was not an option, not in the long-term, it led only to the resurfacing of all those old painful repressed memories. Those carefully targeted heartrending interrogations punished her at each refusal; for punishment, of a sort, it undoubtedly was. Finally she had to answer, had to say something, all she could do was plead innocence, deny everything: They laughed at her! Laughed out loud!

"Do you really believe that to be the truth?" The woman doctor had interjected in the proceedings for the first time, up to then having been happy to let her colleague handle the questioning.

"I,I,I, d,don't know"

"What do you mean you don't know? Are you really asking us to believe that you have never masturbated at any time in your life?"

"I…I, I…"

"You know what I think? I think you are lying to us, its as simple as that. How are we supposed to help you if you can't tell us the truth you stupid, stupid girl? I'll ask you again. How often do you masturbate and do you think it is a problem?"

"No! No, n,n ,no!", sob.

"You know what?, I know that you are lying." She reached into the buff folder before her, retrieving an envelope from which she unfolded an A4 typed letter. Looking around at the assembled group then back at Susan she announced: "I have here a report from Ms Soames."

The shock very nearly sent her into a dead faint; the room was spinning, closing in on her. She started to sway, first to the left than to the right then back to the left again.

Matron's hands gripped her shoulders from behind, steadying her and then pointedly placed her hands back up on top of her head, her arms having fallen listlessly by her sides. "Aunt Julia?" Susan thought, her consternation and confusion made blatantly obvious to all present by the deep furrows appearing below that sun-blond gamine fringe and the tears welling anew to endow those pretty eyes with the special doe-eyed femininity that only such a vulnerable state could possibly manifest, and the true connoisseur appreciate. And she was surrounded on all sides by connoisseurs, some smiling almost sweetly, some leering, leaning closer still.

The doctor went on: "It contains a somewhat graphic account of her concern regarding what she considers to be episodes of self-gratification taken to a pathological extent. Not only that but she reports that, in addition to taking certain preventative measures, she often had been left with no option other than to resort to the use of corporal punishment". Then, looking directly at Susan: "During your stay with Ms Soames she had no option other than to cane you on many occasions because of your filthy habits *that's* the truth isn't it?"

"I, I, I m,mean, n,no, bu ,but…"

"You had to have rubber covers on your bed and wear rubber knickers because of the staining that's also true isn't it? It must be, it says so here in Ms Soames' report"

"I,I, n,no. No! No! No!" Susan was sobbing uncontrollably now. How could Aunt Julia have written such things, why had she sent this 'report'? Why? Why had she? This was worse than the isolation, this was total and utter abandonment.

"Are you inferring that Ms Soames is a liar then?"

"Ye,y, ye, n.no I, I m, mean, I Oh, I, I d,don't know what I m,m,mean a,any m,more. Why are y,you d,d,doing this to m,m,me? Why? Why? Oh w,w,why!" She broke down completely, slumping forward with her head in her hands, almost toppling forward onto the carpet in the process; she was sobbing her little heart out.

"I feel we should give her a little time to settle down. Matron, would you take her next door, you can get on with the internal exam and the rest of the admission procedures while she composes herself. We will see if she is ready to be more honest when you bring her back. By the way I would be grateful if you would see to her hair and find her a bonnet. Whatever group we decide to assign her to I am sure that they will want her to be properly dressed."

"Yes doctor"

She struggled to her feet, beetroot-red of face, hastily brushing down her skirt front as she did so. Her hands, smoothly sweeping from the top of her pretty blonde head to the front of her thighs, described a heart-shaped arc through the air that hung in the eyes of her observers well after she had gained her full height; more than one present bristled with exasperation that she should have been able to retain such grace under such circumstances.

The doctor in particular struggled to disguise her annoyance; it should not suit her purpose if the patient was to read anything but utter futility in the situation.

There was some modicum of dignity here, an element of self-respect, perhaps even of vanity, and this despite her uniform, despite the fact that throughout they had been at great pains to ensure she only be addressed by her patient number; indeed of the group present only Matron and herself knew the girl's name, the others knew her only as patient 43C. Did the silly little cow not realise just how ridiculous she looked, how she appeared in the eyes of everyone around her, what these men thought of her? Had she no idea how that stammer made her sound, that no one would listen other than in pity, that her muddled thinking and indecision put paid to any likelihood of being taken seriously? She should have been crushed, why wasn't she crushed? Could she not recognise what was happening to her, what was being done to her, what they were *going* to do to her? Well, she had her exam to come yet, her depilation, her first regulation hospital haircut and then another question-and-answer session with the panel. Finally she would be getting her first thrashing and she was going to make sure that it was a damn hard one and the first of many. She was going to be a very different girl by the time she was returned to her room.

Susan, having regained her full height, nervously tugged at the sides of her skirt, gripping the abbreviated hem between the index finger and thumb of each hand. She turned slightly away from the table as if thinking to leave by the way that she had come in. Whether she was, perhaps, thinking to bolt for the door must remain conjecture; suffice it to say that none but futile encounters with locked doors and security grilles lay in that direction in any case.

As it was there stood, close behind her, Matron to her right and the nurse to her left. Matron placed a firm hand upon her shoulder, the other indicating a dark panelled wood door located towards the rear of the room and set within the right-hand wall at the far end of a run of floor-to-ceiling bookshelves, an oil seascape in an over ornate gilded frame claiming the remainder up to the far corner.

As she passed the table's end she felt something brush the inside of her left thigh, an appraising squeeze, a transient exploration of podgy perverted little fingers. The pipe-man's hand? Part of her wanted to turn, part of her didn't welcome the confirmation, the revulsion was enough as it was. Another time, another place she would have lashed out, lashed the palm of her hand across the disgusting old lecher's drink-contracted wrinkled face. Here, now, that was never going to happen, there would be a leering smile met by tearful shaming acceptance. That was where she was right now and deep down she knew it.

Behind Closed Doors

The brass globe handle rattled in its turning. Momentarily she caught part of her reflection in the burnished finger plate and uncharacteristically, at least for the old her, looked away, averting her eyes. Not that there was escape in that direction, there were only the bottle-green and white stripes and the nylon sheen of her dress and below that, below the tan stockings, the patent bottle-green gloss of the Mary-Janes.

Beyond that door lay normality, of a sort. Nothing within in any way threatened the conventional aspect of a fairly typical, if rather more comprehensively equipped than most, hospital gynaecological examination suite. The centre of the far wall was dominated by what at first appeared to be a dentist's or hairdresser's chair although the leg rests and stirrups extending to the front told a different story. Directly behind the chair a floor mounted pedestal supported a hairdresser's basin in black vitreous china. In front of the chair the white tiling of the wall was interrupted by a mirror running floor-to-ceiling and being of perhaps two metres in width.

To the left another mirror ran floor-to-ceiling, this one being perhaps one metre across and separating two windows, each being of around one square metre in area and being of the usual construction, frosted glass lying back from a flush white plastic security grille. A toilet pedestal extended out from the wall at the centre of this mirror. This at least was of a conventional size, but there normality ended. It was the one *real* oddity of the room; the entire thing was of some transparent material, the pedestal, the pan, the seat everything, and the region of flooring immediately surrounding it was mirrored in contrast to the spongy white linoleum flooring that extended across the rest of the room.

Immediately to their right, as they entered, a series of floor mounted cabinets, topped with a continuous white melamine work surface, ran along to the corner. Immediately above this, matching door fronted wall cupboards were mounted and ran along the entire length of the wall. Around one third of the right-hand wall was occupied by a conventional if old-fashioned looking wood framed and brown leather topped examination couch, a single long sheet of white protective paper covering the entirety of its upper surface.

Tucked into the far corner between the end of the couch and the wall was a combination height gauge and weighing scale the like of which she had not seen outside of the medical room at her old school. The near right-hand corner was occupied by a large mahogany writing desk, its top illuminated by the light from a modern wall-mounted angle-poise lamp. A modern swivel office chair, upholstered in some light-grey fabric, was turned side on having been recently vacated by the nurse who now strode across to greet them, her left hand brushing aside a curling lock of silver-blonde hair that had strayed from beneath her cap, her right slipping a blue biro into the breast pocket of her dress.

Her appearance came as something of a shock; not from her presence itself as such, nor was there anything particularly out of the ordinary about her, quite the contrary in fact; it was the very normality of her appearance that was so startling.

190

There was no calf-length white dress with its pseudo-Victorian styling, no face-framing nun-like headdress and no ring of keys hanging from her belt suggestive of a prison wardress. Everything about her was conventional, albeit stylistically suggestive of an expensive private hospital. Her uniform, from her cap to her dress, was in a light, soft, ' hospital' blue.

To Susan, starved for so long of stimulation, denied of the printed word, of taste and flavour, of colour, even, for all intents and purposes, conversation, every detail was important. She couldn't take her eyes off the woman, every nuance, every subtlety was to be studied, memorised and more importantly, experienced.

The nurse looked to be no older than her mid-twenties, not overly attractive of face but with pretty sparkling dark blue eyes and a slightly perky nose. She looked to be slightly overweight yet was curvaceous, her tailored, panelled, button-through dress, having obviously been carefully cut to take account of her full figure, flattered and smoothed without a hint of strain or pulling. Attention to detail was evident everywhere about her uniform; the dress' hip pockets, breast pocket and collar were trimmed with white piping. Its long sleeves terminated in neatly buttoned cuffs that were similarly neatly picked out with white piping. The breast pocket sported the hospital crest and name in finely embroidered red and gold thread. Her blue nurses' cap was edged with white piping to match her dress and had two white stripes running across the front that Susan considered was probably indicative of her rank.

The woman coming closer, Susan realised she appeared to be wearing a conventional nurses' watch on her top pocket, but even with that realisation came disappointment; a mere moment later and the woman's hand was obscuring the dial, in one deft move it had been unclipped to disappear into her hip pocket.

She had known they were coming of course, it was written in her schedule and she could quite easily have taken off her fob watch before their arrival or even have replaced it with one of the adapted ones that only showed the time in seconds. She knew the protocol well enough; the patient was to be allowed access to neither watch nor clock. There had been no slip-up on her part, indeed she had played her part well; this little pantomime had been all for her patient's benefit. It was all part of the treatment; they wanted the girl to *know* that she was not to be allowed to know the time, that she could know nothing, go nowhere, do nothing unless they allowed it, unless they gave their permission.

"Ah, Matron, and this is 43C I assume?" There was just the faintest hint of her native Lothian about her voice, it gifted her a gentle pleasant Gaelic sing-song backdrop to her speech. She flashed a friendly smile in Susan's direction and half turned away to retrieve a plastic hanger that was lying near the front of the worktop. "Just you pop your dress and knickers off, dear. Hang your dress on the back of the door here when you are finished and I'll fetch you a gown." She opened the closest wall cupboard and indicated a coat hook on the inside. With that she passed Susan the hanger and turned as if to cross to the other side of the room adding, as if by way of a afterthought: "Oh, and place your knickers on the side there, if you don't mind, the usual way, neatly folded and inside-out with the gusset uppermost. I may need to take a swab from them."

Susan was a bit taken aback at the rapidity of the developments but nevertheless began to fumble with the first of the two buttons that fastened her belt at the front; there was a sequence to be followed, it was part of her discipline.

Matron's voice cut into her almost immediately. "What do you think you are doing, girl?"

Susan jumped, startled. "Wha...?" Then she remembered, her knickers came first, already she was in trouble. "S, S,Sorry ,M,Matron." Embarrassed in front of the new nurse and red-faced she reached under her skirt and began to wriggle her thumbs under the broad, tight, elasticated waist band, easing it away from the tacky rubber grip-band of her corselet.

"No! No! No! What else have you forgotten? Your manners perhaps?"

That was it, now she realised. It had been that new nurse's friendly attitude that had thrown her. She had forgotten to say 'Yes nurse' when she had been told to disrobe and, worse, she had forgotten to thank her when she had been passed the coat hanger. She looked up from her task, the nurse was standing, no more that a couple of paces away, with her hands on her hips, just standing there, watching, waiting, the smile had left her.

"I,I,I'mm s,so, s,sorry, n,n,nurse."

The smile came flooding back. "That's ok sweet heart, that's a good girl. Now come along and get those things off. You can leave your corselet, stockings and shoes on for the time being."

"Y,Yes, n,n,nurse, th, thank you n,nurse, a,a at w,w,once, n,nurse."

A Sound Velcro Attachment

The nurse had gone to a double-fronted cupboard located in the far left hand corner of the room. Susan was still unbuttoning the front of her dress on her return. Having started at the skirt hem and worked her way up she was awkwardly and hesitatingly fiddling with the last three buttons of the bodice, her acutely uplifted breasts bursting into view, thrust out and up by the old fashioned corselet they made her wear. She placed the dress on the hanger, it irked her having to refasten each button before she could put it away and be allowed to dress in the examination gown' it irked her having had to undo all the buttons in the first place; once the bodice was unfastened she could have simply slipped it off her shoulders and stepped out of the skirt. The sequence was the exact inverse of when dressing; It wasted time, it was illogical but it was a rule, a stipulation, there was no choice involved, it was all 'good discipline'.

The gown was received with dismay but outwardly with the required expression of the deepest gratitude. Hanging over the nurse's forearm the multiplicity of folds had lent it opacity, the blue sleeve of the nurse's uniform below and the puddles of reflection on the surface imbuing it with a hint of colour. Now placed around her shoulders, fastening with a sharp click at the rear of the collar, its true transparency was only too apparent. There was a certain pearlescent quality to the PVC but otherwise it hung in thick near- transparent folds to her calves. A rear zipper fastened it from the waist to the snap- fastening at the collar, the rear being open from the waist down.

192

Susan took her seat when ordered, sinking back into the black vinyl leatherette upholstery, resting her lower legs on the supports that extended out from the front of the chair, the curve of her calves fitting closely to the padded 'U' section leg rests, comfortable support being thus provided from just below her knees to her ankles. As instructed she rested her arms on the rests, the latter being possessed of a gentle concave cross section that both aided comfort and suggested a certain sense of security. The girl could feel herself relax, there was an atmosphere of calm in the room and she certainly was not going to suffer any *physical* discomfort, far from it.

The blue-uniformed nurse slid open a drawer to the right of the mirror. She placed a box of disposable latex examination gloves on the side and then donned a white plastic disposable apron of the sort that Susan had often seen worn in hospitals, the familiarity aiding the normality and calm of the scene and easing her anxiety.

Matron and her companion nurse were each passed an apron in their turn and all three women helped themselves to gloves from the box, the girl craning round in her effort to catch sight of the latter. That there might be visible a manufactures name, some instructions, a slogan perhaps, was a futile hope; the original box had long been discarded and its contents transferred to the unit's own standard plain white packaging. It was yet another stipulation; the patient was not to be allowed access to reading materials, of *any* kind.

It had been explained well enough; the Velcro fastenings were a necessary part of the procedure. The chair incorporated a multi-adjustable positioning system and from time to time in the procedure it would be necessary to change its configuration and orientation without her shifting position. At other times it would be essential that she keep absolutely still. Nothing they were to do to her would entail any pain, although there might be some transient discomfort. Invariably, though, there would, on occasion, be sensations that she might well find unfamiliar or unusual.

The straps were soft, comfortable yet firm and unyielding. The nurse had started at her ankles, a wide band encircling each, before a broad strap was fastened just below each knee. Each arm was fastened at the wrist and just below the elbow before a ten centimetre wide band was pulled across her abdomen and another similarly drawn across her upper chest and shoulders. Despite all their reassurances she disliked this feeling of helplessness, the sensation of being strapped down, and yet there was something strangely reassuring about it all, an odd numbing-calmness that refused to give way to the fears that continued to bubble away below the surface.

It should be said that it was doubtful if ordinarily she would have submitted to such restriction without putting up at least some argument. Undoubtedly the thought of being so powerless would ordinarily have triggered an outburst of panic that would have entailed quite some struggle to overcome.

As it was, in anticipation the doctor had agreed to her prescribed medication being increased by some twenty-five percent to help her through; if continued it risked strengthening the girl's, already growing, dependency on the sedatives of course but it would ensure docility and the thinking was that, as a one-off, it would do little harm.

Besides, the thought was never too far from the back of the doctor's mind that there was little in life more pathetically humiliating then dependency and addiction - in all their variant forms. Still, it was always a balancing act, prescribing the girl's dosage; care had to be taken to ensure that the girl was not so heavily sedated as to risk ameliorating the psychological impact of the procedure.

This was always the quandary from her perspective; the right dose encouraged suggestibility, docility, heavier sedation, though, tended towards having a buffering effect, it tended to guard the mind, the psyche, against damage.

Matron took up her position behind the chair by the basin. Matron's companion, the white uniformed nurse, went to stand to one side at the foot of the chair; she was there in the twin capacities of observer and student, for her this was to be an instructive demonstration. The blue-uniformed nurse, having now donned a face mask, pumped her foot repeatedly on a pedal near floor level and, having satisfied herself of the chairs height, squatted down slightly and began to rotate two handles in unison.

The girl's legs were drawn apart and her knees drawn backward in the same movement. From time to time the nurse glanced up at her patient's face, experienced eyes searching for the first signs of discomfort. Finally there came from the girl the sound of breath drawn sharply through clenched teeth, a quick glance revealed the girl's features to be just beginning to register the onset of discomfort, not real pain yet but discomfort certainly. Carefully and gradually she edged both wheels on, a half turn, three quarters of a turn, ratchet-click by ratchet-click edging closer and closer towards a full turn... Another sharp intake of breath, more urgent this time, the reflection of discomfort more overtly discernible on her patient's face. Deftly the nurse locked-off both wheels.

Returning to the rear the nurse began pumping a second pedal with her foot while simultaneously rotating a wheel with her right hand. Gradually the whole chair tilted back, further and further. The headrest was removed and Susan's head was free to tilt back, her neck locating into the padded cut-out of the hairdresser's basin behind.

That she was to have her hair washed at the same time as an internal exam would have made sense had she not earlier had a shower. Yet, despite the dubiousness of this attempt at time management, she welcomed the distraction that it would bring. Having her hair washed, professionally, had always been one of her little indulgencies; she certainly hadn't expected to encounter such luxury here, not in *this* place.

Behind her, out of sight, matron had combed out her golden locks and, having gathered and piled the full extent of her corn-spun sun-kissed glory in the basin, was proceeding with the shampooing.

Susan's apprehension was dissolving away with each passing moment. Her hair had been handled with surprising care and patience. Combing-out was never easy with *her* hair; it grew thick and wilful with a determination to knot and tangle that at times defied all reason. Now educated fingers kneaded and stretched her scalp, lathered and massaged. Were these ministrations really at the hands of the same woman who rebuked and derided so cruelly, whose spiteful tongue lashed out so readily, whose barked instruction denied refusal.

Her remaining consternation now revolved solely about the other extreme of her person, those once private, secluded and secretive regions. She could see nothing; her eyes were clenched tightly shut with a determination that set wrinkles and furrows curving out to distort her pretty features as if through pain.

True, her groin was tautly stretched but much of the initial discomfort had subsided as sinews and ligaments had stretched to accommodate their unaccustomed conformation and muscles had relaxed their opposing rigor.

Presently there was the sting of shampoo to be avoided but that protective reflex had preceded the latter's application to the tune of two to three minutes. It was the exhibition set before her that had truly pricked that protective mechanism and that she was so keen to avoid.

The section of ceiling abutting the wall-mirror and directly above the chair was itself mirrored. The chair having been now fully tilted, her crotch was orientated directly ceiling-ward and the seat itself, being hinged, had been rotated down and away from her buttocks, providing unrestricted access to her anus.

And therein lay the *present* focus of her concern. She had been shaved with great care, her outer labia manipulated and pulled gently between nimble latex-gloved fingers, stretching the skin so as to expose to the razor the very last vestiges of cover. Throughout, the blue-uniformed nurse had provided a running commentary, outlining the finer points of intimate depilation. Primarily and ostensibly for the benefit of the student nurse, her considered and pointed choice of certain terms and adjectives had seemed suspiciously indelicate and brought to question whether she could truly be so insensitive of the likely negative impact on her patient. And yet, not notwithstanding the latter, undoubtedly considered, humiliating aspect, Susan had somehow got through it. Then she had felt her buttocks being drawn apart and the unaccustomed cool touch of the air against the sensitive puckered rosebud within. The nurse had shifted her attention and her razor's focus. For a moment Susan had caught sight of herself, or more accurately she had caught sight of her now denuded *mons*, the tension in her sinews causing a partial, but exposing, gape wherein the coral corrugations of her inner labia glistened. She had squeezed shut her eyes in response, only succeeding in bringing more acute attention to bear on the sensations diffusing out from that new centre of torment, the sensitive nerve endings visualising, as though through sight itself, the finger that had penetrated her, that was hooking within that puckered sphincter to pull and stretch the flesh under the fine skim of the razor.

Time wore on; Susan could hear the blue-uniformed nurse explaining the necessity of applying a cleansing vaginal douche in addition to a pre-exam lubricant. Suddenly the woman was standing alongside her head, demanding that she should open her eyes, pay attention. In her hand was what at first looked like a particularly anaemic peeled banana, at least in size and shape, but there any resemblance ended. There was a faintly medicated odour about it, a smoothly gelatinous finish to it and a wobbling-flexibility that suggested a firm, yet gel-like, consistency.

"I am going to be using a vaginal suppository rather than the more conventional fluid douche. I'm afraid they appear to have supplied a size larger than I'd requested but there's no need to worry. I know it looks rather daunting close-up but I can promise you that you'll have no problem in accommodating it.

I can guarantee there will be no discomfort whatsoever as long as you relax and allow me to take my time in introducing it. You may find the sensation rather odd to begin with but most women find it quite pleasant after a while. The trick is to relax and let your body respond in its own way."

She went on, her tone encouraging. "Once fully inserted it will take around fifteen minutes for your body's warmth and moisture to dissolve it and then I can flush out any remnants and detritus. In all it should take no longer than it will to dry your hair off. While we are waiting I intend to perform a urethral-sound procedure and then an anal dilation and examination. Neither of these procedures should cause you any discomfort and you may well find the sensations quite pleasurable, if so you can be assured that it is all a perfectly normal part of your body's response to the stimulation of the particularly sensitive nerve endings that abound in that area. I generally *prefer* to carry out these procedures with the douche *in situ* if at all possible, it saves a lot of time later, we can get the entire exam over with more rapidly and then we can get you up and out of here."

So saying, the woman returned to her position between the stirrups. Moments later Susan felt the first gentle strokes of the object's tip, ever so gently, up and down, up and down, brushing backwards and forwards along her inner lips, the touch as light as a feather. Every three or four traverses the range of movement would be extended, the tip momentarily sliding across the head of her clitoris, and then it would start over again. Gradually the pressure increased, there would be a momentary penetration, then it would be withdrawn, then there would come more tantalising stroking and then a slightly deeper penetration. At the same time something began to press insistently against her anus, drawing gentle yet firm circles around the edge of the softly puckered flesh before, ever so slowly, beginning a tentative intrusion, pressing inward even as the object penetrating her vagina began to withdraw, before itself withdrawing as the vaginal suppository again pressed inward and onward, both intruders penetrating deeper and deeper with each repetition cycle.

The gloved finger embedded in her anus had now penetrated past the knuckle and was performing a series of knowing twists, turns and undulations. The banana-like suppository was now remaining embedded to perhaps half its length at the extreme of its withdrawal phase and penetrating to around three quarters of its length at the extreme of its inwardly directed travel. From time to time it would be withdrawn in its entirety as far as its tip, the latter circling two or three times around the edges of her inner labia before it would again slide deeply and smoothly into her; deeper, ever deeper. In short the nurse had now adopted what was to all intents a fully-fledged fucking motion; there was no other term for it, she was blatantly fucking the girl with the suppository as she might with a dildo.

The girl gasped and writhed, images came fleeting back and forth across her mind, gradually focusing and taking shape. There was Aunt Julia standing over her, flexing that cane of hers. Then, slowly, the image morphed, Aunt Julia was wearing a nurse's uniform now, all blue polyester, starched apron and cap. Then it was Matron who was standing there before her, over her, dominating her. It was Matron who was flexing Aunt Julia's cane; it was Matron who was slashing it down across her naked buttocks, again and again and again. Then... Then... It stopped, it was over. The suppository was embedded deep in her, up to its hilt.

196

Her muscles spasmed around it, those intimate lips shone and dripped with stringy gooey moisture, part secretion, part lubricant, part dissolving medicated douche gel.

One more touch, quite literally, was all it would have taken. One more touch, however slight, and the girl would have reached orgasm. She had let the girl come so close, *too* close really; she had so nearly left it too late, too late to stop.

The girl was right at the summit, balanced on a knife-edged-crest between fulfilment and flop, between zenith and nadir, teetering, threatening to topple down to anguish, one last encouraging push, not even that, just the gentlest pat; the slightest-lightest infinitesimal touch an infinite act of mercy. But there was no one in that room with a sufficiently merciful heart, no one in that room willing to tip her over it, the girl was alone with her futility and with all certainty there was nothing that pathetically-writhing, pitifully-whining, panting wretch could do about it.

The nurse looked on with hands on hips, they all looked on; the girl was almost fainting from sensory overload. The nurse smiled, there was some cruelty there and yet some part of her, an ironically merciful part, hoped beyond hope that the darkness would not claim the girl, that she would make the most of it, that she would long continue to savour those rippling sensations, however tortuous, however frustrating. After all she would be returned to the sensory desolation of the unit proper, all too soon. In some ways she couldn't help feeling sorry for the girl, the poor thing was the only one there who was unaware of her deteriorating mental state.

There came a pang, a twinge of guilt; undeniably she had had a part to play in all that, was presently, quite likely, exacerbating the girl's condition and she would undoubtedly continue to do so in the future. What was that oath? Do no harm? She was doing little else, and with no little satisfaction.

She had to be careful in adjusting the speculum, the girl was still squirming, her labia swollen with arousal. She had to be similarly delicate with the placement of the urethral sound - she was determined not to push the girl over the edge. A gentle stretching of the girl's urethra would make it easier to catheterise her if it should become necessary at some future date.

The nurse expertly manipulated the sound, letting her thumb brush across the protruding tip, gently vibrating it with a gradually widening circular movement. Susan gasped; the sensations were building again but now there was something else, almost as if she needed to pee, the sensations intermingling until she could no longer tell one from the other. She gasped, a long sobbing gasp, and the nurse removed her thumb; it had been close, very close, but she'd been in time to catch it.

She counted away the seconds, let sufficient calm descend, then smoothly slid the sound free of the girl's urethra. There came yet another gasp from her patient, then a shudder. Urine sprayed in a golden fan against the plastic of her apron before subsiding to a smooth arcing flow, pooling on the floor before drawing itself around the base of the chair in curling rivulets. The white uniformed nurse gasped in synchrony with the patient.

"Oh my God!, She's peeing herself, it's going everywhere!"

"Yes, that is always a risk of this procedure. I just wanted you to see what *can* happen if you get it wrong.

Ordinarily this is to be avoided at all costs, there is no physical discomfort involved but it is potentially *very* psychologically damaging to the patient, particularly if dealing with someone who has… how shall we say?… a fragile personality."

"I'll get a cloth shall I?"

"Don't worry about it for the time being, I'll have the patient clear it up herself when we're finished."

The speculum was removed with due care and, for the briefest of moments, Susan began to relax, began to regain some composure. Then, again there was something pressing against her anus, again she gave out a little gasp. It was not that it was her first time, of course it wasn't, it was part of her daily routine after all, immediately before bed and again upon arising. It was a familiar sensation, to be sure, but one that had, under these circumstances, taken her by surprise nevertheless. One after another, in quick succession, the three suppositories were slipped into place.

"There we are, all done now."

She felt the seat hinged back up against her buttocks, grateful for the extra covering it provided. Behind her the hair dryer's drone continued for perhaps another ten minutes or so, they had clearly hopelessly underestimated how long it would take for her hair to dry. It made her wonder why Matron hadn't started drying it sooner, why she hadn't completed washing it in one go, surely there would have been plenty of time but Matron had kept going off somewhere, sometimes for what seemed like quite long periods of time. Then all went silent and she felt the chair being returned to the vertical.

Her hair flopped back into place across her shoulders, the foremost sections tumbling down across her breasts. With it came the smell, a pungent odour that she associated with hairdressing salons, with her step mother's freshly dyed hair. With it came the numbing shock; what had they done to her? What had they done to her lovely blond hair? Black! It was jet-black! A horrid artificial, plastic-looking black! A nastily-cheap, nylon-fibre-wig, black.

There wasn't even tears, there would be time enough later. There would be months or even years to cry over it, for it to grow out: Bleaching it back out would not be an option, it would destroy the condition; her hair would never recover. For now there was just a long drawn-out gasp and saucer-wide, unbelieving, staring eyes.

Ruination and Remembrance

Matron had pulled a large white plastic comb from her uniform pocket and, with something of a practiced flourish, she began to expertly and quickly comb through the girl's hair. Deftly separating and bunching the shining black locks to either side of Susan's head Matron's practiced fingers began rapidly braiding, displaying the rapid dexterity that comes only with the most dedicated practice, an expertise that would not have seemed out of place if demonstrated in the most exclusive of salons. Brusquely reminding the girl to sit still from time to time as occasion demanded, she quickly achieved two waist-length plaited pigtails.

Reaching into another pocket of her uniform Matron produced two lengths of green and white striped nylon ribbon that appeared to almost glow wherever the sheen of the fabric reflected shimmering pools of light and shadow across its five centimetre width. In just moments the ribbons had been formed into two large bows, one in each pigtail, tied almost exactly halfway between earlobe and shoulder. To the casual observer this would probably not have made a lot of sense, after all with the pigtails extending to the girl's waist, surely the majority of that length was going to just as quickly unravel.

This was not a question that concerned the woman, this was the correct placement for ribbons and bows, always this position, and if there was one important thing, one thing that Matron really appreciated, it was uniformity, uniformity in *all* things.

Susan was completely unaware of the tiny plastic bottle that next was conjured from Matron's pocket. True she had become aware of a vaguely chemical odour permeating the air but, then again, there was still the residual odour of the dye hanging about her. She certainly saw nothing of the drops of thin clear fluid applied to the centre of each bow, the fluid rapidly taken up by the over-sized nylon knot and soaking thoroughly into the braid within.

Satisfied with her work and smiling to herself Matron popped the top back on the super-glue bottle and slipped it back into its home, her pocket, under her control, as everything should be. Without further word the woman turned on her heel and crossed the room leaving Susan sitting stunned, ever more perplexed, with tumbling thoughts and racing heart.

Behind her the cupboard door slammed shut. Startled, her thoughts and deliberations, interrupted, she instinctively glanced up at the mirror, quickly shifting her focus past her own image as best she could but unable to completely dismiss the blatantly uplifted torpedo breasts staring back at her from beneath the near-transparent plastic hairdresser's cape. The return of Matron, heralded by the, now, all too familiar rustling of her uniform dress beneath the protective plastic apron, brought with it a new dread. In the mirror Susan momentarily and mistakenly made eye-contact with the woman. There was an unmistakable air of professional efficiency about her, it was in those eyes; she was decisive, a job to do, a function to be perform, rapidly and without sufferance of impediment, no argument nor excuse to be tolerated. But it was not what was conveyed in those eyes that brought such soul crushing dread.

The shears, for how else could one have described them, certainly the term 'scissors' would have been insufficiently applicable, had not been immediately obvious, clasped, as they were, in matron's left-hand and carried down by her side.

The girl in the mirror, it wasn't her, it couldn't be her, not her. She was a blonde, a natural blonde, always had been, was born a blonde. And the pigtails? She had been given pigtails like this before, every day since she had arrived here in fact, always she had had unravelled them as soon as she had been left alone; it was a small thing to be sure but it was an important thing, it was one way she could fight back. That girl, that girl in the mirror, she had to warn her. She had the most beautiful waist length hair, plaited now in two thick ebony ropes but that woman, the woman behind her, the woman in the hospital matron's uniform, she was about to slice off one of the girls pigtails, those shears, she had the blades around the entire braid just below the bow, one wooden handle in each hand, she was tensing, beginning to apply pressure, the blades were cutting... She had to warn the girl, *she had to!*

"No! ,N,N,NO! D, Don't, d,d, don't let her!" The girl, the girl in a mirror, screamed back at her and they both struggled in their matching Velcro bindings, both watching helplessly through their fog of denial as each lost at least two thirds of a metre of lovingly cared-for and nurtured growth from first one side and then the other.

Neither had wanted to watch, they shared each others' suffering with a bitterly personal empathy; both had been forbidden to look away.

"It's up to you of course but have you any idea just how many good, legitimate, medical reasons there are for completely shaving a girl's head?" Matron was right of course, she always was, there was no point in struggling; she had to submit, to give in, it was the only way she could help herself. "It's the hospital's regulations, not mine; I'm afraid hair has to be kept no longer than collar length. Is not my fault sweetheart, I didn't make the rules. It's for hygienic reasons; we just don't have the time or the staff to look after hair of this length properly. I have held back from this as long as I could, I really do appreciate how long it has taken you to grow your hair to this length, but we would have had to have dyed it in any case, it's important that all our test subjects appear as similar as possible. We can't have you standing out like a sore thumb amongst the other girls, now, can we?. You'll find that all the other girls that you meet here have their hair in the regulation style, why do you think you should be any different?"

The message had been clear enough and she settled back in the chair. Her eyes went down to her knees and the pearly shimmer of the PVC cape that lay across them, seeking a hiding place or a distraction amongst the plastic folds and the puddles of light and finding none; none was to be allowed.

"Look up, keep those eyes on the mirror, do as you told, now, unless you want me to get the clippers. It would be just as easy for me to shave the whole lot off and put you in a wig. See here? We're bound to have one to fit you." Matron had gone to a cupboard under the work surface to the left of the mirror and now stood with her clenched fist modelling a genuinely dreadful black nylon wig, the artificial sheen of its stubby pigtails matching that of the green and white striped nylon bows at their ends.

200

From behind her two heavy thuds came in quick succession. Two rope-like lengths momentarily writhed in serpentine death agony on the vinyl flooring behind her, all that remained to show for five years of careful and expensive care.

The electric clippers came next. The headrest had been refitted to the back of the chair and now a pair of hands interlocked their fingers across the top of the girl's head, at the front, barely overlapping the hair line and intruding onto the very uppermost of the girl's forehead. The girl's head was firmly restrained within the curving padded confines of the rest, the blue fabric of the cuffs and sleeves fluttering in and out of her peripheral vision telling of the identity of her captor but offering little clue as the reason for that restraint.

Matron leant across and from her right, there came a harsh buzzing. A warm vibration smoothly crossed her face following a gently arcing path just above her eyes, from the right-hand side, across the 'T' zone above the bridge of her nose and on across the top of her left eye. There came a couple of revisits to small areas around each eye and the job was done. The hands released their grip, Matron stood back and the girl in the mirror had become a *something* rather than a *someone*; the extent of the contribution of her eyebrows to her individuality and expression becoming only now truly appreciated in their absence. The doll stared back from behind the glass, its tears aiding its realism.

The Coal-Scuttle Bonnet

From somewhere just out of view she heard a cupboard door open and close. From her left and to the rear there came the familiar rustle of polyester dress beneath plastic apron and, simultaneously in the corner of her eye and the edge of the mirror, she caught sight of the blue-uniformed nurse, the nylon-sheen of the stiffened green and white fabric draped over her right hand and the two trailing tails of broad ribbon that hung down from it.

"I think this should be her size Matron"

She had seen this thing once before, on that girl, the girl in the wheelchair. There had been few other occasions in her life that she had seen anything really approximating that design and they had been restricted to art galleries and the pages of history books. The bonnet was a hideous thing covered in green and white striped nylon fabric so as to match her uniform dress and fastening under the chin with a huge draping bow of matching ribbon. It had a peak that rose up from the chin area, gradually broadening to form a canopy jutting forth over the forehead, before tapering down the other side of the face and that extended out from the entire front of the thing to such a degree as to require the wearer to turn her head in order to look to the right or left.

Indeed she *had* seen such a style depicted; it had been in vogue for a short while in the 18th-century and even then had been satirically portrayed and ridiculed in both caricature and prose as a "coal-scuttle bonnet". It must be said that this was not quite as extreme as some then had been but nevertheless she was dismayed by it, and of her appearance in it. The thing was ridiculous; there was no point to it, no sense in having to wear it. It was little more than a form of restraint and oppression, a form of psychological bondage.

The bonnet, the dyed black beribboned pigtails, the shaving off of her eyebrows, it was all simply the latest manifestation of that rationale that they were always so fond of stating as being 'good for her discipline'.

She hated that bonnet as much, if not more so, as the rest of the uniform. She hated it, yet she would wear it nonetheless, that was what they meant here by discipline. It was part of her uniform now and as such she would wear it day in, day out.

There was a choice, of course, she could wear her bonnet or she could wear a wig over a smoothly shaved head.

A Sunday Roast

All heads turned as they re-entered the room. Twice she had to be reminded to keep her fingertips on her shoulders, to keep those shoulder blades back and those elbows smartly out to the sides. Then the smell hit her, for a fleeting moment there was in comprehension, her starved, shrivelled, senses inundated, overloaded.

A lace trimmed white cloth now graced the table. A hugely-wrought silver terrine in held court in the centre and seven places had been laid and were occupied by richly-heaped roast beef platters. The woman doctor, her male companion and the two obese old men accounted for four, matron and her accompanying nurse for two of the other three set on the side opposite and, accordingly, two additional chairs had been drawn up, one to either side of the diminutive white plastic child's chair. A place had been set before the latter also; she couldn't believe her eyes, it all looked so beautiful, heavenly, the steam rose like a genie, beckoning her, taunting her.

They might as well have beaten her with truncheons or rubber hosepipes. Matron and the nurse had tucked in, the others also, but not her. Her genie beckoned still but remained ignored, her fingertips remained on her shoulders and her elbows smartly out to the sides. Before her, her knife and fork lay neglected, their white plastic identifying their ownership amongst the silver clatter of the surrounding cutlery. She wasn't to be trusted with such adult accoutrements any more than she would be given a china plate or a glass to drink from; the 'adults' had wine in their twist-stemmed glasses, her plastic beaker contained orange juice but to her was as tantalising as the finest vintage. Her turn would surely come but for now she had to wait. There were a few inconsistencies that would have to be cleared up before she could be allowed to savour her first mouthful.

They took it in turns, between mouthfuls, the questions coming from anywhere along the table but only two of her inquisitors were now within her view, her new bonnet's side cheeks now blinkering her field of vision to the exclusion of the extreme ends of the table. Two elderly gents were now outside that field and she had been vociferously reminded several times to remain facing straight ahead if she didn't want to see her plate taken away.

The interrogation quickly became as unanswerable as before but now the impasse was precarious and limited. She felt, quite rightly, that time was limited, she knew, intuitively, that the table would be cleared once the others were finished and her setting with it.

And then there were the suppositories to take account of, already she was shuffling uncomfortably in her seat. Clearly they were a much stronger prescription than she had been used to; they were already taking effect and more and more so as time went by. She felt as if she was trapped in a pincer movement; time was pressing in on her from both sides and still the questions came.

It was galling to think that there was a toilet so nearby, just in the next room, the room from which she had only just returned. She wanted to ask but was embarrassed as much as being too afraid. Finally there came an invitation, the woman doctor having presumably noticed, at last, her squirming discomfiture.

"Are you all right, dear, you look uncomfortable?"

She wasn't quite sure how to put it, not with these men present; she tried to bluff it out. "Y,Y,Yes I'm f,f,fine." But she wasn't.

Soon she was desperate, her squirming obvious to all around the table, her eyes pleading with the doctor, communicative, plaintive eyes, tear-laden eyes. Still the questions came, still she tried to sidestep the answers they clearly wanted to hear, that they needed to hear if they were to satisfy their blatantly voyeuristic curiosity.

"Do you need the toilet, child?" The voice was masculine but mild-mannered, kindly, a grandfather's voice and had floated in on a cloud of smoke from somewhere to her right. One of the old boys, the pipe-man, the old lecher with the wandering hands! The balance had swung, humiliation versus humiliation, hopefully she chose what she thought to be the least:

"Y,Y,yes p,p,please, p,p,please"

Quickly the woman doctor interjected: "Oh no, I don't think so, not until she learns to answer our questions truthfully"...

They had dragged every nuance from her, picked over every morsel, distilled, disentangled and picked apart the complex tangle of an entire lifetime's accumulated subconscious influence. With every disclosure there came from her audience an uncomfortable shuffling and a shifting of weight, perhaps a cough, a wheezing note added to the breath, sometimes a gasp betraying an illegitimate thought or mental image. Then at last they were satisfied. She was empty.

She sat slumped on that exam-room toilet now, having swapped one form of humiliation for another. Matron had taken her leave, presumably to return to her meal, the nurse had remained behind and now stood over her with arms folded, regarding her with a condescending smile playing around her lips and one hand toying with that all-important toilet roll. Despite her eventual co-operation she wasn't to be spared the usual close supervision but here there was a new dimension to it; each plop drew the nurse's attention downward, the sight before her broadening the woman's smile. It was a sight that the girl herself was only too aware of, the reflective flooring offering a view of the transparent pan's contents from every angle and even of the underside of her own buttocks. Nor was she to be spared the bell. She hadn't seen the signal, a certain subtle flutter of the nurse's fingers, but nevertheless there had come the usual tolling of the toilet bell. It was important to always be consistent with a patient's conditioning.

The door had burst open well before the girl had completed her ablutions. Matron strolled into the exam room the letter fluttering like a pennant in her hand. Looking across at the nurse she said brusquely; "this came a while ago, it seems it got mislaid in the secretary's office, it's about time they got it sorted out if you ask me."

A Letter, a Letter

The letter would have been the first thing she had been given to read in well over a month, well, closer to six weeks in actuality as Susan would have been aware, assuming of course that she had been able to retain even the slightest notion of the passage of time. As it was, all this was academic and for a couple of good reasons. For the first part; one may be forgiven for missing the proviso that the letter *would* have been the first thing Susan had read in a very long time, in a different context, from everyday experience, one might simply assume a slip of grammar, that is of course had one not been granted a privileged window into the machinations of a private psychiatric clinic. Secondly, the girl no longer had any grasp of time passing as we would understand it, that is, outside of the routine of the institution, outside of the concept of toilet time, mealtime and sleep time, each delineated by its particular bell. As it was, the doctor had decided that Matron should read the letter out to Susan, not that it had been specifically meant for Susan in any case. Despite this, it had been decided that it would be best for Susan to hear the contents as they pertained to her stepmother's plans and thus did concern her to some extent.

And appreciate it she did, her eyes lighting up at the first mention of a letter, the first glimpse of writing paper, something to read! She felt desperate, excited and anxious all at once, barely able to contain what to an onlooker, at least if unaware of Susan's circumstance, might have appeared as a rather pathetic, childish glee.

Moments later and jubilation had turned to despair, the first sobs coming with the realisation that she was not to view the letter itself, that Matron was to read it to her. A bundle of straw had been held out, the offer of the most tenuous handhold onto another reality, the reality of 'outside'. That she was not to be allowed to physically possess this morsel of news, to read the words, even to *see* the words, was as if a lifeline had been thrown her and then, at the very last moment, withdrawn.

Matron began her reading, her tone deliberate, cold, monotone and impersonal.

The letter was addressed to the institute's head, from Ms Anna Alison Gray. Susan knew that name only too well of course; it was her stepmother's sister writing in her capacity as the family solicitor and on behalf of Susan's stepmother. The gist was simple enough; the family company was to be wound up, meanwhile Susan's stepmother had embarked on a cruise, the holiday of a lifetime it sounded. Apparently Susan's stepmother was considering a move back to her native Australia and was taking this opportunity to mull things over, consider her options and make plans. Ms Gray was to be instructed by phone as and when the various decisions and plans had been finalised. Ms Gray, for her part, would be supervising the sale of the family home if required and organising the transfer and the division of the proceeds of the sale of the business.

In any event there would be no one in residence in the house and in the event of Susan's stepmother deciding to return to Australia the house would be cleared of all furnishings in preparation for the sale. The letter went on to request that, with Susan's upcoming university place being two months away, Susan be allowed to reside at the Institute as a patient until that time.

Her mind in turmoil Susan leapt to her feet, the urgency, the panic, overcoming stiff limbs. She had to get out of here; she had to leave, now, right now! "B,bbbut, I,II I'm" she started, panic worsening her stammer.

"What do you think you're doing, girl? Sit down at once" Matron's authoritative grip was not going to slacken for an instant, that much was clear. A moment's hesitation, a mere moment, and Susan had meekly retaken her seat back on the toilet, wincing inside, in her mind, with the pain of defeat, the humiliation that comes with the blind obedience of an order despite oneself.

Yet she had to do *something*, had to say something, her stepmother was clearly selling her inheritance from under her. How could she do that? Legally? No, Susan had to act now, decisively, tell them once and for all that she was leaving and that's all there was to it. They couldn't keep here, they had no right. And what was all this stuff about being a patient, she wasn't a patient of *any* sort; she was a volunteer, a scientific research subject. Certainly this program had been recommended to her, it was psychological research work that they did here and she had been promised counselling sessions to help her with one of two small problems that she needed to overcome, yes certainly that much was true, but she was a volunteer, not a patient, she had never been registered as a patient at *any* point. It was a psychiatric hospital for heaven's sake; it would be a disaster to have on her record a history of being a patient in a psychiatric institution.

"I, III, I w,w,wwwant to, to..." She could get no further, that damn stammer again! It was getting worse, she was sure of it.

In any case, Matron drew a halt to the proceedings. "That's quite enough of that, no talking, you know the rules." Then, as if to confirm Susan's worst fears, as if she could read her mind, she added as a parting gesture: "Just listen to yourself, stuttering and spluttering, you sound like a retard. Your stammer is getting much worse, girl, I said it would if you didn't do as you were told. The doctor told you to avoid situations that might aggravate your problems; she made it quite clear that the no talking rule is particularly important in your case. You're just making things worse for yourself, you silly girl. I've told you before; if you keep on asking questions, worrying about things that just don't have to concern you, you'll bring on one of your panic attacks, you know that don't you? "

Susan knew she had to answer. As it was she found herself answering automatically with a meek "yes Matron", irritated by the way her stammer always seemed to subside under such circumstances. Somehow she always seemed able to manage "yes Matron" or "yes nurse" without any difficulty.

Surely there had been some sort of mistake, some sort of mix-up but what could she do about it? They wouldn't let her say anything, anything at all, talk to anyone. She was gently sobbing now. Then a new realisation hit her: What had it said in that letter, that sentence? Something about it being two months to go before her university course started, wasn't it? But that couldn't be right. It was three months before she was due to start, not two. Wasn't it?

Chapter 10 | Coiffure, Ribbons & Bows...

There had to be some mistake somewhere, either that or she had been in this place for over a month. But how could that be? It *couldn't* be true; there were just too many inconsistencies.

For one thing, Aunt Julia had said that she would write from time to time while she was on her trip; if it had been over a month she would surely have written before now. Then again, it did sound as if they had some sort of problem with mislaid mail.

Secondly, her doctor had said that she would be able to continue with her therapy sessions while she was here. She said that she visited the clinic regularly and that she would arrange that they met for a session a *minimum* of once a week. She had not seen, or even heard mention of, her doctor since her arrival.

A thought struck her but was quickly dismissed; it was ridiculous, they wouldn't be allowed to do it, after all nothing had been said to her at any point, either before or since her arrival, and she had seen nothing about any such restrictions in any of the documentation that she had been given to sign. Nevertheless, they *had* made her surrender her mobile phone on her arrival and they had told her that there would be no access to a telephone once in the unit; the former she half expected in a medical environment, the latter seemed expedient, at least as far as incoming calls were concerned, if there was a likelihood that some important experiment might be disrupted. Neither had seemed particularly sinister in itself at the time but now... Considering that she had not seen a television or even a radio anywhere in the unit, that there didn't seem to be any magazines or books, no posters or charts, it was difficult not to at least consider the notion.

Were they, perhaps, deliberately withholding her mail? Had she been deliberately cut off from the outside world? Maybe visitors were banned as well, what then?

Matron walked over to the door as if to leave then turned and, folding her arms, simply waited. The bell had ceased its ringing and the nurse, having waited patiently through the proceedings, amusement never far from her lips, unfolded her arms to proffer the toilet roll. "Here, take two sheets, no more. Its time to get that big fat arse of yours cleaned up. Come on! You'd better get a move on if you don't want to miss the meal completely."

CHAPTER 11

END GAME

Caning Her

The doctor interlocked her fingers as she looked up; for a moment there was just the faintest flicker of satisfaction around those subtly-painted lips, scarcely discernable. "I take it Matron has read you out the letter?"

"Yes doctor, b,b,b,ut I,I, d,d,d…"

"Listen, the fact of the matter is this: As it has worked out, the last couple of weeks of your contracted period here will overlap with the beginning of your first semester at university. It doesn't matter one iota *who* is to blame, the point is, someone has to contact the University to make a deferral application. If you were to just turn up, some three weeks late, unannounced, you might well find, quite rightly, that they had cancelled your place. I've already made some casual inquiries and it seems that generally they do not allow new students to start part way into a semester. However, under extenuating circumstances, exceptions can be made. I understand from the letter that they have already deferred your start-date once, I think Ms Soames arranged it for you, but I am sure they will continue to be understanding once they hear that you are in a psychiatric hospital."

"What? Y,y,you can't t,tell them th, th, that! Pp,please d,don't tell them that, p,p,please, pleeesse! It, It ,It's n,not true, n,nnot really, I,II'm not a p,ppatient here I'm a,a v,v,v volunteer."

"Nevertheless, you are currently residing in a secure mental hospital, is that not the case?"

"Y,Yes, b,b,but I,I..."

"And you have been, and are still, under the care of a psychiatrist, is that not also true?"

"But, I,I..."

"Surely it just comes down to semantics in the end. You're not really fit to attend university at the moment; you wouldn't be under the care of a psychiatrist if you were. You are staying at a psychiatric institution, that's the simple truth of the matter and I think they have a right to know, don't you?"

"No, n,no! Please, p,p,please d,d,don't t,tell them, ,p,p,please don't." The stigma, that was the one thought running through Susan's mind, *the stigma*. The university might not want her and in any case how could she face anyone if she did eventually attend if this got out about her. And then there was the employment market to think about: What sort of career prospects would she be left with? Who would employ her once branded as a psychiatric patient, worse, a patient that had been kept in a secure facility? It was clear from the way that the doctor had said it that it was her intention to make the situation sound as dark as possible. For whatever reason, the woman clearly had it in for her. She had it in her power to ruin her life with a couple of pages of headed notepaper or a brief phone call.

The doctor was continuing her tirade, it was important that she pay attention, she had to keep track.

"... ironically, if you actually *were* a patient, even a *voluntary* patient, we would be bound by the rules of confidentiality and legally restrained from making any such disclosure. It would be left up to the patient, in a situation such as this, to arrange the deferment of a university placement, for example, themselves, citing any plausible reason they saw fit".

She had to dig deep, find that determination, she had to *concentrate*; this was important, desperately so, her future depended on it.

"P p,please d,don't tell them, a,anyone, p,please."

"But I have to, don't you see, it's my duty as your doctor here."

Of the three men present, the young blonde man seemed pitying, almost embarrassed, the two elderly men, in contrast, fidgeted in their seats, the pipe man tapping his pipe nervously and licking his lips again... in anticipation?

Susan began to sob anew. Her fingertips left her heaving shoulders, she brought her hands, shaking, around and up to her face, now lying back shaded within the confines of the ridiculous little Victorian bonnet they had dressed her in. Again came the numbing incredulous realisation of her ruined hair, her fingers having brushed past the stubby little pigtails tied in their oversized nylon bows where they would remain permanently fixed, at least until her next 'styling session'. Her fingertips, pressed to her face, now only served to confirm and remind her of its depersonalised plainness, the absence of eyebrows leaving her with all the expressiveness of a pale bisque doll-mask.

"Hands away, now!" The young blonde man's voice this time and the shock all the more acute for it. "Fingertips back on your shoulders, girl! This instant!"

Dumbly she obeyed; this was how she had had to sit since her return from her 'admission procedure', the bonnet precluding the hands-on head posture of previously.

One of the old men coughed, the other shifted his weight awkwardly as if something was now compromising his comfort. Both appeared to be breathing heavily, beads of perspiration forming on their brows. Both were now quite openly leering, their gaze fixated by that transparent plastic gusset and the coral-pink treasure that lay beyond, secret no longer, freshly razor-denuded and glossily cream-moisturised.

Somehow again the girl found the strength to plead, her new found fortitude only serving to excite, still further, her tormentors; it all added piquancy to the delicious anticipation of the moment, surely to come, when there would be no such reserves to dredge, when her fragility would become firmly established.

"Ppp, please." The voice, pitiful now.

Then came a long, silently-heavy, pause. The woman leant back slowly in her chair, interlocking her fingers and clasping her hands together in satisfaction. "Well... I suppose we could consider a voluntary admission." She glanced around the table as if seeking approval from the others before continuing; "perhaps if she were to admit herself as a voluntary patient, then perhaps..." Her flow was interrupted; there came a heavy, snotty, shuddering intake of breath and a bravely stuttering interjection. The girl was distraught, desperate and confused in equal measure.

208

"Yes, y,yes, pp,please, a,anything I, I'll bb, be g,good, I, I p,promise, I'll b,be gg,good, I'll be a g,good g,g,g, girl."

The doctor, clearly irritated by this disruption, pointedly focused her gaze on the shivering-snivelling, girl, before going on: "The trouble I have with that Idea is that, to this point, you have failed to show any sign of wanting to help yourself. You have refused to co-operate, refused to answer our questions truthfully. If you can't even be truthful to yourself, if you have to continually lie to us *and* yourself, why, then, should we go out of our way to help you?"

"B,but, bbb, but…I, I p,p,p,promise, I, I…"

"I'm afraid it's a little too late for that now. I have already drafted letters to the University and your local health authority, we have to make these things official and I can't do the one without the other."

"No! N,n,no! Oh n,n,no! Please, p,p,please give m,m,m,me one mm,m,more chance, p,please!"

"I'm really not at all sure that I can"

"No, p,p,please, p,p,p,ppleass…currrghhth…urrrgh…urrrgh" The sobbing cough had followed on through to retching. Even the doctor was given pause to consider whether she might be pushing the girl too far too fast; perhaps it was time to wrap things up, time to make her move, switch to a more *physical* form of chastisement. After all it was the latter that her guests expected to witness and she well understood their impatience. They anticipated watching close at hand, perhaps even participating, and they had paid well for their privilege.

"…but you've wasted so much of everyone's time already. There are the other panel members to consider."

"P,p,please, a,a,a,anything" She was going to be sick, she knew it.

"Well…you are going to have to show commitment, make amends."

"Y,y,yes, y,yes, a,a,anything, a,any th, th, thing"

"Well, you can start by apologising to the panel and then you can get down across this table. I want you bent over the end here and lying along this table. You've seen the cane here and I know you have been caned before. We've all read Ms Soames' report, you've been caned several times by her, before coming here. Perhaps that's the sort of old-fashioned discipline that works with you, certainly nothing else we have tried here has done. I have to warn you, I won't have you wasting any more of the panel's time; I'm going to start you off with six strokes across that big fat round behind of yours and then I'm going to get that form. You had better be ready to sign it when I get back, young Lady."

There it was again, that reference to Ms Soames, to her 'report'. Ms Soames, her Aunt Julia, they spoke about her as if they knew her, personally. Why did they speak of her with such a tone of familiarity? What did they mean by a 'report' exactly? She knew her doctor had a close connection with this place, it was the reason her doctor had agreed to her coming here in the first place, when she had shown her that flyer, the call for volunteers. But what connection could Aunt Julia possibly have with a place like this? Surely Aunt Julia couldn't have known what went on here, that she would be treated like this, or she wouldn't have let her come and the same applied to her doctor. But then again, how could Dr Ecclestone *not* know? What was going on? She was frightened now, really, really frightened.

Chapter 11 | End Game

The doctor went on: "Make no mistake, I have come to a decision, this is the way it is going to be for you here from now on, young Lady. There's that lovely roast dinner waiting for you, for after you have signed the documentation, but first of all I think we will have that apology from you and then we will have you bent over for your punishment.

Submit to a caning here and now, of your own volition in front of witnesses, and no one need ever know of your stay here. But, and it's a big but I'm afraid, it won't be your last taste of corporal punishment here. I will make sure that you are caned, and caned hard, for even the *slightest* hint of disobedience or non-compliance during the rest of your stay."

Susan could only sit dumbfounded, her eyes like saucers her jaw hanging open in disbelief; ever numbed by sedative and medication she was loosing the battle, an almost catatonic wave of shock was sweeping over her, rinsing her free of the remaining dregs of intellect.

Still the doctor went on, driving home the point, cleansing her patient of the burden of refusal: "Of course you are free to refuse, after all you a free woman, here of your own volition, a voluntary research test subject are you not? In the long term we are trying to help you here but if you can't put yourself out to help yourself I for one am not going to put myself out to go and get that form for you. What is more, I'm sure the other panel members have better things to do than wait around and watch you eat; I'm sure one of the other patients would be happy to make short work of that roast.

You can finish off your contract here, as it stands, and start at university part way through the first semester but I will have to make the arrangements for that, with all the implications that has for your prospects in the future.

Alternatively you can apply to defer your start personally and then they would allow you to start at the beginning of the second semester in February of next year. I can provide you with the necessary documentation for that, already filled out for you and with a plausible set of extenuating circumstances in place. All you would have to do is sign it and, of course, the voluntary admission form. Before you decide I want to warn you want again; I won't have you wasting my time, if you decide to go down the latter route, and I fetch those forms, you will damn well sign them and without hesitation or delay. If not you will find your bottom in intimate contact with my cane for a second time today, or even a third if necessary."

Susan was buckling and every one in the room could see it. There, right in front of her, lay the two opposing facets of the doctor's proposition, diametrically opposing yet occupying the same side of the balance; to her mind the other side was filled with all her hopes and dreams, her ambitions and aspirations, in short, her future. Less than half an arm's length away the golden-roasted meal tantalised, inducing in her an almost debilitating continuous salvation, she was drooling, constantly having to swallow down her own saliva. Directly behind the plate, arranged longitudinally in the centre of the table, lay the glossy white smoothly-tapered crook handled cane, the latter being of around one and a quarter metres in length and possessing perhaps the thickness of a man's forefinger at the point at which the handle's curvature began but no more than that of a pencil at its very tip.

On one side of the equation lay a lifetime blighted by stigma and accusations of mental illness. To the other side lay a way out, that beautiful, beautiful roast dinner but also the humiliating kiss of that cane; she could not have one without all.

The apology had to come first. They were stringent in their requirements, her adherence to form supervised with sadistically detailed eyes.

She had to kneel, squatting back on her haunches before the table, her nose a mere few tens of centimetres from the bounteous roast platter, her hands held either side of her face limp-wristed with palms prone, like some circus-trained poodle. The prescribed formula was grovelling in the extreme; she was ever so sorry for being such a silly, silly little girl.

She had to ask the doctor *very* nicely, ever so nicely and most respectfully, if she would be so kind as to correct her behaviour by caning her. She had to ask each of the three men in turn, again in tones of utmost respect, if they wouldn't mind being present while she was punished and apologise for the unattractiveness of her fat bottom. This latter entreaty in isolation would have been enough to bring her to tears, attacking as it did, her vanity from one of the deepest roots of her insecurity; like many young women of her age she had a particular sensitivity regarding the size and shape of her bottom and in truth her recent inactivity had resulted in a significant increase in the curvature of that region.

She had to stand at one end of the table and bend smartly at the waist, her torso prone, and reach out along its length with both arms outstretched. To either side ostentatious bone china was accompanied by crested silver utensils and held the half-eaten remnants of a most satisfying meal. To her left, and less than half a metre beyond the point at which her head lay, one plate remained untouched and would remain so, awaiting one woman's contrite acceptance of punishment and a brace of signatures on a formality of documentation. They had arranged her to lie so as to face that plate; she couldn't take her eyes off its mocking contents.

The doctor drew her hand back, up and behind her right shoulder, her braced stance stretching her hip-hugging knee length black leather skirt, causing a series of horizontal rippled shadows to flow across the front of her thighs and the under-hang of her buttocks where the fabric was stressed. In one flowing movement her arm extended and her wrist turned backward and outward. For a moment she waited, letting the tension build in her arm, and in the girl's mind, the cane curving subtly downward along its length under the gentle urging of gravity, such was its plastic man-made flexibility. She was well out of the girl's eye line, the blinker-like side cheeks of the latter's bonnet saw to that, she would use that to build on the girl's apprehension, stretch her nerves to breaking point.

The first three strokes slashed in with a viciously-repeating quick-fire whip-like snaking action. A rapid triple pistol-crack filled the air but in isolation, not a sound from the girl, beyond a sharp gasp coinciding with the first strike. Her knickers had been left on, they offered little if any protection, but even through the white latex three parallel curving ridges were gaining in prominence, one across the centre of her buttocks, one across their very top and one across the overhang, just above the crease of her thighs. Already angrily-reddened, the colour was developing before their eyes, becoming purplish and revealing the extent to which the whippy-flexibility of that cane had allowed its kiss to extend around the curvature of her bottom.

211

The doctor's thumbs were in the waistband of the girl's knickers, hurriedly pealing them away from those swelling globes and down the girl's thighs to hang just below her stocking tops.

She quickly stood back, simultaneously swinging her arm smoothly back and up, over her shoulder, before, at the extreme of its travel, whipping it back in, the cane curving back on itself as it whistled through the air. There had been no pause this time, she wanted this, the fourth stroke, to slash in as quickly as possible, before the pain of the first three had become fully apparent to the girl. She knew *exactly* what she was doing; she knew that the immediate effect of a stroke, as viciously applied as any of the first three had been, would initially be a numbness rather than pain *per se*.

She had stepped back slightly to slash in this fourth stroke and whipped her wrist forward fractionally before the moment of impact; she wanted to land the very tip of the cane at the centre of one of those fatty cheeks, split the skin, permanently mark the girl.

The girl had begun to struggle. A strong male hand pressed down on the small of her back, another between her shoulder blades, yet another pair grabbed her wrists.

The first stroke had taken her breath away, then there had been a throbbing numbness, the next two had landed before she had begun to realise fully the ever-growing agony, the shear utter unbearable agony to come. But now, now! The fourth brought its own momentary numbness before its branding iron burn joined into the building crescendo. The fifth and six were well spaced both in time and positioning. The doctor was allowing for the development time now, expertly guiding the girl beyond anything she had the capacity to withstand; the strokes were being neatly interdigitated, now, between the existing wheals, permanently marking her body and mind in one. She wriggled, struggled, screamed, writhed and begged; it was unbearable yet they made her bear it. And it broke her.

Of News and Views

It was the way her expression had changed, the abruptness of it. And it was that lovely smiling nurse, the really pretty one, the one with those wonderfully-smiling twinkling blue eyes and soft, lilting, Devonshire accent. It was the nurse that always wore that special uniform with its jewel-like buttons and their myriad hues, that watch, with its fascinatingly-spiralled rotating face, swinging gently from her breast as she glided about the room. It had been in that lilting tone of hers, all softness and serenity "can I get you anything?"

She had been standing directly in front of Susan subtly shifting her weight from foot to foot, a dance barely perceptible but enough; the girls gaze had already been captured by the brilliant shards of glittering colour as the collar button of the woman's uniform caught the light. Susan found herself required to exert substantial effort in order to snap herself out of the daydream she had seemed to have drifted into; as so often when in the presence of this woman she seemed to have been robbed of the very ability to think.

"I, I, I www ,w,wonder i,if, I m,m, might h,h,have a ,a b,b, book"

The nurse's smile had collapsed to an expression not exactly of anger nor of any real irritation but more, almost, of disappointment.

"A ,a,a, a m,m,magazine t,then or a a,a,n,n,newspaper, p,p,please a,a n,n,newspaper, j,j,just a,a n,n,newspaper, pp,please, i,i,its bbb,been s,so ll,l,long – sob- p,p,please."

She had begun to cry, quite pityingly, not really knowing why nor how something as commonplace as a newspaper should have come to grow to such importance.

At this the hardest of hearts could not have failed to have melted; the nurse's changing expression again told of the story about to unfold. There had been a return of the smile but now betraying an underlying sadness, even hinting at pity. "Now what could you *possibly* want with a newspaper you silly girl?"

She had half expected an answer in the negative, although she was not sure why, but not clothed in terms of such derision nor accompanied by a patronising girlish chortle.

"B,b,but I,I,I ddon't n,n know w,w,what's g,g,going o,o,o on" she protested, desperately trying to retrieve some dignity from the precipice of the childhood tantrum she could feel was fast approaching, struggling to forbid her foot from stamping and her tears from falling.

A comforting arm was around her shoulders drawing her head to rest on that ample bosom. The words, when they came, were as soft as clouds, words that outside of the context of this institution would surly have provoked the most vigorous of protests from even the most docile of girls.

"You don't need to know what is happing out *there* sweetheart. It has nothing to do with you, you are not out *there*, you are in *here*, safely away in an institution"

"B,b,but I,I,I d,don't e,even n,know w,w,what d,d,day i, it is. P,p,please ,w,w,what d,day is iii,it, pp,p,please, p,p,*please* t,t,tell m,m,me." Despite the nurse's comforting embrace she had broken down again, all pretence of mature dignity displaced by childhood tears.

Chapter 11 | End Game

She had already begun to stroke the girl's forehead with the long fingers of her right hand; those of her left were dextrously unclipping her fob watch from its home on her uniform's breast pocket, manoeuvring it subtly to catch the light. It had already caught the girl's attention and it would hold it unerringly, she knew.

"There, there, now we'll have no more of *that* nonsense. That's a good girl, such a good, good girl. Such lovely, lovely colours going around and around and around, there you are, that's so much better now, you *are* being a good girl and good girls always listen to their nurse"

The weeping had subsided to a gentle snuffle the girl's features loosing their distorting emotion to slowly take on the very epitome of serenity. "There, there, there, that's *much* better, you have been such a *silly* little girl, *that* is why you have been so upset isn't it?"

"Yes nurse" the voice small, timid and yet calm, surrendered."

"you are *such* a silly girl to worry about such silly, silly, things. You are so, so, safe here, you are so, so, safely all locked away in an institution, well away from all those awful, awful things that go on outside. We keep all those things locked away outside; they have nothing to do with you. You are just an institution girl in an institution, you should not concern yourself with things you can do nothing about and that have nothing to do with you. You don't need to worry about what day it is; it has nothing to do with you. You mustn't concern your self with it. You are safely away from all that in an institution. When you think about the awful, awful, things out there you are helping them to get in, to get to you. Those thoughts come to you, that awful panic, the dizziness, the head aches the fainting.

You can feel it happening now, can't you? You can feel the panic now; you can feel your head beginning to throb, can't you?"

"Yes, nurse". The voice had changed; there was a note of distress, of pleading, to it.

The girl was sweating profusely now, an expression of fear and pain crossing her pretty features. She was learning her lesson now, learning to try to shut out all those thoughts and memories pertaining to her old world, the world beyond the institution's walls, steel bars and security grilles.

Ms Soames and the doctor had done much with the girl even before she had been brought here, some fine work indeed. In truth the girl had come into her hands already well hobbled and restricted.

Although security bars, walls and locked doors all had their role, and it would take many, many repetitions of today's tableau, in the end it would be she who would be the arbiter of the girl's true confinement.

Externally were all the physical trappings of imprisonment. Internally, and still only partially constructed, were more covert structures of restraint and confinement; in time the girl's mind would carry the subtle chains of her psychological imprisonment.

She was to construct a prison within a prison for this girl, that was the task entrusted her. It was work, that was all; she had no pity for her. They were all the same, her type, prettily-pouting spoilt princesses. She was just another spoilt brat placed in her hands to be tamed; it was just work, but for such sweet reward.

Retrospection, Reflection and Repercussions

Susan sat, waited, her future mapped out before her as on some Möbius-strip treadmill of futility, tedium and repetition. Just what had the woman been talking about? It was none of her affair? Nothing to do with her? She would have liked to have felt indignant, to have experienced anger, that at least would have represented some semblance of normality. In the event there was only dismay, an overwhelming urge to weep and a strange logic-defying inner belief that, in some manner, the woman was correct.

If only she were more confident, not given to these ridiculous bouts of uncontrollable weeping. If only she were not hamstrung by a stammer that, despite the best efforts of her therapist, was clearly worsening daily.

If only she had the fortitude, the strength. If only she hadn't signed that form; she was no longer a test subject, a guinea pig, she was a voluntary psychiatric patient. What were the implications of that?

If only she had refused, but they'd had that cane there, there had been her future to consider and then there had been that wonderful steaming roast dinner just sitting there before her, waiting, practically under her nose. The smell, that delicious smell, that *gorgeous* smell; she could almost taste it, even in recall, it had been so close, so, so close. She had had to make a decision and she just couldn't make decisions, not just not that, not there and then, she needed help, guidance.

And then there had been the second caning, just for having hesitated. Of course she had hesitated; the documentation hadn't made sense. The deferment form for the university, the part about starting in the second semester, 'February of the year following', it hadn't made any sense; she had *already* had her entry deferred until the second semester.

If she had been in residence here for over a month then they were already *in* the new-year. Then, there had been the voluntary patient committal form, this definitely hadn't tied up with the deferment date and, what was more, it covered a period of six months, not the three months she had initially registered for as a research subject.

When she had tried to query these inconsistencies she had been rebuked for talking before being spoken to first. The doctor had become angry, lecturing her about wasting every one's time again, telling her that it was a standard committal form and that she was to sign it and that was all there was to it.

There were to be no more questions. She had simply been told that she was to be under the doctor's discipline until such a time that she started her university course; there was to be no argument about it, it was just how it *was*.

It had been so unfair; that she had been punished so just because she had been unable to make up her mind, that she had had to suffer the pain, the bitter humiliation so, so, unfair. Of course she had had to sign, there would have been many, many, more strokes of that cane had she not, she had been in no doubt about that.

But why hadn't she signed sooner? Why had she been so stupid, why had she delayed, held back, for so long, too long?

That wonderful roast dinner, sitting there, taunting her with its aromatic promise of flavours and textures almost beyond her imagining.

Those thick slices of juicy brown-red beef, the golden sizzling slice of Yorkshire pudding, the steaming Brussels sprouts and oozing thick brown gravy. Oh why, why had she even hesitated? She had taken too long, it had all gotten cold, too cold to eat, *they* had said so.

That lovely, lovely meal, how she had broken down when the nurse had taken it away; she had been a good girl, she had signed all the documents they'd wanted her to and still they had taken it away. How cruel they were, how cruel they all were. Now she was back to those bowls of tasteless porridge, those tepid white drinks.

Then again, what *now* of her future? She had been assigned to join an experimental trial, what had they called it, the protocol? The workhouse protocol? Yes, that was it; they said they were going to place her in the workhouse...

But what did *that* mean?

And then they had said they wanted her to see their dentist, an orthodontist. Why? What for? Certainly, the nurse had taken a quick look at her teeth, but what would *she* know, a nurse, and apparently a gynaecological specialist at that! She had always had regular checkups; there had never been any mention of a problem with her teeth, bar a few minor fillings. What was *that* all about, what was *any* of it about?

Where did she go from here, what could she do about her step mother while she was stuck in this place? What had happened to Aunt Julia? Where was her doctor? What was going to become of her?...

She wept and waited, waited and wept, what else could she do?...

GLOSSARY

'At home'   A rather archaic term meaning an expected, planned and
                 scheduled reception of visitors at one's home by invitation.

Bloomers   Used as above in some cases here. Wide, loose trousers gathered
                 at the knee and formerly worn by women and girls as an athletic
                 costume. Girls' underpants of similar design.   Named after
                 Amelia Jenks Bloomer (1818-1894), feminist reformer (USA)

Brussels sprouts The small, cabbage-like heads of Brassica oleracea gemmifera,
                 cooked and eaten as a vegetable.

Coal scuttle   A receptacle for coal usually kept at a fireside with the
                 appearance of a cylindrical or truncated cone shaped bucket with
                 an open slanted top

Corselet   Sometimes spelt, corselette. An old fashioned woman's
                 lightweight foundation garment comprising a brassiere and girdle
                 combined in a single garment, sometimes incorporating
                 suspenders.

Diaper   Nappy

Gymslip   A sleeveless tunic once worn by English school girls as part of
                 their uniform. The USA Jumper definition is probably the best
                 guide to what is meant here, though: A one-piece, sleeveless
                 dress, or a skirt with straps and a complete or partial bodice,
                 perhaps bib-like, usually worn over a blouse by women and
                 children.

Jumper   See gymslip

Knickers   (Here used fairly interchangeably with pants panty or panties or
                 even, on occasion, bloomers) women's underwear. British
                 Informal. a woman's or girl's short-legged underpants.

Napkin   An abbreviation for sanitary napkin, a pad of absorbent material,
                 as cotton, worn by women during menstruation to absorb the
                 uterine flow

Pad   Panty liner, a more modern slim-line or low profile version of
                 the old fashioned Sanitary napkin or towel.

Glossary

Pants
(Rather than
trousers)   An abbreviation for panties, i.e. women's underwear.

Skivvy   A female servant, particularly one charged with undertaking more menial tasks.

Speculum   A speculum is a device designed to gently open up the vagina or anus for examination.

Tampon   A plug of absorbent material, typically inserted into the vagina during menstruation to absorb blood or secretions.

Towel   An absorbent cloth or paper for wiping and drying something wet here used as an abbreviation for sanitary towel, British : sanitary napkin.

Urethral Sound   Occasionally, sond. A smooth medical instrument designed to enlarge the urethra. In a non-medical setting they can provide for highly pleasurable stimulation

COMING SOON...

VOLUME 2: CONFINED IN THE WORKHOUSE

Lavinia is returned to the 'Schoolroom' and soon mysteriously seems to be putting on weight, a nightmarish portent for a young woman still entertaining aspirations in the worlds of fashion-modelling and dance. We learn of her past life under her aunt's discipline and of her hypnotherapy sessions with her doctor.

Meanwhile, Susan, having now been catheterised, finds herself confined in the mysterious 'Workhouse'. Worse still, her dental exam hasn't gone too well and there are irksome repercussions! Meanwhile, Alison Springer takes up her post at the clinic and is soon supervising girls undergoing Matron's 'comparative self-criticism and reflection therapy', including her own cousin, Susan. It goes without saying that Matron's cane is frequently wielded, and chubby buttocks are bared.

Elsewhere a young woman awakes to find herself in a hospital bed, immobilised and with her arms and legs in plaster. She has apparently been involved in a road accident but of this she can remember nothing. What she does seem to remember is disconcerting in the extreme; apparent sexual abuse and punishment at the hands of an elderly man of the cloth. He comes to her in her dreams, wielding leather tawse and whippy cane in his effort to drive the devil from her body, to save himself from temptation as much as her. Immobilised in a Hospital bed or whipped in a parsonage and her tender young bottom abused by an old man; both scenarios seem as surreally unlikely, can she really be as deluded as she is continually being told she is? What is reality? Why won't the nurses listen to her accusations? Why will they only ever discuss her 'accident'? Why do they walk away, ignore her, if she ever speaks of anything else?

www.ingramcontent.com/pod-product-compliance
Lightning Source LLC
Chambersburg PA
CBHW020317260626
47156CB00004B/1260